DETHRONED

Books
By
Branka Čubrilo

The Mosaic of the Broken Soul
Fiume – The Lost River
The Lonely Poet and Other Stories
Dethroned

DETHRONED

Branka Čubrilo

SPEAKING VOLUMES, LLC
NAPLES, FLORIDA
2017

Dethroned

ISBN 978-1-62815-350-7

To my father
Milan Čubrilo

Acknowledgments

Many thanks to
Irina Dimitric-Stojic and Althea Kuzman

I

DREAMTIME

Gregor's Metamorphosis

"When Gregor Samsa woke up one morning from unsettling dreams, he found himself changed ... "

When Gregor Truba woke up on that mild April morning in 2017, from a long unsettling dream, he found himself changed. Indeed, he found himself manipulated – altered greatly.

Gregor Truba was an ordinary man. He always portrayed himself as an honest, hardworking man with a sharp sense of justice and belonging. Belonging to his country, to the dream. *The Big Dream.*

***

His first disappointment, bordering with rage, edging with shame, calling for justice, was when he was only seven. At school, he learned that his father was '*on the wrong side*' in WW2.

It was 1968 and his small world consisted of: Mother Elsa, so far his favourite person, sister Veronika, little brother Hugo and his strong-jawed father Anton. He would have preferred it if his father were something else, not *'just a car mechanic'* so, often, he would adorn his job description with complimentary titles like *'a doctor for fine apparatus'* or *'a machine-wizard'*.

Mother Elsa was of German origin. To be precise, Elsa's mother was a pure German, though her father was a Croat, a little bit too proud, but his pride even though oversized, still remained within the confines of acceptable behaviour and orientation. Still, there is more to say about Elsa's German heritage. Not only was her mother German, but her Father's great-grand father was born in that proud land.

To many Elsa was a dear woman, hardworking, obedient and quiet. That stood as a predominant opinion in the neighbourhood. Blond, with two long braids, as cliché wants it, but the family loved her golden thick locks tidied and tamed into two parallel braids.

For now the story about WW2 will be skipped as those stories are more or less correctly written in various, numerous history books.

But I shall weave my story around the Truba family from that moment in the year 1968 when Gregor had a nightmare: his dream was nearly destroyed, but the authorities interfered, as it was written in the Book of Law that authorities can, could and should interfere in such circumstances.

Mother Elsa, a healthy woman of German origins, packed Gregor's sandwich (not in a box, but rather wrapped it in brown paper) and walked him out of the house (a small, small house on the edge of the town) and gave him a hug, then she ruffled his blond hair. Gregor considered himself so lucky to have such a sweet mother and luckier he would consider himself if she gave him a kiss instead of ruffled his hair.

Veronika was ill on that day and little Hugo was still asleep being just a baby in 1968. Gregor's father went out an hour earlier; still, there was an empty cup of coffee on the table left behind for Elsa to take care of.

***

Subject: History.
Lesson: Tripartite Treaty
Date of Lesson: 21 May 1968 (Springtime)

"On 25th May 1941 Yugoslavia joined the Tripartite Pact, but soon with the help of England a coup in Belgrade was organised and accession was cancelled. That was the reason for Germany, with the help of its allies (Italy, Hungary, Bulgaria) to attack and to break and divide Yugoslavia in the 12-day war. The Independent State of Croatia (NDH) was created from Croatia, Bosnia and Herzegovina with the help of these countries, especially Italy,

which itself had taken a big part of the Croatian coastline, many islands and cities, while Hungary took Medjimurje."

Those were the exact words Gregor uttered, all those sentences learned off by heart, all said in one long liberating out-breath.

Bravo!!!

Bravo Gregor!

But, there was silence.

No bravo.

Gregor sat down and the teacher approached slowly, with a carefully, neatly arranged bun on top of her head, and with a sentence equally carefully arranged:

"That would be correct Gregor, that would be correct."

Though that was all she said there was some sort of forced silence that fell heavily onto the kids' heads, then a loud voice from the back of the room thundered:

"Mother's German, father's a traitor. Black Shirts."

Gregor stood up and ran to the back of the room, jumped at the thunder-voice-boy and broke his nose with just one mighty hit between his eyes. Done!

He asked Father about his whereabouts at that time and his father told him not to bother with the past. Mother Elsa said the same but Gregor felt as if he were, somehow marked, regardless of the fact that the incident was forgotten and something of that kind had never happened again. After that incident he had decided to be *'the best person he could ever be'* and was keen to show by example how an honest and brave boy acted. He had many friends during that period of history as people appreciated and encouraged honesty and purity of heart. Let's sum it up: as a young boy, Gregor had a reasonably happy life, no big questions, no big dismays given that he had overcome the disappointment with his father; as it is known children tend to forgive and forget, plus it was something that happened long ago, then after all, his father was an excellent mechanic ... who really cared about WW2?

DETHRONED

But, alas, in that country people have the memory of an elephant, as he would learn much later in his life. Would he benefit from that or not, was yet to be seen.

Often he would wake up in a sweat, as if some sort of nightmare had crept under his duvet and talked to him in the German language. Sang to him. Mighty hymns. Back then it looked to Gregor as if it were some sort of omen. Yes, Omen with a capital *'O'*.

What was going to happen to the people who lived good lives, so good that it was beyond their possibilities and beyond their logical minds and the logical minds of the rest of the world?

He grew up with his German Mother Elsa and his *'mechanic-wizard'* father in a reasonably stable household. Veronika was a crackpot as she smoked marijuana 24/7 and everybody pretended that they never noticed *'anything strange'* in regard to such a habit. Mainly she was sedated while constantly dreaming that *'one day, she'd go to a country, a capitalist country, where milk and honey flowed in abundance.'* Ah, Veronika and her dreams, they talked to her in the English language when she dived under her duvet, yes, in English with a strong American accent. Gregor would hear, some years later, the verses coming from the cracks and holes in the walls of her tiny room (or under the door):

"It's coming through a hole in the air
From those nights in Tiananmen Square
It's coming from the feel
That it ain't exactly real…"

Yes, she dreamed about Democracy (with a capital *'D'*) coming from that glorious land. She had been to Trieste, more than eighty-eight times, she had been to Florence, Padua and twice to Milan, but what she dreamed of was some *'real Democracy'*, some *'real capitalism'*, as her cousin worked in Trieste for an owner of a *'Gelateria'* who never paid wages on time, nor the correct earnings.

Her dad, Mr. Wizard worked for a government body, he looked after a park and cars and anything else that dealt with mechanics. He had a guaranteed wage, he was given a house (though quite small, but still, he got it from the government!), he had paid holidays and the resort on the coast free of charge for the workers of that particular government firm. Ah, how boring, how average!

"No, no, what we need is Democracy!"

Those were the wisest words she could deliver and kept repeating them, proud of two things in the sentence: the firmness of *"No, no"* and the determination in her otherwise weak voice.

"It's coming from the sorrow on the street
The holy places where the races meet
From the homicidal bitchin'
That goes down in every kitchen
To determine who will serve and who will eat
From the wells of disappointment..."

Gregor opted to leave her in the safe bubble of Cohen's lyrics, smoke and partial truth about democracy whether it was written with a capital *'D'* or just in lowercase. Long ago, Gregor determined, that saying anything to Veronika was a plain waste of time. She'd *'figured it all out'* especially early in the morning prior to lighting her cigarette. Yes, bright ass!

Well, years sailed pleasantly: there was an air of comfort, abundance and camaraderie among his family and friends; high-school passed almost without any conflicts, or inner conflicts; here and there, in the early seventies someone would mention his father's past, but, alas, those ghosts from the past were well behind, hidden, thrown away, only sick minds thought about the past, especially his father's past as he was an easy-going man with a number of friends.

The last year of high school when he was supposed to study the most, as he was contemplating philosophy as his chosen profession, Gregor formed a punk-rock band. Then, right then, he met her.

She was a songwriter. A poetry-machine. A pin-up beauty. A speechless desire. A creature of every boy's dream in the mid-seventies.

Pia.

That was her name.

Pia meant – desire. Pia meant: improvement, thirst, inspiration and – pain. Yes, pain. Pain, pain, pain.

That was all he obtained from Pia and carried it into his future as a rare gift from his *'misfortunate deal'* that the dealer had dealt.

He met her at a poetry evening. Dressed in black from the top of her head to the very bottom of her boots. Her hair was long, thick and dark, freely falling onto her shoulders, black leather jacket with silver buttons and buckles, tight dark skinny jeans and knee-high black leather boots. She never smiled.

Mesmerised he was!

He just stood there with a glass in his hand and open mouth. The cigarette was hanging from the corner of his lips and he urgently needed a stiff drink. She saw him gazing and turned her back to him. She walked away and sat alone in a corner. After some time someone called out the name *'Pia'*, and she stood up. She read the poem about withered flowers and a black crow eating the dead petals. Her voice was deep, velvety, prolix. Her dark green eyes shone. She looked mysterious, unearthly with a touch of indifference. No smile. Ever.

'Pathetic! Phoney. Just a poser!'

Those were Gregor's thoughts when she walked out.

Then several weeks passed and he came across Pia again. At some party. She sat there all alone, no smile on her face, no sparkle in her eyes, no desire to communicate with anyone. Hermetic world.

'Nonsense.' He thought he would never like to befriend such a cold phoney beauty. *Arresting,* that's the word.

As by some magnetic force he was pulled closer and said:

"You write lyrics?"

She shrugged only one shoulder and the expression on her face never changed. Not a tiny tick on her face. But when she looked into Gregor's eyes his knees weakened. He sat next to her without invitation and started to breathe heavily.

"You'll get a heart attack." she said without looking at him.

"Exactly how I feel."

Pia had a boyfriend.

His nickname was Barbarossa. Yes, he had reddish hair and a few barely visible red hairs on his chin. At twenty he had already published two collections of poems and was writing his first, much-talked-about novel. Gregor knew Barbarossa well, one could find him everywhere, literally everywhere: in dark cafés and bars, alternative and underground scenes, at poetry evenings organised and ran by him; at least once a week he was a guest speaker on different youth radio programs, almost a demigod of that generation - outspoken and physically unattractive, nevertheless, he was massively popular and sought after.

Given all that, Gregor really thought that Pia was unapproachable, someone who would stay out of his reach forever.

The third time he met Pia was at the most unusual place that he could have ever imagined or dreamt of.

The doorbell rang. Mother Elsa was busy in the kitchen, Veronika – who could guess where she was hiding - thus Gregor went to open the door, and his jaw dropped when he saw Pia, with her long, black, thick hair, with her black leather jacket and her knee-high boots. She didn't smile; her velvety voice said one word only:

"Veronika?"

'She was a friend of that crackpot? Pia, my sister's friend?'

"Veronika, Veronika!!!"

She came out of her room looking indifferent, yet annoyed, if that makes sense at all, but when she saw Pia she ran to the door and hugged her. Pia just stood there unable to lift her arms to hug Veronika, as that would imply that she had feelings.

Off they went into Veronika's room and he heard Leonard Cohen's versed melancholy coming out through the cracks.

That was a very difficult afternoon, it never ended; he thought that she would never come out of that tiny room. They couldn't be heard, just the Velvet Underground and Iggy Pop.

They went out that evening; on her leaving she didn't say anything. *'Annoying bitch!'*

But that wouldn't do (the *Annoying bitch* remark).

The next day he tried to bribe Veronika but Veronika wasn't willing to tell him anything about her friend and their whereabouts. *'If bribes don't work, then something else will work'*, so he threatened Veronika to expose and name the brand of her *'tobacco'*.

The story was brighter than he ever anticipated.

Barbarossa wasn't *'a real boyfriend'*, they were *'just hanging around together'*, and they *'hooked up occasionally'*.

Then, for the first time in his life he thanked his Mother Elsa for her heritage, as his genes proved to be the winners of all wars!

Pia loved tall, blond and blue-eyed boys. That was him!

Thanks Mother Elsa! Thanks to all worthy ancestors and warriors; this war he was going to win as he had the winning combination passed down from the Germanic heavens.

To prevent a potentially lethal discovery that the cigarettes she was rolling were not coming from a *Drum*-inscribed bag as it served to be only a plain décor for the dumb or ill-informed, Veronika organised a meeting between her brother and the poetess Pia, all with, one and only, good intent: he needed someone to write lyrics for his songs.

Purely business.

On the next day he received an envelope. It was from Pia. A note, perhaps a poem, it read:

Oh, leave me
Leave me
Leave me alone:
It's sun, it's sun, it's sun –
It's storm
Oh, it's storm; it's storm
Again it's storm
I run, I run, I run:
It's sun - it's storm
Oh, leave me
Leave me
Leave me alone
I don't need another Heathcliff at home.

What was he supposed to do with it?
Loudly, he said:
"Bugger off, you crackpot!"
He thought that Pia wasn't any better than Veronika was, *'just a bloody depressed junkie. Right, write her off, and finish that Pia-Story-Obsession!'*

***

Anton ended up in jail.

Not for too long, just several weeks, but the whole town knew it. Once again Gregor felt as if he were marked, as if the whole family were marked.

He cried when his father was jailed.

Anton never said what the real reason for his short imprisonment was, but Gregor always thought that his father wouldn't harm a fly; he had so many friends, a broad, sincere smile and hands of gold.

Communists – crackpots! *'In the end'*, he thought, *'perhaps Veronika's right. We need a revolution; we need democracy.'*

His father came out of short imprisonment angrier and after a short-while he lost his job. Not that he completely lost his employment, just his supervisor's position. He went back to where he had started, down on his knees, under the cars, to be a mechanic. With him on his knees his wage went down and the family's standard of living accordingly.

Mother Elsa suggested renting out their weekend house on the coast. She had a German mind; once again it proved that life was easy and solutions were at hand only if one was willing to find them.

It was summer and everyone worked that summer. Even Veronika. She worked at Pia's cousin's café as a waitress. Mother Elsa was busy with her rental business, Father was a mechanic again, but with fewer jokes, and the band had several places where they played for some money.

When summer ended Gregor enrolled into a university course. Bachelor of Philosophy.

Guess what?

There we have her again – Pia, a student of the Faculty of Comparative Literature and English and Italian Languages. The same class. The same old Pia: smile-less, stunning, with a black leather jacket, black knee-high boots regardless of the season or temperature.

She was the centre of everyone's attention.

Aloof, cool, distant … but - breathtakingly beautiful.

Like a queen, like a queen with the attitude: *There will never, ever be a suitable suitor for her Majesty.*

A red-bearded man was waiting in his car; she sat next to him fixing her dark sunglasses on her perfect little nose.

Gregor despised her! He despised him!

A Short Chapter on Freedom

Veronika's ideal view on freedom was, a sort of, anarchy. Urban Anarchy. Amsterdam was on her mind because of the liberty to smoke marijuana. Hmm. American freedom was less appealing the more she watched American shows and films. They were shouting, shooting, speaking their mind blatantly, women were portrayed as whores as they made themselves available any time to anyone: just pants down, let's do it, don't complicate life, move on!

'Why? Were they exactly like that? Was that an American woman? A modern woman? Who portrayed American women as sluts? And why?'

She wanted to be free, to express herself in a way she wanted, she wanted to make decisions, but she knew the difference between a pure slut and a modern, free woman.

Dead corpses on the streets, revolvers and *'Greed is good'*. Freedom to choose death or debit.

She was only eighteen at the time and had deeply engraved the wrong conception of justice, fairness and equality.

Absolutely wrong!

The distinguished award for such an achievement she placed into the lap of Mother Elsa. She could have found so many reasons why she would opt in favour of marijuana, but the first and the strongest one always was – Elsa. She blamed her mother for her good upbringing and believed that the *'modern woman'* had to have some sort of liberty, namely to smoke, to say *'no'* when she felt like saying so, to wear revealing clothes… something like that, no, not that extreme American-shows-woman-liberty to jump in anyone's bed, no, not that kind of freedom.

But, Mother Elsa, she had so many rules that started with the sentence, *'A good girl doesn't…'* or *'Good girls never…'*

Therefore, Veronika had decided not to be *'a good girl'*. It was: boring, average, un-cool and un-popular, at least, in her world, in her mind, hence marijuana was the number one sign of disobedience, a sign of anarchy. A sign of Freedom – the holy freedom.

So, Veronika's freedom came at a cost, that's for sure!

It is not necessary to stress that Veronika was an exceptionally intelligent and gifted girl.

A wide array of interests she had, that ranged from music through fine art to classical literature. Not only because Mother Elsa encouraged the strong influence of the holy German culture, no, but, art strongly spoke to her soul, and the soul was the most important aspect of herself to be cherished and nourished, as she would claim.

Disobedient, disobedient, a disobedient child she was.

No amount of kindness, advice or good will was ever sufficient to influence her choices. They were extravagant and different by any definition.

If the word 'weird' were to be used to describe her choices and acts, let's present this simple story to support it:

She was only seven when she cut off her mother's plaits while Elsa was asleep. She took the scissors and cut them off, put them into a plastic bag and threw them into a rubbish bin. When Mother Elsa saw her reflection in the mirror she almost fainted. If it were not for a little old cabinet underneath the mirror, she would have ended on the bathroom floor. When they asked Veronika, 'Why did she do it?' she said – no reason! No reason at all!

Mother Elsa was painfully obsessed with tidiness and that was what Veronika hated; she wanted a mother living in an untidy place while sitting on a sofa, smoking cigarettes with a vacant gaze as her best expression; a depressed housewife in desperate need of a psychologist at least; she wanted a mother that would come up with original and different interests and stories, a mother that travelled the world, sold stories to ruthless publishers, or maybe to be an unaccomplished dancer, slightly neurotic and ready to argue at any moment.

But Mother Elsa was just a plain, boring housewife, almost always happy on demand, and as a German Shepherd - obedient, obedient, obedient, as a good Christian is, a churchgoer and a priest-admirer.

What happened after the *'cutting-off-plaits-incident'* took place?

Well, after that Mother Elsa took Veronika to see a psychologist, the only psychologist she could possibly have taken her to: the school psychologist. (*'Oh, how inventive'*, Veronika thought). Plus, that woman, the psychologist, was her friend's mother. Hell no, Veronika would never talk to Marina's mother!

All Gregor said to that incident was:

"There's no one who can help you, Veronika. You are a lost freak."

After such *'an incident'* Veronika withdrew even more and her heart grew impenetrable; she listened to loud music locked in her room and her brown eyes were almost always on half-mast like some sad flag of a defeated country.

Another display of her freedom: a few years down the line landed her in jail, just for one night - she labelled it as *'just a passenger'*.

There were three of them: Veronika, Laura and Leo.

Sitting on a park bench. Rolling cigarettes and singing loudly. A few cans of beer around the bench. Teasing passers-by. Swearing and throwing pebbles at stray cats.

Two cops came and asked them questions.

Veronika said:

"Is this a free country or is this a prison?"

They found a bag of grass in Leo's pocket and each of them had a joint – Veronika's second joint was tucked behind her ear.

The policeman instructed them to follow him to the station but Veronika went on and on:

"I want to see my lawyer, what kind of freedom is this? What have we done wrong? In America they would kick your arse if you took people to the station without letting their lawyers know about it. Let me call my brother! Let me call my family, you motherfuckers!"

After one of the officers told her to *'shut up'*, she continued:

"I am free to say whatever I want, whenever I want, no one will stop me! Ever! I can smoke whatever I want. I can do whatever I wanna do, you arse-

holes, you scumbags, standing in the way of human rights, freedom of speech and expression."

The next day they were let off from such a luxurious abode and angry and exhausted she came home. Ashamed? Never!

Police pressed charges against all three of them for disturbing public peace and order and possession of illegal drugs. Additional charges were pressed against Veronika: offending police officers on duty.

That was Veronika's way to freedom.

She was most surprised when her father commented:

"Bastards. Plain bastards!"

Well, she wasn't guilty at all. She knew it! To rebel against authorities was equal to rebelling against *'plain bastards'* as her father nicely put it.

At last, for once, Father was on her side.

Long ago Gregor had given up on Veronika and her weird ways; long ago till the moment he opened the door and met the beautifully sculptured face of Pia the Poetess on the other side.

***

What was slightly disturbing for Gregor, slightly weakening his spirit, was the fact or the feeling that, somehow, Veronika had a stronger character, a stronger will and fewer fears and considerations. She appeared at the same time a strong character and a joint-eater and that was in opposition, but nevertheless, he secretly envied her for exactly that! Exactly that combination of fearlessness and apathy, nihilism and anarchy.

Ah, Veronika, the shame of the Truba family!

And that was the card she was playing!

Anything but the mirror of the obedient, tidy Mother Elsa.

When people would dress up Veronika had to dress down. When everyone was quiet she had to scream, when umbrellas were up Veronika was drenched in the rain, in summer heat she wore boots whilst in winter she went out barely dressed. Always astonishing family, friends, teachers and passers-by.

In the early spring of 1983 Gregor met Veronika on the terrace of a local café. The sky above the terrace was covered with the tops of century-old wild chestnut trees, and the patrons were shadowed and darkened - unrecognisable, especially if one was exposed longer to the sunlight as Gregor was, prior to stepping into the thick shade formed by the treetops. Nevertheless he recognised them. He recognised Pia at once, as his heart started to race uncontrollably, then to his delight he spotted his sister, and an older gentleman was comfortably sitting between them.

They greeted him, though indifferently, but he sat down at the table even though no one asked him to.

The man who was sitting with them was in his early fifties, probably, but he was dressed tastefully with a dapper neat haircut, neat fingernails and an air of importance about him. With a silky shawl he had disguised his sagging neck. But still, the man looked interesting, familiar and somehow *'important'*.

When Gregor heard his name Simon Odak, he remembered him. He was a renowned theatre director and an actor. Yes, Simon Odak. Veronika was all over him, hugging, kissing, teasing and pinching him whilst he had a little mischievous smile on his lips, barely nodding his head, and Gregor wasn't sure if he was nodding in agreement or in disagreement.

Pia kissed his bare hand twice, and when the girls got up Pia kissed his forehead and just said, *'See you around, Simo.'* Gregor's sister planted a wet kiss onto his lips and he licked it off and said to her, *'Come over soon.'*

Gregor was left alone with Simon, who took the papers as they left and started to read as if no one was there any longer.

Gregor's thoughts were: *'Both of them are his lovers! Old bastard! A pervert! Only because he was a theatre director, some ol' dandy fart!*

But, he wasn't right.

The truth was quite different and when he learned it, he looked at Pia with different eyes. Loved her even more.

A Page from Pia's Diary

When Gregor entered the room it was empty. Mother Elsa told him, *'The girls are in the room'*. But, no, no one was there, the door was ajar and the music was on, *'Well, they shouldn't be too far'* was Gregor's thought.

He tiptoed anyway and looked around the room. There was a big black leather bag on Veronika's bed and he knew that bag well - it was always on Pia's shoulder.

The temptation was too strong and he couldn't resist it - he looked through it. He started slowly to examine the bag's contents and excitement grew as if he were going to discover something of epic proportions.

What else could be found in a young girl's bag but some make-up, a wallet, several hair clips, a pack of cigarettes still unopened, a little mirror, an envelope quite crinkled – the letter was probably in it as it was addressed to her name (but what would come later to his awareness, when excitement wore itself out - would be her surname), then there was a book covered in black leather and he suspected it to be a diary. And he was spot on! It was Pia's diary: the first page was dated 7th February 1973 (Sat). The last, current page was dated 11th May 1983. *'Only yesterday'*, he thought.

Gregor was faced with a difficult task, a quick decision: whether he was going to read the first or the last page. On the last, he dreamed, he might find his name somewhere in those crammed sentences, but what enhanced his unbearable curiosity was that the whole of the first page was framed around with a thick black marker.

It looked like an obituary.

It said:

"February 7th – three years have passed without you. Still missing you and still it hurts everywhere, even my eyebrows hurt, my eyelashes, my eyeballs as you were my sight and my light, you were my dawn and sunset, you were the brightest star in my sky or in the entire sky. Everything hurts: my fingers when

I write about you, my toes when I walk the path to your crypt, my fingernails hurt when I dig them into my thighs when I cry and when I need no witness to my tears. My breath hurts when it passes through my throat as I know this passage is closed forever and when I utter your name it won't reach you, oh, how much my lips hurt as they will never plant a kiss onto your cheeks, and my soul will hurt forever... " Gregor heard voices; he quickly shoved Pia's diary into her bag and started to whistle. The girls came in and looked at him with an air of boredom or of animosity.

'Was it a poem?'
'Was it really an obituary?'
'Was it just fiction?'
'Was she sane?'
'Who was the person Pia had written those lines to? Was it all real? Or just fiction?'

"What were you doing here? What? Are you some sort of spy? A police informant? Get out of my room – now!"

As an obedient little puppy off he went.

But the story from Pia's diary never left him. Not for days, not for months or years, it had never left him!

The next morning upon waking up he examined his dreams. He thought that he might have dreamed of her. But what came clearly to his mind was her surname. He could see the inscription on that envelope, *'Pia Odak.'*

Without success he tried to reconstruct her words. The only thing he remembered was her surname and it was the same as the surname of that old fart, the dapper man whose hands she kissed, whose old lips Veronika kissed – Simon Odak. Was he her father? Perhaps her uncle, but surely not some old paedophile fooling them into something sinister and repulsive to his mind.

That very same day he tried to bribe Veronika.

18

Poor soul, she always wanted to sing, but talent was not there and it looked like it simply would never emerge even with mighty efforts of thousand experts trying to help.

"We need a female voice for one of our songs, would you be interested before I offer it to someone else?"

"Why? You said that I was dumb and talentless, didn't you?"

"Well, you've grown, your voice has changed. Give it a go."

She came and it was a major disaster: her voice sounded horrible, high-pitched, insecure; she looked awkward with her legs spread wide and she was holding the microphone like it was a huge cone of an ice-cream ready to be swallowed by her inexperienced mouth.

The boys were frustrated and they never agreed that he bring his sister, but gave in as he promised it would be, *'Just a one off'*. Driving back home he told her that *'she wasn't that bad'*, and when he asked her about Pia's parents she just lost it.

"Is that why you gave me a chance? To get closer to Pia? Why on earth would you care about her parents? Keep your nose out of her business. Let me out, you freak!"

***

Their first single was a chart topper.

No one really expected it: no one, including him. He knew it was something different but he never imagined that it would take the country by storm, actually never dreamt about it. But it did happen and it did change his life overnight. Even Veronika softened.

At the end of that year he finally got over his dreams about Pia. They travelled a lot from town to town, they spent a lot of time in the studio, interviews in papers on local and national TV; he hadn't had time, not even to think about the neurotic self-professed poetess.

It was late summer of 1983. Paradoxically, life was intense but easy. It smelled of adventure, of youth, of young girl's bodies, it smelled of promises and success, it was like some sort of dreamland, as if he had taken an elixir that brought everlasting energy and ecstasy. Everything worked in his favour even the sun was rising up to greet Gregor that summer of 1983. He had big plans, a big head and a big heart.

He met Tina. A ballet dancer.

No, not that Tina was a simple character, but, after all, he never liked simple characters. Such a repulsive idea it was: a simple, ordinary girl. Tina had what he needed: physical beauty, thick long honey-blond hair, eyes of a dreamer, the body of a Nymph, the intelligence of a philosopher and a very, very fine talent.

He would never settle for less. The theory that *'everyone was the same'* would come later, much later when he himself would change, when he became *'just another brick in the wall.'*

But this late summer of 1983 was the sweetest summer he had ever experienced in his life and as if he knew it he lived every second of it, inhaled every atom of it and integrated it into his being.

He had *'the most promising band'* in the country, he had a girlfriend who matched the girl from his dreams and who was Pia? He thought; he never even knew her.

He never met Pia that summer, it might be that he travelled a lot or simply that Pia took off and went on her own adventure.

But by the end of the summer when the first leaves started to darken on the edges, again, he met the man whose name was Simon Odak.

They met in the theatre. Tina had introduced them and Simon never remembered that they had met. Simon Odak offered cooperation.

Alas!

They agreed to meet, exactly on September 1st at the theatre café between 5 and 6 pm.

For a very uncertain reason Gregor was unsettled, restless the whole day. He was choosing his thoughts carefully, his clothes, his shoes, as if that were going to determine the outcome of their meeting.

He made a huge effort to avoid thoughts of Pia.

Why was she back in his mind? He loved Tina and he knew it. Who wouldn't love her and who wouldn't want her? Tina, Tina, Tina … he kept on repeating, remembering her name every time Pia's name came out of the blue. In the end, he thought, he was probably thinking about Pia only because he was meeting her father. There! Full stop!

But out of the blue the words walked into his head, yes, they walked into his mind as if on a promenade, they walked slowly, in slow motion; without any effort he saw them imprinted on some inner greenish screen, the letters painted with dark ink and nostalgia, a heavy dose of Pia's pain and mystery:

"Still missing you and still it hurts everywhere, even my eyebrows hurt, my eyelashes, my eyeballs as you were my sight and my light, you were my dawn and sunset, you were the brightest star in my sky or in the entire sky. Every-thing hurts: my fingers when I write about you, my toes when I walk the path to your crypt; my fingernails hurt when I dig them into my thighs when I cry and when I need no witness to my tears. My breath hurts when it passes through my throat as I know this passage is closed forever and when I utter your name it won't reach you, oh, how much my lips hurt as they will never plant a kiss onto your cheeks, and my soul will hurt forever…"

'Ah, Pia, a mysterious or disturbed girl?'

He came a little later than he intended as Simon Odak was already com-fortably seated in one of the armchairs. He was late because Tina dyed her hair. Yes, they came together, looked like he needed her support. Perhaps he did need her support. After all, she knew Odak well - they worked together and were extremely at ease in each other's company.

"Isn't he Pia's father?" he asked Tina while driving.

All she said was:

"He is."

21

After a while Tina said:

"I never knew that you know Pia."

"Veronika's friend."

He asked himself why he was nervous. He pretended not to know the answer even though the answer was the loudest thought in his head on that particular late summer day.

On that particular late summer day he met Pia again.

As they sat down the conversation started to flow with ease. Odak was such a charming man when women were around. With the corner of his eyes Gregor caught a shadow of a tall, thin woman in a long flowing black mantle. His heart raced and he hated the fact that he couldn't control his heartbeats.

She held a glass in her hand while slowly approaching. Behind Simon's back she came, bent down and planted a little kiss onto his forehead and said:

"Hello Simo."

Simon offered her a chair and she sat down silently.

"Are you hungry?"

"Don't ask me silly questions. Don't talk about me. I am fine."

She looked at Gregor's eyes and there was a little, barely detectable, smile on the corner of her lips. Unease crept under Gregor's shirt and he started to scratch his bicep. Then the other one. Then again, the one he had already scratched but this time his palms were moist, as moist as Pia's deep green eyes. Awkward silence set in at the table as their eyes were playing some sort of game seemingly without rules. Pia looked at Gregor's eyes, he looked down at the floor, Pia looked at Tina's eyes and Tina kept her gaze onto Pia's eyes, Simon looked around first into Pia's eyes, then into Tina's and finally into Gregor's eyes and he started to smile wider and wider but without uttering a word. Pia was like a high priestess of some unusual religion: domineering, penetrating into souls and silently setting the tone and atmosphere without any effort.

Simon took control over the conversation and proposed several ideas that Gregor agreed with mostly.

What he noticed was: just as the first time when he met Simon and Pia (not knowing he was her father) she took his hand and kissed it several times. Each time she kissed his hand he would take her hands into his and kiss. Each time he kissed Pia's hand Gregor noticed a different expression on Pia's face.

'*She needed reassurance*', Gregor concluded.

'*Was she still a child inside?*'

'*Was that image of hers just a façade she was hiding behind?*'

He wanted to know, he wanted to know, oh, so badly and desperately he wanted to know who Pia was.

At any cost he wanted to know who Pia was.

But it seemed that no one wanted to talk about Pia: his sister never wanted to say a word about her, Tina only said, *"Can't stand her, everyone knows she is guilty"*.

"Guilty of what?"

"I don't want to talk about her. You should see yourself; you just acted like any average stupid teenager. What do you, men, see in her? What is so 'special' about her? Poor Simon stuck with the lunatic."

"Tina, stop it! You sound just like a jealous bitch. Stop it right now!"

He drove her back home and that evening he went out all by himself. He knew exactly where he would find Pia.

And he did find her there. Seated in the corner with her drink, with Barbarossa and the three slim, sleek figures dressed in black, with sleek black-coloured hair and black-painted fingernails. His thoughts and his hands trembled.

***

When Gregor Truba woke up from a long unsettling dream, he found himself alienated from his original self. Indeed, he found himself manipulated – manipulated by someone. Was he '*the someone*' that had manipulated himself? A quick decision arose, without a second thought he made a phone-call.

"Tina, I wanna know what love is…"

"You want me to show you?"
"I want someone else Tina, don't call again."

***

Mother Elsa brought breakfast in.
"Is there anything wrong, Gregor?"
"Mother, why did you leave Germany?"
"I met your father."
"Did you love him?"
"Absolutely. That's why I left. I would go anywhere just to be with him."
"Have you ever regretted your decision?"
"I haven't. What is it that bothers you, son?"
"There is a girl, Mum, that I can't take my mind off. When I met Tina I, kind of fell in love, she is such a great person, but I have never stopped thinking about the other girl and she has been constantly on my mind, almost like a heavy obsession."
"Does she know that you fancy her?"
"I don't think so."
"Tell her. Oh, my gorgeous boy, you are a stunner, you look even more handsome than your father ever looked, and believe me he turned many heads when we would walk together down the road. You look like uncle Eginolf, plus, those constant phone-calls, those girls they call all day long. Who is she? Do I know her? Do I know her parents?"
"You met her, Mother. She is Veronika's friend."
"Oh, not the Goth girl, for God's sake."
"She is just a girl Mum, that's the image, not her real self."
"Do you know her 'real self'? Do you really know who she is?"
"Forget it, Mum."
"You know, son, you were born into a modest family. Your father was only a car mechanic, and I come from a small village, your success was unexpected and quick, you are almost famous, aren't you? But for me, it is all - unreal, you are just my son, my little Gregory, you travel a lot nowadays from one side of

the country to the other, there are all sorts of people out there. Some are jealous, some are really nasty; some girls are chasing you just because of your sudden fame. All I want is that you keep your head on your shoulders, what else can I say? That girl, Veronika's friend, I heard weird stories about her and that family, I don't like her coming over; as much as we know that Veronika is rebellious and unbalanced I can tell you that she's been even worse since that girl walked into her life. I can't understand what they have in common. Gregory, I thought Tina was your girlfriend. What's wrong with her? She looks like a normal girl, she is pretty; she is a ballerina, petite and pretty. Gregory, keep your feet on the ground, son. Please, sonny."

"I never said I was going to marry any girl, Mum. It's fun. I am after fun."

"And that is how it should be, son."

***

On the very same day Tina came over in tears. She walked in quietly and sat on his bed. On the bed where only yesterday they were lovers, where he whispered in her ear sweet words, some of them even smelled like sweet promises. Tina sat on the bed and wanted to start a level-headed conversation, but she burst into tears.

Gregor never knew how to cope with women's tears.

He remembered the time when Father went to jail. He said something, something that had disturbed important people. The small gods of a small town.

Mother Elsa bitterly cried on that day.

Gregor came home an hour earlier from school on that day; they were let off as the teacher was ill. He felt ill on that day too; his stomach was all knotted as if he had a hazy precognition that he was going to witness something disturbing. While he was walking he had a strange feeling that someone was following him. That was probably his fear, the same fear that caught up with him about half an hour after he passed the house threshold.

The sound he heard at once was one of loud sobbing. He thought of Veronika at first, but as he rushed into the lounge room throwing away his backpack, he saw Mother Elsa huddled on the couch, and tears were running wild as a wild unbridled river which was breaking down all the bridges that Mother Elsa had built with humanity ever since she could remember.

Gregor's heart sank. What could have possibly happened to throw her on her knees, to throw her in the abyss of despair?

"What happened Mum? What on earth has happened Mum?"

He was overwhelmed by the panic and Mother's inability to say anything coherent. He never wanted to see his mother's tears, never wanted to see so much distress and despair for he thought that he wasn't equipped with the right tools and mechanisms in such extravagant and out of order situations.

Deep inside he knew he *'had to be a man.'*

Well, that was exactly what Tina said through her tears:
"Why can't you be a man?"

Oh, it was so difficult for Gregor to be a man in both of those situations. What would *'a man'* do faced with so much emotion?

While Mother Elsa was uncontrollably crying he was repeating one word - *'strong'* and he looked into his, not yet, manly hands and hugged his mother tightly trying to control and calm his own heart believing that by calming his own heart he would calm Mother's heart too.

And it did happen! He just held her in his arms, pressed her onto his, not quite yet, manly chest and fewer sobs came from distressed Mother until it was all gone and she was able to lift her face, look into his eyes and give him an uncertain smile.

He felt like a hero.

When Tina started to cry her body shook as if grabbed by some mad fever coming from the deep inside; Gregor tried to catch her, hug her shoulders, but she shook and shook and kicked her arms and legs disabling him from coming any closer.

All that Gregor understood through her sobs was that Pia was an evil girl, that her father was a pervert and that both of them were guilty.

After a while when she couldn't cry any longer with so sad an expression on her face she stood up and said:

"You ripped my heart out."

Gregor stood frozen knowing that any word would be just the wrong word, so he stood there almost patiently awaiting what would happen next.

And the next was a – slap!

She came closer, he even thought that she might kiss him, but she lifted her hand and slapped him – five fingers left a mark on his left cheek.

***

Gregor threw himself on his bed and went down the memory stream that he embarked on when Tina was crying:

Mother Elsa told him that Father was taken to the police station. She didn't tell him why as she said that he was *'too young to understand what was going on in the country'* but she promised that she would not cry again, and she even promised that *'everything was going to be alright'* whether that concerned the situation in the country or the dire situation in which his father had found himself.

He recalled Mother Elsa telling him *'it wasn't our country'*, but he felt absolute belonging to the town, to the people and to the country, hence he blamed Mother's German heritage for feeling displaced and not belonging.

Gregor heard her saying something similar on another occasion. Friar Marag came over and told her to close the doors and windows for *'even the walls have ears'* and while she was closing everything he heard her saying, *'Friar, we've always been superior to them, those devils have to go back where they came from.'*

Yes, the doors had closed almost hermetically, the voices turned into whispers, music on the radio went up and the children were forbidden to enter the room while Mother Elsa confessed her sins to Father Marag. The sins no one knew about.

Are horrible, hostile thoughts sins too?

Yes, they are.

Was it known that Father Marag informed Elsa about it?

No, that wasn't known. Father Marag would come quietly, they would close the door hermetically and after a while he would leave quietly with a gentle smile on his seemingly benevolent face.

No one ever knew his original thoughts, his real feelings. His face was like a sculpture: always a benevolent smile (that fake smile from abundance of forced kindness), eyebrows slightly up as if he were curious or slightly surprised, a penetrating gaze and if it were not for his watery eyes he could have passed easily for the fresco on the wall behind Elsa's bed.

There was something in Friar Marag that Gregor disliked immensely as a child, then after that as a young man: something sinister, manipulative and no, not benevolent, but quite the contrary – malevolent.

Friar Marag

He was born and grew up on barren land, the son of a peasant without any land, the second oldest of seven sons. Three sisters always remained skeleton-thin and grey, almost invisible, almost as if it were a shame to be born a girl. Well, it was a shame in the household where the Friar was born, in the part of the country where he was born.

He was born with a mark across his face - it looked as if a dog had left his ink-wetted paw on his left cheek. Somehow it made him bitter from the start. Or was it that?

Franko, that's how his father named him, with the probability already in mind that he would give him away to Franciscans, to study to be a priest.

That was the practise of pauperism: the oldest went to the priests.

Even though Franko wasn't the eldest, but second in chronological order, his father had decided that he would be given to the priests, because the eldest, Miro, was not the brightest child. He would stare into the distance for hours with a smirk on his face, or, often he would climb the tallest tree, sit in the treetop and sing at the top of his lungs till late night hours.

Franko showed anger and disobedience from an early age, therefore his father thought the gain might be doubled up: they would teach him obedience, and prayers would transform or ease his anger, plus there would be one less mouth to feed. He wasn't the brightest either, but what Father believed was - if Franko was exposed to wisdom he might well grow to be wise and intelligent.

"One never knows!"

Franko Jere Marag was born on a crisp December day in 1939 in a village whose name even God had forgotten, where people lived in houses with tiny rooms together with goats and sheep underneath their bedrooms, and had no winter clothes and not enough land to plant anything else but potatoes. There were some fig trees here and there, knotted, beaten by icy-cold bitter winds that bowed them to the ground.

Franko was like that wind: icy-cold, bitter but unwilling to bow his head, he went against things, against anything. He went against his father's will when he was told he was to go to the priests, he was whipped to the bone, like an animal he was whipped. In that part of the land the biggest sin was disobedience to hierarchy. Father almost whipped out of his head the strong will which resided there, but whipping gave birth to some sort of primitive intelligence: he was no longer as disobedient, he listened, but he stored anger and hatred for future reference. Right there behind his icy pale blue eyes, right there beyond the reach of any kind thought. Like a tangle of snakes those feelings were cosily nested in his young heart.

The harsh, barren land left an imprint of poverty, shame, violence and hatred in his young soul and that was exactly what he carried in his heart when he had entered the Seminary.

In his first year he didn't make any friends. In the second he was thinking of running away, in his third year his will was almost broken, in his fourth year he thought he might be a priest one day, perhaps only out of spite or to have the right to exercise power and authority.

For some reason, he never talked about his days in the Seminary, but surely there was a good reason why he would seemingly lightly change the topic of such a conversation when or if it arose. He had learned that smile, mastered it – *'the most benevolent smile'* and it stood there for years as if it could cover up unpleasant issues or accommodate to any taste. A priest should be a wise one, his smile should be mysterious, leaning towards benevolent, but definitely mysterious.

That was the kind of smile mother Elsa loved and that smile often assured her that *'everything was going to be all right - according to God's will'*, and *'the Almighty, our holy Father, knew what we wanted even before we thought of it.'*

His hands were somehow womanly: soft, pale, protected from deterioration by long rests in his lap. His index finger was somehow disobedient and would give out his malevolent streak: pointing a finger was something that Friar Marag never unlearned in that fine Seminary. Hmm? How come? Could it be

30

that they never taught him how to get rid of that unholy practice and habit? Could he have been encouraged? No! That would have been unholy and evil.

He pointed his finger at citizens, choosing and accusing who was a good Catholic and who wasn't, who was a good honest person and who wasn't, who were communists and bastards, then enemies, then disobedient and wild youth, single mothers and their bastards. Often he called people *'lost causes'* and that group he pointed his finger at as *'dangerous and malicious'* and it was better for him not even to think of them as those thoughts would provoke such a rage and hatred that he felt as if his heart were going to be set on fire in which he could easily lose his mind. But Mother Elsa was his mirror. No one understood her better than Friar Marag did, and in all honesty - vice versa.

He was a regular guest in the Truba family, baptised all three children, brought appropriate literature and made jokes at the expense of some neighbours, whispered something soft in Elsa's ear prior to leaving and reminded her of the Sunday sermon at 10 am sharp.

Suffice to say – Veronika always disliked him. No one knew why; Mother Elsa blamed communists, school and peers; father Anton would say, *'Leave her alone'* and Gregor Truba never had any opinion about anything that hadn't had connections with music, but his guts, and his quite open-to-all-possibilities mind, told him to keep away from the *'little-sly-old-fashioned-man.'*

He started his piano lessons when he was only five and playing Father's guitar shortly after. He listened to every kind of music and would learn all notes off by heart when he heard it only once. The second time he could play it himself. God or no God he had a gift and he couldn't care less about Friar Marag's comments and observations.

When he grew up he would comment, *'Up his arse'* to any of the Friar's benevolent pieces of advice.

Gregor understood, much later, that he had a much greater influence over the Truba family and over his own life, in a very sinister, sly way – planting a bug into Elsa's ear. Elsa would act as directed, as to her he symbolised all that she had (for some unknown, untold reason) lost: pride, superiority over others, an infinite intelligence and wisdom that only a good German would be generously given as it were already engrained in genetics.

But for the love of a man a woman is capable of doing just anything, that's how she had found herself in this land with customs and temperaments much different to her own. Although in a blink of an eye, she had learned to hide her feelings, her real thoughts and opinions. She would portray understanding and kindness while inside she would judge and criticise everyone from a little child to an old person, consequently she had never found any friends, but she claimed, *'My family are my best friends'*, a statement which was not true to the letter. Especially Veronika; she was not a friend of the Truba family members, other than little innocent Hugo. From the beginning it was obvious that she had a solitary character and as she grew her heart failed to show softness, especially to her mother Elsa.

When Hugo Truba was born, Friar Marag baptised him with much delight and this was the first time Veronika had seen such delight in his eyes, and such excitement which looked to her as if it were genuine, not just like his mask of benevolence. He never missed a chance to come and visit mother Elsa and little Hugo. Veronika felt she could bite him as if she were a little animal. That was exactly what she did on one occasion. He came closer and said:

"Well, Veronika, when am I going to see a smile on your face? A young girl shouldn't be so gloomy, that is not good for the soul." Then he tried to stroke her face, and yes, she bit him. All teeth went deep through his soft, lax hand. The thin trail of blood came out from each tooth mark and started to drip onto the floor and on father Marag's black robe. Panic-stricken mother Elsa ran quickly to his rescue, but on father Marag's face there was still that mask of a benevolent smile, although Veronika saw something different in his icy-blue eyes. She saw an abyss of nothingness that could easily suck her in, and she bet she would find herself in the full glory of his own internal hell.

Her face was burning for days after mother Elsa, without any questions or interrogation, with an open arm hit her across the face several times, and only stopped when Friar Marag told her to. He was calm and collected and Elsa was shaking and apologising countless times in countless differently arranged sentences.

"Godless child, godless child, ah, ah, what a godless child!"

But Veronika wasn't the cross mother Elsa bore.

It was little Hugo.

At an early age they noticed that he was somehow *'slower'* in his reactions, his eyes were unfocused, it troubled Elsa. Tremendously it troubled her when he wasn't smiling at her, as the other two kids were when she would lean over the cot and show her face. Tremendously it troubled her when he showed no sign of awareness, a sign that he was interested in the world around him. At two he would barely say a word. He liked Veronika best, that troubled Elsa too, *Why would he like Veronika best, she, Elsa, was his mother!*

At three he would recognise her and he would smile to anyone, he had that same smile as Friar Marag – benevolent but sincere, a smile of a child that was developing slowly, far too slow. At three he would endlessly ask and repeat:

"Mummy loves Yugo, yes?"

"Yes, Mummy loves Yugo."

And he would clap his hands, his little tongue hanging, and he would yell with excitement:

"Mummy loves Yugo!"

Then he would run to Veronika saying:

"Lonika, Mummy loves Yugo. Lonika loves Yugo, yes?"

Veronika would hug him and sing a song to which Hugo would clap his hands and swing his little blond head.

The unbridled satisfaction, though never publicly shown, came to Veronika when her mother tried to take Hugo away from her arms and Hugo would say:

"Yugo loves Lonika mo."

Could it have been that Veronika stopped altogether loving her mother after this accident? She came back from school and had found Hugo in his cot. His face was almost coloured purple-blue as his favourite blanket was wrapped around his neck. He looked like a purple balloon ready to explode; she wanted to scream but regained her senses and unwrapped the blanket and started to massage his chest, breathe into his mouth, smack his little cheeks, and while she was doing it no one came in as if the house were a ghost house.

It wasn't.

Her mother was sitting on the veranda with Friar Marag sipping coffee, whispering and laughing at his *'benevolent jokes'*.

They revived him and Veronika ran to her room and cried. No one saw her crying, Father was at work, Gregor was at school and no one else mattered.

That afternoon Mother came into her room and told her not to tell about this accident to anyone. She said that *'nothing really happened'* and that *'it would be best not to upset anyone'*.

That night Veronika cut off her mother's braids.

Everyone was puzzled; everyone thought it odd.

Veronika was a sinister child. She always had been!

Gregor told her:

"I hate you for what you did to Mother."

Veronika shrugged her shoulders. Not a word. Mummy had forbidden words. But, she couldn't forbid Veronika's feelings.

When mother would say, *'We are superior'* Veronika would play with Gypsies in the street. When mother would dress her up as a *'real girl'* Veronika would sit in the puddle and dirty her white socks and pastel pink dress with white dots. When mother would say *'God loves obedient girls'* Veronika would wander off and wouldn't come home; the entire day she would walk, walk, walk the streets of her town and get familiar with each and every house, with every garden and stone, she would talk and greet dogs and cats as she liked animals better than the people she knew.

They said, *"Veronika was a troubled child"*.

No one knew why.

Not even the omniscient Friar Marag; the only thing that he would say to console Mother Elsa was:

"Often God gives us challenges."

Yes, that's all God gives us – challenges.

Isn't life itself just an endless series of challenges?

There were times in her youth when Veronika would feel genuine happiness, and it was always in connection with Hugo's visits to her room. She would always seek the solitude of her room. She knew when Hugo was at the door, as he would scratch it like a little puppy would.

"Push Hugo, push."

"No push Lonika, 'eavy."

Then Hugo would jump onto Veronika's bed and say:

"Lead Yugo."

She read him fairy-tales and he would enthusiastically participate with comments and show a plethora of emotions:

"Yugo hates witch."

"Yugo loves Mummy" pointing to the drawing of Gretel, and Veronika said:

"Yugo, this isn't Mummy, this is Gretel, that's Mummy" pointing her finger to the hunched-back witch and Hugo clapped his hands laughing, laughing, laughing, while Veronika was dead serious.

They would end afternoons confirming their love to each other:

"Yugo loves Lonika, yes?"

"Yes, I know you love me."

"Lonika loves Yugo."

"Forever sweetie."

"Polebel tweetie."

It wouldn't be right and fair to say that Hugo didn't love Gregor with sincere and deep love, but Veronika and Hugo shared a special bond.

Hugo would often enter Gregor's room where he was practising the guitar. Hands open wide saying:

"Go-goooool, Yugo comes, yes?"

"Come in little alien."

"Yoiyon commin'!" running right into Gregor's arms. Then Gregor would sit him on the armchair, his little legs hanging down while Gregor leaned

against the armchair with the guitar in his lap. Hugo always rubbed his foot against Gregor's face or his shoulder.

"Let me play, you little devil."

And the cascades of crystal clear laughter came from above.

"Go-gooool, Yugo guital, yes?"

"Yes, now Hugo is going to play. What do you wanna play, little alien?"

"Yugo pyay lil yaiyon."

"Oh, you'll play the little alien song, show me how it goes."

And Hugo would bang on the guitar, pulling at the strings under the careful eye of his brother.

When he was a little bit older and sleeping in a single bed, his visits to Veronika's room got more frequent. He would sneak out of his bed, take his blanket and walk the dark corridor without bumping into furniture, he would open the door, climb up Veronika's bed and nest in her lap. He could endlessly touch her face while she was sleeping, draw little circles on her cheek or her back with his finger and giggle.

Sometimes Veronika would pretend to sleep and when he started to draw little circles she would catch his index finger with her mouth saying:

"Aw, monster, I'll bite off your finger."

"Ha-ha-ha-ha Lonika, that's me - Yugo, yes?"

One day, without apparent reason and without knocking Mother Elsa walked into Veronika's bedroom and sat on a chair.

Veronika didn't lift her eyes from her book.

"What are you reading? I hope it is something inspirational."

"None of your business. It isn't a Bible, just to inform you."

"Gothic literature, isn't it?"

"Why would you care, leave me alone."

She stood up and said in German:

"No more Hugo in your room at night, all right!"

"Whatever."

But Hugo did come. The following night. He climbed up Veronika's bed, they hugged and huddled and an hour later Mother Elsa walked in and tried to untangle Hugo from Veronika's embrace. Hugo protested when she said that he had to go to his bed, he started to kick his legs and arms and cry but Elsa didn't show any mercy while trying to wrench him from Veronika's tight hold.

"Why are you doing that, you witch?"

And Hugo through tears said:

"Doin' dat witch?"

Elsa said nothing just carried him out and laid him, all in tears, in his bed, then she locked the door.

The next morning she found Veronika at the kitchen table with her hair cut off and painted in blue.

"You are mental Veronika." to what Veronika replied:

"And you are not?" and continued to butter a slice of bread. Beautiful thick German rye bread baked by her devoted Mother Elsa.

She hated that dark, thick bread and never took it to school but bought a sandwich on her way, a sandwich made with nice, snow-white, still warm locally baked bread. While eating she stumbled upon Friar Marag; he opened his mouth to say something but she turned her head to the other side, turned her back and ran across the road; she liked the devil himself better than this wicked, wicked sly man.

Pia in the Window

One of the days in the first week of April in 1984, as the spring sun enticed him out of the house, Gregor Truba passed by a jewellery shop. He had passed by this shop countless times in his life and had never paid any attention to it, as he never had any interest in visiting such a place. What caught his attention was the woman who was fixing something in the window. Without hesitation he shot in as he had recognised her long black hair, her delicate long fingers adorned by rings, her turtleneck black sweater and her cherry-rose sealed lips.

The little bell rang as he walked in and found himself face to face with a dark-haired beauty standing there, speechless and confused, as a schoolboy would be in the presence of a beautiful but fear-inspiring school teacher.

She fixed her liquid green gaze onto his face while his mind stood still-frozen. All he was aware of was - it was Pia, a perfect replica of Pia. Even the clothes were identical - dressed impeccably in black from the top of the head down to her boots, even the stones in her rings were black. Black agate. But, the woman, the replica of beloved Pia was at least twenty years older than the original piece of art. Even though she could have been in her early forties, she preserved the beauty of her youth as some women do (without making ridiculous fools of themselves by tacky facial surgeries), as if God were full of mercy when he generously gave her such a gift to extend, to be everlasting. Only a few lines around her eyes and her lips hinted that she was well over Pia's age. However, everything else was Pia's: lips, beautifully crafted when closed and open, perfect teeth, a little nose, straight, an abundance of hair and long, long eyelashes, alabaster flawless skin. She even smelt like Pia.

Without any doubt in his mind, Gregor Truba was positive that the beautiful woman was Pia's mother. God otherwise couldn't have created an absolute replica, the same features, the exact look, if they hadn't been blood related.

The look in her eyes was stern and it aggravated his discomfort. While he was standing, his eyes fell on the paintings hanging on the main wall with a price tag underneath, hence he said:

"Fantastic paintings, are they for sale?"

"Sure, please, take a look."

Closer he came and with undivided attention started to examine the un-framed canvases one by one. There were eleven oils on canvas and three of them followed the same theme and a trail of blood had a continual flow from the first to the third.

In the first painting of the triptych there was a blade stained by blood, three oranges and there was a portrait in the picture; a closer look revealed it was a self-portrait of the woman he assumed was Pia's mother. In the other painting there were letters inscribed with an address, the only visible words were *Pablo* and *Andalusia* and the trail of blood ran through the letters, while in the third painting there was a naked body with face turned downwards, only her hair was seen, hair thick and dark as a starless night somewhere in the wilderness of Andalusia; her wrists were cut but they were not bleeding; the trail of blood was coming from her heart with no sign of any violent act that the heart had been subjected to, like stabbing or a bullet, just a tiny trail coming out. A white dove in the distance, a dusty suitcase and a shawl. There were two letters on the mauve-coloured shawl: one painted in dark purple and the other in bright red: letter *"G"* and *"O"*.

Quite mesmerised he stood there not knowing how to read the paintings of that extravagant and morbid triptych, but deep inside he *'knew'* that those paintings, indeed, had some significance and connection with Pia's life, or her past, or anything, just anything that talked about her.

The woman, as Gregor took her for Pia's mother already, was rearranging some jewellery without further interest in her customer. He started:

"Powerful images. Who did them?"

"Some are mine and some my sister had painted."

"What about the triptych?"

"No, those are not for sale. All others are."

"Is this your gallery?"

She nodded her head without lifting her eyes. Her eyes were cat's eyes, they were Pia's eyes and he almost asked about Pia, but when he wanted to utter her name he felt weakness in his knees, in his heart, his stomach lifted and he felt like he was going to vomit, as if there were countless worms in his belly rising up like a storm, and he feared that they would pour out and embarrass him in front of Pia's mother. To prevent such a disaster he ran out of the jewellery shop as if chased by devils, worms, wolves and bad memories. The sun brought him back to his senses but his hands still trembled as if ready to play a guitar. Off he went to Dino's garage for a rehearsal that afternoon. When Dino asked, *"What the hell happened to you?"* he answered with a question:

"What do you know about Pia Odak?"

"Not much, not more than you, but I can ask; there are several guys I know who went to school with her. I know her father, people talk silly things."

"What silly things?"

"I don't know, I heard he is a pervert, but as little as I know him he comes across as a really cool guy. Just a bit different, creative dude, different to an average arsehole."

"What do you really mean by – pervert? Tell me, what do you know about them?"

"Listen, man, I don't know much and I don't care about petty talks of me-diocre minds. Man, he is super-talented and creative; Pia inherited his talents surely, such a creative chick... and, yes, you too have caught the 'Pia-fever' as we all did at a certain point. She has some sort of relationship with Barbaros-sa, doesn't she?"

"I don't know."

"I talked with Tina yesterday, she told me you left her for Pia. I don't blame you but just be warned."

"Warned of what?"

"You know, Pia – The Queen of Cool, or even simpler – No Heart at All. She takes what she wants or needs and leaves you with a broken heart for another hundred years. That's what I think, no mystery at all, she is just a cold beauty, a heartless little bitch.

Listen, on Saturday there's a big party at Quick John, the little Beatle, there will be some hot chicks, loads of booze and good grass, forget about her."

And, yes, Gregor wanted, sincerely wanted to let go of this obsession, but simply he – couldn't. She haunted him, and followed his every step, he wrote lyrics for her, unexpected, uninvited she came to his dreams, sometimes beautiful and surrendered and on some other nights she came with her wrists bleeding and sadness in her green eyes.

That week he met her twice in Veronika's doorway; she nodded her head and quickly walked in, and the other time she said a quick *'Hi'*. Just her long black hair was flowing behind her like dark wings, waving seductive but unspoken words, and Gregor couldn't decide or decipher if those words were inviting him closer or signalling *'stay away'*.

Yes. Gregor was invited to the party, but no one really told him it was a pyjama party, hence he came in his usual attire: black jeans; white T-shirt and unbuttoned linen shirt. Upon his entrance he was greeted with lots of screaming, cheering and laughter as the girls demanded that he should go back home and return in his pyjamas, or otherwise – that he undress down to his undies, or even better go the full monty; he complied saying to the crowd that, anyway, he slept in his undies. He took off his clothes and showed his German-God-like-body, then he took a microphone ready to perform and said:

"Don't salivate girls, you'll drown us all."

He went to the bar followed by several female fans and loud cheers as other guys took off their pyjamas and stayed in their underwear too. Loud calls for the girls to take their pyjamas off were coming from all corners. Some girls immediately started to undress giggling, others waited for later hours when alcohol took away all their inhibitions. Just showing up dressed, disobeying the party theme from the beginning, he initiated and promised a very merry party.

When he finished his second song he rolled his cigarette comfortably reclining on the armchair. By that time his eyes were perfectly accommodated to dim light so they could detect, a short distance away, naturally, clad in black silk pyjamas, Pia immersed in deep conversation with a man sporting longish dark hair. The man with longish, well-cut dark hair was his friend Davor, Barbara's boyfriend, so somehow he felt relieved without knowing exactly why. Or, was it so?

"Man, that was good!" Davor said when Gregor sat next to them.
"You know my friend Pia?"

"Yeah, I know Pia."

Pia said nothing. She just sat there in her black silk pyjamas, with rings on her fingers all with black stones in the middle and with secrets in her deep eyes.

What came to Gregor's attention this time, that Pia wasn't aware of, was her careful and thorough examination of his bare chest and his broad shoulders.

Davor stood up to get them a drink, then Gregor moved closer to Pia and asked:

"Where's your boyfriend tonight?"

"I don't have a boyfriend."

"Then let me take you home in the wee hours", as she said nothing Gregor took it for a *'yes'*.

In the sky touching cypresses the day was born red as they watched it from the veranda. In the early morning Pia appeared to Gregor as an unearthly beauty, in her black silk pyjamas edged with dark pieces of delicate lace around the sleeves; her collarbone against the blackness shone with fine pearl colour; a tiny silver chain around her neck, a pendant with small letters *'Pia'* and the letter *'P'* was glossed with dark enamel.

They stood next to each other, shoulders almost touching, and looked as perfect secret lovers who just got up from a bed made of rose petals.

She shivered as dawn was just born still wet with dampness of the unseen womb, the air was cool, so he put his arm around her shoulders and with her gaze fixed on the rising sun she quietly said:

"Don't!" and it was apparent that Pia had intimate friendship with no one. When she turned her face to him their eyes met as she was almost as tall as the German God of Beauty, if there were such a one, and if there wasn't, Pia just named him in her head – Gregor, that'd be his rightful name. Even a little smile twitched her lips as this thought entertained her imagination.

"Pia, may I kiss you?"

"No!"

"Pia, why are you rejecting me? You know how much I long for you."

"Tell me more."

"Since I saw you I can't stop thinking about you."

"That's good."

"May I kiss you, Pia?"

"No!"

"Are you trying hard to be faithful to your boyfriend?"

"No boyfriend!"

"Barbarossa?"

"No boyfriend."

"Anyone else?"

"No boyfriend." she said it for the third time and left Gregor standing on the veranda to cool down his heart. He yelled behind her:

"You are heartless, you little beautiful witch." and he reached for a cigarette from the packet that was left on the table. After finishing the smoke he found her curled up on a sofa covered with a little white blanket, *'Snow White'* he thought, then he said:

"Pia, let's get drunk now."

"Five o'clock?"

"Forget the clock, let's get drunk together and make love all day long."

"Pig."

"I am. But all I can think of when I see you are just those sinful thoughts. Pia let me examine what's under your silk pyjamas."

"Pig. Stop talking."

She was tipsy; he was more than tipsy.

"I don't wanna stop talking, I had too many sterile conversations with you. Let's talk sweet or dirty perhaps. Sweet talk would be 'Oh, Pia, I fell in love with you at first sight', or let's talk dirty..."

"Stop! Stop it! I don't care about you as I don't care about anyone else. I simply don't care. You don't even know me – just go away. Go, go!" She pulled the blanket up and covered her face. There was no one left in the house, none but a few who were sleeping somewhere in bedrooms, but the majority had already left.

"Call a cab for me."

"I'll give you a lift home, you don't have to kiss me as a favour, I was just teasing you, Pia."

She gave him a little melancholy-charged smile and softly said, *"I know you were."*

While driving he was thinking what would be a common interest or a trait of character that Pia shared with his sister. Maybe, after all, Veronika wasn't such a *'freak'*, a *'weirdo'* or a *'misfit'*. As Pia was highly intelligent, sensitive and talented there should be something really substantial in Veronika's personality that Gregor had probably overlooked or ignored.

He knew two things: Veronika never had a close relationship with Mother and he could not ever understand why, and the second thing he knew was that Veronika hated, from the depths of her being, Mum's *'angel'* – Friar Marag. Passionately, as one can love madly, she despised him with the same might. Once, just recently, upon his leaving mother's morning quiet talks Veronika said:

"Oh, your Angel has left, the blessed immortal winged creature, but the wings are as dark as the ones of those shadowy demons, tempting us to err, he is constantly whispering wicked thoughts into your ear. Be aware sweet Elsa, be warned, little blond darling."

Neither did he himself like Friar Marag in all honesty, but alas, if mother had found in him a good companion, and perhaps, some sort of divine counsellor – *Why not?* He never perceived their friendship as wicked, like Veronika did.

Now, he remembered the first incident that laid the path to a mutual mistrust and aversion between the two of them.

That particular summer, Veronika was about five, while Gregor was almost nine; they had an invasion of ants in their kitchen. Ants would form a long line and obediently march to different sources of freely, though not deliberately, offered food. Particularly, they loved the crumbs of mother Elsa's thick German rye bread, but there were always plentiful sources of nourishment everywhere: on the kitchen table, on the floor, on little Hugo's chair, on his cardigan, in his hair, around the sink and on the cutting board. They had a navigation map inbuilt and wherever German bread was cut they would mobilise the army and diligently press on with their hard but rewarding work.

What was Veronika's blind obsession with ants, runs as follows:

She would put her finger in the middle of the tidy line and the ants would spread around in semicircles. Then, she would press those semicircles sometimes with her index finger, sometimes with her thumb, then gather the ants in the palm of her hand, lick them off her palm saying, *'Hmm, yum!'* to the uttermost disgust of mother Elsa. It would easily land her into a pink rage and she shrieked so loudly that all the birds would avoid their house for an entire week. Everyone would react in this or that way offering words of advice or disgust. Everyone reacted except Veronika and little Hugo. And no one could ever stop her. In the seasons that brought the ants to the kitchen table Elsa even tried to bandage Veronika's index fingers and thumbs (yes, both hands, for when Elsa bandaged only the right hand Veronika used the *'spare one'*, as she would say), but it did not stop Veronika performing her duty using her elbow, then leaning against the table licking off the fallen army. She enjoyed this unusual play and loved to witness the panic her elbow bestowed upon them and then, the mad run of the surviving little creatures.

No one, no one ever knew, except Veronika and Gregor (only occasionally, only when deserved) that in Elsa's household corporal punishment was in practice. Gregor witnessed it twice, both times in connection with innocent victims, namely – ants.

Gregor never took Veronika's side, never felt like defending her, for he believed Mother Elsa to be perfect, hence always right. That feeling was mutual as Mother Elsa thought that her boy was a picture-perfect boy, with all noble genes transferred and delegated in divine order. Well, she adored him!

On the contrary, Veronika was born dark, with a thick dark mane on her head and her face was covered in small dark hair. When a nurse brought her in, Elsa screamed and was absolutely certain that the child had been exchanged by some mistake of a drowsy nightshift nurse. But, it wasn't the case as she was told that such a scandal had never happened in the hospital. Never ever had any child been misplaced or exchanged - she had to overcome this shock and denial of reality.

Anton tried to soften it:

"That is what mother said about my sister Veronika, that she looked like a little monkey, all covered in dark hair. Don't lose your heart, as you know Veronika was a gorgeous girl later on. Let's call the child Veronika and rest assured that she'll grow to be a real stunner."

Occasionally, Mother Elsa would refer to her as *'a little Gypsy'*. When Veronika grew a little bit bigger she turned into a lovely looking child, with rosy cheeks, cherry-red lips and big, big honey-coloured eyes. All her facial hair fell off a week after she was born, while the hair on her head turned thick, pitch-black and silky. She really looked like her aunt Veronika in those old black and white photographs that their grandma kept in a cardboard box hidden under her marital bed.

When any kind of incident in the Truba family happened, Anton Truba was never present. He was at work for the majority of the day but when he walked through the door harmony would walk in with him and as if by magic everything was tranquilised and transformed: Mother Elsa's face and attitude would significantly lighten up and she acted like those sweet mothers one could watch on TV shows imported from the land of freedom and happiness – from the U.S.A.

Therefore, very early on, Veronica deciphered and understood the meaning of (in Mother's case poorly hidden) hypocrisy. The majority of children learn that lesson much later in life, for to master that skill one needs a mature and sharp mind. And that was exactly what Veronika had: a mature and sharp mind that could detect hypocrisy as soon as it winked at her.

Well, let's go back to that date when Veronika and Friar Marag signed the secret, yet obvious, pact of mutual aversion that would grow steadily, from Veronika's side, into plain hatred. She hated him!

But, was he really that bad?

Such an opinion was formed by one child's unpolluted eyes and, still pure heart.

Veronika's belief that he was *'really that bad'* would be revealed through his actions that the future would bring along, the actions that would be of inevitable nature as they were born out of his language, out of his character as an inheritance from his past.

Veronika looked at the trail formed by the tiny soldiers keen to conquer a mountain made of dark and thick breadcrumbs. When the little soldiers surrounded the mountain and strategically started to load it onto their backs, the edge of Veronika's palm flattened them with a mighty blow – the majority of the army, plus the breadcrumbs, were glued to the edge of her palm. There was a little wry smile on her lips and as she brought the palm to her lips to lick them off Friar Marag took her hand, squeezed it hard, very hard and said:

"God Almighty created those ants the same as He created you. They have their holy duty to perform in the scheme of God's plans. Don't do that ever again. It's evil!" He said that sentence with a stern voice while holding her hand in his so tight that she felt his fingers penetrating into her bones leaving their poison there, yet on his face there stayed that ever-present benevolent smile, his signature benevolent smile.

Seemingly embarrassed she asked:

"May I sit on your lap?"

His smile became wider as would be expected to be from the one who just conquered the inferior and in the most agreeable voice he said:

"Repeat Holy Mary three times and, yes, come I'll give you a cuddle if your mother agrees."

Mother agreed without any hesitation, she just smiled approvingly. Then up Veronika climbed, onto Friar Marag's lap and she didn't hug him, neither did she bite his nose as mother Elsa probably worried might happen, but she sat there peacefully and her real intent was revealed when everyone witnessed a puddle under Friar Marag's chair.

She peed on him.

"The Devil's daughter!", shrieked Elsa while dragging her off by both hands into her room where she had locked her in for the rest of the day without any food or a sip of water. Veronika heard her apologetic steps going back to

soothe the wounded priest and she heard her mother mumbling, *'wicked, wicked child.'*

And when it came to apologising Elsa couldn't find words to express her regret and shame but all she met when she came back was his benevolent smile on his ever-placid face, just contrary to what one would expect to meet in such circumstances from be it a priest or not.

From those frequent lock-ins Veronika developed a solitary character hardened by harsh criticism for her extravagant and unacceptable antics. Because of those traits she was always very careful when choosing her companions may they be humans, animals or some other entities that she had been caught sporadically talking to. Even such a private practice as talking to unseen creatures was strictly banned by Elsa so as not to embarrass the family.

While driving and thinking of Veronika's troubled soul, the most powerful images, words and deeds came to his mind: last year's christening of Isabella, uncle Tomo's daughter.

The whole family gathered in their little garden after the christening and as always the guest of honour was none other but – Friar Marag.

Mother Elsa prepared a feast fit for a king; hence the family was gathered around the table. A professional photographer was called in.

When family members and guests settled with their plates and glasses on various chairs and little garden tables, Veronika meekly asked if she could read a passage from the Bible. Mother Elsa was standing next to uncle Tomo while the peaceful eyes of Friar Marag were resting on the back of her neck: a tender, loving look in his placid eyes.

Veronika was encouraged; they even gave her a round of applause.

Veronika opened her little book that she always carried with her in case she got to write in it something special that came to her mind:

"It was said that Jesus, to whose theology, our inevitable friend Friar Marag, has been a highly respected interpreter, taught us that the sin of lust could be, as well, carried out mentally and spiritually through an impure heart, and He, Jesus, said it as follows – Whoever looketh on a woman to lust after her hath committed adultery with her already in his heart."

48

Yes, a holy hail of silence fell upon the gathered group and the sunny day seemed to sink into the shadow of Veronika's words, mother Elsa's breathing became shallow but fast, Friar Marag kept his benevolent smile fixed on his face, he kept his eyes on his glass, only father Anton found words to utter:

"Veronika, here, take this money and go out, go to the cinema."

She took the money without any other comment, put the little book of wisdom into her pocket and walked away. The shadows she caused and brought down from above stayed after her departure, lingering for the rest of the day, which had promised to be sunny and bright earlier that morning.

***

Gregor sighed a deep sigh and parked his car as Pia said, *"You can stop here."*

"OK, Pia, see you around."

When Pia walked out of Gregor's car it was 5:30 am. Gregor started up the engine, then he felt a strong urge to light a cigarette. He turned the engine off, leaned back in the seat and for the first time an idea occurred: *'Maybe, after all, Pia wasn't an arrogant, stuck up beauty, maybe she was genuinely timid or sad."*

It rang loudly through his mind – *Timid or sad.*

Or maybe it was just wishful thinking.

From his thoughts and dulled awareness caused by the sleepless night, he was brought back to the present moment when through the open window a hysterical scream erupted. He recognised Pia's voice at once and ran out throwing the cigarette away. There he found her cornered to the wall by a man with red hair and red beard. He held her wrists up and against the wall while he continued to push her.

And then, he, Gregor Truba, a proud son of German ancestors, with a body of *Apollo* and the anger of a starved wolf, charged in. He thundered:

"Let go of her. Right now, let go!"

"Who the hell are you? You have nothing to do with us; don't interfere. She is my girlfriend and this is none of your concern."

"It is of my concern because she has spent the night with me. She might have been your girlfriend but she has just learned that she needs no pussies that are brave only when facing the weaker. Come over here, I'll show you how I deal with motherfuckers like you."

He came closer but in no time he found himself spread onto the asphalt: nose bleeding and the left eye stinging as hell. He tried to get up but Gregor hit him once again across the face, then helped him up and while Barbarossa was leaving Gregor said:

"Stay away from her, and stay away from me."

Pia was standing unable to say a word; Gregor took the keys from her hand and asked, *"Which floor?"*

"Third." she whispered, and with his arm around her shoulders he walked her into her apartment.

Pia offered a strong cup of coffee but he suggested he should make it while she took a shower. When she came out two cups were on the table. She sat next to him and her silk dressing gown fell off from her knees revealing her slim, long and beautifully shaped legs. Before Pia managed quickly to pull it up and cover her legs, Gregor noticed blue and blood-red marks all over her thighs. The marks looked like bruises still swollen with blood.

Her eyes were tired and reddish when she said:

"Thank you Gregor, you can go now."

In the doorway she touched his hand with her long fingers still adorned by several silver rings with dark stones in the middle and, even overly tired, his body trembled with pleasure.

And this episode marked Pia Odak's and Gregor Truba's friendship, which commenced on that April morning around 5:30 am in the year 1984. For Gregor Truba it was almost simultaneously the beginning and the end of his happiness.

Another Page from Pia's Diary

The next time Gregor infuriated Pia was when he asked that forbidden question.

"I went to the jewellery shop and the woman I met there is an exact replica of you, just some twenty years older. Was that your mother?

Then she lost it!

She pushed the glass and it almost landed on the floor and if it hadn't been for Gregor's quick reflexes it would have smashed onto the tiles. His jeans were painted red with *Bloody Mary*; she banged her fist on the table and screamed:

"How dare you! How dare you pry, you sticky beak! Why are you following me, investigating me? I owe you nothing! Leave us alone!"

She stormed out and all eyes were fixed on him. Hmm villain!

'What did I do?' he asked himself. *'What a reaction, no wonder she is friends with Veronika. They are both mental.'*

But that thought wasn't enough to calm his fears. He feared she'd be mad with him forever; she would cut him out for eternity.

He left a note in her mailbox.

"I know nothing about you, Pia, and never wanted to intrude into your sealed privacy. To explain myself: I want to say that I just met that woman by chance, hence forgive me for being born in the same city as you were, forgive me for meeting people you wish I had never met. Forgive me that I met someone I wasn't supposed to meet because that chance meeting had upset you unbelievably. Sorry for trying to be a friend and for not knowing that the certain topics and the certain people were forbidden to be brought up. If you wanna stay friends, please write a list of topics and people that I would be allowed to mention or discuss. I am on my knees, your Majesty! If you decide to forgive me, I have two tickets for our concert on Saturday, so you can bring a friend along.

The biggest sinner ever, the man who dared to challenge Pia, the Queen of Coolness, your loyal admirer and blind servant, Gregor Truba."

That night when Gregor came home late, under his bedroom door he found an envelope Veronika pushed through.

Pia answered with a poem.

A few sentences preceded:

"She had stolen everything: my oranges and my suitcase, even the letter from Pablo of Andalusia she had stolen, and all I was left with was my signature underneath."

Three oranges
Three candles: red, white and a black one
The letter there, in the middle
From Pablo of Andalusia...

A knife...
With a long, smiling blade
Anxiety...
A rainy day...
Horizons in the past and
A stiff bread-roll halved for you
In case you came back
Hungry ...
Like a hungry wolf
And the shiny blade
Smiling
Unforgiving
I am begging it
I am begging my memories and the rain
I would never beg you

DETHRONED

What do you know about forgiveness?
Kindness?
Blade naked
Lip dripping and the blood
As a rain
Warm and
Welcomed
Perhaps welcomed, on the secret page
Where a password never was given
Don't remind me
Don't ask me to put 'please' in my sentences
I cut out those 'please' with the bleeding blade

Forgive yourself

Eat oranges, one by one,
Blow out candles, and the black one too
Blow the wind from the source of your coolness

Cry!
In your heart
Don't let her hear it!
Don't! (without 'please') just – Don't!

(for Luna, 1981.)"

Gregor somehow read that Pia has forgiven him his intrusion into her privacy, but from that note and the poem he had divulged that she hadn't forgiven *someone else for something that had been done!*

Or was it just another Pia's poem?

'*Where did it come from?*' he wondered, '*the dripping blood, the blade, unforgiveness and heaviness? What kind of dreams did she have?*'

***

He knocked on the door to Veronika's heaven.

She painted the ceiling with stars: red, yellow and mauve. Among the stars she had written in Gothic letters *Veronika in the sky with diamonds.*

She still had a teddy bear in her room. She found a good excuse for having it at seventeen – Hugo liked to come into her room and she kept it for him to play with. She said without knowing who knocked on the door:

"What do you want?"

And the other, sweeter voice repeated it:

"Yeah, what, what, what do you want?"

Gregor said with a grin on his face:

"I want to play with my little brother and my sister, may I come in?"

"No!" said Veronika.

"Yes!" said Hugo and smiled at Veronika leaning his blond head onto his left shoulder, his tongue out, wet and dripping. Veronika wiped off his saliva and said in a low voice:

"Don't get too excited, you little puppy."

"Little puppy, funny Lonnie."

At that age his speech had improved much, but he still felt the most secure when he just repeated other people's sentences, when in agreement, and he still kept calling Veronika *Lonnie.*

"Lonnie, do you know, you probably do, that... people, far there, like, like far, I think Far East, they look like me... Yugo might travel there, mingle with them and no one would find Yugo different. Ha-ha-ha Lonnie, you come to visit. They all look like... like... I think they are good people, as they look good and smiley. Ha-ha, Lonnie would you let me go?"

"No Hugo, I would never let you go. Who would wipe off your saliva, who would tuck you in?"

"Lonnie, not for real. Just for a story, then we travel together just in a story... and then ... and then, and we meet people that look like Yugo, but not with blonde hair, but black. Ha-ha-ha, Lonnie, can you see Yugo dark? Ha-ha, Yugo likes being blonde, Lonnie's dark, Yugo loves Lonnie. Lonnie loves Yugo?"

"Guess."

"Hmm, guessing, guessing, guessing... let's see... ha-ha-ha, I gotchya, you are worried, you think Yugo doesn't know Lonnie loves him? You think that? You think that! Ha-ha-ha, Lonnie's a funny gal. Lonnie loves Yugo and Yugo loves Lonnie the best. Ever. Forever Lonnie."

Only Veronika talked his language, only she understood his language and only Veronika made him feel special by treating him as *not special*.

She would tell him:

"Bugger off, you little shit." and he would laugh his head off, while her mother would run to the rescue, to heal the scars, to scold Veronika who would walk out and let her be *the best person in the whole wide world*. But Hugo would run after her saying:

"Lonnie, Lonnie, the little shit wants to play with Lonnie."

Veronika's kisses onto his head were the sweetest kisses for Hugo, even sweeter than the daily *Kinder* egg Veronika would buy for him on her way home from school.

Veronika knew that mother prayed every night to their tongue-tied God asking to *'improve Hugo, to make him, somehow, normal, to take that shame away'* and asked God in her intimate conversations, governed by the meek Friar Marag, *'Why such shame had befallen their family?'*

To Veronika Hugo was just a sweet brother, a little angel, a *Unicorn*, as she would call him; he was pure hearted, innocent, full of insatiable energy and warm to the extreme.

Gregor walked in and found them head to head lying on the bed and looking at the stars on Veronika's sky. Hugo said:

"Come, come, lie here, next to Yugo and Lonnie. We are looking at the sky. Lonnie painted it for Yugo."

"Bullshit. Lonnie painted it for Lonnie. You see, it is written Veronika in the sky with diamonds, isn't it? Where does it say Yugo in the sky?"

"Ha-ha-ha, Lonnie, you little devil. Yugo is going to come up to your sky and paint Yugo in letters there. Yugo and Lonnie forever."

"What about Gogol? May I write my name in your sky, guys?"

"No, you are already a star, Gogol. Mum said that you are a star, you play your guitar and lots of girls ring home and ask Mummy where's Gogol. No one asks for Yugo, no telephone calls for Yugo, ha-ha-ha, me and Lonnie, we have our own sky where we are stars, aren't we Lonnie?"

"Yes, Yugo. We are each other's stars."

"OK, then, Lonnie, up you go, go, go... up you go and write it up – Yugo and Lonnie."

"I will write it up there Yugo, but not today. I promise I'll write it by the end of the week."

"Yeah, when your tall Pia comes she can write, she is clever. Yugo loves Pia, she is pretty and very funny, and she loves Yugo back, doesn't she Lonnie?"

"Oh, yes Yugo, Pia loves you, she always asks about you and sends Kinder eggs."

"And... and, and she sends, she... she sends, what is it called, Lonnie, what she sends?"

"She sends origami birds for Yugo."

"Oh, yeah, loligami birds for Yugo. You see; she loves Yugo."

"Everybody loves Yugo."

"Not everybody. There are boys that make fun of Yugo, they say Yugo looks like those people from far away, not knowing now what they say exactly, but they are not always kind to Yugo, and Yugo gets, he gets, very, very... he gets..."

"OK, Hugo, now calm down, all's well. Lonnie loves you, Pia loves you, Dad loves you..."

"Gregor loves you, too."

Hugo hugged Gregor hard and said:

"Gogol, you never said you love Yugo."

"I did."

"You did?"

"Sure, I did!"

"OK then, everyone is happy, aren't we? We are all happy Lonnie, are you happy?"

"Yes, yes I am."

Hugo laughed and clapped his hands the same way as he did when he was five.

Veronika's love for Hugo was deep and inexhaustible. Hugo was the only person that Veronika loved without hesitation, without judgment, without expecting anything in return: yes, it was unconditional love.

"Veronika, do you want to come to the concert on Saturday?"

"Why? Is it that I can bring Pia along?"

"No, Pia's already invited, she'll come anyway, but I thought that you'd be happy to come."

"And Yugo?"

"There will be far too many people, Hugo, it wouldn't be safe."

"You never invite Yugo. You invite girls but not Yugo. Why? Why? Why?"

He started stamping his feet and Gregor tried to reason:

"Hugo, I'll record it and will bring it to you and we can watch it on Sunday."

"No! No! No one ever calls Yugo. Ever! You are not my favourite person. You are not Yugo's good brother. Go! Go, now!"

He was reduced to tears but Veronika took his face into her hands, looked into his distressed eyes and said:

"What about Lonnie takes Yugo to the cinema? Right now Yugo, just you and me, hey? How about a big bag of popcorn? Let me see the smile. Yes, I can see it. Don't hide it, I can see it." Hugo buried his red face into her embrace and hugged her with both arms tightly.

Just as he was about to leave the room someone knocked on the door, opened it ajar and he saw her long dark hair hanging and covering half of her face.

"Pia, Pia, Pia, my sweet friend, Yugo is going to marry you one day."

Pia hugged him while Hugo kissed her on her cheeks and then on the forehead. Gregor had never before seen such an expression in Pia's eyes – the expression of kindness and deep empathy.

"Pia, are you going, are you going to bring, to bring.... Hmm, are you, Pia..."

"Yugo, look at me," Veronika said in a commanding, yet kind, voice, *"Calm down; breathe, breathe, breathe! Good boy. Yes, hold hands, yes; deep breath-in. Fine, what did you want to say? Calm, now go ahead."*

"Thanks Lonnie! Thanks, my sweet Lonnie. Pia, are you going to bring your crayons and write Yugo in Lonnie's sky?"

Pia lifted one eyebrow, looked at Veronika, Veronika shot her eyes up to the ceiling and Pia smiled in a way that Gregor never saw her smiling – she showed all of her teeth and only one dimple on the left cheek:

"What do you want me to write?"

"Yugo loves Pia."

"This is Veronika's sky, she has to decide, but, no, no, don't get upset, I will write your name up but will leave mine out as this is only Veronika's sky, it isn't nice to intrude into someone's sky uninvited. Hang on, no, I won't ask Lonnie, because this is a family sky and I shall write your and my name in my sky, OK?"

"Yugo loves Pia. Pia you are a beautiful, beautiful gal. Mum said you are Gof, Yugo doesn't know what the Gof is but you must be a very beautiful Gof, like a Smurf, like Sassette Smurfling just with dark hair, but more beautiful than Gof Sassette Smurfling."

"OK Hugo, let's get dressed and we'll take you to the cinema at five."

Hugo clapped his hands and ran out calling his mother:

"Mummy nice clothes for Yugo, he is going to the cinema with Lonnie and the beautiful Gof."

Veronika went into Hugo's room to help him choose his clothes, Pia said:

"Excuse me, I gotta go to the loo." And she left her bag lying open on Veronika's bed.

What temptation!

He wanted to steal at least one more page from her black notebook. He counted that he had approximately three to five minutes, and started frantically to look through the book as if he were going to find something of absolute importance. There were a number of poems; he leafed through trying to find something that stood out, something like that obituary he found last time.

There was no obituary but there was a date circled with a black marker and the first sentence was underlined.

No day passes without hope of reconciliation, you and me, without guilt and secrets, without pain and longing, without the past, just everlasting present going into an infinite future. I miss your hands with countless fingers that touched my hair and my nose, I miss your stories and origamies, and I miss the dawns that aren't red as they were red only when we watched them together, when the sun kissed the sky as you kissed my forehead, your kiss like a feather's touch so gentle and unearthly, oh, kiss me, kiss me, kiss me in my sleep in my walking hours, be my shadow, my breath and my secret page where we can meet and exchange pain, pain, pain, as rain drumming on my face, don't go, don't fade, stay, stay, stay... teach me how to carry that pain, how to count those days without you, faced with indifferent eyes full of reproach and..."

He heard her footsteps, shoved the diary back into her bag and leaned against the window. The expression in her eyes had changed: there was no more kindness with which she looked at Hugo, just that usual expression of indifference.

"Are you coming on Saturday?"
"Is Veronika coming?"
"Yes, I believe so."
"Good. Then I'll take Barbara with me."

Hugo came in accompanied by Veronika, dressed in his best clothes; his hair was combed over his head and behind his ears. Pia said:
"Now that you are handsome we can go."
He clapped his hands and hugged Pia again; Veronika half-whispered:
"Calm down, calm down."

Gregor wasn't invited; he stood at the window looking at that unusual trio with a faint smile.

'Who is Pia really and what was she hiding?'

'What or who was she afraid of?' Those were his thoughts before Mother called him to answer the phone.

***

When Veronika and Hugo came home it was about an hour later than Gregor anticipated. He heard from his room Hugo's sobbing and walked out only to find his favourite red cardigan all in tatters, Hugo's face snotty, eyes teary and Veronika red in the face, shaking.

"What on earth has happened?"

"Go away!" screamed Veronika but Hugo said through his sobs:

"He called Yugo a retard. Yugo's no retard, is he?"

"Who? Hugo, who called you a retard?"

"That man, that boy, he called Yugo a retard and laughed and pulled Yugo's cardie, and called Lonnie a freak and called Yugo a freak, and called everybody freak."

"Veronika, what happened?"

"Leave me alone! It's all because of you." she said and ran into her room.

Gregor took a handkerchief and started to wipe Hugo's snots and tears.

Mother came in panic and, when in panic, her strong accent sounded like barking:

"What happened! Where's Veronika? What happened? I told her not to take him out, especially not with that Goth. Where's Veronika?"

"Calm down, Mother, I'll find out what happened and don't worry, someone is going to pay for this."

Hugo said:

"He squeezed Pia's hand and pushed her."

"Who, Hugo? Do you know his name?"

"No, he said that Yugo's a retard", said Hugo and started to sob again.

"Did he have a red beard and red hair?"

Hugo nodded his head; Gregor ran out into father's garage, took a crowbar that served to lift the front of the car and went out with the crowbar on his shoulder. He knew where he was going, he knew where he would find him and yes, he was exactly there, sitting and sipping his beer.

Without a word he grabbed him by his shirt and pulled him up. With panic in his voice he said:

"Calm down man, what have I done to you?"

"I'll kill you! Right now, I'll smash your head with this crowbar."

"What have I done to you?"

Gregor hit him across his back with the crowbar and Barbarossa let out the shriek of a wounded animal.

"What have I done to you, you idiot?"

"Idiot, ha? And who is a retard?" And he lifted the crowbar to hit him, but Babarossa lifted his arms preventing his body, and the crowbar hit him across his forearm.

"What did you do to my brother?"

"I don't know your brother, what's wrong with you?"

"My brother came home crying, my sister was with him, where's Pia?"

"Ah, you care about Pia. So, the little retard is your brother."

Then Gregor lost it and started to hit him with his crowbar wherever he could reach him, but soon two policemen walked in as someone had called for intervention.

They took him with them.

Late in the evening the Truba family learned that their oldest son, Gregor Truba was arrested for disturbing law and order.

He was taken into custody.

It was nine o'clock in the morning the next day when the guard came to take him into a room where, he said, his lawyer was waiting to see him.

'A lawyer, I don't have money for a lawyer, who might it be that dad had organised?'

A tall man was standing there, dressed in a black suit, a snow-white shirt and a neutral tie. He had black hair neatly combed backwards; he was in his mid forties, a handsome and self-assured figure. He looked familiar and when he saw Gregor he smiled at him and said:

"Gregor, I am your lawyer, call me Boris."

"A lawyer?"

"Yes, you have found yourself in a little bit of a pickle my friend, haven't you?"

"Yes, but who sent you? My dad?"

"No. A young lady, Pia Odak, my niece. She came last night, it was past eleven, and told me what had happened. She asked for help, and here I am. Pia never asks for anything, and I never work pro bono, but it looks like miracles do happen: Pia asked a favour which is a good sign, and I am willing to compromise my stand regarding pro bono work. Tell me what happened?"

Gregor was retelling the story and Boris listened carefully taking some notes. Then he asked:

"What's your full name?"

"Gregor Bernard Truba."

"Hmm, Truba? Is that Truba, the mechanic guy, your father?"

"Yes."

"Hmm."

"What? Anything wrong with it?"

"No. He isn't an easy fella, is he?"

"What do you mean by that?"

"He himself has been here a few times. Hard working man but quick in judgments. Nevertheless, now we are concerned about you – how to get you out of this hole as quickly as possible."

"Can you?"

"Sure. And... Pia, how do you know Pia?"

"She's my sister's friend."

"Sure?"

"What do you mean by 'sure'?"

"She never asked anything from anyone. She would come to me only if it was a matter of ... never mind. Are you her boyfriend?"

"Not really, I wish I were, but I am not."

"OK, sign here, we'll talk soon and I believe the file will be in my office today and you'll be out by lunchtime."

And he was out by lunchtime.

He went to find Pia.

She opened the door sporting only shorts and a T-shirt. She was barefoot and her hair was wet. She smiled.

"Thank you, Pia."

"That's OK. He has to pay for that."

"May I kiss you, Pia?"

"No. You've got to earn my kiss."

"How?"

"Be different, not ordinary, be extraordinary."

"Am I not?"

"Not yet."

"Do you think that I have what it takes?"

She only shrugged her shoulders and slowly closed the door right in his face. She did it, though, gently with a smile on her face.

He knew there and then, when Pia Odak closed those doors that he was going to love this woman as none other ever would.

He knew that Pia Odak was running through his veins like some wild dark river, he knew that her poems were rhymes to his breath, that he could listen to her poetry and her voice till his last day.

Pia Odak, his Muse and his Ode.

***

When Gregor walked in he found in the living room his mother, father and Friar Marag. Mother ran to him almost in tears, hugged him and said:

"What did they do to you? Oh, Jesus, now they want my boy, now they are after my boy."

"No one's after me, Mum. I beat the shit out of him, that's why they kept me."

In a low voice Friar Marag said:

"Indoctrination, you see how indoctrination works, he believes they had a right to torture him."

"No one tortured me Friar. I beat the shit out of a man, I am lucky they have let me out, all thanks to a lawyer."

"A lawyer?" father Anton stood up from his armchair?

"What do you mean by – a lawyer? They gave you a lawyer?"

"No, Dad. Pia's uncle came."

"Who is Pia and who is her uncle?" asked Anton in disbelief.

"The Goth girl?"

"Mum, don't call her Goth-girl, her name is Pia. Yes, her uncle is a lawyer, he came this morning and shortly after they let me out."

"Sure they did," said Friar Marag with one eye half-closed and fingertips touching on his chest, then he turned to Anton saying:

"That's the Odak clan."

"What do you have to do with them, with the Odaks?"

"Pia's Veronika's friend."

"Even better, I told her that from that girl nothing good could come, but one never was able to reason with Veronika."

"That is the same lawyer who always covers her father's arse, isn't he?"

Friar Marag crossed himself several times quickly as if protecting him and the whole family from unholy forces.

"The lawyer, the public prosecutor and the third one, is the Devil himself. Sorry Father, for mentioning the unholy name but I have no other words for him."

"The famous brothers Odak, nothing passes unnoticed by them. Was it all because of that devil's daughter?"

"Mother, please, calm down. I don't even know what you are talking about. Nothing happened because of Pia. I went out and kicked the arse of a man who called my brother a retard, he ripped Hugo's cardigan and ridiculed him in public. He was with Veronika and Pia. When I heard what happened I

ran out, found him and broke that club on his back. Pia's uncle came only because she asked him to help."

"Ah, poor fool! Don't let them fool you, son. He came because he is an operative, a spy. He knows who you are, don't you worry. He knows who your father is." Friar Marag barely finished his sentence when Veronika took over:

"Oh, kind Friar, God's emissary and the protector of the weak, he knows that the Odaks are not the creation of God, they are not possessed with the same beautiful spiritual body and mind with which a manifestation of the Almighty is endowed – 'Raging waves of the sea, foaming out their own shame; wandering stars, for whom is reserved the blackness of darkness forever.' Be warned, Mother, be warned by God's meek representative."

In the room silence stood frozen.

It was broken like glass by a cheerful voice:

"By God's meek representative," Hugo clapped his hands and hugged Gregor saying:

"Wanna play chess with Yugo?"

"That'd be the best choice Hugo, let's play chess."

The Odak Brothers

In the household of Jure Odak three boys were born. It was an honour and privilege to father boys. Jure Odak was a doctor who married a young woman who studied midwifery in Vienna. When the war ended he continued his studies commenced in Vienna in 1939 and on the day he came back home there was an omen in the sky. He left the train at the crack of dawn and looked up to the sky: there was the number three formed by rosy clouds, there were three stars aligned above it, the stars that he could swear he had never seen in the sky before.

He married a woman he loved, even though his father, a district judge, said, *"If she were of the same faith it would be better, but let's hope that it'll turn out for the best."*

It turned out that she gave him three boys in the first five years of their marriage. The eldest, Ivan, showed high intelligence, the same his grandfather was endowed with from the moment the child showed interest in the world around him. Jure said to his father, *"This one's going to be like you, a top brain, probably a judge, yes, just like you."*

The prophecy came with such precision, but given that the family was highly intelligent and wise it wasn't a real surprise that Ivan became a well-respected and feared public prosecutor.

The next son born to Jure was Boris, who almost outshone his older brother with intelligence and wit. Even though his father wanted him to be a doctor he showed interest in the legal field, too. Anything that had to do with disputes, investigations, litigations and negotiations, he was called to get involved in since his early youth.

In the eighties, it was known, there wasn't a brainier or more aggressive lawyer in the whole country. He was involved in the biggest cases be it of criminal or political nature. Impeccable by all means.

DETHRONED

The third son born to the Odaks never showed anything in particular, not any distinguished talent or interest … yes, he read a lot, but was not cut out to be a writer or an academic. Then, of what use would be all of those books that he had read? Probably stored in his mind as a dowry for the future.

He had two openings to his future.

The first one was when he formed a little theatre group at his university. That secured and sealed his future, just with one precise decision he became the God of Theatre for many years to come.

The second opening to his future was caused by his uncontrollable lust for young and pretty girls and that vice mapped his roads of extravagant voyages.

Ivan and Boris looked alike, they looked like brothers: both were tall and of solid build, with dark hair and longish straight noses. They spoke with determination in their voices and were prone to think before talking. They both inherited Mother's grace. Not Simon. He was short and stumpy, yet his face was the face of a handsome man though his nose was somehow short and snub with a few freckles, and he had lighter hair. His temperament was of a more sanguine nature, he tipped towards all sorts of arts, his clothes were fashionable, outrageous sometimes; he enjoyed an excess of everything, a good-timer. Though, it wouldn't do him justice to say he was shallow or superficial. Well educated, well read and from an old family where good upbringing and manners were absolutely instilled and encouraged way back.

He never, really, had a problem with approaching a girl or taking her out for a date. But he had a problem with accepting the fact that some girls never wanted to go out with him. And that fact didn't add to his willingness to modify his character and his ways, but quite the contrary; it made him more assertive and arrogant expressing to the world unknown modes of being.

The upper limit for the girl that he would fancy was fifteen when he was twenty years old. And it stayed for quite a long period of time.

He wasn't the faithful type, the one who would marry, have a couple of kids and live happily ever after. No, not really. He liked the kick of excitement, the adrenalin when courting a beautiful young lady. Yes, beautiful, for less wouldn't excite him, less than beautiful was just invisible, plain, boring and average, so, he left *'the average for the average'* as he knew that he was entitled, always, in any circumstances, in any aspect the human experience only to – the best. Surely, the family name and reputation of generations of noble, kind people, added to such high self-esteem. One can imagine, that a man like him, wasn't really much liked by the wider community, but he never really cared about *'the wider community', 'society', 'norms'* and *'what was acceptable'.*

And as it happens often everyone finds their own match sooner or later.

He met a beautiful young woman, a student at the School of Dramatic Arts, a future actress and his heart gave in the moment his eyes met hers.

Yes, she was an extraordinary girl of such delicate beauty; she looked as if she had come from some far-away land, her complexion one shade darker to what was normal in their town; the colour of her eyes was neither green, nor blue, nor grey, but her eyes would change between those three colours as the sky would change its colours during the daylight hours. Her teeth were big and healthy, white and often on display, she looked like she was just ready to take a shoot for some high-fashion magazine. Her hair was a bit darker than the hair of an average person in their town - it looked like some hordes from the depths of the Balkans lost their child on the way to the wide seas and oceans.

She was sitting at the back of the little theatre and was eating an apple, when she lifted her eyes he left the script and in his most arrogant way said:

"Stop eating here!"

"Yes, sir!" she said teasingly and lifted her right hand next to her forehead in some sort of salute.

His knees went weak and he couldn't understand what had just happened with his arrogance and high esteem, as he said:

"And your name is?"

"Sapphire."

"Sapphire?"

"Yes."

"Mine is Lapis Lazuli."

She giggled:

"No it isn't."

"What kind of name is Sapphire? It is a gemstone not a name."

"Well, then, call me Gemstone."

"I'll call you Gemma."

"Oh, you are so clever, my real name is Gemma; Sapphire is my nick-name."

"Is it because of your rare beauty?"

"Probably."

After WW2 Gemma's parents stayed in Istria while the majority of Italians left the country which used to be Italy prior to the war, but as the borders had changed the Italians left their homes to the newcomers. Those that couldn't part with their ancient hearths stayed hoping to adjust to the new regime, regulations, language and new culture.

Even though the parents were wealthy they stayed, their family going way back, countless generations back; they belonged to this city.

But, alas, from being wealthy industrials with a mansion in the city and a villa in the country they became just *'ordinary citizens'*, almost second-class citizens to Croats who came from the inland. Their wealth was *'seized and generously shared'* as the new regime was kind to the poor, especially when it came to sharing the wealth of the wealthy, the wealth and money that never belonged to them.

The Bonifacio family had adjusted but they never liked the *'new occupants'* of their land. They had two young daughters and stayed aloof, apart from daily affairs, speaking Italian and instilling a sense of superiority into their children. Pride and superiority! Grandfather's factory was seized and nationalised and the villa in the country was given to the party leaders for their needs. The mansion in town was halved and a family somewhere from a passive part of the land moved in to enjoy city life and the fantastic sea view. They were loud and kept their habits of country folk forever as if to spite the former owners. They had the same rights as everything belonged to the state and all were treated as equals. Seemingly.

There were those who were equal and those who were more equal. More than equal. That was the Odak family – more than equal. They fought for the right cause. Not down to every member of the family, as Jure's brother was on the *'wrong side'* at the beginning of the War, but towards the end, when he had understood that his heart should be silenced in order to save his head, he changed his ideology and political views and ended up being the biggest partisan the country had ever produced. He was loud and proud but his good fortune was the fact that he carried that surname, the surname that could open any door.

The Bonifacios never wanted to mingle with Croats and hoped that their children would stay loyal to their roots and choose wisely. Those hopes were hidden deep in their hearts and souls, never spoken loudly as they knew that their home was no more theirs and they had to obey the new laird.

But they were more adaptable than they were willing to admit, for when they learned that the *Theatre Guy* was the grandson of a district judge, a respected doctor's son and the other brothers were young lawyers, they decided to show humility, change their language and accept the new regime with a little more kindness.

Yes, that was what they did when Gemma told them that the boy she liked wasn't of Italian origin. As long as he belonged to the most powerful family in town!

Gemma fell pregnant. Simon never would have called it rape, but neither did she willingly give in!

They had dinner after one of his plays and he made her drink more than she wanted.

She told him to stop but he always liked to do what pleased him; they got drunk and he took her to the hotel on the corner with a beautiful view of the harbour. He undressed her while she protested, she even bit him but he laughed it off, he took it lightly, as a game, foreplay. Her eyes were full of tears, she even begged but he laughed, he was a man, a man that women always begged: they begged for a role, for attention, for advice, for friendship, for a date or ride. They always begged him, what was the difference if women begged with tears in their eyes? Maybe she desperately wanted him?

But she didn't.

They made love, he took her as if he would take anything that belonged to him: carelessly, without attention, without respect or gratitude.

He took her virginity, and while she was crying he said:

"Don't cry; the first time is the worst. You'll get used to it!"

She refused to see him for several weeks and when she learned that she was pregnant she spoke to her sister.

"What am I going to do?"

"Tell him."

"And what then?"

"Marry him."

"Marry him?"

"Yes, marry him."

"I don't love him."

"Marry him. Love comes later. He is such a good catch."

*** *

Simon said, *'probably, maybe'*, or *'it couldn't possibly be mine'*. He was in denial of paternity, but he wasn't in denial of love, he told her he loved her but he wasn't ready for fatherhood, they were too young, he said a lot of things, but Gemma went to see Boris. He was outraged. First he talked to Simon, then to Ivan, then they talked to their parents and all of them agreed that they should visit Gemma's family. Yes, marriage was on the cards. It can't be said that Simon was unhappy with the deal, he loved Gemma, but he wasn't ready to settle down, to have a wife and a child. But he set his foot on this road and there was no return.

71

When Simon Odak married Gemma Letizia Bonifacio, nicknamed Sapphire, he was twenty-two years old and she was just eighteen. She looked like a porcelain doll in her white dress, with her dark long hair scooped on top of her head, her green eyes on that day were not sad but they were not happy either, hence their colour was a much darker green; as a matter of fact they were never that dark-green, they never had that colour of ripe-for-picking olives. It looked as if some deep but disturbing thought settled into her eyes and no one noticed it, not even her sister who always knew and read, with natural ease, each and every one of her moods. She saw her happy because she believed she must have been happy to marry Simon Odak, oh, how lucky she was, how lucky... if only she were as lucky.

Seven months after the wedding the most beautiful little girl was born, they named her Pia Letizia.

First Ten Years of Pia Letizia

When Pia Letizia was born on that golden spring day, in the early morning of 1961, birds ceased to sing as if their song, or their breath, were taken away by magic. There was absolute silence in the air; no one noticed the difference except her mother who, after the lengthy agony, gave birth to a silent child. She didn't cry.

Pia Letizia was born with three gifts: the gift of unearthly physical beauty, the gift of weaving fine words into rhymes and the gift of reflexive solitude.

The first gift, the gift of unrepeatable physical beauty was obvious from the moment she was born; she was crafted as if the finest artist took time and all his skills to create her to perfection. The second gift started to show when she learned to speak, then it was perfected when she started to write, which was exactly at the age of five. And the third gift, the one of reflective solitude, was easy to assume it would develop as the signs appeared and showed since she started to build her fragile life and personality day by day. She never needed company, the only person she ever needed was Gemma; she kept a distance from her father and had a profound need to be in the vicinity of her mother, immersed in silence but sheltered by knowledge that her mother was within eyesight.

She grew up speaking two languages, exposed to two different cultures, two different worlds often colliding: a strong lineage of intellectuals versus ex-industrialists, the communists versus capitalists' minds.

The constant struggle to prove who's who: *'Who had more knowledge'*, *'Who had more wealth in the past'*, *'Whose culture was the cradle of civilisation and class'* and *'Whose culture was a culture of slaves'*.

Her natural inclination was tipped towards solitude, and that was the way by which she avoided identification at the cost of denying the other side of her own self and her heritage.

Her mother's father, her *Nonno*, would say:

Branka Čubrilo

"Don't let them fool you into thinking that we are all the same, for we are not. Understand? – Not! Capisci? – No! Non siamo tutti uguali! These people don't believe in God. But, let me tell you, God has created us all different and that is for a good purpose. Look at the people around you: some are tall, some are not, some are fat and others are slim. Some people have talents and intelligence while others are not so sharp. God has created even little mongoloids, cripples. God gave us different talents, tasks, languages, skin colours and skills. Don't let them fool you that we are all the same as communism teaches. We are not the same; some people have very fine souls while others are still in the darkness of ignorance and evil. We are not the same, bambola, look at you, how beautiful and fine you are, and all the credit goes to our family. We always bore the best-looking females, we have always run the best businesses, we had the best culture prior to those devils who came from the mountains. Don't forget your roots. Don't let them fool you!"

Her other grandfather used to tell her:

"Pia, my fine girl, you are going to be a doctor, just like me. You are kind and thoughtful, and to distinguish one from plainness one has to educate oneself. There were people in this city who just wanted to accumulate wealth and they hadn't had much education, just plain pretentiousness that they were cleverer or more artistic. But, what I want for you is good education and you can carry our family's tradition of being a doctor or a good lawyer, like your grand-grandpa, he was the finest lawyer, a district judge, oh, I can picture you being a brainy lawyer. Brainy? The brainiest one, my sweet puppet! Aren't you my little puppet, just nodding your pretty head? Come over here and I'll read to you, we can start with Grimm Brothers, how about that?"

Grandpa Jure always fed her with stories. They would start with Andersen and Grimm Brothers, as Pia liked them best. Shortly after, he read her Chekov's short stories and fine poetry. The poems rhymed and they used to announce verses together, Grandpa in a deep voice and Pia, in a tiny little voice, like a little bird, which had found a fountain of everlasting nourishment.

But, Pia never liked to stay longer than ten minutes with anyone else but her mother. That was real nourishment. No, not the conversation or the loving words, it was just her presence that made Pia whole.

Nonna Oriana always talked in Italian and never wanted to learn a word from *'that language'* and when Pia used to visit she would play Mario Lanza's records and talk to Pia about their worthy ancestors; she talked about money, possessions that *'those devils took away'*, and she even christened Pia in church, where she was christened herself, without anyone's consent and anybody's knowledge. Just the two of them went out, then Signora Urlich and her granddaughter joined that quiet but important event; everything was hush-hush, only *Nonno* learned about it later and gave her, apart from the gifts, a handsome sum of money. Pia hid this money into a box, which she hid under her bed. Their maid had found the box and showed it to Gemma. When asked about the money Pia naively said that she had found it somewhere, but Gemma took that money away, so no one ever learned that Pia was christened in the Italian church by the Italian priest, the same one who had christened Gemma when she was a child. Somehow Pia believed that being christened was a great shame. As her grandfather would say that religion was a privilege of naïve housewives and weak men, it looked to Pia that those two groups were the most embarrassing and undesirable. She knew early that she was going to be *'someone very special'* as everyone would point that out as soon as they saw her, and being a housewife never fell into that category. She knew nothing about weak men, as from the very beginning she was surrounded by a bunch of opinionated, strong male characters. Her own father appeared to be the weakest one, since being involved in art and theatre he never matched up to the other ones – the two lawyers.

His weakness was often expressed in his eyes when they'd meet a beautiful woman, but Pia was too young to read and decode those messages. Her mother, however, was versed in reading those sparkles in his eyes, read him with unbelievable ease and she, really, never knew whether that made her sad or simply – tired. She grew tired and old before her time. Somehow, she always kept her appearance and looked as if she followed in the footsteps of Dorian

Gray – everlasting youth and beauty was sculptured on her face. Pia adored her gentle ways, her elegance and sophistication in everything she did.

"Do you love me, Mum?"

"Very much Pia, very, very much."

"You look sad sometimes."

"No. I am never sad when you are around."

"I feel the same."

"Good. Then all's well."

"Mummy, often, more often than not, I dream about you and I'm going somewhere far, just the two of us, without our family, yours or Dad's. I dream we are somewhere where just us, you and me, can sit and enjoy the silence. Where you can paint and I can look at your beautiful pictures."

"Let's hold hands and hang onto that dream."

"Are you happy when you paint?"

"Yes, for me painting is communicating, just as it is for you with your little rhymes. I understand, Pia, when you put words together, no one understands, but, you know, sometimes I paint your words, do you know that?"

"Yes, Mummy, it makes me happy."

Pia's paternal grandmother, Granny Sava, was born in a small village at the foot of a mountain which blocked the splendid view of the Adriatic Sea. She was the daughter of an Orthodox priest whose family was related to the famous Tesla family and was proud of such kinship; hence they would gladly mention that fact, if the topic became apparent. Sava was sent to Vienna to study. There she met Jure.

When Jure said he was going to marry her, his father said that he sincerely hoped that faith would not stand in their way. And it never did, as both heads of each family were wise and clever men, above profanity of vulgar attitudes, customs and assumptions. They kept together for every important event, decision or discussion.

Granny Sava used to sing while cooking and taught Pia numerous folk songs. She would sit Pia up, on the table, and while cutting onions and vegetables she would tell her stories and sing folk songs. After ten minutes Pia would say:

"Granny, take me now to my Mummy, I miss her."

"That's all right, sweet bunny, but you have to get used to walking around without your mummy, she's fine painting her pictures."

"Do you know, Granny, that she paints my words?"

"Oh, that's lovely! What words did she paint so far?"

"Dawn, dawn, dawn for my little Faun!"

"... and, who is the Faun?"

"Grandpa Jure read the story about the Faun. He was kept in the dark, he was lonely... and I wished he had some light in his lonely life, so I wrote, 'Dawn, dawn, dawn for my little Faun!' and Mum painted the picture. Next time when you come I shall show you, only if Mummy agrees."

When Pia was ready to go, almost at the doorway, Granny Sava said:

"And what about a kiss?"

"I only kiss my mummy, you know that, Granny."

Even though Granny Sava was Pia's favourite person after Gemma, she never liked to share intimacy. All her emotions were reserved and saved for Gemma.

They were like one artist in two bodies: one constructed the words whilst the other gave a form to those words; it was almost perfect, the ever-running flow of a silent creativity.

"I Love You, Pia"

After Saturday's concert they went to an after-party at someone's home. It was a beautiful house, on the edge of a cliff, full of art and antiques; later Gregor learned it was Igor's late grandmother's house. The view was stunning and with the pregnant moon in the sky; people were loud and if he hadn't been troubled he would have enjoyed that evening and most probably got drunk and flirty with all those girls who pronounced his name with so much sweetness that even the most-immune-to-vanity-guy would smile at his ego being this flattered and inflated.

There were two things that played in his mind: *'Was he going to be imprisoned or charged over that incident with Barbarossa?'* and the second trouble was presented right there – Pia was sitting with the very same guy, Barbarossa and they were chatting, smiling. *'What on Earth does this woman think! After all, she might be on his side, maybe it was all a set up as Mother pointed out.'*

Just recently he had learned that Pia belonged to *royalty*. A very powerful family indeed, they made laws and rules and they ruled the city and decided *Who's Who* in the hierarchy of the pyramid. And his father, Anton Truba, was right there on the widest, flat side of the current pyramid, right at the bottom. Plus he was imprisoned, if Gregor was right, twice, for unknown reasons and after the second imprisonment he had lost his job as a supervisor at the garage. Back he went where he had started – a car mechanic. And he never spoke of it, he never allowed Mother to mention it, and he checked the road thoroughly up and down, when Friar Marag walked into their house. *'Why?'* Gregor asked himself.

He was standing on a big terrace that offered a beautiful and peaceful view; he lit his cigarette and sat on the floor. Shortly after someone behind his back said:

"Do you want a chair?"

Next to him Barbarossa sat with two glasses and said:

"I have apologised to Pia. I'd like to apologise to you, too. I have known her since we were in Kindergarten, I loved Pia all my life and don't want to lose her as a friend. I was tipsy that evening. I didn't mean to harm your brother, I sincerely apologise."

"No harm done, man!"

"Yesterday I went to the police station and changed my statement. I just said that I was drunk and had annoyed Pia and your brother. I said that you just told me off. Just the way it happened. No bad feelings man, no bad feelings OK?"

"Yeah, OK."

"The concert was great. You should come to the poetry evenings down in the Club and join us, some good people gather there."

When he left Gregor was even more puzzled. *'Her uncle told him to change his statement, yes, but why?'*

When he came in after a short time Pia was no more. She had left, together with Barbarossa.

He sat in the car and drove around the city, slowly, as if he were looking for someone, searching for something that would soothe his soul. All he had found were lonely early morning figures that missed the last bus and it was still too early in the morning to catch one. All he met were stray cats and papers dancing on the pavement to the rhythm of the morning wind.

When he wanted to turn his car left, at the lights, towards his home his hands steered the wheel to the right and the road took him to Pia's house. He stood there smoking his cigarette not knowing what he was waiting for.

He wasn't waiting for anything; it was that strange feeling that he couldn't go home prior to finding out where she had gone. With whom had she gone? Why didn't she even come to say *'Hello Gregor'* and why did Barbarossa come to apologise?

***

On Monday morning Gregor came into Pia's uncle's office. A brass plate was standing on the most prominent building in the centre of the busiest part of the town. It read – *Boris Odak – Lawyer.*

He struggled to push the door: red, polished and heavy, it looked as if it were made of mahogany wood; he walked into a middle-sized reception room. The room was adorned with a number of diplomas and awards; some photographs of Boris with prominent political and contemporary literary figures; there were three armchairs and a little table, red and bare, and the big desk where a young girl with heavy make-up was staring at him. He said:

"Hi there!"

She put her hand up to cover her open mouth, then stood up, tall, slim and elegant, and said:

"I can't believe it! You are Gregor. Gregor Truba, aren't you?"

"Yes."

Redness coloured her neck (as her face was covered by heavy dark-brown foundation) and her sentences became fast, fragmented and high-pitched while she tried to explain how much she enjoyed Saturday's concert, what a fan of his she was and that she kept his poster in her room, and finally admitted that she had a smaller poster even in her bathroom, to which admittance Gregor crinkled his nose.

She told him that Mr. Odak hadn't arrived yet, but she was expecting him to come any minute and offered Greg a cup of coffee and ran to the desk to answer the phone that was ringing for too long.

Boris walked in without saying a word, perhaps *'good morning'* to the blabber-girl if not to a client he hadn't even noticed. The girl asked him about his appointment and when Gregor said that there was no appointment booked she, then, crinkled her nose and said:

"OK. That's not good, he won't let you in without an appointment... but, let me try."

She came out shrugging her shoulders.

"What did you tell him?"

"He said 'Truba?' Who the hell is Truba? How am I supposed to know, and why should I see him without an appointment? Book him in and don't bother me anymore.' Sorry Gregor, I tried."

"Try again! Tell him that I am Pia's friend. The one he had visited in custody last Friday."

Pia's name was the key that unlocked the door to her uncle's kingdom.

"What did you do sir?"

"Look son, all's good now. Go home, play your guitar and don't cause problems any more. And don't play the hero, she has never been impressed by heroes."

He said that, opened the file and at that moment no one existed for him any longer. Gregor walked out without saying a word but he was no less puzzled. Still, he thought that he might have been framed, or simply, that Pia played him like a game. *'What the hell was she doing with Barbarossa again, and where did they go together at four o'clock in the morning?'*

Gregor remembered the lawyer's words, *'And don't play the hero, she has never been impressed by heroes.'*

But he was not one to give up easily.

He went to her mother's jewellery shop. When he came in the woman was sitting in the high chair sipping coffee and leafing through the morning papers. She was elegantly dressed, but again, all in black. She had her hair tied up with a wide black band which emphasized the delicacy of her features.

"Can you make a necklace for me?"

"Sure. What would you like? Silver, you don't look like a guy who can spend a lot, come over here I'll show you a few lovely chains. Is it for a lady?"

"Yes, for a very delicate lady, with superb taste and unpredictable nature."

A little smile escaped and played in the corner of her lips. She looked just gorgeous, ageless and oh, so self-sufficient that, apart from her appearance, judging by her attitude she couldn't be anyone else but – Pia's mother.

They chose the chain and he said:

"Can you make a pendant for me?"

"Sure I can, but I'll show you what I have already, you might like one of these..."

"No, no, I know exactly what I want."

"That's easy then. What shall we do, then?"

"Letters that simply read – I LOVE YOU, PIA."

She put down the chain she was holding and looked Gregor directly into his eyes. She said nothing but just kept looking into his eyes. There was no expression on her face, but Gregor saw kindness or sadness in her green eyes...or was it something else? It could have been that Gregor saw exactly what he wanted to see, but in her empty eyes there was no kindness, no sadness, no empathy. She kept looking and then said:

"Yep, it can be done. When do you want it?"

"Well, whenever you manage, I suppose. End of the week?"

"That'd be fine. But...it'll cost you, my boutique is quite expensive and particularly if I make things to order."

"You tell me your price and I'll pay right now. Shall I come by Friday?"

"Yes, your beloved Pia will have it by Saturday, but...are you sure she is going to wear your necklace?"

"Why wouldn't she? Do you know her?"

She just gave him a little smile, told him the price for which Gregor swore he could have bought a second hand car.

What did he hope to achieve with the necklace? Was this woman her *'mother'*, as Gregor called her in his mind, when she imposed that question with a poorly hidden sting?

When Gregor came to collect the necklace the pendant wasn't the one he ordered. Yes, it read *I love you Pia* but the letters were the wrong size, too small, they were shiny black with red blood-like drop above the *'i'* in Pia.

They decided to re-do it for, yet another, small payment. This time Gregor gave her detailed instructions, he even drew it himself on the pad that she offered him in a slow movement and a little smile on her lips. While he was drawing it her long fingers were drumming on the counter as if they were bored, they were drumming as if they were drumming some war-calling march, some disturbed melody, while her face was the face of a porcelain doll; her emotions, if they were existent at all, were probably hidden in the drawer underneath the counter. When he finished his drawing he wrote next to it –

Please, no blood dripping (no red!).

The next week when he came to collect it he checked it out thoroughly: everything was the way he drew it, the way he wanted. He turned the writing on the backside and there was engraved a stamp – *Luna Gallery.*

When he walked out neither of them said a word. She stood at the window looking at his back with that little wry smile of Luna. She always had this little smile on her face, even when she was a little girl she had that smile of a disappointed, bitter adult.

***

When Gregor Truba came in front of his house, with a small box with *Luna Gallery* engraved on the top, and a necklace that read what burned in his heart, there was a car parked across the road. Nothing in particular that would draw his attention to the car, but as he slammed the door, both doors of the car opened and two men, as two trained robots, in synchronised steps were approaching. One had a wide smile and said:

"Gregor, how are you?"

He stayed puzzled as he couldn't recall knowing either of them and the man continued:

"Maybe you don't know us, but we know you. Come over here, please."

They just stopped him for a *'friendly chat'*.

They wanted to know *'How often Friar Marag visited his family, how and if he had ever directed attention to what they were talking about and finally how often his mother's father visited'*.

The other man, the one without a smile on his face, didn't say a word but he jotted down in his diary-like book a few sentences.

The smiley figure told him not to bother with this conversation, not to disclose it to others, as it wasn't really of any importance. He even said that he had enjoyed Saturday's concert and that Grgor was really a great musician.

What Gregor was thinking when he walked into the house was how he would present this gift to Pia and what she would think of it. He pushed it behind the chest of drawers made of walnut wood, still neatly wrapped in the paper of that fine *Luna Gallery*.

'This strange, strange woman can't be her mother.'

That was his thought prior to the blast of a tornado that swept away the room – Hugo rushed in saying:

"Yugo listened to Gogol playing on radio. That's my Gogol! Yugo's happy. Yugo loves Gogol. Gogol's the best brother."

"Let's play a game of chess."

"No, you let Yugo win. Yugo's not stupid. Yugo like to play chess with Lonnie, she never lets Yugo win. She is fair, you sing well but you don't get Yugo."

And off he went to find Veronika and left Gregor with the memory of the two *'friendly men'* that met him in front of the house.

'What did they really want from me?'

He threw himself on his bed with head full of unanswered questions: *'Who's the owner of Luna Gallery?'* *'Did Pia set him up while still being Barbarossa's girlfriend?'* and the final question, *'Was there a warning in the man's voice when he said that Gregor was really a great musician?'*

He went out again as he couldn't stay alone with his buzzing head and the singing questions. They sang, out of tune, an unusual *Song of Future*.

Not because of fear, but he resolved not to say anything about the visit of those two men, it could be that he didn't want to upset his father, or maybe his mother, he just resolved to put it aside, hoping that their excursion to his concert was a mere chance.

Was there someone that was checking him out? Monitoring his moves?

Why did his father never talk about his short imprisonments?

DETHRONED

Who was it that made the telephone ring very early each and every morning? Anton would just listen and say, *"Yes, I understand".*

If Gregor would ask him who it was that just rang, Anton's answer was, *"Never mind, go back to sleep."*

Mother whispered to Friar Marag just about everything, but the whispers were so low when she'd mention names such as *'them', 'they', 'us'* and *'ours'.*

Yes, there were two sides, shadows that Gregor feared might overshadow his days some time in the future, some time in the not so distant future.

The last thought before he let himself freely into that warm velvety darkness of sleep was, *'This strange, strange woman can't be her mother'.*

Luna, the Dark Side of the Moon

Many men had loved Luna, but Luna loved only one. The one she could never love openly and freely. Many men had slept in Luna's bed, but her soul had never registered any number in order to conserve the lowest amount of her dignity and self-respect. Many men helped Luna get where she had arrived but they were just a vehicle to her destination that, once reached, lost its meaning and the sweetness of the original illusion. She never broke up with her numerous illusions but kept them wrapped in fine cellophane very similar to the one she would wrap her customer's gifts in that finest *Luna Gallery* of hers.

She wasn't supposed to be a troubled child as she had everything that might keep a young child happy: a loving family (though, a little bit too proud, slightly arrogant and quick in their underestimations of others), a beautiful house on the edge of the sea, the advantage of speaking two languages from the very moment she started to speak, and she received beautiful gifts from her aunties that would arrive *'from the other side of the border'*. Oh, yes, and she was such a beautiful girl that anyone would stop in their step to pay her a compliment.

But none of the compliments would do.

Luna felt as a dethroned queen. She felt as if, wrongly, by some horrible mistake, she never got what was hers by birth right – absolute attention and obedience, yes – from anyone she came in contact with.

How come?

Well, in retelling this story we should go back, which means not to her date of birth, through her childhood, first loves and so on, but to the moment she appeared in that gallery of hers.

Back in the spring of 1971 Luna came into the mayor's office.

They sat down on leather sofas with their coffees, cakes, oranges, lemons…and who knows what else there was to greet her decision to pay a visit to the mayor. Without much introduction she said:

"I'd like to open a gallery. An Art gallery, where I can show my art: my paintings, my jewellery and sculptures."

"What a fantastic idea!" said the fat man slowly stroking his beard, *"How can I help you, Luna?"*

"I set my eye on that space under the town-hall."

"No, no, that is not possible. Not possible, understand? That space has been reserved for Olga, attorney Marin's wife. She is going to have her practice there and that has been decided, pick somewhere else."

"No! That's what I want."

"It isn't possible. Absolutely impossible! Absolutely!"

"So, you are saying – NO!"

"A firm – NO!"

"You are saying 'No' to me? To Luna?"

"Yes. This time I have to say 'No' Luna. This time. But, any other location you pick I'll see what could be done, my darling."

"What if I don't want to pick another location?"

"You have to, this time, my dear, nothing can be done." He was still stroking his beard peacefully.

Luna stood up without touching her coffee or cake, or any of those offerings put in a neat order by the lovely secretary. She said:

"Well, then, I'd better be going. I bid you 'good-bye' and I shall ask some of my other influential friends to see what can be done. You are just a pathetic puppet."

"Darling, you are wrong. No one, I said NO ONE would make it happen. It is impossible. Please, do not hurry sweetheart, sit down and think it over. I can offer some very attractive locations…"

"And what would happen if your wife, let's say, set her eye on that location? Would you knock her back the way you knocked me?"

"I didn't knock you back, sweetie. I am telling you that some things are not possible, not even for me. That location is out of the question."

"Fine. I'll go and talk to Alessandra."

"Alessandra! Are you sane, why would you wanna talk to her?"

"Tell her about us. Tell her about your lies. You lie to her, you lie to me, you lie to everyone: judges, employees, the public. You are a liar."

"Calm down Luna! Calm down, your temper is uncontrollable. I know you are angry with me, sit down, sweetie, sit down and finish your coffee."

"Are you saying that I am angry, or are you saying that you are going to do something about it?"

"Sit down, Luna, sit down!"

By the end of the year 1971 Luna had moved her furniture, imported from Italy, her paintings, her sculptures and her fine jewellery into the most prominent building on the main square of the town. It was refurbished, not at her expense though, and a big sign painted above it read – *Luna Gallery*.

She loved men of power.

She had that magnetism that would instantly draw anyone, but men in particular, into her, at the same time bizarre and irresistible world. The magnetism of her eyes was so strong that often only one look into the eyes of her victim was enough to cast a spell. She was Lilith, a dark beautiful lover who offered her delicious fruit with an equal proportion of impenetrable ice. A powerful spider who weaved her strong web of sweetness, hopes, sexual extravagance and false promises around her little flies until she sucked out of them all she ever needed at that moment. Even though she appeared to live for the moment she was set up for an eternity, led by a hidden master who gave her everlasting power and confidence.

Luna – like the dark side of the Moon.

She read each and every man who walked through the door as an open book, as an easy read, and was able to adjust to their level or frequency only if she wanted, only if she saw any sort of gain. Whoever crossed the threshold of the gallery she saw them as a potential pot of gold or as a helpless victim.

Her beauty was simple, yet obscene; her voice was velvety, yet harsh; her green eyes shone like cat's eyes, the long lashes made them seem soft but they were made of all the strongest crystals, like a nephrite jade, two shiny stones set to endure all sorts of upheaval.

Another powerful man who was just a little fly in Luna's web of magic was Marin Tintor, a general attorney. Marin had married Olga Laris in 1966. Olga Laris was Luna's best friend, same as Alessandra Primo was. The three of them went to school together, went out together and chased men together. To put the record straight – Olga and Alessandra chased men, and thanks to Luna they had success to a certain degree. Where Luna went they followed. The trend Luna set women followed. She played the cat and mouse game and when she got bored she would leave those little mice to the other as chewed up leftovers.

No one knew that Leo Maretti would become the mayor. No way! He was kind of a nerd, the boy who studied hard and played little. Before he became the mayor and got himself into the trouble of being corrupted and before he learned the fine art of fraud and deceit, he was a pleasant companion: well read, had sound knowledge of art and theatre and had a weakness for beautiful women. Luna's calculations were sound when she speculated that one day he might be a good lawyer, someone she might be in need of. She never wanted him as a boyfriend or, God forbid – husband, but to keep him under her spell for the rest of their lives. She knew she could have him forever as an obedient soldier who would never refuse any of her desires for his service. His sexual appetite was unquenchable and only Luna knew how to fulfil his hidden needs. She helped Alessandra to get to know him better and when their romance flourished she stayed at bay knowing that soon she'd be his queen again, yes, she knew it and that was exactly what had happened only two months after their honeymoon – he called her and said:

"I miss you, my dark angel."

The other man she shared with her best friend, Marin Tintor, was in agony for years. He was the only official boyfriend of Luna. When she met him she was only sixteen. Marin was six years older and they embarked on such an emotionally charged relationship that she ran away with him when her parents forbade her from seeing him as they wanted to preserve her dignity and virginity for an Italian man, the son of Father's friend who was heir to his father's factory in the vicinity of Venice.

The lovebirds were not caught and brought back to justice or anything along that line. No, Luna grew tired and bored of Marin, who, after only two weeks, exhausted his repertoire of extravagant fun, and became just a plain young man, incapable of doing outlandish things for Luna – to take the Moon down for Luna to see what it was made of. She came back home tired but with well-planned tactics. She came with tears, apologies, accusations, promises and remorse. They took her in but the marriage to the heir of the factory in the vicinity of Venice was out of the question. And that was Luna's real victory! Her real aim hidden behind the cheap theatre of the Prodigal-Son-Play.

Again, a short time had passed and Luna grew bored with the plainness of her life. She waited for him knowing what time he would walk uphill to his university, she crossed the road. His heart skipped and in spite of his decisions and hurt pride, he stopped and said:

"I miss you so much Luna."

They never went back to being boyfriend and girlfriend again, but Luna informed him that her family said they would kill her or him, if she only went back to him, so she told him that they had to keep the relationship secret, hidden almost forever…but, as long as he was sure that they could see each other he really didn't care if the relationship were to be a secret of not, as long as he knew they could be together. No matter how; no matter what - as long as Luna was his again.

And no one knew that Luna had two lovers: as for Leo, he was a *'happily married man'*, and Marin, he feared Luna's fears – they might be punished by her family who were absolutely disgusted by their runaway antics and the fact that he had *'ruined Luna's chance to marry into a wealthy family.'*

She played them as a dark queen would on a chess-board moving them as wooden pawns from one place to another, from one task to another and from one achievement to another, yes, her achievements.

To hide their relationship and keep it alive she suggested to Marin he should start to date other girls. Initially he was reluctant, but when she said that she might stop seeing him as they drew attention and suspicion, he gave in. She had introduced Olga to Marin and they started to go out, sometimes all three, sometimes just the two of them; with time Marin started to appreciate that arrangement, it gave him a strange sense of self, he felt to a certain extent like a local *Casanova*, a sort of man who goes around women with ease. It was a completely erroneous assumption as all his arrangements were led by Luna's careful hand, wisely, meticulously calculated to the last miniscule detail.

Even when Olga asked her to be her maid of honour Luna said:

"With absolute honour."

Yet another victory for her invincible tapestry which she weaved with the threads of her colourful and hidden madness.

And for Leo, the mystery of *How Luna got that hall for her Gallery* stayed locked away forever, yes, forever, because Luna's footsteps were always covered with thick layers of snow, or of dust, or of silence. Or, it might have been that Leo had learned that asking about Luna's affairs would be just foolish, too foolish.

Show Me Slowly
What I Only Know the Limits Of

When Gregor Truba woke up, sometime in the early morning on a crisp November day in 1984, from a long but unsettling dream, he found himself asleep alongside Snow White. He rubbed his eyes in disbelief wondering if a torn out page from a fairy-tale was directly applied to his reality, or was it still a dream?!

But a dream it wasn't.

There was a woman sleeping next to him and she had the face of the most beautiful angel and the body of *Calypso* a demigoddess, a beautiful long black-haired nymph – *She Who Hides.*

He looked around him still unable to figure out how he found himself in this beautiful home, full of antique furniture and exquisite paintings. There were yesterday's papers on the table, a pair of reading glasses, a glass of wine with a dark oily rim running through the middle, a fruit bowl, sharpened pencil and an open book.

He looked through the window and from his lying-down position he saw a cape, pine trees, several fishing boats and red roofs in the distance. He heard her even breathing and some birds singing, he heard a church bell from afar, and he heard his own heart beating faster.

He could not remember how he had found himself in this house, next to this woman naked and voluptuous. His head was hurting; the hangover felt as a thick blanket over his mind so he could not remember when he had come here and above all – how did he come? How the hell had he found himself in her bed?

The woman he secretly lusted for, the woman who looked at him as a predator looks at her prey, the woman he, under the rose, wanted so badly that he could not hide it any longer.

While she was still sleeping with her dark long hair scattered on a pillow, Gregor stood up and started to examine her room that looked more like a gallery than a bedroom. The *Luna Gallery.*

On the main wall there were exactly seven portraits of a young woman and he wasn't sure whether those portraits were portraits of Pia or of her mother. The woman in the portraits was very, very young, most probably in her early teens with few years apart, only one portrait was a portrait of the same face, but probably in the future. Distant future. She had penetrating green eyes, soft eyelashes, a perfect nose and her lips like rose petals. The colouring was superb while the signature was unclear. In yet another painting there was a naked body, probably of the same woman, one could only see her bare back half-covered with long dark hair – she held a violin with her long fingers. There were only four fingers on each hand. On the middle finger on the right hand there was a little snake coiled, a ring with two dark eyes, two onyxes. There were three semi precious stones holding a book of notes opened on page 11, the two smaller gems were heliotropes, bloodstones, green gemstones dotted with bright red spots of iron oxide and the third one, and the biggest one was a sapphire, a precious gemstone.

The signature in this painting was clear and readable, it read – *Sapphire.*

There was something unearthly in this room; Gregor felt as if someone were standing next to him, breathing behind his back, telling him to run, run, run away and never come back. But he didn't.

He went into the kitchen and made himself a cup of coffee. He sipped his coffee while trying to retrace his memory. The second cup of coffee he took to bed. The other he left on the bedside table next to the Sleeping Beauty and covered her nakedness. It was cold in the room, not just because it was late November morning, not because the room wasn't warmed, but that coldness radiated from the woman lying next to him. He felt like he was locked in on a page of a story of the Ice Queen, not knowing who wrote his part and why?

***

When she opened her eyes it was well past midday. She wasn't surprised even the slightest. She stretched her long lean body as a sleepy cat would and curled onto Gregor's strong chest with a leg across his waist. She said:

"You have the physique of Adonis."

Gregor said nothing as she took his hand and led it slowly down her lustful body. He felt unbearable heat in his groins and followed each of her moves in such an ecstasy as he had never experienced before. A volcanic eruption, an earth thunder, the sound of a million harps, a primordial sound, a screech of a thousand flamingos, a *Puranz's* thunder – that was what Gregor felt at three o'clock in the afternoon after almost two hours of unexhausted love-making.

When he lit his cigarette lying on his back with her head on his chest he said:

"How did I end up in this House of Everlasting Love?"

"A House of Everlasting Love, that's the thing!!! You've named it! You did! A House of Everlasting Love. Bravo! You are a sensible artistic soul, aren't you?"

"Yes, I am, but you haven't given me the answer, so, how did we end up together?"

"Mystery brought us together... and, there's always a reason why people are brought together, don't you think so?"

"Probably."

"Not just probably, but most certainly. Give it time and it will be revealed to you."

She fed him with strong coffee and frozen cake and they made love one more time, then when he exhausted all his strength she smiled and said:

"You can go now, I have to get ready for the theatre."

"Who you are going with?"

"That is none of your concern, now you can get dressed and you can go. My advice to you would be – just forget what has happened today as if it had never really happened If you meet me on the street, cross the road, and don't come to my gallery again. Never again. Auf Wiedersehen."

DETHRONED

At six o'clock on that same November afternoon Gregor Truba put on his jeans, his shirt, a jumper and a leather jacket. The last of his belongings that he had brought to this house was his wristwatch. He put it on; he zipped his jacket and pulled the collar up. He went out into a cold day, drizzly with rain and left in this room something, but he wasn't quite sure what it was. Was it his innocence or was it a part of his soul? Was it freely given or was it stolen? He couldn't distinguish it on that particular day.

But it would take many more days for him to come to terms with what had happened on that quite unusual November day, it would take many more days than he anticipated while walking his confused walk and smoking his cigarette.

When he entered he heard voices coming from Veronika's room: Hugo and Pia were singing a well-known tune, Veronika was laughing, he knew that it would be the wrong time to join them. He would feel like an intruder, a liar, he would feel as if all of them would read the bad news written on his forehead.

He didn't want to look into Pia's eyes.

He had a shower; half-naked he was lying on his bed and the most surprising visitor knocked on his bedroom door. He said:

"Enter!" through the door ajar, Pia's head popped in; in her extended hand was an envelope:

"You are invited."

He stood up deliberately leaving his bathrobe on his bed. He came closer, took the envelope, put his arm around Pia's waist, pulled her closer to his bare chest and kissed her passionately. She did not resist his kiss, yet she didn't kiss him back. She turned around, then she turned back, came closer, up on the tip of her toes and touched his lips with hers. Then quickly, she went out.

When he opened the envelope there was no invitation, but a piece of torn out paper where, in Pia's handwriting a paragraph was written. The sentence looked as if written in haste, some sentences and words were crossed out; some were in bold handwriting. It read:

"We used to walk hand in hand and look at the world with the same pair of eyes. I'd tell you my dreams, you painted them all and left me with pictures that I don't know how to read anymore as I have forgotten the meaning of words, the meaning of hearts and the meaning of hands. I miss your beautiful face that I could touch with my hands, with my eyes and with my heart, and I don't know now what mission my heart has because without you its rhythm has slowed, its rhythm has skipped the most significant beats as the heart of a tired, old girl reluctant to repair what is considered to be irreparable. Oh, come to my dreams, and come more often, and hold me, hold me, hold me in your arms, paint me on your canvases wherever you are, and sing me lullabies, sing me those old songs, with your sweetest voice, the voice that whispers every night, the voice that disappears every morning while my insides are left empty, deserted and hurting, oh, come to my dreams and come more often.... I can't keep all the memories alive and I often fear they would turn into powder at the touch of my frightened mind."

He went back to Veronika's room, and saw them through the window as they were leaving the house. He called her holding the envelope and she ran to him. Seeing her running towards him his whole being strengthened and weakened at the same time and he heard some melody in his soul. When he told her that there was no invitation in the envelope, her face, her eyes darkened and eyebrows lifted up and touched:

"Give it back, give it back, give it back to me!"

"Here you go, Pia. You gave it to me, I haven't stolen it from you, don't panic."

"You are a loser."

"What have I done wrong now?"

She shoved in that envelope, opened the other one, checked it out and said, *"Here"*.

Then she ran back and caught up with Veronika as if it was difficult to catch up with her – she always walked as if she were sent to meet her own Death.

From the back she looked exactly like the woman he spent the night with. He quaked at the thought of her – *'Is she Pia's mother?'* he asked himself in disbelief, a double disbelief: he couldn't believe that Luna was Pia's mother, any more than he could believe that he had spent the night with her. *'How did it happen?'* he wondered. *'Was I that drunk?'*

From the invitation he learned that Pia Odak was awarded as the most talented emerging young poetess, hence her first book of poetry was going to be presented in the oldest bookshop-gallery on Saturday 20th of December 1983.

The next day he left a note in her letterbox. The note read:
"You are my pride! ... and my Goddess."
She never replied.

***

On Saturday December 20th, Gregor's attention was interrupted by the noise coming from the living room. He was taken aback as he heard china breaking and Hugo's unclear sentences, it looked as if he was cursing. He would use impolite words when upset, but he never knew the real meaning of some quite ugly curses. He would label his mother as a *'whore'* not knowing the strength and meaning of the insult.

When Hugo saw Gregor he ran to him crying:
"She isn't Yugo's favourite person. She is mean. Whore! Evil witch. Yugo wanna go. Gogol, tell her Yugo wanna go."
"Where do you wanna go, Hugo?"
"Pia. Beautiful Pia."
Veronika was in the hallway.
"Aren't you taking him with you?"
She pointed to Elsa:
"Ask your holy mother."
"Mum, I'll take him with me."
Hugo ran to his mother, kicked her in the calf, crying:

"Stupid mother! Stupid woman! Yugo goes with Gogol. Yugo loves Pia. Pia loves Yugo."

Mother said an unfaltering *'No'*, Hugo screamed as if he were cut with a knife; he took the tablecloth, pulled it down and all china went down into pieces regardless of the thick carpet that served as a buffer, the cups bounced off and broke onto the parquet.

Mother Elsa screamed:

"You evil, evil child!"

Gregor said:

"Mum, I'll take care of everything."

"Gogol's my favourite person, not you! You are a whore! Yugo hates you!" and he ran to Gregor putting his arms around Gregor's waist.

"He is not going anywhere, Gregor. He has to learn a lesson."

"No lesson! Yugo hates lesson! Yugo hates you; you are not Yugo's favourite person! You are a loser!"

"Stop it, Hugo!" Stop it, otherwise you won't be going anywhere."

"You'll take Yugo with you?"

"Yes, I'll take you with me, but you have to apologise to Mother, and you have to promise that you will behave as a good boy would. Pia doesn't like bad boys."

"Yugo's not a bad boy. Pia loves Yugo."

"Say sorry to Mum."

"Say sorry."

"Say – Sorry Mum."

"Say sorry Mum."

Elsa walked out; Gregor knelt down and started to collect the pieces. Hugo stood next to him rubbing his hands, saliva dripping from his lower lip, he said:

"You are Yugo's favourite brother."

"And how many brothers do you have?"

"Just Gogol, but you are the best! My favourite."

"What about Lonnie?"

"Lonnie's my favourite person."

"You said I was."

"Yes, today, you was."
"Say – you were."
"Say you were."

While Gregor was cleaning up he saw a shadow pass by the door. It had a long black robe: he didn't know that Friar Marag was present when the accident took place. He was the black shadow, the man whose face wasn't present at all times but his thoughts and deeds were often present by being expressed as Elsa's own thoughts and deeds.

Breakfast at Pia's

On a very cold late morning of December 21st in 1984 Gregor Truba woke up in a cosy room, next to yet another ebony-haired, ivory-skinned beauty. But this was the right Snow White. The one he passionately desired with each and every atom of his young being. Even though he desired her the most one could ever possibly desire any person, even though he did wake up in her bed with his hand across her body, he never made love to Pia that night. How come?

December 20th was Pia's day.

The local press advertised the event, there was her picture, her eyes cast down, not a direct gaze at the camera; she looked like black and white desire. There was a short interview with *The young Pia Odak, a student of Comparative Literature and Languages at the University of Philosophy, a young talent born only once in a few generations. Pia Odak, the only daughter of the renowned theatre director and actor Mr. Simon Odak. Pia Odak, the poetess, amateur artist, linguist and the best student of her generation. Pia Odak, who skipped a year, passed all her exams with 'distinction' – four semesters in one year. Pia Odak – the voice of her generation received the prestigious national award. Congratulations Pia on so many achievements at that age!*

There were so many young people gathered as if she were an international rock star. Even Gregor was overlooked when she showed up. She was immaculately dressed, her signature black clothes laced in places that hid and showed exactly what was meant to be hidden or shown. Her hair let down, minimum make-up, lips cherry-red but sealed. There was just an uncertain smile on her lips.

Her father was there, a prominent figure; he read some poetry, probably Pia's poems Gregor assumed; some other actor read her little biography and she stood as a proud porcelain doll at the same time with ease and anxiety shown in unnecessary movements of her hand while smoothing her hair or touching her nose.

Back home, Gregor helped Hugo to get dressed. He chose a pink shirt with tiny white squares and he wanted to wear a tie. Gregor tried to talk him out of that but Hugo, as always, did what he wanted letting him know that otherwise he might throw a tantrum and spoil the afternoon, or the entire event. Gregor let him choose his clothes and helped him to put gel onto his thick blond hair. He was a handsome fellow, just poor soul, he couldn't stop dribbling when excited. And excited he could easily become like a little puppy when shown a cookie. Gregor told him to stay close to him at all times, and not to run to talk to Pia as that was a very important evening for her and there would be a lot of people who would like to talk to her. Those people, would most probably be journalists and some academics, so he told Hugo, *'We'd better keep to ourselves this evening, you'll see Pia another day and be able to express your happiness. OK? All clear? Is Hugo going to behave as a good boy? You and me, cool, cool, cool? OK?'*

Hugo nodded and wiped his runny nose with the sleeve of his freshly pressed shirt. Gregor gave him a handkerchief saying:

"Keep it in your pocket, wipe your nose and lips with the hankie, OK?"

When they arrived Hugo had forgotten all of Gregor's instructions and advice. When he saw Pia, he started to clap his hands yelling, *"Pia, my Pia, Yugo's here, Pia!"*

Everyone stared at Hugo, a few *'shh'* were thrown towards them, but Pia quickly came, gave him a little smile and a quick hug. She looked at Gregor and whispered, *"Thanks"*, and Gregor didn't know was the *'thanks'* for him attending the event or was it because he brought his brother? To him it was obvious that Pia was fond of the weak and misfortunate, that she was fond of his brother, and childishly he wished he were more Hugo-like, more helpless and a man who would evoke Pia's tenderness.

But he stood there, with his fantastic physique: legs apart, back erect, long-ish blond untamed hair hiding one eye, strong teeth; he stood like the one who knew that all the lights belonged to him! He was comfortable with the atten-tion, with the screams from girls, with journalists taking photos of him and with the atmosphere and an aura surrounding his presence. He held Hugo's shoulder and when his band-mates came Hugo had more guardians to look after his unpredictable ways.

Hugo pinched a girl's bottom, she screamed, turned around and wasn't sure who had pinched her. They all had a smirk on their faces while Hugo was laughing out loudly pointing his finger at his brother.

Pia didn't prepare a speech. She received the award and the copies of her new collection; she smiled and said, *"Thank you all for coming, thank you for the award, thank you for reading my poetry."*

Then she opened the book and read only one poem with tears in her eyes, and Gregor wondered to whom it was dedicated, for whom those tears were shed.

Sapphire

She put her words and thoughts in her final act
Neatly, orderly
She kissed
A blue, blue sky goodbye

The wind was blowing on that day
Readily helping to carry her belongings
Elsewhere

The world got poorer and cooler
For few painted stories and few unordinary lines
But truly it never knew it

DETHRONED

The sky got richer for a shimmering star
A sapphire
And it welcomed it by
Painting itself red.

A long cheer followed. Her father came close and talked to her while she gently shook her head. Gregor couldn't hold back the feeling that he might be needed, hence thrust Hugo into his best mate's hands and came to Pia.

"I am so happy for you, Pia."

"Why would you be happy for me? No one's happy for me, they came just because of the event itself, not because of me. My father was the centre of attention; he said I shouldn't have read it. He said I should have chosen another poem, but I've picked what I, if not liked the best, but then at least, felt the best. I wanna go home, Gregor, can you take me?"

"You don't wanna stay? All those people are here because of you."

"Maybe they are, maybe they are not. Maybe they are here because of my dad, everyone wants something from him. I don't even believe that they liked my poems."

"Everyone clapped and cheered, didn't you hear it?"

"Yeah, I did."

Barbarossa came with a glass of champagne and a wide smile:

"Congratulations, Pia!"

Gregor took Pia's hand and walked her out. She sat in his car; he brought Hugo and took him home. On the way home Hugo couldn't stop asking questions that all started with:

"Umm, Pia, Pia... Pia, tell Yugo, tell Yugo, Pia..."

He had so many questions, all of them she answered with patience and ease. She felt better in Hugo's company than surrounded by journalists.

For the second time Gregor thought that Pia might have never been an arrogant person, but shy.

Hugo didn't want to leave the car, he played with her hair, he told her that he'd like to marry her one day when they grew up, he told her that they could all live together, *'Pia, Yugo and Lonnie'*, he screamed and scratched Gregor when he told him to bid Pia goodbye and in the end they both walked him into the house.

Mother Elsa came to the door, took his hand and almost dragged him to his room.

Pia said:

"She isn't the kindest person."

"Why would you say that?"

"It is not what Veronika says about her, it is the way she acts towards people in general."

"I think she is a good person."

"To you!"

"Where do you wanna go?"

"To the beach."

"And the beach it shall be, my lady."

The moon was high, the wind was cool, they smoked to get warmer, her fingers were cold, Gregor took her hand and kissed each of her fingers. She was silent, lost in her thoughts; again he witnessed what a solitary character she had and how impenetrable her heart was.

He took her home at one in the morning; the wind was strong and he walked her to the door, when she unlocked the door, she said:

"Come in…" and then she closed the door.

He felt a strange melody inside of him; he thought of the chain he purchased for her, the chain he probably would never give her, the chain that had too high a price attached to it. He dismissed the horrible thought and shivered when he thought again about that woman-spider, a black widow where he spent the night not knowing how he had found himself in her house, in her bed, in her arms.

He kissed Pia's hair and her little nose and she was placid and looked like a lost child. There was no sign of passion, no sign of a simple desire; she was calm and docile, but he somehow knew that a storm might come in a blink of an eye only if he tried to muddy those calm waters.

Pia was undressing slowly showing her body without shame, without pride, as someone who knew that they had the precious gift yet never feared it would be stolen and never assured anyone that they were going to be awarded. She belonged only to herself while undressing.

Even though she slipped quickly into her pants Gregor witnessed for the second time the dark bruises swollen with blood around her inner thighs. He wanted to say something but his own intuition said 'No', so he said nothing. He wanted to kiss her but she slipped under the duvet. Gregor took off his jeans and dived under the cover that promised the ultimate reward.

But there was no reward.

She leaned her head against the pillow and in the semi-darkened room she said:

"I don't wanna make love to you, Gregor. You can stay and sleep over, but you are not going to take advantage of my body."

"I never wanted to take advantage of your body, Pia. I thought, I think I love you. I thought, I hoped, that you might want me, at least a little."

"Stop talking, hug me."

Gregor hugged Pia and she fell asleep on his shoulder; her long hair all over his chest. He couldn't sleep. He just held her in his arms while thoughts swirled in his head the entire night. He felt bad, almost guilty when unavoidably thinking about the woman who had Pia's preserved beauty. She couldn't have been her mother…but then, she could have, how would he ever know if he never asked? Maybe her parents got divorced and Pia decided to live with her father; anyway, the man looked more like a sane person than that woman did.

He fell asleep tortured by questions to which he would never find the right answer. He knew that Pia wouldn't want to speak about her family. He never knew why.

✳✳✳

Pia asked him to have breakfast with *'them'* and when he came into the large kitchen where he saw Pia's marks on her thighs for the first time, there was her father seated at the table with a toasted sandwich, a cup of coffee and a newspaper. She came close, kissed his cheeks, then his hands, and said:

"Mornin' Simo."

"Mornin' princess."

He never looked in Gregor's direction, he never acknowledged him; he just kept reading loudly all those accolades written about his daughter, Pia the poetess. When he finished reading he gave her a kiss and said:

"Where's the redhead? You disappeared, he disappeared; I thought you two ran away bored stiff."

Pia just shrugged her shoulders; Gregor felt a sharp pang of jealousy. She put two pieces of toast in the toaster, her father kept on reading; she was humming and Gregor didn't know how exactly he felt in that moment. One thing was sure – he was happy to wake up with her and to have breakfast with her, but he felt displaced. Displaced and unwelcomed. Renowned Mr. Odak, that champion of theatre, well known screen chameleon said it all without many words; he knew how to do it, effortlessly, perfectly.

When Gregor was leaving, Simon Odak said:

"Quickly, Pia, close the door, the coldness is seeping in."

***

Six harmonious, but sexless, days and nights graced December in the diary of Gregor's memory.

They had morning coffees together; he waited for her after lectures; they had their lunch together and in the evening Pia accompanied him to his rehearsals. She just quietly sat there, mumbled and wrote in her book. Six nights she slept on his shoulder and he held her with a burning desire that was quenched only by the thought that the key was – patience.

On the seventh day all hell broke loose!

He took the little box with that *Luna Gallery* logo for two reasons. First, he wanted to tell her how much effort he would put just to tell her how much he cared, to impress her, and the other was – he naively hoped, or suspected, that Pia would open up a little more and tell him more about herself.

They were in a little café eating pizza; he took out the box and gently pushed it with his index finger next to her plate.

It was wrapped in light-blue paper; Pia asked, slightly sombre, as this paper looked familiar:

"What is it?"

"Have a look."

Her fingers trembled while unwrapping. When her eyes met the logo it seemed as if she was hit by thunderbolt – she took the box, threw it against wall without opening it, pushed the plate which broke onto the concrete floor and said, *'You bastard!'* and ran out as if chased by Luna herself.

And obviously, she was chased by the dark Luna, at least in her mind.

Gregor ran after her, caught up with her; she was running and crying; he tried to calm her down and succeeded after holding her tight for a good half-hour. When her rage subsided, she said:

"I hate you Gregor Truba."

"I love you Pia Odak, and I always will."

"I will always, always hate you."

"Because you can't admit that you love me you've chosen to hate me. You are full of shit; you are scared of love Pia Odak. You are scared of people and of yourself. Go back to your daddy and the habit of kissing his hands."

"What do you know about me? Nothing! Leave me alone!"

"Fine! Go to hell!"

"You go to hell! I hate you!"

"You said that. You are trying too hard to hate me. When you decide to tell me that you love me, you know where to find me. Don't forget Pia, I love you!"

He turned his back and headed to his car.

The next morning the owner of the café, a long-time acquaintance of Gregor, called:

"I've put the chain back in the box. Come and collect it any time."

Yes, Gregor came to collect the chain. He wrapped it back in that light-blue paper that Pia, carefully but scornfully, unwrapped and left on the table, and walked to the *Luna Gallery*.

When he walked in, the *Goddess* was on the phone. She smiled at him and waved her hand showing him to sit down. He never sat down; he didn't want to wait for her to finish her conversation but took the receiver from her hand and put it down onto the telephone set. Her eyes widened in disbelief that he really dared to cut her conversation with that simple act, but without waiting for her to recall the words, he said:

"Here's the chain. You keep it. You give it to her. You are sick!"

Luna calmly unwrapped the box, took the chain out of it, and put it into the gallery window on display. In the middle of the window it read, *I Love You, Pia.*

Gregor's rage clouded his mind.

He decided he would never ever come first to Pia and strike a conversation, either at university or any other place. If he met her at his house visiting Veronika, he would just pass by without a word.

It was easy to decide.

It wasn't easy to stick to his decision.

The love he felt in his heart was like a burning fire; at moments he thought that the fire might burn his sanity away. Such was the intensity of his young, still innocent, heart.

And Pia was nowhere to be seen since that evening of declaration of Gregor's love in the form of the chain that came from the famous *Luna Gallery*.

***

Just a few days after that incident in the *Luna Gallery*, when Gregor passed it by again, the pendant which was shimmering in the sun that hit the window, appeared to Gregor as a laughing marker of his past and present path. He went back home calmly, took the very same crowbar from his father's workshop with which he beat the crap out of the redhead, and walked with a measured rhythm to the gallery again. He said:

"Afternoon Luna. I came to repair the Gallery." And he smashed four display windows next to the back wall.

She stood there without a word; her heart never skipped a beat. When he finished, she took the telephone receiver and started to dial, as calm as an innocent lamb. Hmm, Luna: the fine Mistress of Calm Hell.

She said:

"Sweetie, I need your help. Some vandal came into the Gallery and smashed the glass cabinets. No, I've never seen him before. No, he looked like a Gypsy. No, he didn't ask for money, I think he was drunk, you know, one of those. OK, thanks, sweetie, thanks!"

She put down the receiver with a measured movement and gorgeous-Luna-smile; the next day the cabinets were repaired, not at her expense, at the Council's. But, the pendant that read *I Love You, Pia* stood in the middle of the window displayed for all town folks to see what a great artist she was.

As strange as it may appear but the most negative thoughts and manifestations come into life from anxiety, yes, including the awful sin of sadism.

And for Gregor, he couldn't care less that he was again going to be called to the police station and face a banquet of consequences.

Those were the years when eccentricity, impulsiveness, bravery and knighthood were encouraged as desirable qualities of youth.

Defiant youth.

Eccentricity, impulsiveness, bravery and knighthood, were they just expressions of a colourful soul?

Soul, those were the times when people believed that they had souls, and the most beautiful creations came out of that belief and persuasions: beautiful art, music and literature, then all sorts of different expressions of one's soul. People shared more, cared more, and admired more, too. Sometimes openly, more often – secretly.

But in the shadow of fine music, art and literature, dark forces started, once again, in slow steps, to dance their dance of chaos which was approaching slowly: it was sneakily put into speeches of political leaders, of prominent journalists, priests and preachers… only a few understood what was going to be bestowed upon their mild mornings commenced in a local café and to the masses of lulled souls.

The dark frequencies of that music were heard only by those who had fine-tuning that came from faraway Lords, form black-robed *'benevolent'* fathers, who came from the depths beyond human comprehension and understanding. It came disguised and a lie became the truth, and the wicked and perverse started to raise their voice, and the luck of fate sped in through their speeches of hatred creating panic, stress and strains and producing the fruit of bitterness that set itself, almost unnoticeably, among the daily affairs of common people.

First, hope was destroyed; destruction itself was planned and calculated carefully in hushed whispers uttered in darkened rooms, among the walls of holy churches, among the angry and spiteful. Hope had to be destroyed first, for hope joins hands with faith and fellow humans, and what would be a better way to separate humans than deprive them from faith, hope and unity?

Only very few knew it, and those few who orchestrated the events wrote the scripts and played them out. Lords of hatred, Lords of wars fed the nation slowly with *'popular'* TV shows packed with brutal violence and fear, horror movies, use of drugs and alcohol was proclaimed to be *'in and modern'*; pornography, witchcraft and black magic was promoted as a fun pastime. The sad songs the nation started to sing, the cry that no one heard as masses wanted a *'new world, free, democratic and deprived of old, out-dated values.'*

Granny Sava

There was only one person in this wide world that Pia ran to when in trouble, pain, doubt, disbelief or ready to share her happiness.

It was her Granny Sava. That connection was formed on the same day Pia was born as if Pia's soul had recognised in her Granny the kindest soul that had come down to Earth to help ease troubles.

Sava was born as Sava Tesla, in a small village of Raduč in the region of Lika. Raduč was such a picturesque place, full of natural wonders and beauty: chestnut-tree groves, wild walnut bosquets, tall wide oaks touching a mellow sky, elms and poplar trees edging brooks and small rivers, colourful hills under whose feet were red-roofed houses with small flower gardens in the front and in the back, rows of vast orchards, populated by hard working, honest folk.

It was a small village; the entire population would fit into the tallest skyscraper in any European capital.

Milutin Tesla, a Serbian Orthodox priest was born in Raduč in 1819, just as his father Nikola was born in Raduč. Milutin had married an Orthodox priest's daughter, Georgina Mandic, an inventor, poetess and philosopher, and she gave him five healthy, strong-willed and gifted children. His fourth child was named after his grandfather – Nikola, and after his arrival to this world, the world changed rapidly and never stayed the same. An extraordinary mind, unmatched talent and energy originated from that charming little village of Raduč, and the worthy Serb made his name immortal.

He was destined to be a priest as priesthood-like blood ran through the family veins; wisdom and knowledge brought many medals and accolades to Tesla's generations of wise men and women.

His father Milutin was a poet, philosopher and philanthropist helping people selflessly, and as a priest he made worthy efforts to lead by example.

The most unusual mathematics ran in the Tesla family: Nikola had three aunts on the mother's side and all of them had married Serbian Orthodox priests, he had three aunts on his father's side of the family and all of them had married Serbian Orthodox priests, and it didn't stop there. Nikola had three sisters who married, all of them, Serbian Orthodox priests. Almost unbelievable, but unbelievable or not, it is a fact.

Granny Sava came from that lineage; the lineage of wise, kind and talented people. Her mother was married to a Serbian Orthodox priest, too.

They had four boys and only one daughter. At an early age Sava showed unmeasurable ability for empathy and kindness. She wrote poetry and had a sharp mind. She had inherited that distinguished Tesla family height, stature and features: she was a tall, slender, upright woman, one hundred and eighty-five centimetres in height, she had piercing blue eyes and while she talked it was impossible not to look her in the eyes; her face was narrow but her forehead tall and wide, a sign of the highest intelligence, then a thin and longish nose, the one that graced thinkers or mystics. Her hands were always soft, though always engaged in some sort of activity: she held a pencil mostly, or a book, or embroidery when she wasn't engaged in domestic duties, or out in hospitals and hospices as a volunteer or bearer of good hope.

Her father, Milan Mandic used to say:

"If she were a man, I'd send her to study to be a priest."

Few women in that era went to study in Vienna, only those who were from priestly or academic families, only girls from those families that had enough knowledge and money to invest in an intelligent or gifted woman's future.

Among all those qualities to choose from, and the dilemma whether she'd study philosophy or science, her humanistic, empathic streak was the deciding factor – she loved people, women in particular, hence decided to study midwifery.

There, in Vienna, she met Jure Odak, a young worthy man from her own country who studied medicine.

And it was mutual love at first sight.

DETHRONED

Jure was a man of steady character, plain and honest. He was tall and hand-some, a dark-haired man with white skin and big teeth. His nature was rather solitary, he was inclined to enjoy quiet thought and solitude, but in Sava he had found the perfect match, as she was able to engage in any topic with sound knowledge and precise understanding. She understood science, philosophy, literature and politics; she was a very spiritual person and fair in any circum-stances, hence all those qualities matched his almost unmatchable standards.

As the foundations of their love and their house were on strong solid ground, their love and marriage withstood many obstacles and temptations that life itself throws at any couple.

She loved her sons unconditionally, but her secret longing for a daughter came to an end when she received the biggest gift from kind God, as she used to say, when she held Pia for the first time in her arms. There was something about Pia that was different, unearthly; there was something about Pia that Granny Sava had never met in any child. Calmness and maturity grew rapidly and when Pia was supposed to be just a little girl she showed an amazing wisdom, peace and some sort of self-sufficiency that wasn't characteristic of any young child of that age. She would whisper in her ear, *"You might be Odak, you might be Bonifacio, but I know that you are a pure Tesla Girl."*

Instead of reading fairy-tales to her, Granny read biographies of distin-guished men and women to Pia, the one which was the most interesting to both of them, the one they knew almost off by heart was the biography of Nikola Tesla, their relative and ancestor who made their family name known in the whole wide world for many years to come, to many generations that would follow. Pia liked to listen to the stories about Nikola's early life; she liked to listen to the stories about other Tesla family members, the priests and their achievements.

She travelled several times with her Granny to Raduč, a small, small vil-lage populated by kind and curious people who would invite them for lunch and shower Pia with attention and kindness. They would say:

"She is meek and smart, so obvious that she comes from the Tesla line-age."

Pia's other grandmother, of Italian blood, would ask:

"Why did she drag you to that godforsaken village? Peasants! What can you learn there, among them? No manners, village people."

No one ever knew what Pia was thinking. She was a silent child, she wouldn't comment, or she would just say:

"Can I go home now, I miss my Mummy."

Granny Sava liked Pia's mother. She called her *Child*, as Gemma was a child when she married her son. Gemma ate little, was very tall and slim and when the Odak family would encourage her to eat more, to put some weight on Granny Sava would say:

"Gemma's fine. She looks healthy. Young women are supposed to be thin, she looks beautiful like a gracious swan."

Gemma liked Granny Sava. She addressed her as *Sweet Granny*, as Sava offered sweetness with words and her deeds.

Sometimes Pia would say:

"Mummy, Granny; let's hold hands, just the three of us and let's be happy!"

At Granny Sava's there were often lots of kids, as she had seven grandchildren, but when they were all together, Pia would take a book, sit out on the veranda and read. She never liked to join in games or jokes. She never liked hugs or handshakes, she feared chubby kids and felt uncomfortable when someone was talking with a full mouth. She would look at the floor as if she were trying to find an excuse to go home immediately.

The unusual habit people of that land had was to ask kids, *'Who do you love better, Mum or Dad?'*

Pia would answer:

"I love my mummy and I love my granny."

"What about others? Your father, cousins, your other grandparents, your aunts?"

"I love everyone." Pia would quickly answer and leave the room.

One time, on the occasion when Pia came to Granny for a few hours, she sat quietly with a worrisome expression on her pretty little face. Granny Sava sat next to Pia and took her hands.

Pia said:

"I love your hair Granny, it isn't white, but silver. You look like the moon, but your heart is like the sun, and your words are like a little happy brook, they make my heart sing and skip to that same rhythm, Granny, please, please promise you'll never die."

"This is something, Pia, that I can't promise to you. You know, man is mortal, we are all going to go one day, but the soul never dies. I'll look down and I'll follow you, protect and love you, maybe even more than I love you right now. But, you have to develop more trust in God, then you'll be more secure in your heart, you'll know that I'll live in your heart."

"I don't want you to die for a long time, Granny."

"Well, that, probably I can promise, as I don't plan to go as yet. Probably, there are still many years for us to be together. Why do you worry about such a silly thing as dying? Let's talk about something different, let's talk about your words. What have you been writing lately?"

Pia feared that something 'bad' would happen and she couldn't shake off this recurring thought and feeling. She feared that Granny might fall ill and pass away before her time, but it didn't happen. Not that year, for another fifteen years the old woman was her rock. But that year, as Pia's premonitions indicated, something happened that changed Pia's life forever, and only in the arms of her beloved Granny Sava she could mend the fragments of her shattered self. She was the only one who could bear the weight of Pia's pain and guilt. No amount of kissing Father's hands would ease the pain and distress she felt. Only Granny Sava understood; only Granny Sava knew what to say and when to say it to that timid sensitive soul. Pia was made of cotton; Sava knew it.

***

If anyone tried to compare Pia's two grandmothers, taking into consideration only their looks and public presentation of their visible values for what they stood, the difference was vast. Two different worlds where Granny Sava and Nonna Oriana resided.

Granny Sava had shoulder-length silver hair scooped up on the top of her head into a-not-so-big-bun, while Nonna Oriana had a two-layered, sort of bob in a maroon colour, trimmed and coloured by the same hairdresser for a number of years.

Granny Sava never wore jewellery (except for her wedding ring) not even when some occasion would suggest women should take out their best clothes and adornments. Nonna Oriana looked like a wealthy family's Christmas tree: everything in excess and in pairs, several golden chains with crosses and heart pendants, big golden earrings, two bracelets, one on each wrist, two rings of white and yellow gold on the middle fingers, ring fingers and little fingers.

That was her everyday presentation of leftovers of their wealth, and on some occasions which asked to show glitz and glamour, she would always be the winning guest, no mistake.

Granny Sava wore simple dresses, or just one coloured skirt and a blouse with a discrete design; her face was always make-up free. She never used facial creams but rubbed a few drops of olive oil in her hands, then spread it evenly onto her face, the excess of oil she would rub onto her elbows. She never failed to do that when using oil and with a grin on her face she would comment, *"Nothing's better, nothing's healthier for the skin than olive oil. Nature gives us everything."*

She smelled of nature: of olive oil, of lavender fields, of crisp mornings and to Pia her hands smelled of fresh linen and tulips.

Nonna had a different practice and habits established long ago. She still wore her red-hot lipstick that, at her age, looked rather distasteful. She *'modestly'* claimed that lipstick was *'all that she needed as make-up'* but that statement failed the truth, as she daily and regularly applied foundation to her face, some blush on her cheeks and the inevitable mascara.

Her dresses saw better times but due to the best quality and perfect cut they still looked luxurious and confirmed her former status.

DETHRONED

When it came to respect, Nonna Oriana respected Granny Sava solely and only because she was a doctor's wife, but apart from that merit she overlooked all of her own achievements and merits that were numerous but decently hidden behind her modest attitude and nature.

Sava's famous phrase was *'Don't mention it'* whether one was thanking her for her kindness or praising her well-known philanthropic and humanitarian endeavours. There was something warm, humanly soft and caring in her attitude and speech and everyone held her in high esteem, while her husband thought that Heaven looked favourably on him on the day he met her.

This is not to say that Nonna Oriana was entirely a person of faulty character or had a mean, poisonous heart. She talked a lot without thinking prior to opening her mouth. She praised herself practically for everything that went right or smoothly. Her favourite phrases were: *'Hadn't I told you so?'*, *'Smart of you to listen to my advice!'*, *'When I predict something it surely will happen; for everyone's good!'* and the best one was – *'Thank God I was born that clever!'*

She forced and exercised those self-admiring statements onto each and every family member, as well as saying that *'the girls were beautiful because they inherited her beauty'*, they heard this countless times. She talked, talked and talked reassuring herself that everyone heard and downloaded undeniable truths that she was *'smart, kind, beautiful and quick-witted'* and that *'everyone benefited from coming in contact with her'*.

If anyone, ever, happened to ask any family member about the accuracy of her self-assessments and evaluations, most likely there would be some discrepancies. Weird, but factual, she had never heard the truth about herself out of consideration and family kindness, plus she talked so much at such speed that even the fastest and the bravest orator wouldn't dare to match her.

Those two families rarely met by agreement but rather they would meet by chance in the street, in the local restaurant or some store.

Pia's birthdays were celebrated first at the Bonifacios, then, the following weekend at the Odaks where celebrations were less pompous and the guests were fewer. The presents were fewer too, but were selected carefully to last for a long time: the presents that were going to be read and re-read.

117

At *Nonna's*, Pia would be adorned by golden chains and love-heart pendants, while at Granny's poetry was read.

Granny Sava never asked questions about her granddaughter's other family, she would only say, *"Say hello on our behalf."*

Nonna Oriana conducted herself in a different fashion. She couldn't help but comment:

"A book? A book, again? Never gold! Only your kind Nonna buys gold. Books, yeah, they don't cost much, do they? And yet, it's a doctor's house. Come here my angel, I'll dress you up like a princess and we'll go out on the promenade."

That was exactly how she felt while walking with *Nonna* hand in hand – like a promenade pony, adorned and dressed up for a never-ending show.

When Pia struck a close friendship with Veronika and Hugo Truba, she met Hugo on two different occasions.

The first time it happened in the post office where she was with Nonna Oriana to send some parcel to her cousin.

They stood quietly shoulder-to-shoulder in a queue when someone screamed and ran towards them like a hurdling snowball knocking down a postcard stand and laughing:

"Pia, Pia, Pia, Yugo has found you!"

Gently she lifted his almost snow-white head that was leaning against her bosom while his hands were wrapped around her waist.

People looked in their direction; Hugo's mother ran and tried to separate Hugo from his tight embrace, embarrassed, apologetic. The more she tried, the more Hugo resisted and screamed. Pia said:

"Let's go outside. We'll talk outside in the fresh air, it is stuffy in here."

Nonna couldn't hold her tongue:

"Who's that retarded child? So violent! Can't you control him, woman?" she said it to Elsa red in her face, reduced to tears.

Elsa came out while Pia talked to Hugo, promising that she'd come over tomorrow and only then did he let go and sulkily, pushed from the back by his mother, went into the car. He waved at Pia with an uncertain expression in his eyes and Pia waved back. All the time *Nonna* stood on the stairs with the crowd looking at the scene, twisting her head left-right, right-left, both her hands holding a holy cross which hung on her chain to protect her from such kind and misfortunate happenings.

"*How on earth do you know such a misfortunate fool? Look, he crumpled your blouse, poor creature, you shouldn't have let that creature hug you.*"

All that Pia said was:

"*Let's get back into the queue, Nonna.*"

When *Nonna* asked again, in disbelief, '*how come that she knew that little mongoloid child*', Pia finally said:

"*Can't you just let it go?*"

"*Fine! Fine, judging by your reaction he probably is one of Odak's off-spring, I wouldn't be surprised.*"

Not long after that episode an almost identical situation had occurred.

Pia drove past her Granny's house and found her kneeling in the garden. Pia came out and sat on the curb while Granny was cutting lilies. The day was as mild as Grany's smile and once again, like a little puppy, when Hugo recognised Pia, he broke free from his mother's tight grip and ran excitedly yelling:

"*Pia, my dearest Pia! Yugo has found you! Yugo's so happy!*"

He tripped, almost fell onto his knees, Granny stood up with a curious but gentle smile on her face looking at Hugo running, crimson in the face but happy while from his tongue little droplets of excitements were dripping.

Granny asked:

"*Who's the little blond Angel?*"

Hugo strongly embraced Pia and she introduced them:

"*Hugo, this is my Granny Sava, Gran, this is Hugo, a dear friend of mine.*"

"*A friend! A friend! A friend!*" exclaimed overjoyed Hugo to what Granny said:

"*My, my, what a happy fellow! Sit here Hugo, with us, and I'll bring out some lemonade and biscuits.*"

"*Yay! Lemonade and biscuits, Yugo loves Granny.*"

While Granny was in the house taking lemonade out of the fridge and biscuits out of the jar Hugo, once again, was forced by his mother into a parked car. He screamed and cried and called her a *'whore'*, Pia helplessly looked and waved to the teary dear boy, all she could do was to blow a little kiss. When Granny came out Hugo was no more.

"Has he left?"

"He has."

"What a sweet boy. How do you know him?"

"My friend's brother."

"I see. It is said, of such kids, that they are God's children. God looks after them by sending an angel of light who volunteers to embody as a human to assist those unfortunate. You might be one of them, Pia."

"I fear that God had put this child into wrong hands."

"Do not judge my birdie, don't judge God. He knows what's best for each soul, He knows!"

Pia didn't believe in what Granny said, but she never opposed her.

On the seventeenth day of November in 1970 Pia had declared war on God Almighty.

She did declare the war but not a soul knew about it, as Pia was a master when it came to keeping secrets. Especially her own!

Nonna called people, in general, *'Bums'* or *'Slavs'*, while Granny referred to people, in general as *'Souls'*; she would say a *'God's Soul'* or a *'Fine Soul'*, or a *'Poor Soul'*. *Nonna* would say a *'Lazy Bum'*, or just a *'Bum'* that would alternate with a *'Slav Bum'*. *'Slav'* was a generic name; in general it meant *'stupid Croat'* or *'stupid Serb'*.

And because of her careless language or because we attract what we expect and give out, she had regularly encountered one of those that she called *'Bums'*: a young person who wouldn't offer her a seat in the crowded bus, a checkout girl who gave her the wrong change and wouldn't apologise, a careless driver who ran through the pedestrian crossing *'farting exhaust into her face'*, bad-mannered people everywhere: *'Bums, bums, bums, bums! The entire population of bums! Slav bums!'*

And her own daughter, the most beautiful creature, nicknamed *'Sapphire'* because of her beauty, had married the biggest bum of all, she heard who he was, she knew who he was – a cheap actor, a theatre rat!

A womaniser, unscrupulous and a liar, a son of a respected doctor, a grandson of a district judge, a brother to two lawyers and his arse was covered for life. *Nonna* knew all of that because she cared about what people were saying; she cared about small talk and gossip.

In the Odak family only Granny Sava was a religious person. Jure was a doctor, a scientist and a man of common sense: he believed in science, in the visible world and he held that religion, in general, was the privilege of introverted or introspective women and the fallacy of weak men. It should be understood that he utterly respected his father-in-law, a priest, and often would engage him in meaningful conversations and speculations regardless of the fact that the priest's views were never rocked by his opposing stand.

"Science is my religion. Freud said that God was an invention of man who desperately needed security, because we have deep-seated fears of living in a threatening world in which we have little control over circumstances. Hence, he said that man invented God as a protective father. Even Nikola Tesla believed in science, the power of the mind."

"Tesla believed in science, but we shouldn't forget that Nikola said on many occasions – 'The gift of mental power comes from God, the Divine Being, and if we concentrate our minds on that truth, we become in tune with this great power. My mother had taught me to seek all the truth in the Bible; therefore I devoted many months to the study of this work.'

Sava would know more about it; she knows about his stand towards religion and God; that topic was discussed in Tesla's family since we could remember a few generations back. Sava should have been a priest if she had been a boy; she started her life with the belief that one was intended to display self-mastery over oneself, one's own emotions and thoughts, the environment and all aspects of one's life. When she was young she would ask, 'Were Angels ever transformed into beings of flesh and blood in order to help and perform earthly deeds?' Later on, she was absorbed in Tesla's work and his life; she wanted to find out what impact religion had on his life and work, Serbian Orthodox religion. She was proud of his achievements, proud of her roots. And, as you know, her favourite Tesla quote, that all her life was governed by was: 'What we really want is closer contact and better understanding between individuals and communities all over the earth, then elimination of egoism and pride which is always prone to plunge the world into primeval barbarism and strife; peace can only come as a natural consequence of universal enlightenment. Let me tell you now before I forget, in contrast to Sigmund Freud, I can say – He who comes to God must believe that He is. As valuable as science is, it has its limits. Science can't be applied to everything: it doesn't work that way. We can't scientifically prove love or justice, we can't prove anger or empathy, but obviously they are in existence. Even Albert Einstein admitted the existence of a cosmic force in the universe, didn't he?"

"He did, but didn't he say that the force is unknowable?"

Such conversations would be completed by Sava's invitation to the dinner table or by the priest's gentle change of subject:

'Let me now take the board out, and we shall see who is going to be the one to win a game of chess, I think you owe me one."

Soul Mates

Beauty is subjected to various feelings and degrees of feelings. Some adore beauty only for the sake of it, some envy beauty, some are inspired by it and some have an inclination to destroy it. Emotions and their degrees depend on the quality of the observer.

No one could ever deny that Pia's beauty could stop traffic, stop breath, stop a heartbeat and stop thoughts. Thoughts were frozen and only eyes took pleasure in the sight. If an observer had a pure heart and understanding of beauty, he would acknowledge it in numerous different ways. Pia heard all the words and sentences that could ever have been spoken by a person encountering beauty face to face. She was gracious, but always silent, and often embarrassed that she rarely knew what to say, therefore she largely appeared as an arrogant young woman.

Women who were created with God's lesser attention to detail often looked at her with a green eye. Pia never had many girlfriends, just several boys in childhood, and the redhead, from the house next door, who went with Pia to kindergarten. He admired her from the first day of their meeting, which was exactly when they were four years of age. When he was a child they called him Redhead, when he grew up, and started to grow a little beard, he earned a new nickname – Barbarossa. Pia was very fond of him from the beginning as that boy could recite poems and tell funny stories. He never asked her to talk to him or participate, but he was happy that he had a silent, yet beautiful audience. Thanks to him Pia was always protected, as often she was the victim of cruel jokes or nasty comments. She wasn't equipped with a sharp acid tongue, an arsenal of sharp words or a quick remark. When she was seven her mother told her, after she was left without a partner in a school performance, *"There is a price to be paid for being beautiful. Often women don't forgive you for that, but you'll learn with time, you'll acquire new skills."*

***

Pia parked her car near the University. On her way back she saw three girls kneeling next to her car. She stretched her step forward but the girls ran into a parked car and sped off. She came close and witnessed a disaster – three tires were flat. The girls flattened her tires!

"For Christ's sake, why? What did I do to them?"

Pia thought that no one would hear her questions, no one would answer those questions.

But, a young girl came closer and said:

"I saw them. I took their number plate. Two of them I don't know, but the one with short hair goes to my school. I know who she is. One of those girls might be her sister as she has an older sister."

"Why would they do that?"

"Some sort of revenge, don't you think?"

"I haven't done anything to anyone."

"Maybe they just hate you."

"Why should they? I don't even know who they are."

"But they know who you are."

"Sure they know."

"Maybe they hate you just because you are beautiful."

"That's horrible."

"It is. What are you going to do now?"

"I don't know. Maybe I'll call a friend. He'll know what to do."

"Do you want me to call my dad? He can tell us what to do; he is a mechanic. He can send someone to fix the thing."

"Would you do that for me?"

"Sure."

"You are very kind. Thank you. By the way, I am Pia."

"Veronika. I am not kind. No one thinks that I am kind, not even my mother. She thinks that I am weird, a troublemaker, disobedient and who knows what else."

"Your mother?"

"Sorry to bother you with stupidity."

"It isn't stupid, it is sad."

"I don't know even if it is sad. I am numb, I got used to it."

"What do you do?"

"Go to school."

"I meant, what do you do to ease the pain?"

"What pain?"

"You just said that your mother's not kind."

"Oh, that. I have a brother, I love him very much."

"Older?"

"No. The younger one. I love him very much. His name is Hugo and he has Down syndrome. He is a real beauty, I mean, he doesn't look that beautiful but he shines. His inner light touches the sky."

"Veronika, you are an interesting girl."

"No one ever said that."

"What else do you do, apart from spending time with glorious Hugo?"

"Read books, poetry and listen to Leonard Cohen."

"Ha-ha-ha, Leonard Cohen, the troubadour of misery and gloom."

"Is he?"

"Well, do you understand what he sings about?"

"What about you? What do you do?"

"I study. I write poetry. I go to the theatre every day."

"You go to the theatre every day, this is unreal!"

"Yep!"

"How do you manage that?"

"Do you enjoy theatre?"

"Sure I do, but I can't afford it."

OK, I'll treat you."

Veronika's father Anton sent a young apprentice. He came with a pump and hoist. He checked the tires and said that she was lucky as the tires were not punctured, just exhausted. It was fixed quickly and the boy said that *'the boss said no charge.'*

Pia said:

"Thank you ever so much Veronika, I really owe you. Look, how about I take you to the theatre on Saturday?"

"It would be too dear, leave it."

"No! I wanna take you, I don't pay; I have a free entrance to the theatre and people I bring with me, too."

"Cool!"

"Saturday?"

That was just the beginning of a most unlikely friendship that would grow stronger and stronger for many years to come. Slowly they were to discover how much they had in common, how many similar experiences they had had, and how many identical thoughts formed in their heads.

***

No one would ever call Veronika a shy person. But when she got to know Pia better she never censored her stories. On the third occasion, when she said to her mother, *'None of your bloody business'* when she asked what time she'd be home, Pia commented:

"No room for a friendship between the two of you?"

"There's never been, as you said, a friendship, between the two of us."

"How come?"

"You really wanna hear it?"

"Not dying to hear it, but if you wanna talk about it I am curious enough."

"My mother Elsa came from the best land on earth – holy Germany, and she loved only two things here: my father, the reason why she had come in 1960, and her God, my older brother Gregor. He was born on the day when God decided to be generous, hence a perfect little boy was born: he was, just like Elsa, blond, blue-eyed and born with several gifts that would become apparent quite early in his life.

She gave birth to a second child, an ever-angry girl, the girl who never knew why she was angry, but was quite resolute from an early age to find the

126

hidden reason for her anger and frustrations: me, Veronika. I was dark-haired, chubby, chunky and an awkward child, locked in my world of 'bitterness without cause'.

The third child born to Elsa and Anton Truba was a misfortunate child who was born with an obvious fault, my little brother Hugo. The plain truth about him was there from the very beginning. I knew, even though I was a little girl that he was somehow 'different', so I took great care of him. I knew that Elsa wasn't equipped with a steady character required for such a task and that she would bear this 'shame' with little stamina, little dignity and, above all – with not enough love.

When we were young kids this was how things worked in our house. Gegor Truba grew to be a handsome boy with numerous talents; he learned reading and writing at four only; he played instruments with ease and his kind nature and good cherub-like looks brought him the status of an adored demigod. Mother Elsa talked about him with pride attributing all his gifts to their German ancestry. He was a winning bet in whatever he undertook: praises – accolades, praises – accolades wherever he went. Elsa accompanied him to soccer games, to scout camps, music competitions proud and loud, everyone knew that she had 'that son who was a winner and a stunner'.

She had three kids and three different attitudes. Three different hearts. She had three different hearts in her big German bosom, one reserved for Anton, Gregor and Germany. That heart was the heart of love, compassion and pride. The second heart was like a heart of Snow White's stepmother, the Queen. In that heart she stored her undefined emotions for her disobedient dark-haired daughter and her new country that she evaluated from the beginning to be somehow 'still barbaric'; hence, she never made friends, if we exclude the unusually close friendship with a sinister character that we hosted regularly with 'much delight and happiness' – the famous Friar Marag. He was her only friend and confidant, the one who gave understanding, 'spiritual guidance' and some understanding when it came to the 'mysterious punishment from God' referring to my brother Hugo.

I had never felt confortable in the presence of that man in a dark robe who talked under his breath, who gave her advice behind my father's back. He was at our home when my father was at work and it seemed to me that she was only happy, chatty and charming when he was around. He had those kind of eyes that would make one uneasy, somehow agitated, as if wanting you to feel incompetent and wrong, emanating something strange, maybe cold, from his squinted eyes.

Thanks to him I had never believed that God himself had anything to do with people's choices of their profession and their dealings with daily affairs. When I was a little child I bit him several times when he tried to stroke my head with 'that look in his eyes'. He would say to my mother, 'You should teach this child obedience. She was misfortunate to inherit a very bad character. Nothing to do with you, dear Elsa, it isn't your upbringing, this child has something impure within her, only a tough birch is a remedy for such maladies, as we say 'the rod comes out of Heaven'.

The third heart of mother Elsa belonged only to Hugo. It wasn't a sapless heart, but I assume that it was somehow broken, quilted with opposing emotions and colours, I assume there was a stored treasure that she wasn't aware of. All her denials were locked in that heart and she never allowed anyone, or maybe only Friar Marag, the entrance to this sorrowful and shameful abode.

Jealousy and envy prevented me from being close to my older brother. He used to tease me for my dark skin and tell me that I was a 'little Gypsy'. Even though it might have been just a kid's joke I hated it, hated him for calling me names, hated him for being so flawless and admired. I would steal or break his things, rip out pages from his favourite books or hide his picks in an attempt to vent out my anger or, maybe, in an attempt to get his attention. Often I would get my mother's attention and she would remember her best friend's advice 'the rod came out of Heaven' and I would be punished with a wooden spoon. I was the only child in the Truba family who 'deserved a beating'. She never beat me when my father was home, she never beat me hard, just a few spanks with a wooden spoon on my bottom, but it brought to me more anger, a feeling of injustice and unequal love. When Hugo grew up a little, poor kid, he understood that Mother was doing 'something wrong' and he would scream, 'Stop it! Stop it! Not fair, stop it!' Then he would come into my room where I was looking out of the window, trying to keep my tears at bay, and he hugged me and gave me little wet kisses saying, 'Yugo loves Lonnie.' Even today he calls me Lonnie. I often read to him, he liked all sorts of tales and whenever we encountered an evil witch, he would chuckle, 'Lonnie, that's Mum.'

Gregor never shared our stories, our hugs and secrets. For him, mother Elsa was the most dedicated mother one could get, they shared dreams and successes, he wasn't even aware that she treated us differently.

My brother Gregor believed what Friar Marag implanted into Elsa's heart – that I was an awkward and evil child. My creativity was never understood as for them it wasn't creativity but sheer weirdness. Hugo was the one who understood my humour, the paintings on my walls, my haiku poetry and my choice of music. When we had family gatherings or celebrations Mother would come to my room and 'have a chat' with me. She would tell me to 'behave normally' and 'not to embarrass the family'. Especially on the few occasions when we had visitors from Germany. They all adored Gregor, comparing him to some dead and other living relatives who were the pride of their family. They would look at me as if I were someone who might bite at any moment, so they were vigilant, and they talked to Hugo as if he were a little moody puppy who might be happy at one moment and growl the next.

My father worked a lot, later on I understood why. He wasn't that busy, but he had a variety of interests, and one of his greatest passions landed him in a local prison. The paradox was that he was a good-hearted man, but hatred of other nations strongly occupied one compartment of his heart. That hatred came from his unenlightened mind and was passed down by his ancestors who fought a war under the wrong flag. One of his interests was fixing the past, 'educating' people on such topics and getting into trouble for it. He could never let go, as he believed that 'great injustice' fell upon his dream and the future of his kids. He was a hard-working man, kind to kids, women, dogs and Croats. Apart from that he was pretty indifferent. He would say, 'What do I know, I am just a mechanic in a screwed up state.'

I can say that I loved my father, surely more than my mother, but he was uneducated and he had so many prejudices favouring the idea of a 'superior nation' and mourned 'the old glorious days when Croatia and Germany were allies.'

Friar Marag never let himself talk about such a topic in public, but under his breath he would say to my father, 'God will give us glory again, God will provide.'

I can tell you so many stories about our dysfunctional family, the family that the biggest hypocrite, Elsa Truba, tried to portray as 'an average, but happy, family', but no need to go any further. She was a hypocrite, father was politically obsessed, Gregor was a God in the making, Hugo was the shame of the family and I was just – Veronika, a misfit, probably a bigger shame than poor Hugo to the picture-perfect Elsa, as he was born misfortunate while I was born 'sane, but evil'.

I am dreaming of the day I am old enough, strong enough to wave them a silent good-bye. The only reason that I do hesitate is Hugo. What would he do without me? It would break my heart to leave him alone."

"Don't tell me that your brother is Gregor Truba, the Gregor?" asked Pia.

"Yeah, the God of rock and roll! Finally, he climbed the stairs to Heaven, and my jealousy culminated."

"I don't see you jealous, I see you as someone who has never got due attention, your talents, your personality were overlooked. What do you write about?"

"I spend a lot of time alone. I sit in my room, or walk the streets for hours and observe. I observe myself: my thoughts, my feelings, my breath, the way my chest rises up and falls, I observe the rhythm of my feet when I walk, again, when I walk I observe my breath, I coordinate my breath with the rhythm of my feet, with the sounds of nature, with inner melody, and after some time of silent observations I hear verses, then I take them down in written form, or draw them, or paint them on my wall."

"You mean, a real wall, or your inner wall?"

"No, the wall in my bedroom. On one occasion my mother came in when I had painted the stars on my ceiling and said, 'By tomorrow morning I want it all down. All clean, do we understand each other?' Staring in her eyes, I took a *bucket, still with the yellow paint in it, and poured it onto the parquet floor and asked, 'And what about the floor, that part of your demand was unclear, do you want me to clean it as well?'*

She said, 'Friar Marag is right in saying that you are evil, wicked, a wicked child.'

Love, love, love mother Elsa, you've never given any love. No, I didn't tell her that but I heard this sentence in my head and wrote it, with that yellow paint spilled on the floor onto my ceiling – right there among the stars:

'Love, love, love, what Else, but love!'

"Wow! You are crazier than I am. I do so-called weird things, like, I paint my thoughts."

"You write beautiful poetry."

For the first time ever Pia mentioned her mother, the word *'mother'* itself, then added to it the possessive adjective *'my mother'*; for the first time in many years she mentioned her mother without feeling threatened:

"We used to do that. I would write my thoughts, little verses and my mother would paint them onto her canvases."

Mellowness was in her eyes, they got moist and she felt as if she wanted to hug Veronika, but she didn't, she knew that she had earned a friend for the rest of her life.

"Your mother is an artist?"

"She used to be."

"Was she a good one?"

"Fantastic."

"Why did she stop painting?"

"Veronika, my mother died many years ago."

"Oh, I am so sorry."

"No, I am the one that feels sorry. . . I fear I killed her."

***

Deep silence set in between them. Veronika didn't say a word, she just concentrated on her breathing and this time it was quite a task to concentrate solely on her breathing. Thoughts interfered, feelings interfered and questions that were not to be asked interfered.

She kept breathing and Pia heard it as if it were some sort of strange symphony, the symphony coming from past times when life looked like a real thing, when she heard beautiful symphonies in the fragments of her own being.

Veronika kept breathing and Pia sat on her hands.

They sat there for quite a long period of time, twilight darkened the window, Pia saw the reflection of her face in it, she looked like Sapphire she looked like her mother and that notion only intensified her guilt. She couldn't escape from her deeds, from memories, from guilt and from Sapphire's image, in each and every mirror, darkened window or stainless steel cutlery she saw her face, the face that spoke to her in a gentle, loving manner, Pia kept sitting on her hands in order to prevent her nails digging mercilessly into her thighs.

Then Hugo came in, looked at Pia in amazement and asked:
"Lonnie, is that dolly a real one?"
"Hugo, this is Pia, my friend. Pia, my little brother Hugo."
"Pia is a real doll, she moves head and speaks, ha-ha-ha, beautiful Pia."
He came close and gave her a hug, she patted his head and said:
"You are adorable."
He giggled and said:
"Yugo loves Pia."
Pia winked at him and said:
"Pia has to go now Hugo, but I'll see you again."
"Promise?"
"Sure!"
"You promise forever?"
"Forever Hugo, forever."

When Pia left, Veronika hugged Hugo knowing that he was the only person she was at ease with. Maybe the only person, as in Pia's company she felt quite similar: at ease with words and emotions.

She never dreamed that she would gain such an intimate and sincere friendship with Pia Odak, the most beautiful girl in town, the girl everyone wanted to have for a friend, acquaintance, be her boyfriend or just be in her company by chance. She looked and behaved like a Goddess, while Veronika was just a plain looking girl, strange in her ways of doing things, socially awkward and with only one friend – little brother Hugo.

Without knocking at her door mother Elsa came in and said:
"Who's that creature all in black that just left the house?"
"All in black? Isn't your friend dressed 'all in black'? Maybe it was him! Looking for you, run, run Frau Elsa, run after him, drink from his fountain of wisdom and preach to your kids heretical philosophies and from his lips passed down theology."
"How dare you! You..."
"Satan!"
"Stop it!" Elsa screamed ready to explode as her face become crimson, but Hugo's cry prevailed:
"You 'top it! Yugo said 'top it Mum!"
Elsa slammed the door and Veronika asked:
"Do you want me to read to you?"
"Sure!"
"What would you like?"
"Little Yugo."
Instead of saying *Little Prince* in the story, Veronika inserted *Little Hugo* whenever the name was mentioned.

Hugo loved the story and she read it to him often. This time he laid his head on her lap, he held onto her index finger and each time she needed to turn the page over she would say again, *'Let it go'*, and after turning the page she said, *'Here'*, giving her finger back to him as he hung onto it as some kids hang onto their toy or security blanket.

New Year's Eve, 1984

For his crime he was never punished, as Luna never said a word about it. The Gallery got fixed at the expense of the local government and the necklace stayed in the window. Gregor Truba resolved to *'forget Pia'*. He thought that he had had enough of her ways, that she was way too weird, plus, really, one impregnable fortress, why would he bother any longer?

He had found himself a girlfriend: a girl who worked part-time as a TV presenter and occasionally as a model. Yes, prettier than Pia! Smarter than Pia! Friendlier than Pia! Easier than Pia!

He resolved he was going to love her and forget all about Pia and the weird stories about her and her father, the whole family seemed like kooks.

The new girlfriend's name was Margit, she even played the guitar, she was good-natured, she was entertaining, she was funny, she just graduated and was four years older. Gregor met her when she interviewed them, yes: witty and chatty, the complete opposite of the moody and unpredictable Pia - the Queen of Silence. The Queen of Unpredictable Moods!

No, he had had enough; all he wanted was *'just a normal girl'*.

After only two weeks he felt as if he'd known her for ages, he was relaxed, his old self, they went out a lot, played guitars for fun together; she cut his hair shorter, she changed his image by choosing a *'cooler look'*, she organised more interviews and his band played at the charity event that she had organised.

Everyone liked Margit as her personality shone through good deeds and her friendly manner. Gregor said to himself that he was blessed to have her on his side. Plus, they made love as a normal couple would, he was young and he needed a real partner, even in bed, not an arrogant, or frightened, frigid beauty who slept all night on his shoulder.

Margit came over to help Gregor pack his instruments.

Knowing her face from the TV screen, Elsa softened her manner as much as she was able to and welcomed her in. She said:

"Look after my boy."

As they were taking out a bass-guitar, they met Veronika and Pia on the doorsteps. Gregor stopped in his step. Pia smiled. Margit said, *'Hi Pia, who would expect you here.'*

Pia smiled. Veronika pushed through the door, Hugo screamed, *'Pia, Pia, you came, Yugo's beautiful Pia.'* Pia smiled. Elsa repeated, *'Look after my boy, Margit.'*

Gregor nervously wiped the sweat off his brow (though, it was a cold and the last day of December), Pia smiled, he said, *'Hi, Pia!'* and she just kept smiling.

Yes, he was shattered. The extent of her power over him was visible in his shaking hands as his guitar nearly fell off, and it would have if it hadn't been for Margit who caught the guitar's neck and said, *'Watch out!'* Only Veronika was cool and sharp and said, *'Watch out Truba, watch out!'* and closed the door of her room.

Everything went wrong that afternoon.

First, he got a speeding fine, failed to apologise to the officer, bumped into the low wall while trying to park and had a quarrel with Igor; he wanted everyone to listen to him and when they told him that his *'Nazi-blood'* had to be cooled, he even told the good-natured Margit to keep her mouth shut. He drank more than he should have and everyone noticed his bad mood, everyone noticed, but only Igor knew the reason for it.

He was never nervous prior to a concert, he never needed weed or alcohol to calm him, he took it just for fun, but on that afternoon he took it as medication.

No, he never got over her; it would take a long, long time before he could talk about Pia with calmness in his voice and hands resting peacefully on the table.

The concert was on a boardwalk and the technicians were working all afternoon. The big stage was set up, some streets were closed to all traffic from the early afternoon; it was meant to be an open party till the morning hours.

They were the opening act; the crowd started to gather in the early evening hours even though it was crisp and the coolish wind was blowing, the sky was clear and it promised a dry night, everybody said *'as long as it doesn't rain.'*

***

For the New Year's celebration Pia took Veronika to her friend's place. They lived in one of those tall old buildings overlooking the boardwalk and the harbour. At midnight, the ships and boats anchored in the harbour made a simultaneous display of fireworks and the spectacle was great when seen from near by, especially from a higher building. The stage on the boardwalk was as if on the palm of the hand and the music was loud. They took the tables outside, placed food and drinks on them, ate, smoked, danced and drank. Veronika felt very special that evening as she was a part of such a *'cool crowd'*, Pia's crowd, creative people and intellectuals yet so mad, funny and fun-loving while she was still a high-school student. She admitted to herself that she did admire Pia for all she represented, and it was clear to her why her brother almost dropped his guitar – Pia's magnetism was so strong, whenever she entered any space the energy would shift, it was as if a million harps were announcing the entrance of someone that would change people's awareness and behaviour.

Veronika stood next to Pia and whispered in her ear:

"God's playing. We have to admit he looks hellishly hot."

Pia smiled holding a glass of bubbly in her hand.

"Do you like him, Pia?"

"I don't. I don't need a man in my life. The main challenge for me is to understand how my consciousness works. I don't wish to explain it away, as contemporary neuroscience and philosophy of mind try to do. Science or established religions can't tell me the meaning of my life."

"Isn't the meaning of life love?"

"Oh, look who's talking! The expert in the field. What do you know about love Lonnie? The only person you have ever loved is your little brother Hugo?"

"And you."
Pia hugged her and said:
"Let's get sloshed!"

When Pia woke up on the first of January 1985, precisely at 4:45, the apartment was full of people still chatting and drinking. Some were singing while others were rolling on sofas in a delirious embrace, some with old, some with new partners. She didn't remember, neither did she ever see her father there, but when she went out for fresh air, she saw him cuddling Veronika. She just said:

"Happy New Year, Simo."
Veronika smiled, Pia smiled. Just another year; old habits die hard.

She decided to walk home alone in the crisp dawn of a just born New Year. As she was walking, a car pulled over. A man opened the window and shouted:

"Happy New Year, Pia!"
She sat in his car, there were two other girls, all students at her university, they offered her to join *'for a last drink'* and she said, *"What the hell, let's go."*

They came to another party that was slowly dying down, the atmosphere was a little bit washed out, enthusiasm was on the low side of the scale; she took the offered drink and a cup of coffee and her eyes met Gregor's. His arm was around her waist, they looked good, relaxed and happy – Margit and Gregor Truba; she smiled at them and Gregor said across the room:

"Happy New Year, Pia!"
"To you too!"
She left an empty glass on the table and walked out.

While waiting for the lift to come, the door opened. He walked out and said:

"Hug me!"
She came and gave him a hug. Tightly he pressed her against his chest and said:

"Let's go. Let's run away together and hide under your duvet."
"You are drunk."

"I am always drunk when I look at you, Pia. And you know it. So, play me as a game, you know you can do it, take me, use me, discard me, but be mine tonight.

The lift stopped, Pia said nothing, they walked in together and when the door closed behind them they found themselves in a passionate embrace, kissing each other breathless. Gregor pulled down the little handle where *'stop'* was written and the lift stopped, they kissed and laughed and celebrated the New Year, the new dawn and the new beginning.

When he was undressing her he saw the marks on her thighs but he didn't want to spoil this perfect early morning with any *dark marks.* He didn't want to create any discomfort; all he wanted was to give her love, not even thinking about asking her to love him in return. He thought that his heart held so much love for Pia that it would do for both of them.

When they were in bed, almost naked, Pia said:

"I don't wanna make love to you, Gregor. I just want to sleep."

"Why?"

"This is what I wanna do. There's no answer to your why. Simply, because it is so."

"Let it be, Pia, let it be."

Once again he felt played by Pia.

She fell asleep and he looked at the ceiling, *'What am I going to do to make her love me'*, or *'Was she capable of love, at all?'*

To get anything out of this extravagant deed, leaving his girlfriend without any explanation, he wanted to gain something. He got up and started to search for Pia's bag or, more precisely, for her diary.

He was adamant to find out what was written there.

While she was sleeping like Sleeping Beauty he started his search through her bags and drawers. Yes, he had found it. Quietly he went to the bathroom, switched the light on, sat on the toilet seat and opened the page, the one that had that black rim around it - the page that resembled an obituary.

It read:

"And this is not life but existence, nor is it creativity but a mere cry. I cry through my poems in an attempt to touch your soul, to get an answer or to please you. I know that you are here, in my mirror, in my steps, in my breath and my sorrow. I know that you see me, that you hold my hand when I can't write, that you stroke my back when I can't walk any longer. I feel you around; I see your eyes, the eyes that looked at me on that day pleading with my soul to let you go. What could I have possibly done other than let you go, when I believed that you'd take me with you? You never did, but I still dream about the day when we would finish our last painting, oh, I miss your gentle brush strokes and gentle strokes of your hand against my cheeks I reserve all my words for you, in that, still childish, hope that you'd be able to paint them and put them up for an exhibition in Heaven, in Heaven you had gone to, as all your deeds were Heavenly guided, including the last one, including the last one, including the last one..."

It was 7:30 am on that first of January 1985 when a strong knock on the toilet door startled Gregor. A male voice said:

"Are you OK, Pia?"

"Oh, oh, it's actually ... someone else."

He heard the echo of his heels rebounding off the walls of the tall hallway, he heard that he had put some music on, Mario Lanza, and then Gregor, shoved Pia's diary in his pants, he took one of her bathrobes hanging on the back of the door, put it on and went into her room, again on the tip of his toes. Quietly, he put the diary where he had found it, he put his clothes on, kissed Pia's forehead and left the house.

***

The next day, on the second of January, Pia came with a cake.

She pressed the doorbell and Elsa opened the door. She said:

"We are sleeping." And closed the door. Pia stood as if she was hit by a thunderbolt, not believing that this woman just shut the door in her face. She turned and slowly walked towards the car when she heard through the window:

"Pia, my beautiful Pia, come, come to Yugo."

He ran out of the house, his mother followed, Veronika came out of her room, Gregor stopped eating, only Anton Truba was peacefully reading the morning papers.

"What has just happened?" Gregor asked. His mother was dragging Hugo indoors telling him that he'd *'catch a cold'*, Veronika was looking at her with a puzzled look on her face, Pia stood with a tray in her hands and Gregor walked her in.

Elsa said to Hugo, *"Only God can help us."* Veronika addressed no one in particular by saying, *"He doesn't care about hypocrites"*; Pia walked into Veronika's room and said:

"I brought some cakes, my granny baked them for me, they are still warm, I wanted to share them with you."

"Who else?"

"Well, Hugo."

"Yugo loves Pia's cakes."

They sat together eating cakes, listening to the music and laughing at Hugo's jokes. The previous evening he heard some jokes on a state television show and he was telling them without order and mixing all of them and *'inserting random shit'* as Veronika nicely put it.

***

Gregor was keen to know if Pia was going to call him – ever, after that night they spent together, so he left it up to her! But, she never called. Not the first week of the New Year, not the second, but then, on the third week he met her at the University cafeteria eating a *'tramezzino'* with blue cheese and lettuce. He sat next to her and grabbed her hand. She smiled and he said:

"Why are you smiling?"

"Not for any particular reason, probably just an expression."

"Pia, do you have any feelings?"

"For you?"

140

"For anyone, just genuine human feelings."

"I do have feelings."

"But, you don't know how to express them, yeah?"

"Hmm, never thought about that. Don't trouble your head with such topics, Truba. Stay cool, stay relaxed."

"I want to help you, Pia."

"You want to help Pia? What kind of help are you offering?"

"Obviously you are full of problems."

"Oh! Splendid! A Saviour! You think that I can't solve my problems myself, but rather wait for a Saviour. Truba, you can't do much for me, it's up to me to work it out, if there is any problem. You see problems; I see freedom. I am as free as a bird, and being free isn't a problem for me. I love being free, Gregor Truba. It's me. Such a solitary creature, Pia the Hermit!"

"You kissed me in the lift. You wanted me."

"Yes I did. I kiss boys. Is that strange?"

"It's strange that you kiss boys, yet you are afraid to make love to them. That is strange."

"Don't play God. Don't you think that it could simply be because I am not so keen, Truba. Pick some of those girls that are mad about you, Pia is not the one."

The very same evening he met her in a bar holding hands with Barbarossa. He knew it now, that holding hands meant nothing. Nothing to Pia!

A Short Visit to Jail

Gregor was absent for a few weeks touring local towns.

The more he wanted to escape from memories of Pia, the more she haunted him, especially when he was tipsy or high he would do everything to *'prove to her that he couldn't care less about her'*. Namely, he would charm in no time any local beauty, get into her pants and put yet another *'tick'* into the book of his achievements that wasn't hidden in his heart, but rather revealed in his drunken speeches. When drunk he was not a gentleman, neither was he one when sober. He was only 23 years old, he was as popular as a young star could be, *'fame'* got to his head, he behaved as if the world had been invented for his entertainment, hence he couldn't grasp – *'Why Pia resisted his charms, his charisma and him, the God of rock and roll, the most handsome guy in town?"*

Cold and arrogant Pia! He said to himself that he could and he would sleep with the most beautiful girls out of spite, as he really never wanted her for anything else but for sex. For what else but sex?

When sober, he would regret long-legged-beauties-with-nothing-to-say, girls who giggled, talked rubbish, looked artificial and were endlessly boring. Then he would sit with his guitar and quietly compose lyrics and music with Pia in his mind.

He always kept away from politics and political figures, be they the present ones or the ghosts of the past. He kept away knowing that it could only land him in trouble as it did bring a few storms his father's way, plus, he knew that being Anton's son never helped when it came to *'law and order'*. It was like, *'Ah, you are Anton Truba's son!'*

The town where they played that evening was small, more inland, a part of the country where young people rarely got much entertainment but amused themselves with daily politics and tales from the last two wars. They discussed *'who did what and who owes what to whom'*. They had the memory of an elephant and never cared for: beauty, culture, literature or kindness. It was just the way it was, they hadn't had much of a choice as it was their way of living and no other way had been invented or shown to them yet. They drank heavily and fought heavily.

After the concert Gregor and his mates were invited to some party in the only hotel in town. They had a few drinks with local young men who adored them for what they represented and just kept on bringing more and more drinks to the table. A young journalist was drunk and loud. He took several pictures of Gregor, and when he learned that his mother was of German origin, the young lad took a picture out of his wallet of *'Adolf the Great'* and initiated songs that were forbidden in 1985. In honour of Gregor Truba, the great musician, the son of a German mother, the journalist started with *'Lili Marlene'* and the salute. Others joined in and the journalist kept taking photos with the *'famous guys'*, he kept bringing more and more booze and in a short time the local hotel resonated with marching songs that were glorifying the Nazi leaders from WWII. Not long after the hall was in dead silence. Several policemen came and the songs died, they were sitting as defeated heroes, all with their identity cards in front of them answering questions while policemen gathered requesting information.

They were all detained in the local jail.

***

When Gregor Truba woke up the following morning he experienced the worst hangover yet. He had a splitting headache, but then he found that his ribs were hurting; he touched his face and screamed as his prominent cheekbones were swollen and painful.

He recalled what had happened only several hours earlier.

He thought of Pia's uncle. He thought of her. That journalist took pictures of him. There was a photo of Hitler on the table, a swastika drawn with blood of one of the blokes. He feared it would appear in the morning papers. He asked for the papers but was refused. He asked if he could call home. That was allowed. He called Pia instead. He didn't mean to but he dialled her number.

It was seven o'clock in the morning and the telephone rang for a long time. He feared that her father might pick it up, but he was wrong. He never knew that her father would not go out of his way to do anything for anyone. His approach to telephone calls was – *'If they need me, they'll call again'*, or *'They need me, that's why they call'*. He never needed anyone, or anything in particular, he got it all on the day when he was born: social status, doctors, lawyers, teachers, free entrances to anything, free access to any event or information, or for that matter any girl.

The telephone rang and rang; Gregor was about to hang up when he heard a soft sleepy voice:

"Hello."

"Pia?"

"Who is it?"

"Gregor."

"For Christ's sake, what's the time?"

"Seven in the morning, I am in jail."

"Why are you calling me? What do you think I can do for you?"

"Maybe give me your uncle's number."

"It's Sunday morning. Where are you?"

When Gregor told her where he was jailed she just sighed. The silence filled the gap, finally she said:

"What have you done this time? Beat the crap out of someone who looked at your girl?"

"More complicated than that. Pia, please, can I have his number?"

"If it is not urgent, I'll give him a call after nine."

"Thanks."

"Yeah, thanks."

"Pia, you are the only person I wanted to talk to..."

She hung up and went back to sleep.

***

The cliché of *'good cop, bad cop'* was played out as they interrogated him again. One tried to intimidate him with his bad language, calling him names and threatening with long imprisonment, while the other *'understood'* where he came from, being the *'son of an offender and politically incorrect man, and son of a German woman who had close ties with an ultra right clergyman'*. But his understanding was stretched to the following:

'All of this doesn't look that bad, as long as you cooperate, you can name people your father associates with and off you go. How often does that priest visit?'

To Gregor the whole thing was ridiculous, a farce, a show where two men gave too much importance to trivial matters. They just got drunk and sang songs that were considered to be bad propaganda and criminal behaviour. Gregor saw the incident as the plain stupidity of several young men, an incident he was tricked into, was an unwilling participant in, even though he had his guitar in his lap - he always has it with him. Always when he was out and about. But he had never sung those songs before. He wondered, *'What did his father have to do with it? He wondered why Friar Marag was such an important topic and person; he was just a local priest. Yes, Elsa's friend, everybody knew that, but they didn't do anything wrong. He was a priest, and petty-bourgeois gossip went around, but he would brush those insinuations off, Friar Marag was a good-looking man, surely an erudite and an expert in a vast range of topics, he built that close relationship with Elsa only because she couldn't find anyone in this town who would understand her. Friar Marag was fluent in several languages, including German.'*

Gregor thought harder, but all he knew was that everyone liked Friar Marag. Or, at least, everyone they knew. Or, hang on! Veronika didn't like him, quite the opposite, she hated that man passionately, but didn't he, Friar Marag, say himself that the best way to deal with Veronika would be to perform some sort of exorcism? Veronika was a troubled child, always! She even hated her own mother. Gregor couldn't understand - why? In his eyes, in his books, there was no better mother than their kind mother Elsa. Veronika did all sorts of horrible things when she was a young girl that no one ever understood. Why? Why was she so spiteful? Friar Marag said that she was born that way, like a *'bad seed'*. He said it under his breath, he spoke then lowered his eyes, he felt sorry and sad for mother Elsa, for the entire family. Taken out of context, one day he said:

"To this very day the seed of Belial is embodied among us."

He was a clergyman, a man who understood people; he was never in any sort of conflict with anyone, least of all the police, as a priest should keep out of conflict and strain.

On that occasion Veronika had commented:

"Yes, we see those spoilers everywhere, in any arena, including the churches. Mrs Truba, as your illustrious Friar Marag serves as the guide and the anchor of your absolutely innocent soul, rest assured that he will forever keep you from drifting away from your path of righteousness; he is leading you towards light and wisdom."

Yes, Veronika; she was a troublemaker; was she born that way, or was that malevolent streak developed under the same roof without Gregor noticing it? Was he just taking things at face value: *Dad had always been a hard-working man and kept his business to himself, Mum was a real sweetheart that wanted everyone to be happy including Friar Marag who would have a proper meal only when she cooked. Veronika was born evil, was an envious child, and Hugo was just a misfortune.*

And who was he – Gregor Truba?

That very question he had never asked himself before.

There he was, in the provincial jail, with two men with silly moustaches that were never in fashion anywhere on this planet, who were interrogating him; while he prayed on rare occasions, this proved to be the right one, that somehow Pia would be on his side, again. The little, cold-hearted witch who had stolen his heart for eternity.

Pia's Journey

"It's Sunday, Pia."
"Yes. But can you help? Do you want to help?"
"Yes, if it is for you."
"It is."
"Who will pay for it?"
"They'll pay, they have money."

He picked her up at 9:30 am and they went slowly down the road. The road was empty on that quiet and cold Sunday morning; Pia had put her headphones on, lowered the seat and drifted off.

While she was drifting off she dreamed a dream:

She dreamed that she was nine years old and was carrying a backpack full of books and ideas. She dreamed that she came home and left her schoolbag in the corridor, she heard soft music and as she was walking she saw blood coming from the gap underneath the kitchen door. She ran there and found her little feet dipped in blood and she walked with blood-stained feet around her house, leaving blood-red leaf-like shaped steps that were leading her into darkness. The colours had disappeared, leaving only blood-red steps against the encompassing blackness and the soft sound of music that was coming from the cracks in the dark walls. She found herself in the small dark room, even the red steps had disappeared, only darkness was real and palpable, and only her breathing kept her in that realm. She tried to call someone, she tried to run or scream, but she stood there unable to move or to reason. She stood there in surrender, naked and ashamed; in that room the doors disappeared, the windows disappeared and there was no air anymore for Pia to breathe, and she surrendered, surrendered, surrendered.

She didn't scream because of the dream; it was quite a pleasant dream to Pia, but she screamed because her uncle stopped the car and started to shake her. He said:

"*Wake up, Pia, wake up!*"

"*What happened?*"

"*Look at your hands!*"

When Pia looked at her hands there were blood marks all over her palms and the top of her hands. Blood was pouring slowly and uncle Boris gave her a handkerchief and said:

"*Was it a nightmare?*"

"*Not really.*"

He looked deep into her eyes with a worried expression and asked:

"*If there's ever anything you want to tell me, please Pia, let me know.*"

"*There's nothing. All's well. Let's go.*"

This time Pia closed her eyes but decided to stay awake, no drifting off. She put her music louder and looked at the scenery as he drove.

Now she was thinking of Gregor. She asked herself, '*Why was she helping him again?*' But to that question she couldn't find the answer. She didn't feel anything in her heart, but in her mind she felt secure when with him. She felt different. She felt something, but she couldn't put a name to that feeling.

***

She grew close to his sister Veronika even though they looked like the most unlikely match. They were so different at first glance, but under the surface beauty was discovered from both ends. All their hidden treasures were exposed freely and sincerely. Pia found in Veronika a girl who thinks deep thoughts and experiences deeper emotions and she was delighted that she could share her thoughts and poems with her as we, humans, need a friend, a mirror that reflects our both sides. Pia liked Veronika's sharpness and direct approach to anyone; her sense of humour was plainly weird, so different, and Pia related to it from the first laugh they shared together. The first laugh they shared together happened when they shared a seat in a packed theatre. A heavy woman, dressed as if she were a part of the acting crew, stepped on Veronika's foot; she cast a scornful look at Veronika and Veronika said:

"Please, feel free to step on the other one and when you get tired of your elegant dance, you can freely repose in my lap. There's always room to squeeze in one more character."

"You are a real character! A Goth, or whatever!"

"Whatever will do, thank you!"

Pia whispered:

"You are crazier than I am."

"I know I am. I am the Devil's daughter, that's what my family believes instructed by the famous priest."

When thinking about that Pia smiled, she never said what she really thought in her head, she never acted out her fantasies, but Veronika was a champion, seemingly without any inhibition, but then when she met Hugo, she discovered the real Veronika. Veronika could surprise one endlessly, and Pia was in awe of her abilities to recognise and name any behaviour, emotion or a lie, she was like a human detector, a scanner whose accuracy was astonishing. Knowing that, Pia had never doubted Veronika's evaluation of her brother Gregor's emotions.

"He is shallow, a man who thinks with his penis. What else could one expect from a God of his proportions? Mother's Golden Boy, he was the favourite one and there was never any doubt about it. He grew up knowing how gorgeous he was, how talented and 'kind'. I hate that word 'kind' when it comes from my mother's lips. That 'kind' is the kind of an obedient mother-worshiping adherent, meek and adorable, yet so strong and desirable. Oh, mother Elsa, if one didn't know you one would pay a high price for you and your favourite son. He, Gregor Truba, just like his mother, the merciful Elsa, wasn't even aware of his brother's existence apart from the fact that his tongue was sticking out, dripping with saliva, that his eyes were squinted and unfocused; they were not aware that Hugo was a being, a beautiful human being

with the most generous heart, with an outstanding sense of humour, with determination to do things in his own way. No! Just obey, Hugo, and don't make anyone edgy or embarrassed, scornful or impatient! Hurry up, Hugo! No, don't unbutton! Don't button up! Don't unzip! Yes, zip it up! I hated them for treating him that way, Gregor perhaps not deliberately, Elsa deliberately; I hate them still for hiding Hugo when someone pays a visit, especially that devil in black robes, who comes and 'comforts' Elsa, telling her that she has to 'carry the burden with dignity and humility'. I hate my indifferent father Anton, who pretends that he doesn't know anything, pretends that he is 'just a mechanic' whenever it comes to any serious discussion or decision. For him, his bloody nation is much more important than his own family. The nation above anything, above God! I would pack my bags right now and leave this country, this city and this shitty family if it wasn't for Hugo. He would be a broken soul if I went, no one would treat him as a human being but as a 'bag of bones and belly that is a burden'. My mother said once that he eats 'like a horse', that's correct; she said that her own growing child is a burden because he eats like a horse. Bloody cold-hearted German bitch! I taught Hugo the word - I told him 'When we are together we can call her bitch.' He laughed and laughed and concluded in the end, 'Lonnie, Elsa is not a bitch. Elsa is an evil bitch.' Then he laughed again and I swear that he laughed out of sheer happiness that I had understood him. Finally, his thoughts were validated. He hugged me and laughed saying, 'Lonnie you are so funny. You understand Yugo. Yugo loves Lonnie.'

And the other brother, he sits in his room and plays the guitar. He played the piano and the guitar as Elsa 'knew that he was exceptionally gifted.' We listened to his music and occasionally clapped at her request. Her German relatives would visit and they would clap and cheer while Hugo and I sat combed, in uncomfortable but presentable clothes. I used to wee on my dresses selected by meek mother Elsa. I weed on my shoes, on my socks; I threw away sandwiches that she made according to her 'best German recipes'. Oh, I can fill up pages; paint millions of walls and ceilings with loony-stories of my family. The only one that was sane, humble and kind was Hugo and he was the one who taught me what love is like, I used to tell him, 'Hugo, love has squint-

ed eyes', he would laugh and clap his hands saying, 'Lonnie, you are right, Lonnie you are so funny, and, and Lonnie loves Yugo, yes?'

While those memories travelled through Pia's head she thought of Gregor. She couldn't determine why she was thinking of him more than she wanted to, why she wanted to help him for the second time, and why she was travelling with her uncle instead of just passing on the message.

No, she wasn't in love; she knew it. She had never been in love, she allowed some boys to admire her, but she never ever wanted to love anyone, least of all someone like Gregor Truba.

The feeling that he was a fake deep down was the strongest feeling that she had about him. Something undefined about him, some sort of self-admiration that she never really wanted to discover.

While thinking about Veronika's mother, after a long, long time, that train of thought took Pia into a stormy landscape, into Luna's land, the valley below.

For it was useful that Pia understood the origin of evil, even as she understood the origin of good in order that she might effectively eliminate the cause and core of *'that which seemeth to be but is not.'*

***

Oriana Letizia de Amicis had married Ernesto Claudio Bonifacio in the most sumptuous wedding in 1936 and the cause of this marriage was, in the first place, the marriage of the two powerful, wealthy families in that region, and secondly because *'the kids liked each other'*. Oriana grew up with maids and governesses, and private teachers in a big loud house. She demanded the world to bend her way from the very beginning of her life, and it did! It really did! For the best part of her life, then WWII tore up this picture-perfect dream.

In the year 1939 she gave birth to twin-girls and named them Gemma Letizia and Luna Averna; in 1941 a son was born, but died of pneumonia before he turned one.

The twins were identical. They looked alike and no one, not even their own mother could tell them apart in the first twenty seconds. After twenty seconds passed the mother could tell which one was Luna Averna as she had one eyebrow slightly higher. It was barely noticeable, and if Oriana pointed out to anyone the difference, the family would shrug their shoulders in surrender as no one really noticed any difference. The difference between the girls started to be apparent with the first signs of their personalities.

Gemma Letizia was born first and Luna Averna came twenty minutes later. Even though Gemma hurried to come first, she was a placid, self-contained child who could look at her own hands and fingers for a long time. Luna Averna came out with a mighty cry and the world stood frozen for, at least, several seconds. They said that Oriana was stunned by the capacity of her lungs, and out of shock she stood up and her insides healed instantly, but her hair rose up and stood up for days and she wasn't able to comb the hair back to normal. Not even her hairdresser could do anything about it and he advised her to *'wait as this was sometimes a normal thing to happen after childbirth.'* She took his expertise in the field for granted and banned all the mirrors in the house until her hair went back to normal. When the shock raised by Luna's mighty cry had passed, her hair lay back on her temple in surrender as if accepting that the screaming child was there to stay.

Gemma had a compliant nature; Luna was the winner at any cost, regardless of whether it was innocent play or school activity, or the applause earned after performing on the old family piano.

Forceful and argumentative, envious and vindictive, that was Luna. She had to be *'The most beautiful, the most talented and the most popular'*, but as paradox had it, all talents really, belonged to Gemma. She was an effortless piano-player, she would doodle and draw sketches while sitting in the sunny garden; she kept a little diary that was hidden and torn apart several times by Luna who always denied it, teary, offensive, defensive and kept the record of everyone's each and every deed.

Later Gemma and Luna could be told apart by their characters, by their deeds and interpretations, the tone of their voices and their remarks.

Gemma loved Luna without any discrimination, Luna loved Gemma because she couldn't help but love a twin as it was embedded in the psyche, in the code, but she envied all her achievements, her pleasant and atoning ways, the capacity to be admired by friends without any effort. Luna did everything with immense effort but never received any prize, or at least not the prize she wanted to get – that grand recognition of her uniqueness, power and beauty.

Gemma did everything with grace, Luna with force. Gemma was the first to offer a hand or a kind word when Luna went mad attacking Gemma for anything, *'Stop being stupid and meek as a sheep'*, *'Stop trying to please everyone, you are phoney'*, *'Stop trying too hard, you are not an artist, they're fooling you'*, *'Stop saying – I am sorry, you don't have any personality'*... the list was long.

Gemma had a short memory and always quickly forgave her sister for any insult and that too would infuriate Luna easily. Luna always thought that Gemma received a better present; that she had more attention and more love. Even when Gemma offered to swap the presents, Luna would reject the idea, because she wouldn't be happy with that either, for her happiness, or unhappiness, never originated from a source that could be seen or from the things that could be exchanged.

They attended the same school; Gemma excelled, especially in creative fields. Her friends, because of her kindness and readiness to help, admired her. By this time it was easy to tell them apart, as their characters were antipodal and their deeds sent loud or silent, but utterly different messages, and their inner circle of friends remained different.

They grew up into real beauties; when standing next to each other they would take a passer-by's breath away: tall and slim, dark-haired and green-eyed girls with perfect facial features, together they looked like a mirage.

But Gemma was the popular one among the boys, Luna wasn't. Luna's poison was difficult to hide, it came from her words, seeped through the look in her eyes – it was apparent in each and every comment or remark. Sleazy, ambitious and unscrupulous boys would be attracted to Luna, as the same qualities were mixed in the glass of the elixir that she was offering to her victims.

She was always up to evil deeds: spreading gossip and lies, ready to break up couples in love, stealing her sister's drawings, scraping off her signature and signing her own name underneath; she went to church and told her priest lies about her family and neighbours; she sent anonymous letters to wives and lovers… As she grew older the list of her misdeeds grew longer and her heart grew colder.

At sixteen she fell pregnant to a prominent doctor's son, but no one wanted that marriage except Luna, so the doctor organised a hush-hush abortion after which Luna's heart withered away, not because she pitied the unborn child, but because of the painful rejection as the young lad never wanted to see her again. She plotted retaliation, but she wasn't yet as sophisticated in using the means that she'd learn as time passed by. But she knew that she would master the art of vengeance and that she would even the score with that family.

The time for revenge came faster than she could have imagined.

Simon Odak was a known actor and aspiring theatre director who fancied Gemma the Sapphire for a long time, but Gemma feared that her sister was some time earlier in love with that young man. She even asked her, but Luna said, *'Take his heart out!'* Gemma didn't really like him, but he was so persistent and charming, he would do a variety of extravagant deeds in the sole attempt to make her smile or feel good.

Simon Odak was a man who was never rejected by anyone, not even girls. He came from that prominent Odak family, he was good-looking and belonged to the upper class of artists; he had his way with girls and always promised a good time. Gemma was the only girl who really didn't care much about him and that just added to his determination to get into her pants, though, that wasn't the only reason as he genuinely liked her, at least, that summer.

He admitted his love when he was pressed to marry her, the only thing he feared was – they were so young and he couldn't swear that he would never stray. She never admitted that she loved him, but she was ready to marry him, so as not to expose her family to the shame – she was pregnant. Simon never assumed that she unwillingly gave her body to him as he got her drunk, but he thought, as countless times before, that he was simply irresistible.

The most beautiful girl was born out of that union, Pia Letizia her mother named her.

***

What Pia remembered now, as she was journeying to the jail to rescue someone she knew, were the sketches from her youth that she had blocked out of her memory for a number of years.

She blocked out this woman who hated her mother; who hated her, Pia, from the beginning. Sapphire would never think that her sister was capable of hating her; she was a dreamer, the one who denies truth in an attempt to hang onto an absolutely perfect illusion.

When she was very little, let's say five years of age, she wouldn't understand or detect the crazy shine in Luna's eyes when she would shove her head into Pia's face and say:

"Pia, you are my daughter, not Gemma's. Gemma is a freak, she is weak, you need a strong mother, not a cry-baby that Gemma is. Understand? I am your mother."

"No, you are not. You are Zia Luna."

"You were supposed to be mine, and mine you are."

"You are being funny, Zia Luna."

"Gemma's funny, not me. She is just a silly person, I am the right one for you, call me Mummy."

"I have my mummy, Zia, and I love her best. I love my Granny, second best."

"She is a freak, too. You only love freaks. Pia, you are destined to become a freak yourself if you don't recognise in time who's who. If you, in time, don't come under my guidance you'll become as useless as your favourite people"

That was how she talked to Pia when she was only a young child. On the other hand, Pia never confided in her mother, as she never wanted to cause her more pain. She sensed that her mother wasn't very happy or that she was the happiest when she was alone with her easel. Her father supported Gemma's art and organised exhibitions in the town, exhibitions Luna never attended. The stories Gemma painted came from Pia's verses and Gemma believed that they were both creators of her fine art.

Those were the happiest days of Pia's life. Those were the happiest memories she stored in her book of memories: two artists, mother and daughter effortlessly creating stories on the canvases of their love.

But soon, the storm would come, no one had predicted it, no one had sensed it, the storm that would change Pia's life forever, the storm that wouldn't leave any hope, as it would shatter everything in Pia that she called 'I'.

The storm was called Luna.
The storm was brought by Luna.

Pia opened her eyes as her uncle Boris said:
"We have arrived Pia, do you want to go in with me?"
"Yes!" Pia said and put the dark sunglasses back on her nose.
She was ready to see Truba, she still wasn't sure why she wanted to see him, what she had to say to him. She followed her uncle and soon the jail doors opened wide.

***

Even though he wanted to be strong and hold himself as a *'real man would'*, when he saw Pia walking behind her uncle he broke down. He started to sob like a little child, the way he, actually, never sobbed before. Pia stopped like a frozen figure hit by a mighty blow of an icy wind. She stood not knowing what to say or what to do in such circumstances. Her hands trembled; the scene took her way back, when she was holding Sapphire's hands looking into them, frozen, without any emotions. She just looked at her hands, her wrists, and eyes, and as if in some distant reality she only heard a faint voice telling her to *'hold, hold and hold'*.

Her heart started to race and while she was unable to walk she managed to say:

"Hold, hold, hold!"

Boris was the one who knew exactly what to do in such circumstances:

"Hold on, son, nothing's lost. We are here to take care of everything."

Gregor threw himself in Boris's arms as a little child would when finding relief in his father's embrace; Boris turned his head to the standing frozen queen and said:

"Pia! Please open that bottle of water. You have some first, then hand it over to Gregor."

Quickly she asked:

"What have you done?"

"I am not worthy of you Pia."

"We know that", said Boris, *"but you know that is not the subject, tell me what have you been up to this time?"*

While Gregor was recounting scenes of the previous evening, Pia, now and then, quietly repeated a few times, *'disgusting'*, to what Gregor said, *"I haven't done anything wrong, I was just sitting there with my guitar."*

"Gregor, if you want my help, you've got to tell me the truth. You can't go on with that shit 'I was just sitting there with my guitar', as that would be the same as when your father said that he never knew those people from Australia back in 1972."

"What people from Australia? I don't know anyone from bloody Australia."

"OK. Tell me the truth."

"*What truth? There is no other truth, sir, and you have to believe me. If you won't believe me, then we are wasting your precious time.*"

"*They took advantage of you?*"

"*Yes. I was photographed with a swastika and Hitler's photo.*"

"*Hmm, Gregor, Gregor, you should change the story, don't repeat what your father used to say.*"

"*My father has nothing to do with this! If you came here only to accuse me, then you'd better leave now. I have done nothing wrong. Understand – nothing!*"

Pia touched Boris's sleeve and said:

"*Wouldn't believing him be a good start?*"

They stayed in the provincial jail exactly one hour. Boris promised that he'd do his best to bring him home by tomorrow afternoon. While he went to visit other members of the band, Pia went to the only café in the small town. Prior to going out Gregor told her:

"*Promise you will not say anything to Veronika.*"

"*None of my business.*"

"*It is your business, otherwise you wouldn't be here. Thank you, Pia.*"

He whispered, no one heard:

"*I love you, Pia, and your unreturned love aches more than being locked up in here.*"

Father's Sins

And seized by his hidden but tangible anger, did he respond by revenge, on a subconscious level, there, where his father had planted a small poisonous garden of his own resentment? Resentment against the country that wasn't his as he never fought for it, resentment for the lost paradise crowned by a mystic symbol – swastika, the symbol of evil and the fallen ones who have drawn many into their soulless camps of lost humanity. In the Truba family, it was obvious that there was a deep gap, an abyss that separated two different, opposing beings: people of light and those who mourned a temporarily lost darkness.

Anton Truba's father Tomislav was a petty thief and a troublemaker. He fancied troubles out of sheer excitement, he got himself into uncountable misfortunes just to make his life more bearable as honesty and decency bore boredom. Plus, no one ever took the trouble to teach him how to separate good from bad, virtue from evil.

He never had *'a proper family'*, he ran away as there were too many mouths to be fed and too little food to meet their needs, there was too much noise and too many slaps. He worked as a manual worker or stableman when he could find some job, but he was happiest when the opportunity arose to pickpocket or to rip off people with card tricks and games.

He was imprisoned countless times for petty thefts or outrageous drunken behaviour; he spent time in jail or hiding in the woods during WW1. He found a farm; a wealthy widower lived there with three young daughters and, on Truba's request, he offered him work in the stables. Tomislav Truba hoped to survive those years hidden without attracting any attention. The farmer's youngest daughter was sixteen, the prettiest one; he chose her to soothe his restless groins in the night, but when the father found out that his worker was sleeping with one of his daughters, he greeted him in the morning with a pitchfork. He came to the stable with a pitchfork in his hands, pressed it against his neck and nailed him onto the wooden pillar:

"I'll kill you! Right now, right here, and no one will know that you've ever existed."

He couldn't speak, he couldn't swallow, but his eyes looked into the older man's eyes with such intensity that the farmer thought the man had something to say before he killed him. The farmer loosened the pitchfork and young Truba, bathed in sweat, moaned:

"I swear on my life I love her! Don't kill me, I'll marry her and I'll stay. I'll take care of all of you!"

"Now we are talking. But, you are a penniless nobody. What will we gain?"

"Everything! I'll work day and night without a dime. I'll take care of all of you, when you grow old I'll take care of you, too. I promise! Please, reconsider it! She loves me, ask her!"

The old man thought, *'What if she really does? These are difficult times; another man in the house could be for the betterment of the whole household. He is young, strong and capable of many tasks while I am growing slower and more tired.'*

"All right! But, you have to prove who you are. If you do anything wrong, I'll nail you with those forks onto the wall, I won't have mercy if you do anything wrong – to her or to any member of my family."

"Consider your family to be mine for now on. I would never wrong my family, never."

And that is the story of how Tomislav Truba got married.

Ana was her name.

She was a strong girl, of solid build, almost as tall as Tomislav, dark-haired, with a noticeable lisp, but it added to her charm somehow or, at least it was seen as a charming trait for the first year of their marriage. In that, first, year of Tomislav and Ana's marriage, Anton Truba was born. Veronika a year later, and the following year another boy was born – he was named Tomislav after his father.

DETHRONED

Three years had passed quickly and one early April morning, a constant hooting awakened Ana. There were two owls on the oak tree branch that was touching her window. They were staring into her eyes, she opened the window and screeched, *'Shoo, bloody, shoo!'* but to no avail. The owls stayed there synchronised in their sad song.

The sad song the owls were singing was to be deciphered and understood that very same day.

When she got up, her marital bed was empty, as it used to be empty each and every early morning, so that didn't trouble Ana at all. When it was time to come back from the fields, only her father came. He asked her about her husband's whereabouts, but Ana knew nothing of it. Since that day, that warm and pleasant April day in 1935, no one had ever heard about Tomislav Truba senior. It looked as if he had been swallowed by the fields. It looked as if he had not taken anything, but later on, they had discovered that three silver thalers that belonged to her late mother were gone with Tomislav. He never said good-bye to his children; neither did he walk in again, or ever send a word to anyone.

Ana's father's only words were:

"I should have known that. I should have killed him that morning."

Ana never had the time to moan or to cry as she had three mouths to feed, and there was no man in the house apart from her aging father therefore in order to redeem the sinner's sins, she rolled up her sleeves and started to act as a man: in the early mornings letting the herd out to the fields; days full of heavy chores in the fields; then cooking, bathing the kids in the evenings and retiring when the sun set in the field. It was a hard life; compassion wasn't a word in the vocabulary of that region, never used, as if it had not been invented yet.

From early childhood Anton worked hard, but he never feared hard work, the harder the work, the prouder he would be upon its completion. He believed that he'd make his grandfather proud if he showed what his father had failed to show or possess: work ethics, steadiness of character and enormous physical strength and endurance. But he failed to make his grandfather proud, as he somehow directed his anger towards the child, blaming him for just about anything, for everything, including the bad weather that spoiled the haymow. Veronika was very close to her mother, but a child of very few words she was. They hoped she would marry early to bring some ease to the household. She was quite pretty, her lips were full and red and her speech quiet, without a lisp, her face was plain, but attractive, she had a strong back and she could carry a bucket full of water on top of her head. She was her grandfather's favourite child and he showed his affection only to her, openly. He thought, anyway, why should anyone show affection to the boys: they should work hard and be obedient to elders.

He had beaten Anton several times. Regardless of whether it was a *'deserved'* beating or not, resentment steadily grew in Anton's chest. He planned to run away sooner or later. His father did! He never knew him, but often, in his daydreams he would construct the most amazing stories that he could come up with. He would imagine his father being the strongest man in the region, in the country, in the world, some sort of wrestler, brawny and manly, the man everyone feared, including his grandfather. He would lie on top of a haystack and laugh at all those possible scenarios – *'What would his father do to Grandpa if he only knew how he treated him?'*

He knew that his father was a strong and righteous man because Grandpa would scold him by comparing him to his father:

"You aren't any better than this rotten devil that made you. The apple doesn't fall far from the tree."

That's how Anton Truba knew that his father was a good, strong man. He had forgiven him for his departure, justifying it by thinking, *'Who wouldn't leave this bloody devil? I'll go as soon as I grow a little bit older.'*

One day, unannounced, Grandfather's brother came in and said that the war was about to break out any day. Anton listened carefully. He didn't fear it; he just couldn't grasp what would happen to his family. About his grandfather he couldn't care less, but he did care what the future would bestow upon his family. He was the eldest and felt responsible for his siblings and his mother.

The uncle said:

"*Our men are gathering. This fine young man has to go to the right side. Germany is strong and they are going to liberate us, just pray to God they come and bring order to this country.*"

Anton's cousin came over and said:

"*We've got to go to the forest. I want you to meet some good people, I call them Black Brigades; we are all strong and ready to fight that Red Plague that's threatening our country.*"

"*Well, whatever it takes. What will happen to my mother?*"

"*Now, what's most important is our country, it is above anything, above anyone.*"

"*Yeah, sounds powerful.*"

"*And powerful it is, we've got to sacrifice our lives if need be for our fatherland.*"

"*You are so wise.*"

"*I know; you have a lot to learn from me. I'll come by tomorrow when it darkens.*"

The next day Anton walked out of the house led by his older cousin into the woods. It was in 1941 and he was twelve years old but inside he felt like a real man, a man called to liberate his country from the potential Red Plague, not even knowing the real meaning of those words. He was ready to fight, ready to hate; ready to kill in the name of his holy fatherland. They roamed neighbouring villages with rifles, knives and other tools, with the Bible and some, with little pots. Yes, a little pot for the victim's blood that came out of slashed veins on their necks. There was a man, a local hero, who got himself a fine title: he was called *Luka the Vampire*, as it was known that he would cut the throat of his victim and he'd gather the pouring blood into his pot and drink it, on the spot, while it was still warm, while the bleeding man was still alive, aware of his monstrous deeds. And only by mentioning Luka's name, blood froze in the veins of many who opposed his views and his *'philosophy'*, many hands trembled.

He would wipe off dripping blood from his lips and with thunderous laughter call out:

"Next one! Next one, faster, faster!"

Initially, Anton's stomach would turn upside-down, he would feel as if he were about to throw up everything that he held inside, but after some time he got used to it, he grew indifferent. No, Truba never laughed at *Luka the Vampire's* jokes, he never commented, and yes, he indeed feared him, everybody felt fear in case their name got to be written in Luka's bad books as they knew that the names written in those books were written off in no time. There was no end to his sadism, he raped equally very young girls and old women; when he could not do any harm to his enemies he would pick on his brigade mates; he would catch a squirrel and bite off its head with his strong teeth.

Anton got used to it. His stomach stopped turning upside-down and on some occasions he would hold the victim for *Luka the Vampire,* when some strong men would fight for their life, as they were physically stronger, *Luka the Vampire* would call Anton:

"Son! Hold the motherfucker! Look, I am going to take his heart out, put it on fire, that'll be a good dinner for you, you pussy. You remember when you came; you were a pussy. It looks like you are learning fast how to become a real man. Hang around son, hang around and learn. We'll clean this beautiful country of ours from the scum."

Three years he spent roaming the villages rounding up locals, killing and helping himself with the Fatherland, then he fell ill and no one knew what name that illness bore. He was taken to the monastery, a big monastery with a school for future priests, and spare room for visitors or wounded soldiers. There he had met Friar Marag. He was a student, a young man in his second year of studies, he was quiet and distant, but with time he grew a little bit more empathetic when he learned that Anton was a brave and dedicated soldier for the highest cause. Back then, no one called him Friar Marag, his colleagues called him *'brother'* while Anton got the privilege of calling him simply – Franko, then Frane.

They prayed together; they dreamed together that their land would soon be liberated and free for them and their kind only. And that was God's will and God's kindness, and His grace. They were waiting for their God to bestow grace upon them: grace and glory!

But, no glory!

As 1945 came, the streets of main cities were crowded with people waiting with flowers, flags and shouts of happiness for their real liberators. While the country and the world celebrated, Friar Marag and young Truba hid their real emotions, hid their hatred and disappointments. They hid their original selves and morphed into this nameless mass of overjoyed citizens, knowing that this was not yet the end of their dreams. Dreams are to be dreamed for life, sometimes postponed, sometimes put on hold, but they were embodied in one's life as guides and inspiration; they give hope and inspire even when one thought they were about to end.

Dreams. Hidden dreams! Postponed but never betrayed.

Their ways parted as they wished each other *'good luck'*, not knowing that their paths would cross again.

***

When Anton Truba came back to his village he was greeted by his sister, frowned upon by his brother who said:

"You'd better leave as you have left before. Go where you belong as everybody in the village knows where you have been, which flag you've fought for."

"I was not in the war, I was hospitalised."

"Yes, because you couldn't witness any longer what your pals were doing. Killing people as if they were chickens. Cutting their necks, taking their hearts out, raping women, get lost, you are the shame of our family, get lost now!"

Veronika said:

"Tomo, don't! We don't know, people talk rubbish; people always talk whatever they wanna talk. He was only a young man, almost a child; he had

never harmed anyone. He had spent the remaining three years in hospital, he was a patient, not a soldier."

"What kind of hospital? We know that, as well. Look, you'd better go and not come back to my door ever again. Grandfather was killed because of you and that worthy cousin of yours, too. We found a bullet that went through his eye and ended in his pillow, and his face was not recognizable, I heard a gunshot but didn't have the courage to walk into his room. Mum ran in, she screamed and someone shot again. It was like a shower of bullets, all over the house. I jumped under the bed, Veronika next to me, I held her tight as she wanted to run to rescue Mum. We found her later, in blood, tears and with a vacant gaze. She drowned a few days later. Who knows if she fell into the water or someone pushed her? Who knows whether she did it because she couldn't take it anymore? And still, you fought; you fought for your pals. Get out of here, I don't want to see you ever again."

It was a common occurrence that in some families, two brothers would fight for two opposing armies or ideologies. Even though they were only kids at that age, the circumstances aged their minds and they reasoned beyond their age. Tomislav, towards the end of the war, when he lost his mother, took to the woods but he went to a different party – Tito's young courier he became, immersed himself in the Marxist ideology and anti-fascism, hence when the war ended he saw his brother as a traitor, as the shame of the family and someone who had to be unquestionably punished.

Anton Truba had left the small village and tried to find better luck in the north-western port town of Rijeka, liberated from the tight grip of Mussolini and D'Annunzio. It was there that he wanted to start his life all over again.

When one tries to run from their not-so-honourable past, the past takes something like an ethereal entity of the person itself, like some shadow that follows the person reminding him of his deeds, misdeeds actually.

His work ethics were established when he was young and when he started to clean car parts for a mechanic whose wife gave him a little room. Soon the mechanic realised that the young man was naturally bright, a fast learner, discrete and of few words, but above all – very fast and reliable. He took him under his wing and taught him his own art of looking after fine machinery. Anton was almost like a replacement for this man's own son who lost his life in the war several years earlier. Anton never told him that he had fought in the war when the man used to say:

"War only brings misery to everyone. War is fought by and for those in power not for ordinary people. We are fooled into the belief that we are somehow different, but we are all humans, trying to survive, to raise a family, to live our short lives on this planet as best we can. My son was a brave and honest young man, just a year over twenty, he had a heart of gold but the mind of a child. He believed that communism would bring out the best in people, that after this war milk and honey would run freely. I was proud when he went; when he was killed a part of me died forever. Stay clear of troubles Anton, life is too short to be spent in hatred or remorse."

Anton would only nod his head without saying a word.

On some days he was ashamed, on some days his heart was full of rage. The former days prevailed in the first few years.

Prior to meeting Elsa he was locked in his own head, his young heart resembled the heart of an old man, without any sap or happiness, he was locked in a puddle of blood that was still slowly pouring out of the slashed veins of victims, the blood that his pal *Luka the Vampire* drank from his little pot tied with a red rope to his belt. To that belt, with a thin blood-soaked rope, some other relics were tied like severed fingers, teeth or ears of all those people who were born in the wrong nation, or were of the wrong religion.

Years after the war, Anton would wake up in the middle of the night and look at the lights in the port unable to sleep, unable to wash this blood out of his mind. It stained his mind, it blocked his arteries and it never gave him the opportunity to have sound sleep, unpopulated with unknown faces and uncluttered with names, screams and pleas to which no one ever answered kindly.

His deeds spoke to him at night in horrifying, yet familiar, pictures but during the daytime he was a *'Shy mechanic with golden hands that could fix any problem'*. He feared that people, even here, might recognise him as a former pal of the death brigades led by *Luka the Vampire*. To soothe and ease his conscience he would repeat Veronika's words, *'I was only a young man, almost a child'*, but he really never, ever regretted belonging to the elite killing troupes, he believed that he fought for the right cause. He justified his hatred; his friend and adviser, a young priest-to-be, Frane, had justified his hatred, then, he had done nothing wrong! Plus, he had never cut anyone's throat, never raped a young girl nor drunk anyone's blood from the dirty little pot that had passed many hands as requested by Luka. For that reason Luka had christened him with the name – *Pussy*, only when he was drunk on the rye-brandy or too much blood he would call out to him:

"Pussy, come here and learn how to be a real man! I don't need pussies in my troop, come and show the low-lives of what stern stuff we are made of."

Anton feared him so much that he fainted a few times when he was called to drink the blood, then Luka laughed, swore, caused brawls and fired his machine-gun randomly into the dark sky and horizon.

In this new town he learned how to be a town person, he learned new skills, new customs and refined his behaviour a little bit more. He improved his speech and his strong accent mellowed a little and people stopped asking him where he was from as he looked and behaved more like a local. He learned how to swim in the tranquil Adriatic sea and he learned about cinema, but chose to watch only foreign films, since those made by local producers were coloured red, the colour he still dreaded, which might have been because it resembled the blood that always flowed fluidly through his dreams, or, it might have been that red was the colour of the comrades, the communists. He lived in their world, but he kept quiet, he kept to himself.

He had completely lost contact with his brother, who, as he heard became a policeman, wore a uniform and had a good wage. He thought, *'What a sold soul'*, and to his brother Tomo, Anton was *'a lost soul'* and there was never ever any chance of reconciliation.

But Anton's sister Veronika kept calling and asking about his affairs, she never gave up on him.

One day she had appeared on his doorstep.

He came out as the mechanic's wife called him to come and greet his visitor. When his eyes met Veronika's smiling face, some sort of unbearable softness entered and he went down on his knees, hugged her legs and cried like a child.

She just kept ruffling his hair saying, *'Look at you, look at you, my big, handsome brother.'*

She came and stayed. He made her enrol in a nursing school and helped her until she finished and found a job in the near-by hospital. They were both proud of their joint achievement. They shared this tiny room above his boss's garage where they put another mattress near the one he was sleeping on; she brought a small hot plate where she cooked simple dishes for the two of them.

In the early fifties they were still so young and in the country there was such a strong feeling of enthusiasm and renaissance, there was plenty of work for everyone and for Anton the future looked a bit brighter since Veronika moved to the town. Being a nurse and having a very agreeable personality, she became a popular girl in the district and in the hospital, too. She never rejected any request for longer hours or night shifts; she was compassionate and kind to patients and to the hospital staff alike.

In the hospital she met a young cook who was full of wit, sometimes to the extreme, and in the beginning he appeared to Veronika as rude and blatant, but meeting him on a daily basis she started to understand his humour – she understood that his heart was kind and unburdened, so when he asked her out she said:

"You've got to talk to my brother."

"C'mon Veronika, we don't live in the dark ages, who asks brothers for permission any more. Not even my granddad asked…"

"You've got to ask Anton."

"Ah, people from small villages! I only want to take you out to a dance."

She kept on repeating, *'You've got to ask my brother's permission'* and he understood if he ever wanted to take her out, he had to ask her brother for his blessing. But, Anton was kinder than he had imagined him to be. He was faced with a young, quite timid man, gentle in his manners, who just nodded his head to everything that Veronika's date proposed.

Soon they became good mates. All three of them. Together they went bowling, to the cinema or sunbathing, but when Saturday came, Veronika went alone with her friend, as Anton would regularly find an excuse not to join them so as to give them a chance to grow closer.

Matija married Veronika one year after they had met. He said to Anton:
"Now is your turn, my brother, but I am warning you, you won't find a prettier girl in this town, mine is the one that wears the crown."

Anton knew that he wouldn't find anyone prettier, he feared he wouldn't find any girl in this town. Even though he was exceptionally good-looking the town girls overlooked him, they were haughty, spoiled, they wanted a man who danced well, who was well dressed and well spoken. He was a country boy, a mechanic, someone who couldn't come up with anything original, smart or interesting when with women.

He thought that he might spend the rest of his life alone, but fate had written for him a different story. Probably it was written in some hidden book or in the stars that he would meed Elsa Dodig and that she would change him to the core of his being in a split second.

***

In the mid-fifties, on one fine day, Anton Truba was stopped and greeted by a man in a suit. It was an unusually warm late May day, the sun was at its zenith; Anton wore a light short-sleeved linen shirt; he ran across the main street in search of more shade, he noticed a man running after him with the same intent – to find deeper shade. Or was it so?

When Anton turned around he met a man's smile and his extended hand. The man said:
"Hello Anton, what unbearable heat! How are you?"

Anton looked in disbelief, trying to put the face into any context, any environment; he asked himself if the man was their customer, but he couldn't remember him.

"I am sorry, but it seems to me that we haven't met before. Do we know each other?"

Now the man came closer and he put his arm around Anton's shoulders, he lowered his voice that was still somehow cheerful, as a voice of someone who was glad that he had found an old friend, and said:

"Anton, weren't you the closest friend of Luka?"

"Luka? Luka who?"

"Oh, hang on... I don't know his surname... let me think a bit..."

"I think that you have mistaken me for someone else. My name is Anton, but it might be a coincidence as I am quite positive that we have never met, and I really don't know any man by the name of Luka."

"Oh, I know his nickname. Maybe it would help you to remember him. He was called Luka the Vampire."

Anton felt that the ground under his feet was shaking as he looked in the eyes of the man who still had a wide smile on his face. He was smiling, but his eyes assumed a different expression: they grew darker, more peculiar and penetrating.

Anton started to stutter, but the man, still smiling, tapped his shoulder and said in that cheerful voice:

"Anton, you don't have to know me, but you'll see me around. You'll meet me often, you can choose to be a friend and talk to me, or you can choose otherwise. We all choose our friends freely – up to you, my friend, up to you. And, I would add, no one really pushed you into your close friendship with Luka, that was your choice, wasn't it? Maybe it was a wrong choice, but still, it was solely your choice. I heard that you were his right hand. He used to carry a little dirty pot tied up to his belt, do you remember that?"

"I remember nothing. I don't know any Luka in this town or anywhere else."

"Good-bye my friend, take care, you are a good mechanic, a very good mechanic."

While Anton walked away the man in the suit kept looking at his back, called his name again, and as Anton turned the man shouted:

"Young people were falling prey to leaders who had no right to be leaders, who had evil intentions and minds; you are still young Truba, very young, it is never too late to repent; see you next time."

Anton wanted to run, not to walk, but he held his horses and his step was slow and steady, unlike his heart.

His heart was beating like a wild animal's, he felt as if it would jump out and dance in the pebbled street, it raced and he thought that he might never catch up with its rhythm, but what happened right there was that he bumped into yet another man.

"Young man, watch your step!"

"I do apologise, sir... I mean, comrade."

"Ha, ha, comrade! Call me sir, I prefer it that way."

"Yes, sir."

"My name is Josef Dodig, I was born in this country a long time ago, I came here to the funeral, yesterday, my father passed away."

"Sorry to hear that."

"It was his time, one can't live forever. What I wanted to ask was the direction to the Franciscan Church, it looks as if I have lost my way; I haven't been here for a long, long time."

"You are going in the opposite direction, sir. I can walk you there, it is not far, some five hundred meters or so."

They walked together, and Anton was trying to figure out who the man might be: he was finely dressed, he looked like a wealthy man; he had a strong accent; his 'r's' were sharply pronounced, it sounded German. He didn't want to ask anything, he was still under the impression of that other man, but somehow, he found the presence of this man to be very calming, grounding, as he was of a solid build; the aura of superiority and authority was around him, he would have never thought that this man had anything to do with the comrades.

When they came close the young girl who was sitting on the bench in the church garden stood up and ran towards them. She said something in German and the man said:

"*Speak Croatian, so that this fine young man can understand you.*"

"*Oh, but it is so bad, so bad.*" She excused herself and blushed.

Anton blushed too.

Her father said:

"*Would you like to have lunch with us?*"

"*I have never been invited to lunch with such fine people.*"

"*Come, come young man! Tell me your name.*"

"*Anton.*"

"*Have you ever been to this church, Anton?*"

"*Not this one, but I've spent several years in another Franciscan Church during wartime.*"

He felt a surge of pride, but he couldn't understand *why he was opening up to the unknown man and telling him that, why he accepted his invitation to lunch and why he felt so good in his presence.*

Elsa Dodig was his daughter's name, she had honey-blond hair neatly braided, big blue eyes, dimples when she smiled… he couldn't stop smiling, Elsa was different to any girl he had met so far.

Josef said:

"*Well, you sound like a good, honest Croat!*"

"*I certainly am, sir.*"

"*Good, good then. Excellent!*"

While they were walking slowly Anton glimpsed the shadow that followed them; the shadow wore a dark suit on that fine sunny day.

During lunch they talked about general topics; Anton talked about his whereabouts, never mentioning the war; he talked about cars and anything in relation to cars and mechanics. He looked quickly in Elsa's direction, but he couldn't look longer than a second as he would start to stutter or get red and sweaty under his hairline. Elsa just looked at her plate and kept quiet.

Her father talked about their farm, kids and life in Germany.

He saw Elsa again three months later.

When he thanked Josef for lunch, when they shook hands, and when he exchanged a timid *'good-bye'* with Elsa, he thought that he, most probably, wouldn't see Elsa ever again, regardless of Josef's, *'See you again, son'*, and regardless of the fact that he felt deep in his bones that Elsa was *'the one'*.

Even though he was very young, he knew that he was an ordinary man who didn't deserve anything more than an ordinary girl; in his eyes Elsa was an absolutely divine creature worthy of a man who had never yet set foot in this town: probably some blue-blooded man, but not him, a man from a tiny village with the past that followed him like a frightening shadow.

The shadow left the restaurant after they become just tiny dots at the end of a long road. He folded the newspaper he was hiding behind his back, wrote something in his notebook, scratched his nose and smiled. He winked to the waiter and left without paying his bill. He never paid his bill, no one ever requested that he should, even when they didn't know him personally; they sensed that it'd be better to let him go without paying and with an uncertain smile.

***

Seven days had passed and he couldn't stop thinking about Elsa, then on the seventh day a man came to the workshop. He had never met the man before, but he too, was wearing a dark suit. He asked:

"Are you Truba?"

"Yes, sir."

"I am not sir to you, sirs are no longer in this country, comrade. Come over here."

He was told to follow him and he did without any question when the man showed him his badge.

They walked into a building next to the police station and he led him into a small room. There was another man waiting; he greeted them both, offered a glass of water, as it was a hot day, showed him a seat; he said:

"Nothing important, don't be apprehensive, just a few questions."

"Yes, sir." said Truba and the two comrades exchanged looks and smiles.

"On the 28th of May, this year, at one o'clock in the afternoon you met up with Josef Dodig and his daughter. You walked to the restaurant, ordered a meal and you sat there exactly two hours and ten minutes. Given that you walked for ten minutes, it was ten minutes past three o'clock when you left. In those, approximately, two hours you talked a lot. My question is – What were you talking about?"

The three men sat silent. There was a big, round clock on the dirty white wall and the picture of the president. Truba heard the tick-tocking of the clock and he was aware of his heavy breathing. The silence lasted long, and it looked to Truba that it was the longest silence in his entire life: the longest, the heaviest and, somehow, the most meaningful. After quite a long period of time of which Anton wasn't ever able to point out the exact number of minutes, the other man said:

"Well, then, you don't want to talk to us? You can go home, but it seems to us that you have a secret."

"I don't hold any secrets."

"Even better. Then share it with us."

"Share what?"

"What you two were whispering?"

"We were not whispering; we were talking in a normal tone."

"So, no secrets?"

"No..."

"Then, you can tell us what you were talking about now that we have established the topics were not secret. You can share it with us now."

"We talked about cars and the mechanical nature of things, about things that can be repaired."

"So, what would it be, that you can repair, Truba? What has to be repaired?"

"I don't know... cars, I suppose... cars can be repaired."

"Anything else you would repair with your friend Josef Dodig?"

"No, sir... I mean... no..."

"Comrade!"

"Nothing else needs to be repaired."

"OK, you talked about repairing cars, and what did he talk about? What was that that he needed to repair?"

"Nothing. He talked about his farmland and his children."

"And that was all?"

"Yes, sir... I mean, yes... that was all we talked about."

"Two hours and ten minutes you talked about repairing cars and about his farm?"

"We talked about his children and life in Germany."

"What did he say about life in Germany?"

"Nothing in particular."

"OK, Anton, that'd be all. If anything else pops into your mind, you can find me here and we can refresh your memories."

Anton got up and left the building without saying another word. He looked behind his shoulder, there was no one there; he walked back to his room in a brisk pace. He resolved that he would never talk to anyone about this interview, not even to Veronika.

That night his dreams were populated by mighty beasts led by *Luka the Vampire*. He dreamed that Luka used his own hands to cut throats of animals and people alternatively, pouring their blood down Anton's throat. He woke up soaked in sweat, shaking whilst his heart raced like the wildest lynx; he thought of her, for when he thought of Elsa his heart would take on a different rhythm. *'Oh, if only she were real'* those were his thoughts. It looked as if those nightmares would never step down from the invisible throne built behind his headboard.

Only when he thought about Elsa, could he see the blue sky above him.

DETHRONED

***

But he met Elsa again, sooner than he could have anticipated, sooner than he could have dreamed of.

It was the end of that summer, of the same year when he first saw her again. Leaves started to rumple with rust on their edges, and with the weakened sun the mornings turned from mild and pleasant to crisp, almost cold.

He just finished his breakfast and was about to go down the stairs when he heard the voice of his landlady.

"Anton, there's a gentleman waiting for you, hurry up!"

His first thought was unpleasant. Customers never turned up earlier or unexpectedly, it must have been some snoop. He knew their ways by now.

When he reached the last step, he was greeted by a friendly smile and cheerful words:

"It wasn't difficult to find you, you are famous for your skills."

He wanted to ask about Elsa, but he didn't want to make a fool of himself. They met at lunchtime, and once again, Anton was treated to lunch. He said:

"I tend to trust you, but, you know, the last time we were seen together, I was summoned to the police station and was interrogated. Make of that what you will, but they were keen to know what we talked about."

"Don't worry, son. They are not as smart as they appear to be. This is my country too, and I have the right to come and go as it pleases me. Always tell them, remember – always, 'I haven't done anything wrong'; let them prove otherwise. Bastards."

He met up with Elsa later in the afternoon and when they saw each other they both blushed, Josef said:

"Elsa wanted to accompany me."

"That's nice of her."

"She likes it here."

"Yes, it is a beautiful place."

"Not ours anymore, not anymore, but not theirs either for a long time. We are stronger than they."

On Sunday he accompanied them to church. Anton noticed the same man, dressed in a dark suit, leaning against the building across the church, pretending to read the morning papers. He said nothing.

The church was small but still, almost empty: just several souls and a priest. The priest was a close friend of Josef.

In the church Josef took out his bag and envelope that contained a bunch of leaflets.

He said to Anton:

"Shove it into your pants. There's my friend's address in the envelope. I don't visit him when I come here, so as not to provoke too much curiosity. But you go tomorrow and give him this envelope. You can take several leaflets, study carefully what is written there and try to get them out. But you have to be very careful. I noticed that man with the paper, don't you think that I haven't, but you have nothing to fear. If they ask you again about our meeting you say that you fancy my daughter."

All the blood from Anton's face ran down to his trembling feet and his face became as pale as the face of a gravely ill man. Josef asked:

"Don't you?"

"Hmm…"

"Don't you fancy Elsa?"

"Sir… I, what can I … oh, sir!"

"You do fancy her, and she does fancy you. She came with me in order to see you again, I know that."

"Are you sure?" asked Anton in disbelief.

"Absolutely sure."

Anton took the envelope and they agreed when they walked out their ways would part, they'd walk in different directions waving empty hands.

He wasn't called to any interrogation, no one followed, but a few notes were written in his file that was steadily growing with information.

Josef Dodig visited two more times before the official announcement that he would give his daughter's hand in marriage to Anton Truba. He said:

"I know, Anton, that you are poor, but you are an honest Croat, just as much as I am, you deserve my daughter's hand, I know you'll look after her."

They made a stunning couple, like movie stars, like heroes from Roman or German mythology or simply like the two most gorgeous young people in love.

When their first son was born he had forgotten his own past. The future looked bright and light, full of promises for him and his young family. He got a new job, a government job; he believed that everyone had forgotten about the war and the misfortunes that it brought.

Elsa was the proudest mother one could find; she wanted her son to be christened and Anton gave in on her insistence and pressure.

When they walked into the church in order to elect the day and talk over the details, it marked the reunion of old friends.

Elsa told him several weeks earlier that the old priest had retired and was replaced with a young one, a man who spoke little, but his speech was clear and sharp. Elsa said that she liked him since he commented, *'Hmm, a German lady. Well, welcome to our community, to our church and our... let's call it, our country."*

They shook hands and that shake sealed their everlasting friendship.

But when Anton walked into the church with his young wife, the priest walked towards them in a slow and steady walk. Anton said:

"Frane!"

Elsa said:

"That's our new priest – Friar Marag."

And the Friar said:

"Anton, I knew we were going to meet again. So, that fine lady is your wife. I am glad that God was kind and generous to both of you I will personally christen your son, and all of your future children with much pleasure. Have them many, as good people like you two have to breed."

The Unsettling Dreams

When Gregor Truba woke up that morning he felt more exhausted than ever before. He didn't have a deep sleep, but a rather shallow one, the dream to which many ghost-like creatures flew and danced a dance that he had never seen before. It was like some ritual-dance, with drums drumming loudly while he was in the centre of a circle, and there he saw his father and chopped off heads of small and large animals.

He looked around him and remembered the day before.

All he really remembered was Pia's face, the fact that she came and supported him stood out in his memory. He believed that he hadn't done anything wrong and he believed that Pia's strength was lent to him. If he had Pia on his side, he wouldn't fear anything.

Early in the morning he was taken in a car, driven to the jail in his hometown. It was a district jail, big and important, not like the one where he was kept in custody overnight. It was a huge, old building, built in times of Franz Joseph, built to last for centuries. When he saw his house through the window, his eyes were filled with tears. He couldn't go home to his kind mother Elsa and to his guitar. He thought of his misfortunate brother Hugo who was, probably, still trying to button his shirt at this hour, he even thought about Veronika, his indifferent sister absolutely dedicated to her room and to marijuana. He thought that everything in the Truba household was in perfect order as on any other ordinary day. Yes, everything was like the everyday routine and rhythm; only he, Gregor Truba, was thrown out of his routine and rhythm; what he feared was uncertainty – how long was he to be out of step with this rhythm that he now recognised as his precious life?

His town looked different through the tinted windows and through the fear that had tied this bitter knot in his empty stomach.

"I am not a criminal! Let me go home! I have done nothing! I am just a musician!"

"You are a piece of shit, shut up!"

Gregor thought that his heart wouldn't withstand the pain and wild beating as he was fighting for air.

Almost through the tears he yelled again:

"Let me go home!"

"Oh, shut up, or I'll shut your mouth up, you bloody Nazi!"

"I am a musician, not a Nazi!"

"You are a fart, don't make me stop the car and show you what I think about you, you piece of crap."

He was kept in prison for two days. Those were the longest two days he had ever known as he counted each and every minute of them. Time was dripping as if it were made of small droplets of water, and they were falling onto his head, one by one, at small intervals, he felt their moist touch, he heard their soft, but frightening, sound.

His daydream was that Pia would come and tell him something soothing, but – she didn't come. His mother came accompanied by Friar Marag. She was crimson in her face, she hardly held back her tears, and Friar Marag didn't utter a word. Just barely noticeably nodding his head as if in agreement, or maybe in disagreement – as if it meant, *"Yes, that's what they are doing to us, son."*

When he was let off, the first thing he did was to visit Boris Odak. He came in unannounced, ignored the little secretary who protested, walked into the office where Boris was sitting with two men and said:

"May I have a word with you?"

"Now? Can't you see that I am busy?"

"Now!"

Odak said:

"You've got to find another lawyer, I had to drop your case."

He learned that Boris Odak had to let go of his defence due to the fact that Boris's brother Ivan was the prosecutor. He didn't know any other lawyer in town and he didn't know who was that invisible and mighty force that withdrew the indictment. He just got a letter, the letter that ended his agony, but lit new fears, *'Who would do that for me and why?'*

After this incident he understood better what people in authority really meant when labelling him as *'Anton Truba's son.'*

That afternoon he searched for Pia. She wasn't at university, she wasn't home, she wasn't any place where he thought he might find her. He asked Veronika, she scoffed; he rang several friends inquiring about theatre rehearsals and programs for that evening. He even went to Barbarossa's house and rang the bell. No one gave him an answer as to where he could find her.

He went to *Luna Gallery*; in the window there was still written in neat filigree work *'I love you, Pia'*; he walked in and Luna stood up with her hand stretched out, palm facing his face:

"I told you not to come to my Gallery ever again. I can call the police for obstruction or trespassing..."

"Who are you, you bitch! Who the hell are you?"

"You don't have any clue who I am, don't try me out! Go out and don't come back here ever again."

He left, he ran through the town, he peeped into each pub or café where he suspected that he might see her, but he could not find her. It looked as if she had disappeared from the face of the earth.

But he was so determined; he sat in front of her building with a bottle of wine in his hand and waited, waited, waited.

After midnight a car pulled in, she came out with two men. One was her father, the other one he recognised as a young theatre actor. They came closer; he stood up and said:

"I was looking for you all over town."

"You shouldn't have."

"Can I have a word with you?"

"Not now."

"Please, Pia."

Her father came closer and said in a low but harsh voice:

"She said – not now, isn't that clear enough for you?"

"I didn't ask you. Back off, I want to talk to Pia."

"Young man, you are too brusque…"

"I couldn't care less about your opinion of me, I came here to talk to Pia, not to listen to your preaching."

He went up, the other man followed with a bottle of champagne in each hand, Pia looked at the pavement, stood there and waited to hear what Gregor had to say.

"I haven't done anything wrong, Pia. I want you to know that."

"What difference does it make?"

"They dropped the charges, do you know why?"

"How would I know?"

"Just asking, in case you have some knowledge of it."

"You are not as important as you'd like to be. I don't dwell on your troubles, Truba. Now, clear off and don't intercept me again, especially when I am with my family. Don't do that, Gregor."

"Pia, I love you."

She turned her back and walked into the building.

He sat on the pavement and sobbed out of frustration like a child. He was afraid and at the same time helpless and hopeless – she was like a statue made of glass. He couldn't cure his misfortunate love by going to bed with other beautiful women. It just didn't work, and he knew it, it never would. He ached for Pia.

Days passed and Gregor never heard a word from her or about her. One day he read an interview in the papers, she said that she had two exams left and she would graduate. Two years before her peers. Then she mentioned London as a possible destination for postgraduate studies. She was nowhere to be seen because she was either studying or writing her poetry, he never saw her coming to Veronika's either. He read that she won yet another award, just a month ago.

But where he really met her was at the most surprising place, as fate often has it. He went to Belgrade. To a concert.

It was a huge garden party, it was summer; she was sitting next to the fountain sipping a red cocktail. There were several men around her. Her hair was pulled back with a wide hair-band. Her cheekbones shone as if they were polished with alabaster polish, her green eyes shone too, her teeth shone; he came closer and said:

"Pia, how come?"

"Truba, what a surprise!"

"A nice one?"

"Yes. A nice one."

She came to the ceremony where her latest collection received an award. They danced together, they kissed, they drank and laughed.

They went to bed in the early hours; it was five o'clock in the morning. He said:

"Are we going to sleep as innocent kids do?"

"Let's make love" she said and giggled.

She took off her summer dress; standing in front of him in her white underwear and a bra; her thighs were full of bruises, bloodshot, he hesitated as if he wanted to comment, then she said:

"Pretend that you see nothing."

"I see nothing, Pia, when I am around you, I am blinded by your beauty and my love."

He made love to Pia and all her wounds opened up that morning; she bled from those wounds but she kept loving him. They slept the whole day and in the evening they went out hand in hand as a perfectly functional and loving couple would.

They came back home holding hands, they kept on holding hands and Gregor would never ask more from life, but it was never written in the book of destiny that Pia was going to be his; the wind blew Luna's indignation his way again.

This time it was a mighty blow!

Averna's Wrath

The year was gripped by the cooler months and it looked as if it would finish on a fantastic note for Pia. She was preparing her last exam. Gregor was busy with his exams and his music; they would see each other but always on Pia's terms, always when she had time.

They went downtown hand in hand, Gregor was proud to walk with Pia; he would look at their reflection in windows as they passed by and smile.

She was still an absolutely closed oyster to him, but at least she started to express some wishes like, *'I'd like you to come over and help me with something.'*

He looked at their expression in the windows but when they approached the infamous Gallery, he looked to the other side.

He didn't look in that direction, but lovely Luna saw them from the darkness of her Gallery.

She just smiled.

Yes, Luna just smiled with one corner of her tight sealed lips. Then, a little bit later, she took the chain with a pendant where it was written *'I love you, Pia'*, the one she made with her own hands, and she put it back into a small black box coated with silky red material. She closed the box and lay it down into the dark corner of the top drawer. Then she smiled again and lifted her eyebrows.

Luna fixed her blouse and sat down, took out a clean piece of paper, a sharp pencil, and put the bottom of the pencil between her teeth. She lit a small tea candle and started to play with the pencil as if it was alive, biting it and talking to it perhaps in an attempt to inspire the pencil's best abilities. But she knew that she had to charge it with poison, the pencil was a mere, innocent vehicle that would express her own thoughts and feelings. The vehicle needed fuel and she knew exactly how to deliver the best quality of the fuel.

She was Luna Averna, and no one knew better than she did how to charge events with powerful emotions, no, she never learned this art – she brought it encoded in her blood when she was born twenty-four minutes after her twin-sister greeted the world with her placid smile, for sin of pride required a physical body to fulfil itself, and in an invisible laboratory the poison was inserted into her veins and she came out screaming as if warning the world of her coming.

Her little candle kept on burning and her pencil started to lose its sharpness with each new line, her smile got sweeter and sweeter and only she knew when her smile was so sweet, it was overcharged with bitterness.

She wrote a letter to her one and only niece, Pia Odak, and she commenced the letter with words:

"My dearest, one and only niece, who was supposed to be my own child..."

The further she went with the letter, the quicker the candle burnt, the quicker her heart burnt, and the poison was discharged as puss would from a festering wound.

The Postponed Graduation Party

She didn't need, nor wanted any party, but the families requested it. All sides for once were united by the idea of a party that would mark Pia's great achievements. She was the youngest student ever to graduate from the University of Philosophy at the age of twenty-two, all exams passed with the highest marks; it had to be celebrated in the way that the families envisioned it. And each family envisioned it in a different light.

The Odak family was ready to publicly announce that worthy addition to the family name, pride and tradition in producing top intellectuals; the Bonifacio's were ready to splash money and glitz in the form of choosing the most expensive venue, expensive and extravagant clothes and gifts, while the Tesla family wanted something quiet, decent and immersed in the spirit of the former intellectual, scientific and spiritual outstanding achievements of distinguished members of the family.

As always they were divided by: their level of education, tradition, taste, nationality and religion. They were united by Pia's achievement.

***

But the first person she ran to when she finished her last exam was Gregor. She rang the bell and his mother opened the door, looked at her, mumbled, *'She isn't home yet'*, and slammed the door in her face. Pia's face was painted the colour of Luna's last painting, blood red, but she wouldn't let her spoil her enthusiasm, so she pressed the bell again. No one answered; she pressed it again. Like a little puppy, Hugo ran to the door and when he had opened it he couldn't contain his excitement and happiness, as always he screamed:

"Pia, Yugo's beautiful Pia is here. Come, come Pia, give Yugo a hug."

Pia hugged Hugo, his mother came behind and started to drag him into the house saying, *"I told you she isn't at home, go away."*

Hugo screamed as a little piglet would, he tried to bite his mother's hand, Pia stood there without any intention to leave, Gregor opened the window and jumped out with head-phones on his ears and asked:

"What the hell is happening?"

"Your kind mother is helping Hugo to get into the house."

"Yugo wants to hug Pia!" screamed Hugo while Gregor came in telling his mother:

"Let go Mum, I'll deal with it, let go, and go into the house."

She did let go of Hugo, shot a terrifying look at Pia and through her clenched teeth said:

"This devil will cost you your life."

"Please, Mum, go into the house."

She left and Pia said:

"Lucky you!"

"Lucky me!" said Hugo and hugged Pia while burying his head into her chest. Gregor suggested they go out for a coffee, all three of them, and when Hugo promised he wouldn't hug Pia every few seconds, Gregor took them to a near-by café.

"Pia, one day Hugo will marry you. No matter they say Pia's evil."

"Pia's evil? Who said that, Hugo?"

"Priest Malice and Mum. They say Pia's worse than Lonnie. Lonnie is not worse; she is good and kind. They say Pia's bad for Gogol. They never say Pia's bad for Yugo. Pia can be Yugo's friend."

"I always learn new things about your family from Hugo."

"Leave it, Pia. Tell me the news. Good news?"

"Good news!"

"Love you, babe!"

She shrugged her shoulders and pulled back.

Hugo said:

"Love you, babe!" to what Pia said:

"You are my bunny, Hugo."

Hugo kept clapping his hands an repeating, *'Yugo's Pia's bunny, Yugo's Pia's bunny..."* endlessly.

While they were talking Veronika was approaching on her walk back from school, Hugo stood up and started to run screaming, *'Lonnie, Lonnie, Lonnie...'* Gregor was holding Pia's hands in his and listening to her dreamy voice overjoyed by the fact that he was the first person she came to share her excitement with. Yes, he heard the loud breaking, the louder sound of a blow, the even louder scream, the sound of broken glass, Veronika's scream; all sounded as if that was coming from some far-away reality; he left Pia's hands on the table, stood up, looked at the scene in disbelief – his knees started to shake, his legs too, his heart started to pound wildly, he screamed:

"Hugo, Hugo, Hugo!!!" and ran towards the car that had smashed into the window of a shop, with Hugo's body between the tires and the broken window in thousands of pieces. His body was covered in red. Blood everywhere.

Pia was just sitting there unable to stand up.

Her heart was racing too, then she sobbed, *'Mummy, Mummy.'*

Pia stood up, looked at the scene – Gregor kneeling over Hugo's blood-covered body, Veronika still screaming with her hands covering her face – then she turned her back and started to run. She ran and ran and ran, and when she stopped, the scene was still there as it was always in front of her eyes, all those years - the scene was still there!

***

Gregor was holding him in his arms, he was still breathing but all of his body was covered in blood, his body was limp like the body of a withered flower, Gregor started to cry, he heard the sirens of an ambulance, he called his name through the tears; Hugo opened his kind, squinted eyes one last time and said:

"Tell Lonnie Yugo loves Lonnie.... Tell Pia Yugo loves Pia... tell... tell... Gogol, tell..." then he closed his eyes and he never opened them again.

Gregor was kneeling, holding Hugo in his arms and crying as a wounded animal, Veronika knelt next to him and screeched, screamed, sobbed and shook

190

her arms and legs. They both kept repeating, *'Hugo, Hugo, Hugo'* countless times as if that united chant would bring back their already departed brother.

This was the only time in their lives that their hearts were united: never had it happened before and never would it happen again.

Gregor hugged Veronika and this time she didn't throw his arms away. They were not aware of the crowd, the ambulance, the doctors and two police officers. When their mother came accompanied by Firar Marag, Veronika screamed at him:

"Go away, go away, you evil, evil man!"

***

Pia found herself on the doorsteps of her Grandma's house. She sat on the steps and sobbed. It was meant to be one of the happier days for her; after seeing Gregor she intended to visit Granny Sava. She was unable to walk into the house hence she just sat there paralysed. After a while she saw her Grandma walking a dog. Granny Sava came with a light step, but the expression on her face took on the shape of worry as soon as she looked at Pia.

"Pia?"

Pia kept sitting on the steps looking at her shoes. She remembered when she ran to Granny Sava, she bore so much pain and guilt that only Granny Sava could be a soothing presence.

Pia said:

"I have graduated."

"Those are, rather, happy news, aren't they? Why the tears?"

"Granny, someone I cared about just died."

Granny sat down next to Pia and hugged her. She stroked her hair the way she used to when Pia was a little girl. Pia kept sobbing and Granny kept stroking her hair.

After a while Pia said:

"Granny, do you remember when Mum died?"

"Not now, Pia, not now my child."

191

She kept sobbing for little Hugo, she kept sobbing for her mother.

Granny Sava sat there holding her as she did thirteen years ago: tightly to her chest, stroking her head and mumbling, almost chanting, a wordless melody, summoning her Orthodox healing saints to intervene.

When Pia cried her eyes out for the memories of kind Hugo and when she cried her eyes out for the countless time the bizarre passing of her mother, she started to worry about Veronika. She knew to what extent she had been crushed and decided to go and visit her regardless of the circumstances.

When she came to her room Veronika was lying on her bed, dressed in black lace from the top to the laced stockings below; she had a black bow in her hair and eyes open wide, staring at the ceiling where she had written in fresh paint, *'Hugo is Lonnie's Bunny.'*

Pia sat next to her and squeezed her hand.

Veronika didn't say a word, but when she felt the presence of her one and only true friend, her tears just flew down her cheeks, right into her mouth, and she was drinking them as one would the sacred nectar.

When she stopped crying she said:

"Pia, nothing's the same anymore."

"I know how much you are hurting."

"No, you don't, no one does."

"I know Lonnie, my mum died when I was nine years old and I never, never got over it. While she was dying I was looking at her unable to do a thing for her. She just said, 'Pia, hold me tight, and I did. I was just a child, and it never occurred to me to call someone, a doctor, or my fricken dad, I just sat next to her, holding her hands, unable to say anything... I have never spoken of it Veronika, but my mum slashed her wrists..."

Pia stopped talking she laid next to Veronika and they gazed into the ceiling where Veronika had written, *'Hugo is Lonnie's Bunny'*, they held their hands like two little frightened girls who lost their most precious people. They kept holding hands, and after a long silence Pia said:

DETHRONED

"I came back from school. The door was unlocked, uncommon for my mum. She was the only person, apart from my Granny that I felt at ease with, and with whom I felt loved for who I was. I left my schoolbag in my room when the strong smell of something unfamiliar grabbed my attention. There was a heavy silence in the house. It was early afternoon but the shadows were already elongated. I had promised her to hurry back home as we were working on a piece of painting together. Have I ever told you how we painted together? My mum was a fine artist, a very sensible soul; I felt each and every thought of hers, every emotion. I would write a little poem and she would paint it onto her canvas. We would discuss it and add colours or shades, sometimes some symbols that held meaning for both of us.

I was walking, sort of warily, as if I were expecting to face something unusual. That was the feeling, almost like a premonition. I feared Luna's presence. Mother's twin sister, she would come out of the blue and demand things. She would say, that particular piece of antique was promised to her by our Nonna, or she would claim that my dad told her to take the collection of Eco or Machiavelli, or she would simply steal Mum's paintings claiming that she had painted them. She was a strange creature and I have never managed to grasp, how on earth it could happen that two souls and bodies were born out of the same egg yet so different, so vastly different and estranged from each other. They never shared anything in common, she was the embodiment of evil; she plotted and alienated family members, friends and acquaintances.

I didn't meet Luna then, I didn't hear her, neither did I hear my father... I just kept on walking slowly and felt weakness in my knees for no apparent reason. I felt as if something very unearthly was in the house itself, and I called out Mother's name – no answer. Didn't find her in the living room, nor in her little atelier; I went into the kitchen and there I found her sitting on the floor with her hands leaning against her knees, bleeding, sadness in her eyes, total helplessness; my heart sank into my feet, I came closer, still with a very slow step but my heart was racing; I looked at her melancholic eyes and said, 'Mum, what, what?' and she said, 'Nothing, Pia. Just sit next to me and hug me.' And I did. She bled, and I kept on hugging her while she leaned her head against my shoulder. The blood kept on slowly, but steadily, pouring out of those two symmetrical cuts; I was staring at the pool on the floor holding her as I was told, my mind absolutely blocked, blank, no idea what to do, no conclusion as to what was happening; I just remember that she kept on repeating, 'I love you, Pia', and I kept repeating, 'I love you, Mum' and kept on squeezing her body closer to mine as if convincing myself that if I held her tighter she'd last longer, or forever, perhaps.

Then I heard the voices, my father walked in, Luna walked behind him, Dad separated my hands from her body, Luna said, 'I'll take the paintings', she said, 'As she called no one it means that she killed her', my father was telling me something, but when I saw that in Mum's eyes there was no sign of light anymore I refused to hear the words. I didn't hear any words any longer. Luna kept packing the paintings and some other things, Dad talked to me, but I just kept on kissing his hands, and Luna talked in a fast pace, but I never remembered what she was saying; all that stayed with me at that time was her accusation that I took as very logical and reasonable, 'As she called no one it means that she has killed her.' My guilt was established at that moment because I knew that if I had called someone, I might have saved her.

I've carried that guilt all those years, I see her, I speak to her, and she is always kind to me, telling me that she couldn't bare it any longer.

I refused to talk to anyone except for my Granny Sava. When she came, she put my shoes on, washed my face and hands, and took me to her home. There, I sat on the doorstep and wept.

Veronika, I killed my mum."

"You killed no one, Pia. She took her own life. You couldn't save her."

"I could have, only if I had been smart enough. But I was a dreamer, always in the clouds' I couldn't grasp the severity of the situation. I was petrified. Petrified! Still, I am petrified; Hugo's death brought it all up again. I know how much pain you are suffering. To make things worse, I learned a lot about my family; the weirdness, my father's infidelities, Luna's perversion, my Nonna's turning a blind eye to everything. People talked about my family, they would say that everything always came to pass only because we were the Odak

clan, that clan of the powerful and right connections. People said that my mum killed herself because my father abused me. They spread rumours that me and my, weird enough, dad were living in sin, that that was the reason why my mum took her life. I refused the help of a psychologist and coped sometimes with more, sometimes with less ability to cope. I've never trusted men, or women since. I never trusted anyone but my Granny Sava, the rest of the family just kept on looking after themselves, all of them: my dad, my uncles; my granddad was a mystery as he always thought that my mum was a melancholic child; her parents, the Bonifacio family, with Mum's death become more distant, Luna became crazier... and I was left with only one person to trust and to love, my Granny. She talked to me about the nature of life and death, she taught me everything I know, not the schools, not the university, but she was the one who passed on the knowledge and treasured heritage of Tesla's family, that sensibility and wisdom that rare people or families possess. She taught me kindness and how to rely on myself. I had her as my rock, not my father, the fool who tried to portray himself as my rock and my friend. He was never aware of the proportion of disaster he created, he was never aware that I was an intelligent and gifted young woman, no! He was the one! He was Simon Odak, the offspring of the powerful Odak family, a theatre director, a capable single father; an influential figure in the cultural life of the town. He is none of that. He was a father by accident! He was never there when I was growing up. I had a mother, while he was ever absent. He was a guest, someone who came late to a dinner, when it was already too cold to eat, then he would walk out to look for a warm dinner elsewhere. Mum was silent, never protesting, not because she feared him or of the possibility of him leaving us, she never said anything because there was nothing to say. She picked the wrong man, a vagabond; a pretentious prick who ruined her life. I believed, and still do believe now, that he and Luna had a long standing affair; once I challenged him, but, as always, my father just smiled when it came to women, believing that women were there just to give a man pleasure, a good time, entertainment. And my mother was much more than that; he never deserved her; she knew that! I never understood why she married my father; she was sensitive, intelligent, creative and she had a deep reflective soul. Why she wanted someone like him will always be a mystery to me, a mystery that will haunt me to my grave. I love my father and I loathe him at the same time. I love him probably because his blood is coursing through my veins, because he had never been bad or nasty to me, but I loathe him for who he is; for all those innocent, yet stupid, women he had in his life. Veronika, he slept with almost all the young actresses, with almost all my girlfriends, he is a disgusting pig, but still, he is my father, the only one I have, he is the son of my beloved Granny Sava, and with much wisdom she once said, "We can't be proud of good and successful ones in the family and deny love, guidance and friendship to those who are not as virtuous. We have to concentrate on the less virtuous and help them more."

This is who my father is Veronika. This is the story of how I lost my mother. Those wounds have never been healed, and most probably they never will be. I live with my past and the people who caused so much pain. The only person I never wanted to see again was Luna. She caused so much trouble in the following years, stealing from us; my puppet-father gave her whatever she asked with the most transparent excuse that Luna was Mum's twin sister, and that only she had the right to own Mum's work. Mum had more than fifty paintings, more than fifty poems; she had stolen all of that. Mum had at least twenty sculptures. They all found a home in the infamous Luna's Gallery. Yes, that bitch, from Luna's Gallery, that's my aunt, Veronika, she hated me so much, sending on each of Mum's birthdays black cards with black ribbons, telling me that I was the reason 'her sister died prematurely'. She had stolen everything from us: she was furious when Mum was alive, knowing that she would never be able to steal Sapphire's soul and her numerous gifts; she knew that she would never be able to steal the love Sapphire shared with me. She was born that way, nothing could or ever would change her, she just takes advantage of people, of men, of any situation; she is a greedy, unhappy, a creature so evil that even Satan regretted creating her so perfectly wicked. She had outsmarted her creator, nothing would surprise me from her; there are no limits to how far she could go: her wrath, jealousy and insanity are limitless; her determination to glorify death and to destroy all that represents the light and goodness have always been absolute. She occasionally sends 'anonymous' messages; she cuts out paper articles about me, and she puts them in an envelope, and with 'disguised' handwriting she sends it all to me with notes like, 'You untalented freak!' or similar. I know it is her! No one would go out of their way to give me trouble. I feel it in my guts; I recognise her hatred. My Nonna protects her all the time. She tells me, 'She is your mother's twin sister, how can you say anything bad about her, they were the same, identical twins.' No, they were not, and Nonna knows it, everybody knows it, including my screwed up father, but in his weirdness he liked her better, they were a better match.

When my Mum was buried Granny took me to Raduč. Her father, still alive at that time, but retired, returned back to that small village of his origin. They had a beautiful house surrounded by numerous trees: poplar trees, cherry trees and big oak trees. The air was clean and beautiful; the brook near the house produced the most soothing sounds and the most fantastic drinking water. She took me there, and Old Dad, as we used to call her father, took out of the stables an old wooden swing that someone made for me when I was little. He tied it up onto the branch of a mighty oak and they swung me for days, they would take turns and sing folk song, or some chants from the Serbian Orthodox scriptures and I would not cry. Only there, only with those two people I felt protected and secure. My Old Dad, was a Serbian Orthodox priest and he was so learned and kind, he used stories and parables to soothe my pain; later on he invited kind people to dinner and they weaved stories and myths about Nikola Tesla; there were many who knew him and I loved hearing stories about that extraordinary ancestor of mine, I felt proud and challenged at the same time. The stories about the Tesla family, the association with those kind people helped to a certain extent to overcome the worst period of my life. If my life hadn't been overshadowed with such a traumatic event, these six months, probably, would have been the best six months of my childhood. But they were not, and I would cry at night when I believed that no one would hear me, but then all of a sudden, she, my Granny, would walk into my room, on the tips of her toes, she would come under the covers and hug me tight.

I remember her sister, another kind and simple soul; I used to call her Granny Mitzi, as her name was Milica. She baked all the time: breakfast was *baked and lunch too, afternoon cakes and strudels were baked, dinners were baked… then she asked me if I'd like to learn to bake. I would bake with the two of them and learned folk songs from the region of Lika. Granny Mitzi told me stories about Nikola when he was a young boy; for me it was amazing to hear how gifted, yet shy, he was or how fragile his health was at times. There were few pictures of them taken on rare occasions, saved by grace as lots of things went missing during WWII. Those Serbian villages were torn apart and raped; houses, even though very poor, were robbed and many people killed or displaced. But they never talked about those times, they talked about kindness and forgiveness, and as I said the favourite topic that everyone was involved in and proud of was Nikola Tesla and his family, their family, my family. There, during those six months I felt different, I felt a strong connection to this land and those humble and intelligent people.*

My father never came to visit, as he always stated that he never liked to mix with village people regardless of the fact that it was his mother's family. He felt as if he was Odak, only Odak, and he would claim that Odak was his family heritage, especially in public, as if he were ashamed of Granny's background. Oh, he was. Oh, yes, he was, but the more he concealed it the prouder I became of belonging to that family. Strange people, strange places, you know, Veronika, we live in a strange land, here on the edge of the Balkans, on the edge of European civilization; I have my other family having those Latin ancestors, yet we are so different, so unsettled and unforgiving. I am tired of these people and I long to live somewhere where I am not Pia Odak. Where I am just a citizen. It was a heavy cloak for me to bear that surname, to bear those family secrets, to defend my father's weirdness in order to defend my own decency. Yes, I stopped doing it, yes, I pretend I don't care, I don't hear remarks, I don't know what people are saying. The Odak family has always been the subject of speculations: our honesty, our connections and our weirdness and greed. But they ruled this town for generations: we were judges, magistrates, majors, educators… in every Ministry of this country there is one Odak connected back to our family tree. Our name opens the door for me wherever I go, not only in this town of ours, but if I go to another region, people know 'some of those Odaks' in the hierarchy of the country or in the order of things.

DETHRONED

I have been myself, the real me, only with my soft and kind mother, only with my Granny, and in you Veronika, I have found a rare friend, a deep soul, seemingly disturbed, but seeing your troubles, your mother and the people around you, I chose it to be the reason to understand you more and see the similarities between us. I still can't figure out your brother, I don't trust him, he is just enchanted by my physical beauty but I think that it is just a momentary thing; I was a girl he couldn't conquer with ease, so he pressed on in pursuit of me, that's all. That's how I see him. He doesn't have your sensibility, neither Hugo's kind heart. I still can't figure him out, but one thing I can see clearly: he is under a strong influence of his mother yet not aware of it; right me if I am wrong."

"Let me stop you, right here! He is a jerk! He is under the influence of his mother, yes, she is under the influence of this demonic priest who has been hanging around our house since I was born. I can't stand that jerk, but my mother's enchanted by his wit and wisdom. What you said about your aunt Luna, if I had to say something about that weirdo it would be the same. Friar Marag washes his mouth after he speaks to people, that is how much he hates people. Only my holy mother is his Saint Mary.

Yes, I can understand you when you said that you still couldn't figure out my brother. My brother has never been a real friend to anyone. He was always adored by family members, neighbours, teachers, and, of course, girls and women. He took advantage of anyone, not because he calculated it, but just because he was offered things, favours, bodies, vaginas et cetera. He would take 'the offerings' without a second thought. That's my brother: a German God of Beauty and a Musical Talent. Does he have a heart? Well, that would be difficult to determine. His life has always been quite easy just because of his exceptional looks and his ways with words and music. His flattery to everyone was never intentional, he, deep down, knew that it would take him wherever he wanted to go. He would flash his big, healthy teeth, look at you with his penetrating blue eyes, sing a chord and voilà; he was on his way to stardom or to your pants. That's what I know about him. He never paid any attention to any family member but his mother. Father, anyway, was always absent with his 'after-work-duties'; which I never managed to determine if they meant 'other women' or was he really in deep shit with his political views and parties? This or that I only know, he was never there for us, for me, at least. Minding his own business! While he was minding his own business, the creep, the Holy Father, was present. Bloody present! Gregor never really cared about Hugo, either. I can't say he didn't love him, for he did, I know that, but he was always deep in his own activities, playing music, playing soccer, playing cards with his pals or whatever. Later, he was busy with his band and girls, so Hugo was someone to talk to in a hurry while tying his laces or watching the TV. For me, Veronika, no, he never had time as he bought into the home-made-mythology, which read: Veronika's a weird, fucked-up, crazed junkie. He treated me as the situation ordered: with due attention to not being attacked or harmed, or with minimal cordial contact until one day he had discovered that the long-haired black beauty in my bedroom was no one else but Pia Odak. Then he wanted to be friendlier, then he remembered, actually, that the family weirdo who writes poems on the ceiling was his younger sister.

OK? I won't be going any further to put you off. I speculate that you might be in love with the German God; so I don't wish to spoil it. I'll just bow down to him and his chosen one, the selectee, you, Pia Odak... But, Pia, apart from what I've said, how did you get over the loss of your most beloved person how did you make peace with life after losing her, as now that I have lost the only person I genuinely and completely loved I am unwilling to carry on. I will never get over the loss of my Little Alien, my Yugo, I will hear his voice in my ear for the rest of my life, 'Lonnie, Lonnie, Yugo loves Lonnie.'

She started to sob and Pia dug her fingernails into her thighs. That was the only way in which she could cope with pain: to cause more pain, the one that was physical, real, the one that she could see and witness.

"I've never got over it. Do you really think that a child could get over it? I was a child and that part of me has never died. Deep within me, there is still that little frightened, shocked Pia who cries and cries for her mummy, who feels tremendous guilt, you are the only person on this earth that I have told

200

this story to, I have never even talked to my Granny about the depth of my feelings, the abyss of my sorrow. I've kept it locked inside of me as a rare gift, as a sapphire. My pain has been a sapphire, crystalised and solidified in my soul, and it produced the melody of a melancholy that went into my verses. Probably, most likely, I'd say, you will never get over losing Hugo, but the pain will ease with time. Only time heals. I can think of my mum now without that horrible pain in the pit of my stomach, I can see her photos and smile. I miss her terribly, but I've developed coping mechanisms, I've even convinced myself that she comes and converses with me. It has helped a little. I talked to her often and still do. I go to the graveyard and I talk to my Sapphire, especially when the rain's pouring and no one's there."

"The saddest thing, Pia, is, that no one except me and you, had ever understood how sensitive and receptive, how intelligent Hugo was. You should see how shame-ridden my proud mother was while taking him out in public. The more shame she felt, the more I loathed her. The more shame she felt because of Hugo, the more pride she put into Gregor. Listen to this story now. I was about six or seven, and Hugo was just a little toddler. My fair Mother Elsa was sitting on the terrace with her, as Hugo would say 'favourite person', the worthy Friar Marag. They were talking about sin. Things conceived in sin or out of sin. He dug deep down, in most probably, a poorly hidden attempt to find mother's 'deep, dark past', no matter how minor it could have ever been, how partial, but he searched for anything to make it look like an enormous problem, which she could never overcome without his help. I understood that despite being so young. I read him even then. I was the bitter pill that he had to swallow in order to follow my mother wherever fancy took her. To follow her, to make her follow him, to make her understand that truth was within him, and that she was worthy of his mission of taking her into alliance and sympathetic entanglements with him and his doctrines of manipulation. He never ceased in his condemnation of the less worthy than him, making everyone around him feel like worthless sinners condemned forever. He kept on searching for that particular sin for which my mother bore the cross of having Hugo, he kept on pressing, she kept on confessing, they kept on calling him a Mistake, and I came onto the terrace and did a little performance to show them what would

appear as 'normal' but yet to be the greatest mistake. My performance was as follows: They were sitting with their backs turned and I walked in the crisp early evening sunset onto the terrace, took the hose that was hanging from a wooden pole and switched it on. Then I started to wash from the top of my head; then, as I progressed down to my shoulders, I started to take off my clothes. The winterish top, made from the nicest mohair wool, then I took my singlet off, and washed my tiny chest, then I took off my trousers and by that time they turned their faces towards me as I turned the tap up, it started to roar and awaken them from their deep philosophical speculations. I was about to take off my underwear but the pious Elsa got up in a panic that came from the realisation who the real Mistake was, and I, to prevent her from putting an end to my performance, aimed the hose towards her and she backed off. As she did, with the greatest delight I could have ever expressed and experienced in my life, I turned the hose towards the holy, sacred man and soaked his robe which from black went to pitch-black, and there were three voices simultaneously coming out in almost perfect harmony: Elsa was hysterically screaming, our blessed father was cursing in gibberish and my laughter was as hysterical as Elsa's screaming, what a symphony, a divine symphony of extreme emotions! For the first time all three of us were united by the depth and intensity of emotion. Hugo came out on his knees, with his broad smile, I picked him up and said, 'Lonnie loves Hugo, yes?' and he smiled at me caressing my wet cheek with his star-like hands: all fingers spread out warm and at the same time hungry for more warmth. Pia, I don't want to live in this house any longer. Not without Hugo. In a few months I'll finish high-school and I'll leave this town."

"Where can you possibly go?"

"I don't want to go to Germany, although German is the language I speak well. Still, I wouldn't go there, that would only reinforce memories of my mother. But, my English isn't too bad. Maybe somewhere... like, the UK or even America."

"It'll pass, my friend, it'll pass. I'll be here for you."

"You think that I am kidding, that pain talks. No, I am not kidding, nor am I childishly dreaming. I am determined to go, far away, I don't want to see my family ever again. They would never even miss me."

"Do you want to spend several days with me? Come over. We'll attend the funeral together, we'll go and buy clothes together for both of us."

***

The next morning Pia was awakened by quiet buzzing. Worried Gregor said that no one knew where Veronika was. She had disappeared. When Pia told him that she came over for several days, as she needed support and shelter, Gregor wanted to talk to her. He told Veronika that *'Mother was worried'* and asked her to come back home, or, at least, give Mother a call.

"That's something new, completely new. Why would she worry about me?"

"Let's not make things more complicated right now. It is so difficult for all of us, Veronika you are not the only one that hurts terribly. We all do. Please, do it for me if not for Mum. Do it for Hugo. Come back and let's be a family in those horrible moments, we need each other now."

"I'll come Gregor, because of Hugo, but there's one condition attached to it."

"A condition? In this situation? OK. What is it?"

"I don't want that freak to bury my brother. I don't want him, to fricken touch him, ever again. I don't want him to talk about my Hugo; I don't want him to summon his God for my brother. I don't want him in our house prior to the funeral nor at the funeral."

There was a long silence from the other side. After a while Gregor said:

"This is something I can't promise. It is not my decision to make, you have to talk to Mother."

"What about father, did he ever make any decisions? Can I talk to him? Can he ever make any decisions in this house?"

"OK. Wait, I'll call him!"

"Dad, I don't want that freak to bury my brother! Do you understand me? I won't come home unless he is not around."

"Why?"

"He hated my brother! He hates everyone! I hate him, Dad! I hate him!"

"Veronika, you have to speak to your mother. She is so distressed about everything, don't make it worse."

"Can't you ever make any decisions? What is she to you? Your mother? Is she Eva Braun to you? What the hell is she to you? Can't you decide who would bury your child?"

"Why now, Veronika, why now? Please, come back home. Please!"

She hung up and started to cry. Pia hugged her.

"My father never made any decisions. He is just begging. He is begging me. He begged her all his life. I am not going to that house where Hugo's no more."

She sobbed and Pia held her wrists tight.

On the same day, in the early afternoon, Gregor rang the bell. They opened the door and he hugged Pia, then he hugged Veronika. They didn't talk. They sat and smoked and drank strong coffee. Veronika sobbed and ran to the bathroom twice. Pia didn't say much.

Before he stood up he said:

"The funeral will take place tomorrow afternoon at four o'clock. Come earlier. If you wish to come home fine, if you wish to stay with Pia, that's fine too. Mum said that Friar Marag is not going to bury Hugo. Uncle Aaron is coming in the late afternoon, accompanied by a priest, his friend."

He left. Pia said:

"You see; they respected your wish."

Veronika cried:

"I don't want anyone to bury my brother. I don't want anyone to put him in the ground. I want my Hugo; I can't live without his kind hands touching my face, without his dreamy eyes and his golden heart. Pia, I can't live without my Little Alien, I don't want to live without him."

Pia said nothing, just a flood of tears broke the dam of thick black lashes that held the tears back giving her eyes that glassy look, and through this glass she could see some other reality, in some other time, coloured and glassed by the same emotions.

She put Veronika in bed and went out to buy clothes for both of them. On her way she visited her Granny and told her about the sad event. Granny Sava went with Pia to the store and they bought black dresses and jackets; Pia even bought new shoes for Veronika, hoping that they would fit her as they probably wore the same size.

In the evening they drank some vodka, and when Pia's father came after he was absent for several days, he heard the news. He took it lightly, he said that it was sad that she had lost her brother; he said that he was terribly tired and needed a shower; he said that he was ageing; he said some other things, but no one really cared about his random confessions.

At nine o'clock Gregor came and drank some vodka with them. When Veronika was too tired to stay awake and a bit tipsy, they took her to bed and covered her. She said, *"Nothing compares to you, Hugo!"*, then she put her thumb in her mouth and as a sad, sad child she cried herself to sleep.

When Gregor was leaving he said:

"Thank you, Pia. You really are the most kind and sophisticated girl I have ever met. I love you, Pia."

Pia said nothing; she just closed the door.

And behind those closed doors he left two young girls, so close to his heart yet so unknown to him, real mysteries, and he was not even aware of who they were and what kind of pain they bore. That pain unified them even more, he never knew and never would that Veronika was closer to Pia's heart than he would ever be.

***

Veronika woke up with the sunrise; she sat at Pia's desk and started to write a story about *Hugo the Little Alien*, her eulogy. She kept writing and crying, Pia kept pretending that she was asleep.

She helped her to wash and dry her hair, to put her clothes on, to comb and to buckle her new shoes.

Pia bought two similar plain black dresses, for Veronika a finer one, with some discrete patches of lace, and a black small hat. She applied some blush on Veronika's pale cheeks, and at two o'clock they sat in Pia's car. Pia was driving in silence, Veronika still sobbing.

At a small church the family was gathered. In her pain, she was still proud and haughty, Mother Elsa; she hugged Veronika but failed to notice Pia's presence. She said:

"You should have come home."

"I'd miss my brother there."

"You should have come home to your mother."

"It will never be the same without Hugo."

Pia heard her saying to her brother that *'the Goth was responsible for Hugo's death.'* But what she didn't hear was that Elsa held if it weren't for Pia, Gregor wouldn't have gone out, Gregor wouldn't have failed to pay attention, if only she hadn't been there.

Pia shivered. Veronika didn't hear anything; she was just mumbling his name. Veronika wasn't allowed to see him in the coffin.

He was dressed in his favourite red cardigan. They put a pair of black jeans on him, and a white shirt. His hair was combed backwards. He didn't look like a little alien; he just looked as any child that had passed away too early. He didn't look sad nor happy. His squinted eyes were closed, hence they didn't look squinted anymore; heavy make-up was applied under his eyes, and rosy blush on his cheeks. There was such calmness on his dear face. Pia never left Veronika's side.

When the music started Veronika started to shake and scream. Gregor was holding her under the other arm.

She wanted to read the eulogy, but she looked as if she was absent, she looked as if her soul went in search of Hugo's.

Among the congregation Gregor saw a tall, lanky woman dressed in black. Her hair was grey and pulled back. She was holding a big bunch of flowers, she didn't look sad, she looked kind and compassionate, but he was puzzled by the presence of the woman, as he could swear that he had never met her. Was she one of Hugo's new teachers? Pia looked at him and said:

"This is my grandmother."

"Thank you, Pia."

"It was her choice to come."

The service was held by a priest that no one really knew, but there was no sign of Friar Marag.

When they lowered the coffin Veronika cried and wanted to break free from the tight grip of Gregor and Pia's hands. She called out:

"Hugo, my little brother; don't leave me alone."

Gregor whispered:

"You are not alone Lonnie, you have me."

"I want my brother!" she kept on repeating and crying, and tears and saliva poured down her nose, Pia took a handkerchief and wiped off her nose, as Veronika used to wipe off saliva that was dripping from Hugo's tongue.

And after that, for Veronika a long, long silence followed. Hollow and cold silence. She took a week off from school, locked herself in her room, stared at the ceiling where she used to gaze with Hugo and thought of how he asked her to write his name in the stars, to write Pia's name in the stars, to write all sorts of things among those stars that still looked happy, but their colours and shapes couldn't generate happiness in anyone's heart any more.

Veronika stared and asked the same question: *"How can one carry on without the person who meant everything to them?"*

"How can one find the purpose when meaning was cruelly taken away?"

"How can one ever smile when the reason that eternally warmed the soul has disappeared and would never return?"

"Where and how from now on?"

She didn't know where and she didn't know how, but she knew that she had to go. She knew that she wanted to go.

On her bedroom door she hung the message:

"Please, leave me alone until I go."

But when Pia came home from the funeral she felt exhausted, not only from the intensity of Veronika's pain and the emotions she shared, but from her old wounds that opened up and started to bleed like on the most generous rainy day, a day when the sky opens and offers plentiful raindrops that resemble a waterfall, a river that will never stop running. Her wounds were liquid and running, running behind her every time she wanted to break free in any way, they would follow, follow in the rain, follow in the sun, in daytime and wait for her behind her pillow, yes, they followed and whispered. She put her bag on her desk and there she found a letter, perhaps an essay, the eulogy that Veronika had forgotten to take even though she intended to read it. Pia sat at the desk and started to read:

"There was a Little Alien who came to this earth to make people happy. He was supposed to be a source of happiness for others too, so he planted his beauty into Lonika's heart. Their hearts grew together and beat as one, for there were not many who could have read that language of those united hearts. His words were few, but he never really communicated with words but with his smile, and he had thousands of different smiles so that only very few could read their unique language. Hugo, you were the heart of my heart, you were the smile of my depths, you were the softest thought I ever had and the kindest, the strongest Alien that briefly walked this domain. You never belonged here, it looks as if you were put here by mistake, on this planet, in this family, but you brought to my inner realms thousands of suns that will shine for millennia. Life without you will be like a life without the sun, not thousands of suns, but just without one, as all lights will be off from now on. You were the best brother, the best friend and the most beautiful Little Alien. It looks as if I can't live any

longer, dear Hugo, for you were me, not just a part of me, you were me and without you I can't breathe any longer."

Pia thought of her own numerous letters and poems, which she had written to Sapphire since she had passed on. The pain had never ceased, it never really did; it was Pia's shelter: friend and ally, foe and torture.

She knew that life had to go on for everyone; she knew that the next morning she had to pay a visit to the Bonifacio family.

"What an annoying thought!" she said in a low voice while taking off her boots.

The Bonifacios

Once Granny Sava said: *"Take them for who they are, do not judge."*

Pia didn't think that she was a judgmental person but visiting her *Nonna* was never an easy task.

They lived in a hilly and leafy area, steep, but the view was breathtaking. Wealthy people had lived there in the glory times of the town in the not so distant past. Houses were big, spacious, but the windows were small with green wooden blinds. The windows were small because of the bitter, strong winter wind that often threatened to knock the window in, and the second reason was Mussolini's decree to tax houses with bigger windows. Yes, those were the days when light was controlled, it almost diminished; even if one were wealthy, they weren't allowed to see too much light. He feared enlightenment!

There were two Bonifacio brothers and one took over their father's business in the naval industry, while the other, Pia's grandfather, developed his father's other enterprising attempt to get rich and control money in the region – the business of fine clothing. He had the most respected factory of fine suits, coats and male accessories. They exported their textile and goods to the West and East and made a fortune. Their money was kept in the *Banco d'Italia* in Rome as they thought it would be the safest place to keep money at any time, let alone in those turbulent periods when D'Annunzio walked in and proclaimed Fiume to be a free state. They loved the idea of Fiume being a free state and the charming poet to be the governor of the state, but when it came to money they wanted to secure it.

Ah, Empires come and pass, money loses its worth and devaluates, only gold had real value, but even gold was sold for next to nothing in times when chaos took over. After the Second World War Pia's uncle left the country and went to Milan, while her grandfather stayed in the family house. He never wanted to leave.

Pia rang the bell and the maid opened the door. They still kept the maid since Pia's *Nonna* kept some of her bourgeois habits as the last bastion of her past identity and status.

They offered to host a party for Pia.

She never replied, hence she came to visit. When she said the funeral had been the reason for delaying the announcement to *Nonna* as to who had died, the latter commented:

"Is it the little retard who regularly harassed you? Poor thing, they don't live long, nothing to be surprised about. Nothing to be sorry about, it is better for the family as they have been liberated now. It would be such a curse to have a child like that."

"Thank you, Nonna, but I won't plan my party here. I don't like parties. I only wanted to invite several people for dinner."

"And that's exactly what I'll do for you, I'll organise a dinner for as many people as you like. I like people to know that my granddaughter was the best student ever at the University of Philosophy..."

"I wasn't the best student ever, Nonna, but that doesn't even matter. I know you'd like to acknowledge that, but please, let me do it my own way."

"What is your own way? You want to go to the Serbian woman and she'll organise better than us? Better than the Bonifacios?"

"No. I am not going to Granny, she will not organise anything, nor will the Odaks... I'd like to invite some family and friends to a restaurant... we can all share the expense... I mean, Dad, Granny and Nonno."

"How disgraceful! I won't let my only granddaughter celebrate her diploma in some place... with a bill shared between those people... Let me organise and pay for it all, please Pia, you are my late daughter's only child. We agreed upon that long ago."

"If it is to be at your place, then most likely your other daughter will invite herself along."

"Are you talking about Luna?"

"You know who I am talking about."

"What's the matter between you two? She is your mother's twin sister, why, why, why do you dislike her so much? Pia, she loves you, she always asks about you, she means well. Only yesterday she asked when your party was to take place. When and where, she asked. Unbelievable how, sometimes, you can be prejudicial and judgmental. Obviously she asked because she cared, most likely she was thinking in terms of buying you a present. Pia, don't act like that, don't break my heart."

"On that day, Nonna, I don't want her around. Do you understand me? I don't want her to come and ruin my day."

"Oh, Santa Maria del Tersatto, Pia, Pia, Pia! What they have done to you, you used to be my little angel! You used to come and love our family. After your mother had passed away, after my heart was broken, you came so rarely to see us. They have indoctrinated you telling lies about us. Telling you lies about Luna. There's nothing wrong with her, she is your only aunty, yet you don't even want to see her. Who told you all those horrible stories about us? You act as if you are not one of us: you are a part of the Bonifacio family just as you are a part of the Odaks.

They think if they are so well educated that you have nothing to learn from us. We used to be the richest family in Fiume, the most respected before those red devils came and took our country and culture from us. They took our language and money and our rich culture. Oh, Santa Maria del Tersatto, they even took my only granddaughter from me. Che disgrazia, che disgrazia!"

"Nonna, no one took me away, no one even talks about the Bonifacios. You are my family as much as the others are. Please, don't divide, don't tear me apart, I have already been torn for a long time. It is just a simple celebration, why would you not make it simple and enjoyable for all concerned?"

"Me? Oh, Santo Cielo! Me! You are accusing me of being the one who causes trouble and separation? Your family, the Odak family, never considered us to be worthy of their company. Your grandfather only went around with Serbs."

"Nonna, they are not Serbs. They are my family. My grandmother is of Serbian background but she was born in this land, just as you were born here. They were all born here, for generations, just as you and Dad's ancestors

were. Why, why on earth are there all these divisions in this city, in this country of ours!? What does that hatred mean to you? To others? How many genera-tions have to pass before such issues can be buried? Will it ever happen at all? You hate everyone who isn't Italian? They hate everyone who isn't Croat, they hate everyone who is not Serb, yet I am asking you, who is it that owns this town? Give me some breathing space! Stop the hatred!" Pia screamed and left the house running.

Nonna knelt down and started to pray to *Santa Maria del Tersatto.* She said to the saint:

"Ah, this land of ours will be taken apart again. Those devils came to our city and took over. Help us, Virgin Mary, help us as it looks as if they will throw us out from our hearths."

Pia drove to her other grandmother's house. Her door was always open and there was light music coming out as if to greet Pia. She found her grandmother in the kitchen with flour on her hands spreading out dough. When she saw Pia, she said:

"What a lovely surprise! You've come just at the right moment; I am about to put an apple strudel in the oven. Come over, let me kiss my beauty."

Pia gave her a hug and Granny kissed her head, then she asked:

"Is there something troubling you, Pumpkin?"

When Pia shrugged her shoulders, Granny Sava wiped her hands on her apron and sat down next to her:

"Is it the boy? Little Hugo?"

"That too."

"What else is there?"

"Everyone hates everyone in this country."

"Don't concentrate on that emotion. Concentrate on something positive. Leave such thoughts behind, don't evoke misfortune."

"Everyone's evoking misfortune. Why do our nations hate each other so much?"

"Prior to the breakout of WWII Nikola said, 'If hatred of these two nations could be transformed into electric energy, that energy would be enough to light a small town.' Pia, there are many people with a not-so-noble heart and hurtful intentions, leave them in their own world. You have just graduated; imagine what the future has in store for you. You have always been such a sensitive child, don't let negativity get to you; let it go. People are people; hopefully everyone will learn to let their own heart lead them. There are lots of kind people, with generous and noble hearts, you know that, Pumpkin, you know that."

"This Nonna of mine, she doesn't call people 'people', but Croats, Serbs or generic – Slavs. Her superiority is legendary as if God gave her a special place on the day of her birth only because she was born Italian. Yet, she is so much less sensitive, respectful and considerate than you, sometimes it hurts to witness how little she thinks of 'common people'. You remember my mum better than I do, tell me, as I don't think I remember my mother being like her, or like her sister. Mum was a kind person to everyone."

"Maybe it was her misfortune to be born in this part of the world. Yes, kindness and humbleness are not something that people value here. The first thing the majority want to know is one's nationality, then based on such a fact they box you in. They put a label on the box. But, look; strong and intelligent people don't let such things bother them at all. Your mother was very, very different to her sister Luna, that's all I can say."

"Don't even evoke the devil. I'd like to organise a little gathering; she wants to make a circus out of it. A show, where she would show off and tell everyone who she is, and how little she cares for anyone but her name. Oh, Granny, I am tired of them, yet they are my family."

"And that is correct, they are family and let it be that way. It isn't good for one's soul to cut ties with one's family. God placed us in the right family, don't challenge God's decisions, don't question just accept it."

"What is to be challenged? What has God done wrong now?" asked Pia's grandfather as he entered the room.

"Do you think it is necessary to celebrate my graduation?"

"*Certainly! But, you should be the one to decide where, when and who will be invited. It is your decision and we'll obey and follow. No one should or will decide on your behalf. But, one thing I know, the bill goes on my account, right?*"

Grandmother asked:

"*And what is it that your father suggests?*"

Without waiting for Pia to answer that question, her grandfather said:

"*Her father probably isn't even aware of anything, he is too busy being a fool.*"

"*Don't say that!*" said Sava.

"*Why shouldn't I? He is good for nothing, not even for the circus he calls theatre, not even for that.*"

Pia smiled while Granny crossed her chest with three fingers as grandfather left the room, newspaper in one hand, his glasses in the other.

That same afternoon, when her temper was under control again, Nonna Oriana called. She asked if she was '*overly impatient*' but it never occurred to her to apologise.

"*No.*" Pia said, and added, "*That's you Nonna, just be yourself.*"

"*I called to tell you, that Nonno and I agreed to organise and pay for your party. We have a friend, a good Italian man; he has a beautiful restaurant further down the road. It is on the water, spacious and serving good Italian food. Nonno called him and has already talked to him. He said he would close down for the event, he could organise a pianist to play, a fresh sea-food menu, just say 'yes' and tell me which Saturday and we'll take care of everything.*"

Once again Pia found herself annoyed by *Nonna's* initiative. She was hesitant:

"*Let me think...*"

"*Nothing to think about, just let us know when.*"

"*OK. I'll let you know, but you've got to meet two requirements: first, no piano man as I have a friend who will play for us, and secondly, but listen carefully, take me seriously on this one – I don't want Mother's sister to attend.*"

It is my party, it is about me and I want only the people that I choose to be there. Can you meet the two?"

"Why, Pia..."

"If you continue to insist I'll put the receiver down and we will finish this conversation for good. Please, don't call me stubborn again because I am, and I don't really care, Nonna, if you never understand why, but let it be the way I want it to be this time or I won't even consider making anyone happy by attending the party that I don't even want to attend."

"The Odak's blood!"

"No, Nonna, actually, this is very much the Bonifacio's attitude, this stubbornness and superiority."

"You are wrong, Pia, very wrong in making such decisions, but, let it be for the sake of your late mother, let it be. And with the saddest heart do I promise that Luna won't be there. Now, tell me the date."

Then, the next morning in the local, but Italian papers, Pia read, *Dear family Bonifacio, dear family friends and acquaintances of the Bonifacio family, we are proud to announce that our granddaughter Pia Letizia Odak-Bonifacio has graduated from the University of Philosophy, majoring in English and Italian languages and Classic Philosophy, aged 22, which makes her the youngest student ever to graduate there. We proudly announce that she came top in her finals and was given distinction in each and every subject. Pia Letizia Odak-Bonifacio is a talented poetess and writer. She is the daughter of the late Gemma Letizia Bonifacio, an artist of renown, who passed away at the young age of 27. Even though such a traumatic event never healed the Bonifacios' hearts, we are proud to say that she has left this most talented young lady as offspring.*

In honour of our one and only granddaughter Pia Letizia, an elegant ceremony will be held privately. We extend our grateful thanks to all of you who sent cards, congratulations and good wishes.

Proud and grateful grandparents of Pia Letizia Odak-Bonifacio - Signori Ernesto Claudio Bonifacio and Oriana Letizia Bonifacio.

Pia couldn't believe her eyes.

She folded the paper and threw it in the rubbish bin. The telephone rang that morning several times and her friends teased her.

"Yes, I know, stupid and embarrassing." She responded to each of her friends' comments.

She didn't call her *Nonna* - what for? She was her Nonna Oriana, she would do what she wanted, but all in an attempt to show status. They didn't have the money any longer, but her pride was oversized, over-ripe, it was the size of the biggest merchant boat that ever came into their port.

When she called Gregor, he said Veronika was still locked in her room unwilling to eat or communicate. He said that she lived on marijuana; her heavy sorrow was all that came out of the room as the only proof that she was still in there, still alive.

"Would it be OK if I asked you to play at my party?"

"You know it would."

"There will be a strange group of people, my mixed and crazy family, plus some, rather odd, friends."

"Don't justify anything, I am happy that you included me."

"You and Veronika, if we can get her out in some way."

"You'd be the only one that she would ever listen to and agree with. Only you can perform that miracle."

"I'll try."

"Pia, you mean the world to me."

"Ciao!" was all she said.

A few times he said, 'I love you, Pia', with absolute ease and sweetness in his heart, but it was never returned. He didn't even care as long as she was there to hear it. He never suspected that Pia Odak would be the only woman to whom he would say those words: to say them and to mean them from the depth of his young heart.

But when it came to Pia, the words, *'I love you'* belonged to her past, they lost their meaning thirteen years ago. Whenever she heard them she felt uncomfortable, not knowing what to do with the words or how to respond to them.

And All Hell Was Unleashed

That summer when Hugo had died marked the beginning of a long hard period of sadness. For many, those who knew Hugo and those who never heard of him. In the lives of Pia Odak, Gregor Truba, Veronika Truba and some others, the event of losing Hugo brought uncertainty.

Veronika didn't know where to go to survive.

A week prior to the party organised by the Bonifacio family, Pia went to visit Veronika. She quietly knocked on the door and nothing came from the other side. Gregor was standing next to Pia and said, *"Just enter, she is in."* and Pia did.

Veronika was sitting on her bed, knees gathered under her chin, soft sad music coming from her Walkman; she looked at Pia and gave her a little sad smile.

"Pia, there is no more Hugo in this room."

"I know, Lonnie. There is no Hugo here, but only in his physical form. Let's talk about him and he'll be here, believe me, that's how I've kept my mum alive all these years. I just kept on talking to her. Lonnie, Pia loves Lonnie, yes?"

Veronika smiled and hugged her friend.

"You have to come, otherwise I'd feel like an alien. There will be three families at the same event divided by nationality and religion, yet, united by a single person – me, Pia Odak. They are crazy, they can't stand let alone tolerate each other, can you imagine what deep shit I am dipping myself into? If you don't come, I will definitely be feeling like an alien. You said that your mother was weird and crazy; you should meet my crowd. This is a unique opportunity for you to witness madness at its best. You'll see my Nonna, like a show pony in her finest clothes and tonnes of golden jewellery, her husband dressed and combed the way she demanded... my Odak family, lawyers, doctors and bigwigs will be sitting on the other side of the room, far apart from

the Bonifacios with their noses up, touching the ceiling, not even noticing the circus of the Bonifacio monarch. Eloquent Italians and over-proud Croats. Then there will be my Granny Sava, the Serb from Lika, matriarch of the family from where I bear that family connection with the genius, Nikola Tesla, all quiet and introverted as if she were supposed to feel ashamed of who she is. Yes, regardless of the fact that they are the oldest and the most respectable family in the world not only in this, small, provincial country of ours. Please, come, join and witness the circus: the quiet war, national pride, crossing swords of smartness, showing off lost glory... and much more. Then you'll know that every family is actually a collection of a variety of characters and when they are forced to sit at the same table the real comedy begins. Your brother will be there to cheer us up with some music. Say that you are coming and you'll make me happy, and apart from my quiet, modest Granny, you'll be the only one to be really interested in me, the real Pia, without any expectations. Lonnie's coming, yes?"

"*Lonnie's coming, yes!*" said Veronika and wiped her nose.

"*You left your story, the eulogy, on my desk.*"

"*Never mind; it doesn't serve any purpose any more. Throw it away.*"

"*May I publish it in my new poetry collection. There will be a few stories as well. May I call it 'Veronika's Last Words to her Little Alien'?*"

Veronika nodded her head and wiped her nose.

"*You are so different, Pia, to any other person on this earth.*"

"*So are you, we are two Little Aliens on this planet Earth, yeah?*"

"*Yeah, we are.*"

***

The entire week in the Bonifacio household was a busy one: the telephone was ringing constantly as Mrs. Bonifacio wanted to have everything under her control – the venue, the interior, the flower arrangements, the candles, the menu, the pianist… every detail she demanded to be to her exquisite taste and to the minuscule whim of her sadistic need for perfection or, to show off her knowledge in exclusive elegance and decadent opulence. She endlessly checked on: the chefs, the waitresses, the pianist whom she knew personally; she called the hair-dresser several times to remind him of their appointment; she called her favourite clothing shop in Trieste to let them know she was coming; she checked on invitations countless times to make sure that she hadn't overlooked anything. Her hand-written invitations were spotless; every comma checked time and again, the spacing between lines was just perfect; everything that came from the Bonifacios had to be perfect. She knew there would be a great audience and she wanted to shine. It was her time to shine!

The restaurant that was booked was on the promenade; the last one in the row of old buildings and if it weren't for a wall, the tables would almost touch the stones that were immersed in the sea.

White, white, white predominated as if it were a christening. She even demanded a white piano over the black one that was in the corner. A white one was brought in and placed in the middle. The pianist had to be her best friend's son, Giorgio Alessi, a young man who studied music in Milan. She never asked Pia about him playing at the event, but she thought that'd be such a great surprise and who would be better for such an occasion than young Giorgio, a talented, yet modest, young man of Italian descent. She thought that the task of playing the piano so finely, no Croat or God-forbid Serb, would ever be able to take up. Well, at least not at this fine party.

The event itself was scheduled just one week prior to Christmas. Naturally, it was booked on Saturday, and she knew that many people would be out to witness such splendour. Journalists would be invited for a pre-party cocktail at the bar.

She had her hands tied as she promised not to invite Luna. It appeared that she was upset about it, but the feeling that she would have the grand opportunity to show off what the Bonifacio family was capable of organizing for their only granddaughter, prevailed. Though, she did advise Luna very plainly about it the week before. She visited Luna, who was painting her nails purple but when she saw her mother entering the Gallery, she moved the nail-polish away and put her head onto the counter saying:

"Santo Cielo, what happened to bring you here, your highness?"

"Pia's having a party and I am the one organising it. You haven't been invited and you know very well why you haven't. All I am asking of you is to keep away and to be on your best behaviour…"

She never managed to finish her stream of thought as Luna interrupted with her deep voice bouncing through the slow sentences:

"You are asking me to be on my best behaviour? Wow! What exactly does that mean, my dearest Mummy? Is it that someone, maybe you, or your grand-daughter are expecting me to do something inappropriate? When did I do anything inappropriate? When wasn't I on my best behaviour? I understand: I am not welcome. Don't you worry, Mother; I don't even care. I wouldn't come even if I were invited. Do you think that I care about Pia and her party? No, Mother, I do not! Go freely and enjoy your party. Show off! We, Bonifacios are exceptional in the art of showing off, in the perfect art of acting. Pia has always been surrounded by second-rate actors and her father had been such a cheap crew director. Very fine company where Luna Averna has never been welcomed. Go, Mummy, go, and have a nice party, you and that screwed up doll with her 'exceptional gifts'. But, Mum, no one is exceptional in that family; we have all been victims of a grand illusion – a malady that runs through our family. Close the door!"

She moved her nail polish closer and reassumed the previous pastime. She whistled or mumbled a melody while her mother angrily slammed the door. Luna said:

"Yeah, break the glass, that'll cure the anger that's been running through your veins since WWII."

Mrs. Bonifacio had better luck when she travelled to Trieste. She had only two shops where she would set her distinguished foot in. One was a clothing boutique and the other was a shop where the finest leather was turned into shoes, bags, clutches and belts.

After some suggestions and alternations she bought a long beige dress with tiny pearls around the neckline; she bought a waist-long mink fur coat and a silk shawl. In the leather shop she bought a pair of cream shoes with a black bow and the clutch that went with them perfectly.

For Pia, she went into a jewellery shop together with her husband to buy a twenty-four-carat gold necklace with twelve rubies. It cost a fortune. A fortune! But, they were the Bonifacios and they had only one granddaughter. The present was expensive and the wrapping was exquisite: the paper said it all.

***

Granny Sava had only two material things that she considered to be of exceptional value. One was a wedding ring from her mother that she thought she might give to Pia when she got married one day in the future, and the other was a small golden wristwatch that belonged to Nikola Tesla's mother. It never ended up in a single museum but stayed in the possession of that part of the Tesla family.

She took the watch out of the box and checked it out. It said *Gallet* across the round watch; it was not so small, a mechanical watch that Nikola sent to his mother from New York, sometime in 1890, as she was told. The watch stopped exactly at quarter to seven. She wound it up and the pleasant, quiet, ticking brought it back to life. She smiled as the watch took her back under the oak tree; the big wooden table laid out for a number of people; her mother called her in the house and said:

"Open the box." Next to her mother aunt Anka stood with a smile on her face.

When Sava saw the watch, she almost fainted out of excitement stricken with unbelievable beauty of the mechanical watch. It was made of two different colours: the colour of old gold and the copper coloured gold. Its hands were tiny; they looked like laced arrows pointing – the smaller to number two, and the longer to number seven.

The table outside was laid in her honour when she had graduated from the Medical School in Vienna. There were distinguished and less distinguished guests: priests, one engineer and lots of common people – the Tesla family, and they were expecting other guests whom Sava's mother and aunt had never met before. Sava said:

"Mother, I don't deserve it!"

"You do!"

Aunt Anka said:

"Do you know who the watch belonged to?"

"To Mother."

"Nikola's mother, grand aunt Djuka."

"Oh, I don't deserve it!"

The two women smiled, while her mother tried to fix the watch on Sava's wrist. That was the day when the Odak family came over for lunch and asked Sava's hand in marriage.

The day before the party, Granny Sava called Pia to come over.

When she came they sat on the big bed in Granny's bedroom.

"How are you, Pia?"

"I am not looking forward to the party, Granny. I fear that something stupid might happen, we are such a different bunch of people, but I suppose I have to put up with it just for one day. If I had been asked I would never have made a big deal out of it."

"Let it be, make us proud one last time. Don't take things so seriously, keep it light."

Then she handed the box to Pia, and when she opened the box, she started to examine the watch carefully but with awe.

"Wow, an antique Gallet."

"This watch, I wanted to give to your mother, but it skipped one generation. I think you'll be the proud owner of it now."

"Was it yours? I have never seen you wearing this watch, I mean, I have never seen the watch itself."

"No, because I kept it in the safe. I kept it for your mother, but... as she has passed I just waited for the right moment... and here we are, it is yours now. I hope you like it."

"Like it? I love it, Granny! Thank you! Is it the watch that grandfather gave you when you got married?"

"No. This wristwatch belonged to the Tesla family. When I graduated my mother gave it to me. It belonged to her. And you know, it has great value, not only because it is an antique golden watch, but because Nikola bought it for his mother, our grand aunt Djuka, when he was in the States."

"Thanks Granny; thanks! This is the best present that I have ever been given. I am afraid to wear it."

"Well, it is not something that one would wear every day and just anywhere. It is very special; for special occasions, I'd say. I wore this watch only twice in my life: on the day of my wedding, and on the day when your father married Gemma. She noticed the watch and said – 'What a beautiful watch', and now I regret that I never gave it to her."

"You have given it to me, Granny."

"Tell me, who is that young, blond man? Is he the brother of the late little Angel?"

"Yes, he is Hugo's elder brother Gregor."

"Do you fancy him?"

"Oh, Granny!"

"You do, don't you?"

"I think I do, but..."

"Don't say 'but', he looks to me like a good young man."

"I hope he is."

"Go now, Pia. You have a busy day tomorrow. And don't leave without a kiss on the cheek."

***

When Pia had left her Granny she went to the Old City Tavern. Gregor was already there. He kissed her gently and stroking her long hair, said:

"Our kids are going to be the most beautiful kids on earth."
"Crazy?"
"Crazy, why?"
"Because you are."
"Crazy about you."
"Talk about something else."
"About this?" he said and pulled a little box out of his pocket.
"What is it? I don't want any presents."
"It isn't a present, just a declaration of my love."
"Please..."
"Have a look, nothing shocking."

Pia opened the box and there was a little book made of white crystal, and on the cover of the crystal book was engraved – *"Pia, my Poetess'.*

"Wow!" Pia said. He smiled and said:

"I knew you'd like it. I could have easily bought you a ring, knelt down on one knee and proposed to you, I wouldn't have had a problem with it as I know what I want, but, knowing you, I saw the film unwinding: Pia throwing the ring on the floor, all in tears running away – 'How dare you insult me like that, you devil!' So, I gave up on that idea; reserved it for the year 2099 until you gain trust and respect in this vandal. Till then, the little book of honesty will do."

"Are you sure you wanna play tomorrow?"

"Nothing can change reality, Pia. I cry in my heart every day. Life without Hugo will never be the same, it is especially hard for Veronika, I have to admit that they loved each other most, they shared something special, on a level that no one ever related to anyone in our family. They had some mad connection as if they were one soul. She is really crushed, and I thank you ever so much for being there for her as I see that you are the only person she respects. Veronika is much more mature than I had believed. I think I've never really understood her, maybe from now on, as we have both lost a brother, I can make more effort to understand her better."

"Don't try too hard!" Pia warned him.

Pia said that she had a strange feeling, almost a premonition that *'something could happen... something unpleasant...'* but Gregor stopped her. He said, *"Let life flow, you don't have to control it, your relatives are going to behave the way they want to, and that doesn't mean anything to anyone... we are all a mixed bunch in this city, we co-exist, I know exactly what you mean by that, but who gives a shit about their generation, they still talk about WWII, can it get any sillier?"*

"I don't worry about them, I know who they are, or who I am, what annoys me is that I really don't want to put up with all that circus only to please them. No one really cares about me. Tell me then, why did I give in?"

"Because you are too kind."

"Too weak."

"No. Too kind. After this you don't have to participate, ever again, in something like that... anyway, when we get married we won't have all this circus... just you and I."

"Bugger off!" she said and threw his hand that was caressing hers on the other side of the table poking her tongue out.

After a long time, or perhaps, for the first time in her life, Pia understood what that feeling was like – to trust someone absolutely. It was a fine feeling, one that had lifted that constant heavy presence on her chest that caused poor breathing occasionally, and loss of control when it came to verbal expression and where the written word had not been taken into consideration.

***

In the early evening of December 17th, 1986 Pia walked into the *'Seahorse'*, a charming restaurant that served the best seafood in the region, holding hands with Gregor Truba. Her *Nonna* was already there behaving like a conductor of a fine orchestra giving orders naturally, effortlessly as if that were her effortless nature – giving orders and pointing the finger at executors of her will. Workmen were fixing the piano in the middle of the main dining room and for *Nonna* it was a matter of millimetres: shall it go a half-millimetre to the left or to the right and other fine tunings of an obsessed mind.

"We never talked about the piano, Nonna. Gregor just came in to check out the room, what is the matter with the piano?"

"Giorgio Alessi is coming soon to check the piano, it has been tuned but he'll give it a last check."

"Who the hell is Giorgio Alessi, a piano-tuner?"

"No, you know Giorgio Alessi, the youngest boy from the Alessi family, he is going to play this evening."

"Who said so?"

"I said so."

"Come over here, Nonna."

They moved to the reception desk and Pia said:

"Take this telephone, Nonna, and call Giorgio Alessi. Tell him there is no need to come this evening because we are not in need of his fine talent. OK? Do you understand me?

"That's impossible, Pia! He is the son of my dear friend, and I have already talked to his mother, he's agreed to play, he is the finest player one can get here."

"Stop it! Right now. If you don't call your friend and cancel the pianist, I shall call my friends, the rest of the Odak family and I shall cancel the event. Am I making myself clear? I don't want you to make a circus of this event, am I clear enough? No, don't interrupt! I just want to say that I have agreed and let you organise this party, but you didn't ask for anything as if the whole thing were of no concern to me. I don't wish anyone to play at my party but Gregor. Is that absolutely clear to you? You can now call those people and tell them whatever you wish, if you want me to come this evening with the rest of my family that you, despise so much, anyway."

Nonna's hands were visibly shaking and she was red in the face, she wanted to say something, but Pia elegantly turned her back swinging on her heels and walked out. She went to the kitchen and had a few words with the chef, then called Gregor and walked away.

She knew that *Nonna* would follow her instructions, oh yes; she knew that, for *Nonna* couldn't bear not to show her glitz and glamour to her Italian community. It was all about her status, to show that their star had never darkened in those new times under the new flag, but shone even brighter through her distinguished granddaughter, the offspring of the Bonifacios.

At eight o'clock the guests started to arrive at the bar; there was a cocktail-party organised for journalists and anyone who wanted to attend or walk in. Nonna Oriana was at the centre of attention answering journalists' questions; Pia wasn't present yet, as dinner was booked for nine o'clock.

Gregor came accompanied by his best mate Davor just after eight to set up the guitars and amplifier. The piano was pushed against the wall; Gregor and Davor organised a little stage around the piano and fixed two chairs for their guitars.

Slowly the guests started to move to the dining room and took to their seats where the names were written next to the sets of plates positioned on the white tablecloth. Naturally, the Bonifacio family was placed at the outermost distance from the Odaks; in between there were friends while Pia's place was reserved next to Nonna Oriana. She placed Gregor next to Pia's uncle Boris, the most inappropriate place for Gregor, who was meant to play, anyway, and only sit at the table during short intervals. There was no space at the table for Davor, who was to play that evening on Gregor's invitation as Barbara Milich was one of Pia's best friends and Davor was Barbara's boyfriend. Gregor's sister Veronika was seated between Pia's Granny Sava and Sava's son Simon, Pia's father.

***

Veronika never believed that she would ever overcome Hugo's death. She cried every night, she cried as a little puppy does: yelping and whimpering all night long, calling his name reluctant to sleep as if the sleep itself would bring some relief. She was in need of no relief, believing that if she didn't suffer twenty-four-seven she would somehow *'betray her love and pain for Hugo'*. At sunrise, when the first rays lit her room, she would look at the stars that she had painted for him, and she would sing songs that Hugo liked, singing through tears and saliva rolling down on her pillow. Gregor tried several times to talk to her but she was reluctant, Gregor was *'just a brother'* whereas Hugo was *'an Angel, a friend, an Alien and the greatest love'*. The greatest love she had lost and couldn't get over. She felt as if her heart were ripped out of her chest and there was just an empty hole that no future event would be big or loving enough to fill.

Since Hugo went in search of angels she was never able to talk to her mother or to look her in the eye again. Mother Elsa wrapped herself in dark clothes to show the world how much she mourned, but she never had the guts to talk to Veronika. Since Hugo's passing they never had a family lunch or dinner together. Elsa and Anton ate together, Gregor ate, without any order, whenever he would pop in, and Veronika, only when she couldn't stand hunger any longer, would tip-toe into the kitchen, take some food into her room and lock the door again. To her solitude in her tower of tears only Pia had the key. She could enter and sit next to Veronika and hold her hand wipe her tears or nose or tell her without risking the loss of a friendship, *"It'll get easier with time, believe me, I know."* Veronika knew that Pia *'knew'* but somehow, Veronika didn't believe that it would get better, how on earth, could she ever get over the fact that she had lost someone so pure and loving, so innocent and full of light?

But she had agreed to come to Pia's party; she loved Pia. It seemed to Veronika that all the Truba siblings loved Pia in their unique way: Hugo without reservation with the purest heart, Gregor loved her with the might of a young heart and desire, and Veronika loved Pia like a sister that she never had and yet knew that this person would be the best possible sister ever, if only providence had enough sensibility and kindness to bring them together.

Veronika put on a dress and a pair of shoes that were too tight, as if from that sadness and abundance of tears her whole body had swollen.

She came almost last to the *'Seahorse'*, timid and sad, and she hadn't had the guts to walk in all by herself. She asked the man at the door about Pia, but the man said that if she had the invitation she could enter. Veronika hesitated and stood by the lamppost as if waiting for someone. She saw, through the window, the group of about thirty people sitting at the table; there were quite a number of empty chairs and she saw her brother in the corner seated with his guitar, chatting to a man who looked familiar but whom she couldn't recognise from the distance. She felt like crying. Then a car stopped and she saw a long, bare leg, so elegant and finely crafted that Veronika knew could only be the leg of one finely created person – her one and only friend – Pia. When Pia came out Veronika wanted to run away: Pia looked like the most beautiful mermaid sketched on a of a fairy-tale and Veronika felt that she wasn't worthy of Pia's friendship, but Pia turned her head and their eyes met.

"Thanks for coming."

Pia said enthusiastically and hugged her friend. They walked in together and when Pia found out that odd order of placing people, she tried to shuffle what was possible to reshuffle. In the end, she was happily seated next to her Granny and Veronika.

When the guests were seated and the aperitif was poured, Gregor started to sing, a gentle tune of the song that he had written for his girlfriend.

Pia's father stood up and started the evening with his speech, taking away attention from Gregor's fine verses and melody. He spoke about Pia as his own project, about her achievements which came naturally as she was his daughter, the daughter of a gifted actor and theatre director. He spoke of her beauty which was inherited from strong, tall and good-looking generations of women in their family. He spoke of his efforts to give her the best as a single father and of her literary achievements that, once again, came from his talents as everyone knew about his plays, dramas, radio-dramas and operatic librettos too. Yes, everybody knew who Simon Odak was and everybody knew that Pia was his daughter, hence no surprise that she had inherited all his talents. Pia looked at the tablecloth and smiled. Granny Sava looked at Pia and smiled. Veronika, too, smiled and everyone else was clapping. Some were clapping loudly, the Bonifacios pretended to clap, their hands were not touching or making any sound; Simon raised his glass and said:

"To my daughter, to Pia!"

231

Everyone raised their glasses and said in one voice:

"To Pia!"

Pia didn't raise her glass but said to Veronika and Granny:

"Ode to Simon Odak."

He came closer, kissed Pia several times, hugged his mother whilst his brother Ivan took several photos of the three of them.

Jure Odak stood up and said:

"I'll keep it short. My beloved granddaughter has achieved what few of her age have done and we are all proud of her. I wish you, Pia, all the best in your future. Keep on winning, keep on shining, that's my girl!"

Clapping again. Pia just smiled.

Jure looked at his wife Sava and gave her a nod, encouragement to stand up and talk, but Granny just hugged Pia and said something in her ear. Pia smiled and hugged her grandmother without saying a word. On her wrist there was the beautiful *Gallet* watch that her grandmother gave her a day earlier.

Nonna Oriana spoke in Italian. Her speech was lengthy and the truth is that not many understood it, therefore people started to talk amongst themselves which angered *Nonna* who then spoke louder. The louder she talked, the louder the guests became, some started to laugh, Gregor started to play the guitar again, in the end *Nonna* gave up her speech, then loudly, at the top of her voice, in solid Croatian, she said:

"I present you Pia with this beautiful present that the Bonifacio family has planned for you for some years. You are the only child of our late daughter who was a brilliant and talented painter and sculptor, as everyone knows. Our daughter passed away young, due to very sad circumstances, she was way too young to get married and we were of a different opinion when it came to marriage…"

Her husband started to talk to her, to calm her down and took the present from her hands and gave it to Pia. Pia felt sad and confused, she took the unwrapped present and hugged her grandfather telling him how grateful she was. *Nonna* continued to talk to the couple seated next to her, explaining how her daughter, Gemma Bonifacio was a talented and kind person, too young, far too young to marry anyone, especially someone who wasn't ready to get married himself... Then Pia sat next to her *Nonna* and said:

"Let's have a look at the present."

Pia was never really impressed with expensive jewellery, but regardless she said:

"This is breathtaking, Nonna. Only you could come up with something like this."

Nonna nodded her head and started to sob. Pia hugged her knowing that *Nonna* was sobbing not out of emotions, but out of anger: she wasn't heard properly, no one really paid enough attention to her gift and, no one was aware that she was the one who had put so much effort and style into organising such a great party.

Pia whispered into Veronika's ear to tell Gregor to play some happy tunes and the atmosphere changed a little. Dinner was served and conversation took place between people who found themselves at ease in each other's company. The Odaks stayed aloof from the Bonifacios, they only nodded heads and smiled politely when their eyes met. But grandfather Jure went over to shake hands, and Granny Sava congratulated *Nonna* for being a great organiser.

The evening took on almost a pleasant turn; Pia smiled, looked at Gregor several times and winked, blew kisses and smiled again.

It was almost a bearable evening for her.

***

Pia had opened only one present; the necklace *Nonna* bought just to make *Nonna* happy like a little child had to be happy when witnessing the joy of one receiving her gift.

The rest of the presents were taken to the reception. Everyone brought a present and there were numerous bouquets of flowers.

Only *Nonna* noticed and whispered in her husband's ear:

"The Odaks didn't give her anything."

"Shush! How do you know that?"

"They didn't. I was watching carefully. No one: none of the uncles or the grandparents brought anything. Stingy bastards."

"Ah, shut up, woman! How do you know if they have or haven't?"

"If they had, they would show it off."

"Not everyone is a show-off like you."

"Am I? Am I a show-off? I am, actually, the one who has organised this party, the one who has brought a proper present. What kind of people are they? Yet they act as if they were God's given gift to this city, all bigwigs!"

"Will you shut up?"

"OK, OK, I will shut up, but they have showed who they are, numerous times."

Nonna stood up and walked to Gregor, saying:

"Can you sing any Italian songs? I thought here would be someone who played the piano, but… It was Pia's wish to bring two Croats with guitars."

Gregor took the chair under the piano, sat down, back straight, pulled his hair into a ponytail, and started to play. Prior to commencing he stood up and said:

"'Ti Voglio Bene Assai', for my girlfriend, the best person that ever walked the streets of our town". He played *Caruso*. He sang. Pia smiled. *Nonna* sang along; Italians joined in singing and clapping hands; Davor sat next to Barbara and ate the cake; Pia thanked him for coming and once again she concluded: when *Nonna* was happy, and Simon Odak as well, it looked as if the whole crowd was happy.

They were the two strongest personalities that fought for attention and recognition in various ways – her father and Nonna Oriana, but Pia looked at them with a gentle smile and kind of gratitude.

To flatter Nonna Oriana and her distinguished crowd Gregor started to croon loudly, pretentiously *'C'e la Luna Mezz'o Mare'* every time replacing words *'mamma mia'* with *'Nonna mia'* and the Italian family whistled and clapped.

DETHRONED

How could one have a *'festa'* without *'La Luna Mezz'o Mare'*?

Pia was gently swinging her head - was it in approval or disapproval; only she knew. The owner of the restaurant came to Pia's father and whispered into his ear. Simon Odak called Pia, she came up slowly, still smiling and Simon said:

"Apparently, there is a young man at the door, he wants to talk or maybe give you something. Do you want to see him or do you want me to talk to him?"

"I'll go."

When she came to the door, yes, there was a young man, a very young man, not older than sixteen or seventeen, standing at the side of the building. He smiled at Pia and asked:

"Pia?"

"Yes, that's me."

"Here, a present for you."

Pia carefully took the wrapped object unable to form any opinion in her mind, it was covered with surprise; the young boy turned his back and walked away, leaving Pia with the present she held so carefully as if a bomb itself were wrapped in that fine paper and just about to explode.

She walked in, they were still singing, for the second time *'C'e la Luna Mezz'o Mare'*; no one noticed the puzzled look on Pia's face. Slowly she unwrapped the present and found a little box and violet-coloured letter.

She opened the box and there was a chain in it. On its pendant it was crafted: *I love you, Pia*.

Her hands trembled, the voices sang louder *'C'e la Luna'*… she took the letter and turned it around twice, opened the envelope and took out the purple leaf of paper folded in half.

"I wish you many more successes in your future. But be aware of the one that looks like success but might turn out to be a failure in the future. Your boyfriend ordered this chain for you, but being poor as a church mouse he hadn't had the money to pay for it, so we agreed that the payment would be as I

chose, he never hesitated – not for a second, not because he wanted me badly, but because he is a lustful, greedy bastard. But that bastard is the most endowed and gifted lover, inexhaustible and experienced, though not trustworthy. He loves women, especially those that look like Pia, who he claims he loves! On his right thigh, next to his groin he has a rather small mole that resembles a cross, on the small of his back he has a tattoo: several vertical lines, a treble clef and a few musical notes thoughtfully arranged on the lines… very original. All the best Pia Odak, enjoy your evening.

Your one and only aunt, Luna Averna."

'*C'e la Luna Mezz'o Mare'*… continued to sing Gregor Truba, in an attempt to entertain and, at the same time, mock the Italians.

Pia left the necklace on the white tablecloth, took the purple leaf of paper, walked slowly as if she weren't in her epic mood, she came to Gregor, lifted his guitar which was leaning against the chair and smashed it onto the piano. She threw the letter into his face and screamed, *"You slept with her, you awful, ignorant idiot!"* and she ran out through the open door.

'*C'e la Luna Mezz'o Mare'* stopped at once and cold silence filled the room as if cold water had been poured through invisible pipes; the water froze the scene instantly and the people sat there holding the same position they held prior to the freeze that took possession of the room. It looked like a scene from Sleeping Beauty. Only Gregor Truba was turning the violet paper from one side to another unable to grasp what had just happened in this room full of well-wishers, full of seemingly happy people who gathered together to show the continuously unhappy Pia, utmost respect and pride.

"What happened?!"

That was the question on everyone's lips.

The first person to react was Pia's uncle Ivan. He stood up and walked over to the bewildered Gregor.

He simply said:

"May I have this piece of paper?"

"It's private."

"Hand it over, don't make it harder for yourself. Just hand it over."

And Gregor did. He handed over the letter with trembling hands, without a word, for he was not able to speak, his lower jaw danced to the rhythm of the song which was interrupted and stopped in the middle – *'C'e la Luna...'*

II

London

(1987-1993)

Nikki

The telephone rang, Nikki, still sleepy, answered unaware that it was Sunday. *'Who would ring that early in the morning?'* passed through her head as she was reaching for the receiver.

"How on earth did you get my number? Don't call, ever again! Don't call!"

She put the receiver back down and dived under the duvet.

"Who was it?"

"No one, wrong number."

"A wrong number in your language?"

"Strange, hey? Sleep, it's early."

But she had got up. She couldn't sleep after hearing his voice. She didn't feel anything for him, anything, but still, she couldn't get back to sleep. She went to the kitchen, brewed a strong coffee, lit a cigarette and looked through the window – yet another cold, rainy day, *"As cold as my heart"* she said loudly and brought the cup to the window. Rain! Why did rain bring back memories? The only memory Nikki wanted to take with her from her hometown was the memory of her beloved Hugo. There were a number of pictures of Hugo in her house, and she was still in the habit of talking to him. Every day. She would report to him everything, everything that had happened since that horrid evening when some guy, called Gregor Truba, played *'C'e la Luna Mezz'o Mare'* and spoiled the party… spoiled much more than just a party.

***

She arrived in London in January 1987 with just one suitcase and the address of a person who *'might be willing to help her settle in.'*

His name was Theodor Lukas. He was in his late fifties; she had heard of him some years earlier when he performed on national TV. He was an acclaimed pianist, a man from her hometown, whose great talent, in those years, was shadowed by his sexuality. He was *'an openly gay man'*, the title that landed him in trouble in countless ways in the sixties. But his extraordinary talent led him to earn a scholarship, so he had found himself among the world's best up and coming pianists, studying at the prestigious Royal Academy of Music, in London.

He lived in a big Victorian house on the edge of a park, and prior to pressing the bell she felt weakness in her knees, *'What if he tells her off?'*, *'What if he had never heard about Pia Odak or her family?'*, *'What if he had heard about Pia Odak and her family but asks – What of it?'*, *'What if he shuts the door in her face without a word?'*... too many *'what ifs'* were buzzing in her head. When the door opened she stood there unable to open her mouth. A young man in colourful pyjamas and a silky mauve dressing gown answered the door. She looked at him and he said:

"In, in..." and lost himself in a dark corridor. She hesitated; that couldn't be Mr Lukas; she remembered him from that evening show, but the young man behaved as if that were his house, *'Maybe it was'* she thought, but then, *'Could it be that Pia gave me the wrong address?'* and one more loud question in her head was, *'Did he expect me and did his 'room-mate, or relative or butler' know who I was and just let me in?'* She followed him and found herself in a huge living area or a library, with large windows overlooking a bushy garden.

The young man in pyjamas was sitting, reading a book aloud. She couldn't grasp to whom he was reading poetry as she did not notice anyone in the room except for a Burmese cat that was leisurely spreading her fat body on the sofa opposite, upholstered in yellow silk or satin. She stood there holding her bags: her handbag on the right shoulder and the other bag in her left hand. It was rather heavy but she didn't feel like putting it down on the floor without permission.

When he stopped reading, he looked at her and said:

"What are you looking at? Aren't you going to sit down?"

She sat down without saying a word. She was looking around this big decadent place full of books, two pianos, small drums, numerous armchairs, two sofas and countless paintings on all of the walls, literally; the walls were crammed from the ceiling down to the floor, wherever it was possible, with stunning paintings.

The young man continued to read poetry annunciating words at random. Sporadically he laughed, or repeated the verse louder as if he were reading it to someone who was in the other room. *'Well, that's a thought! Maybe he was reading it to someone who was still in their bedroom, or the kitchen, or even in the garden.'* She was more at ease with that thought than the other – that the young man was a little bit odd: he let her in without asking who she was, he told her to sit down as if he knew who she was, and he was reading poetry at midday to his indifferent cat. *'How long shall I sit here without being asked any questions? Shall I ask for Mr Lukas when he finishes his reading?'*

She was reminded that she was hungry when the smell of toasted bread entered her nostrils. Someone called out in a not-so-loud voice:

"Brunch's ready, my Parrot."

The young man continued to read louder, then said, *'Let me finish'* and when he finished reading, he looked at his quiet and confused guest, and said:

"C'mon, let's eat!"

She followed the young man who was addressed as *Parrot* and they walked into the dining room that had a similar view, but from this view they could see the neighbouring house: white, big, well kept, with a splendid garden.

The table was laid for two people; the man who was already seated was unwrapping the morning papers, he looked at them and said:

"Oh, you brought a friend."

The young man or Parrot nodded, which added to her confusion. The older man said:

"Then, my dear, you should get out a plate for the young lady, I am not getting up anymore."

Parrot placed a plate and a cup on the table while the older man was reading the papers and humming.

They never asked her anything, so after they finished their *brunch*, and Parrot served more tea, she said in a tiny, insecure voice and wobbly English:

"Who is Mr Lukas?"

"Who is Mr Lukas? That is a good question! Who is Mr Lukas?"

The older man said that and continued to read. The younger man said:

"I am afraid we would never answer that question. The question is queer."

"Queer? What is queer?" She asked, not knowing the meaning of the word.

"That's another good question! What is queer, anyway? Who is queer, anyway? OK kids, I am off to my room. I have some work to do. Ciao Parrot, don't interrupt me today, feed the pussy, that's the only thing you have to do today. Have fun!"

He simply stood up; breadcrumbs were flying down from his beard to his belly, from his belly down onto the carpet. He was a stocky, short man and he looked older than she remembered seeing him on national TV some years before. But, *'Was that really him?'* that was the question she was not sure she could answer positively.

"Do you wanna give me a hand?"

Without a word she extended her hand towards him.

"What?" he asked.

"You asked for my hand?"

Hysterical laughter followed, he bent his knees and held his stomach with both hands, he laughed as a mean little child would. When he stopped he wiped off the tears, then a new bout of laughter came and he started to laugh again, stamping his foot onto the floor. She stood there and waited. Finally he said:

"So, you don't speak English, do you?"

"Not much."

"I never asked you, who are you?"

"Veronika."

"Nay! Nikki."

"No, Veronika is my name."

"I'll call you Nikki."

"OK, if you wish."

"What's your story Nikki?" he asked as he started to tidy up the table.

"A story?"

"Yes, your story, who are you? Why did you come here? I thought you were Theo's masseuse, but you are not. So, what brought you here?"

It wasn't fear, but some sort of weakness that came over her and she started to sob. He opened his mouth, covered it with his slim hand and said:

"Oh, no, she is crying!" as if he had never seen a person in distress. He didn't know what to do but just waited with his hand covering his mouth.

"What now for me?"

"Where do you live, Nikki?"

"Nowhere."

"That's a common address, I'd say. What brought you here?"

"The man. Is this short man Theodor Lukas?"

"Hmm, never call him a short man, ever. Yes, he is Theo Lukas, but he doesn't know you, does he?"

"I am from the same place as he is, I got his address from my friend. A good friend. My best friend. She gave me his address. He played on TV, I know him from TV."

"Ouch! That's not good. You come here believing... what?"

Her chin started to shake, and she was about to start crying again. Parrot put his hand around her shoulder and said:

"Sit down. Nikki, where do you live now?"

"I came today from my country. I have this address only."

"I see. Why did you come?"

"Complicated story."

"OK. Listen, you can't tell Theo that you came from his hometown with this piece of shit", he said pointing his finger at the paper where the address was written in a neat handwriting.

"He is absolutely, I mean – absolutely, listen to me: absolutely allergic to people who telephone him, come to his door or stalk him in the restaurant

saying that they came from the same country. This is the wrong card. If you had said that before, he would have kicked you out without mercy, no tears would have ever worked. He doesn't like to be associated with his ex-country and its people. Do you really know who he is?"

She swung her head and wiped her nose.

"Shit! Shit! Shit! He said and offered her a tissue.

"What do I do now?"

"Do you have any friends? Anyone you know?"

"No one."

"Shit!"

"Do you have money for a cheap inn?"

"Not much. Just a little."

"Not much – just a little, that's shit as well. So, I don't know what to do with you."

She cried again. In that moment the man walked into the garden. He heard the sobbing and looking at them indifferently asked:

"Parrot, are we going out for a dinner?"

"Yes, yes…I think – yes."

"What am I going to wear, I wonder." He said and walked out.

Parrot said:

"Look, I can help you for just one day. Don't tell him anything. Never mention that you were given his address, don't mention people he might know, don't mention your country or anything. Zip up your mouth and smile at whatever he says. He will never ask about you, as he never asks about anyone, we'll pretend that you are my friend, just visiting. You can stay over for the night; I'll take you to the guest room. We are going out in the evening and you can stay, watch TV or talk to the cat, do whatever and tomorrow you've got the leave, OK?"

"OK."

Once again she was on the verge of tears, she never imagined that it'd be so difficult, so bloody difficult!

Parrot looked like a skinny rabbit. He spent the entire day in his silken pyjamas and velvety dressing gown, he was reciting poems all day long and was talking to the cat.

"I am going to pick up his suit, come with me."

He drove his car still in his pyjamas and his dressing gown, he stopped and she saw only one arm through the window handing him a suit covered in plastic; he drove back reciting odd verses and ignoring her. But she was grateful. Oh, yes, she was so grateful to this skinny parrot who let her in, this late morning, by sheer mistake.

While Parrot was preparing Theodor's shirt and suit, checking out socks, the cleanliness of his shoes, she followed him around. Parrot would give her a little look, then roll his eyes and smack his lips. Occasionally, he would wink at her and she winked back. None of them knew that it was just the beginning of a long sincere friendship, full of ups and downs, drama and swearing.

In Theodor's room as Parrot was helping him to get dressed, Nikki peeped through the door ajar: Theodor was standing like a big, fat child, obedient and annoyed while Parrot was fixing his collar, buttoning his shirt, pulling his sleeves and spicing up the moment with his shameless comments. They giggled like kids when Parrot poked him in his round belly.

When he came out of the room, he quickly said:

"When hungry open the fridge, watch the telly, read books, telephone friends and tell them you'll be back tomorrow."

"Back tomorrow? What friends?"

"I don't know, sweetie, make them up: Peter Pan or Captain Hook or whatever, but bye-bye, see you tomorrow morning, OK?"

Nikki nodded her head and her eyes filled with tears instantly.

"Don't you pull that crap on me."

Said Parrot with his index finger up.

The chauffer parked the car, Parrot helped Theodor into the car, then sat next to him. Veronika renamed Nikki, sat on the sofa and wondered, *'What comes next: Peter Pan or Captain Hook?'*

She learned that evening, quickly, that life comes in small doses, in little stories, in sketches, vignettes, when one door closes another opens. She learned that forcing an answer to an unsolved mystery could only wreck her mind. She took a book and started to read: it was a book written by one of her favourite Irish authors, but the book was written in her native language – Croatian.

Her reading didn't go far; exhausted by the swing of constant shocks of that particular day she fell asleep. The book fell out of her hand as she buried her head into a small pillow.

The next thing she remembered was Parrot's face close to hers, he was rocking her, waking her up:

"Go, go to your room, you silly girl. How old are you Nikki? Are you a bloody child?"

It was sometime before it dawned that Nikki laid her head on *'her pillow'*. She slept like a child.

She was awakened by the strong smell of coffee and some other pleasant aromas. She was afraid to get up, to show up, to say something or to face the day's consequences. When she washed her face she looked for Parrot. She found him in *'the piano room'*. He informed her that Theodor loves to, and always does, prepare his own breakfast.

"Thank you Parrot. I'll go now."

Theodor called out, *"Little Parrot!"* and Parrot said:

"OK, go."

Nikki took her bags and as she went down the corridor she saw them at the table.

They both looked at her, then Theodor said:

"Has she had her breakfast yet?" Breakfast was the most important meal in Theodor's life and he assumed that everyone should eat their breakfast prior to assuming any other activity.

Parrot stood up and hurried to Nikki; he whispered into her ear:

"Have breakfast with us. Don't mention anyone; don't say where you're from…just don't! Eat and keep your mouth occupied with food."

Parrot brought another plate and served Nikki with food; Theodor was eating and reading the newspapers while the two of them ate in silence.

Theodor was reading aloud and Parrot was mimicking Theodor's emotions and expressions as if he had to agree with him absolutely.

"Oh, I nearly forgot. You have to go to the airport to pick up Melinda. Don't you remember?"

"Sure, I remember. She is coming at eleven, don't you worry."

No one talked to grateful Nikki; she just ate as if she hadn't had any food for days. The breakfast was tasty: fried and boiled eggs, fat-free pancetta, prosciutto, smoked salmon and a variety of cheese; some pickles and cherry tomatoes and thick dark bread that reminded her of her mother Elsa for the first time.

Elsa was screaming when she walked out, as if she really cared.

She said:

"The devil woman killed my baby-son, she sent my other son to prison, she tore my family apart and now she is sending you away, too."

"You have your faithful friar-friend! Think about him! Wasn't he the one who tore your family apart? Burn in hell, together with him!"

She shook her head, she resolved not to think about those people any more, that was Veronika's life and just now she had commenced a new life – the life of Nikki: a life full of strange anticipation and anxiety, a life without a future on the horizon.

When they finished their breakfast in silence, Theodor rose and went into the garden looking up to the sky, probably speculating about the weather forecast, whilst Parrot hurried Nikki:

"Pick up your stuff, I'll give you a lift."

While he was driving, he said to quiet Nikki:

"If you wanna keep me company you can."

"Thank you, Parrot."

"Stop calling me Parrot, you silly girl. Call me Caesar."

"Like the emperor?"

"Yes!"

"Is that your real name?"

"Stop asking questions, take things as they come."

She shrugged her shoulders and sank deeper into the seat.

"OK, sorry, sorry, Queen of Sulkiness. Ask, ask whatever you want."

She asked him about the nature of his relationship with Theodor:

"Is he your boyfriend?"

"My boyfriend! God no!!"

"But..."

"Yes, we sleep together, we do things together, but he is not my boyfriend, my boyfriend is in Rome."

"Rome?"

"What's wrong now?"

"Oh! Nothing!"

"Better be! I have known Theodor for some years. I help him out with silly things, like organising social events, buying his clothes, answering his calls, but I never stay longer than a fortnight, then I got back to Rome and I stay with my boyfriend for a week, and then I come back, then I do my other job... happy with my life story?"

"Are you happy with your life story?"

"I couldn't care less."

"Same here."

"Well, whatever Nikki... I mean, if you wish to speak go on, if not, don't bother."

"I left my stupid family, that's all. They are hypocrites, liars, Mother is a religious fanatic, they are national elitists and in general people-haters."

"You come from good stock, Nikki. When exactly did you come to London?"

"Yesterday."

"What?"

"Yesterday."

"Are you kidding? Where were you before that?

"I just left my home. I just finished high school and left my home-town."

"Yesterday?"

"Yep."

"And you said you have no one here, am I right?"

"Yep."

"What are you going to do after I throw you out prior to collecting Melinda?"

"Don't know."

"Shit!"

"Shit."

The London traffic was appalling and to Nikki it looked like disorganised madness, where anybody, at any time, could be hit or killed. Caesar cursed every three to four seconds.

After some time Caesar said:

"I left my home when I finished high school, though not willingly as you did. I knew that my parents were hypocrites and liars, but I never had the balls to leave. To cut a long story short, my father had found out that his son was gay and just told me to 'stop acting out and find myself a girl or leave'. So, being exposed to so much love and care I left. Can you believe, that he said 'stop acting out'? Anyway, I left and found myself in a big, dirty city. Welcome to London Nikki!

"Have you ever seen them since?"

"No! That happened ten years ago. My older brother got married, he has a dozen kids, they are all christened and proper people, surely none of them will turn out to be gay."

"Where are you from?"

"Rome – The City of Love."

"You are Italian?"

"I am free from anything. Don't try to box me in."
"Sorry."
"Stop saying sorry all the time."
"Sorry."
"Shut up!"

Good knowledge of Italian was the greatest gift Nikki could have ever been given; she was able to communicate with Caesar without appearing silly, illiterate or stupid. When they greeted Melinda, Caesar casually said that *'his cousin Nikki'* would take her bags. *Cousin Nikki* obediently took the bags, carried them, then tossed them onto a trolley and with a spring in her step pushed the load.

So far Veronika had a new name and a new cousin. She hoped that her future, for at least several hours, would be predictable.

That late afternoon Theodor Lukas called Caesar and said:

"I am taking Melinda out. Tomorrow prepare the things, I want to check out everything before the concert."

When they left Caesar said:

"Let's call all the crazy people and have a mad party!" He started to make calls inviting people over. In a short time the house was full of people of different ages and different styles. They all knew each other as if they had been partying together since the dawn of the century. No one asked anything about her, she just sat there with a glass of champagne and looked at the colourful crowd.

No one was straight, no one was sober, no one was in a hurry or in a bad mood. Nikki thought to herself:

'Looks like Sodom and Gomorrah, but a very happy one.'

She rolled a joint and exhaled with a sense of ease and relief.

That night she slept in *'her room'* again, but the following morning Caesar said:

DETHRONED

"Hey Cuz, we gotta find you a room or something. You can't stay here end-lessly."

Caesar's *'other job'* was another wonder for Nikki. He was a dancer. A ballet dancer. It was her dream to study some sort of dance, she didn't know what exactly, but when Pia was helping her to obtain a visa through her connections, they stated that Nikki was going to study at a dance academy.

"Easy-peasy my crybaby! That's where I can really be helpful. Tomorrow you'll go with me to the rehearsal and you'll meet the right people."

When she hugged him, he said:
"Don't you dare!"

Destiny works its own course; it never follows one's wishes. Yes, Veronika had got the right address and she did knock on the right door, but, even though it was the address of someone who *'might have been able to help'*, it proved that he never even learned who Veronika was, but the door had opened and Veronika found the right person: *Parrot,* who turned out to be Caesar, the most unlikely friend she would ever earn.

Caesar introduced her to Carla, yet another Italian girl who came to find better opportunities in London. Carla was a dancer for a contemporary dance company, a drama queen who had to be, always, always, acknowledged as *'the best looking'*, *'the best dancer'*, *'the sexiest'* or *'just fantastic'*. Smart as she was, Nikki understood at once that paying Carla compliments would get her far. So she never left out of her vocabulary words like *'fantastic'*, *'breathtaking'*, *'the most beautiful'*, she never stopped clapping and smiling.

Carla lived with several people from her group; Caesar persuaded her and in the end she agreed to take Nikki on board.
"How am I going to pay rent?"
"One step at a time. What are you good at?"
"What do you mean by that?"

"Exactly as I asked – what are you good at? Any particular skill or knowledge?"

"No."

"Cleaning?"

"Cleaning!"

"Yes, princess, cleaning. I might suggest to Theo that he needs another cleaner."

"Another cleaner? He has one?"

"Of course he has one. But he comes fortnightly. I'll tell him that we need someone, just a couple of hours three times a week. Just to tidy up and clean the kitchen, as he hates it when the kitchen and dining room are not cleaned properly for him. The only thing he loves when it comes to domestic delights is preparing breakfast. He knows what he wants and the way he wants it done. He sings and mumbles and doesn't let anyone close while he is in the kitchen. But he demands total cleanliness. I'll see what I can do."

"Oh, Caesar, what would I do…"

"Hey, stop right there!!!"

Soon after Nikki found herself in employment, with shelter and enrolled in the Academy of Dance - she couldn't believe her luck. Did she ever think about her family, her hometown or the friends she had left behind? So far she didn't. The only person she missed was Pia Odak, but she promised that she wouldn't bother her for when she had left she promised a distressed Pia that she wouldn't contact her, but that Pia would find the way to contact Veronika when she thought the time was right. Too many things had happened and Nikki understood that Pia's decision was smart and just.

Carla was odd, way too odd for Nikki, but Nikki learned that she had to accept people the way they were if she wanted to survive in harsh London. Everyone was *'minding their own business'*, everyone had *'the right to do what they wanted to do'*, everyone in this group would easily burst into tears saying *'you don't even know me, so do not judge me'*… she learned that she had to be self-reliant but pleasant to others, she learned that her quick temper and the sharp remarks she exercised on her mother and Friar Marag were outgrown and unwelcome. She did put up with Carla's madness in the knowledge that, for the time being, it was the smartest strategy. She learned that what was important went by the name of – strategy, rather than an act of impulsiveness.

She would clean Mr Lukas's kitchen and the dining room three times a week, early in the morning, prior to his grand entrance into these holy places, then she would leave and attend her classes. In the evening she had found a job in the dirty kitchen of a Greek restaurant. She worked five evenings and never had time to do anything else but work and study.

Slowly, as time passed she had understood why Mr Lukas never wanted to be associated with people from his country. It was clear to her, as clear as a sunny day. Even though he would, probably, meet the better kind, not the ones Nikki met at her jobs and encounters; still, she understood that the best choice was to keep away from those troublemakers, harsh troublemakers.

The best days were when she had an opportunity to catch up with Caesar and spend a few hours with him. They would lie on his bed, in Mr Lukas's house, look out through the window and tell each other weird stories. Caesar had an abundance of such stories, while Nikki often made them up. Even thought, when she came up with some stories about her mother, like cutting off her braids, he said, *'Nay, you made this one up.'* He had many more stories than she had; he was twelve years older, twelve years longer a resident of this colourful, flamboyant and marginalised society of London. Nikki loved his parties, for one could never imagine that such characters existed except in surreal movies.

She never liked to say where she came from when asked by any random person. She reinvented her past, never wanting to mention the country of her origin or her hometown. She said to Caesar:

"I'd like to change my name."

"Change it!"

"I mean officially. I want the name Nikki to appear on my documents. I want to change my surname, too."

"What's your surname?"

"Bloody Truba. What's yours?"

"I have several, which one do you want to know?"

"The real one."

"I've forgotten it. Sometimes I go by Lukas when I am with Theo, sometimes I go by Smith, why not, yet another Smith in London, sometimes I go by Emperor... you get it, Caesar Emperor, ha-ha, that's usually met with a bit of, let's say, disbelief, then I ask – What? Is there something, like, unlikely about that, or what?"

"What does it say in your passport?"

"Caesar Domenico Barlow."

"Barlow?"

"Yes, sweetie, Barlow."

"Who the hell is Barlow?"

"Bartolli."

"You changed it into Barlow?"

"Yep!"

"Can I change mine into Barlow so that we can be real cousins?"

"Crazy, but yes! Let's go downtown and change that crap."

After living in London eight months, Veronika Truba had found new friends, a new career of her first choice, new opportunities and a new name – Nikki Barlow, the cousin of Caesar D. Barlow, *The Queen of Bullshit*, as he would title himself.

***

Beauty is in the eye of the beholder, yes, but no one ever told Nikki that she was beautiful. Not for the reason that she wasn't, but, there are women who don't receive compliments, maybe because they never know how to respond to them with grace and appreciation.

Back then when she used to be Veronika Truba, she never received a compliment because everyone held that she was a tomboy, rather harsh with words and strange in her deeds and preferences. Loners are not beautiful, loners are weird, they don't develop social skills on how to respond to compliments of any kind.

Her mother never told her that she was pretty because she was born dark while her mother's breed were blond, blue-eyed and long-limbed. Veronika was tall, but chunkier than any of mother's female relatives. While she was growing up, in her house the vision of beautiful was in stark contrast to what Veronika looked like. In school she never received any compliments for anything, because kids thought her to be weird. She never smiled back at any boy; they never liked her, as she was too serious and mute. She dressed differently; her sense of fashion was absolutely individual, hence she looked a misfit. In London there were no misfits: everyone had their place, no one was surprised or prone to judge others. Of course she liked that!

After rehearsal, she went to the pub around the corner with a group of friends. It was Saturday evening, she was tired and her hair was pulled in a ponytail. No make-up at all. She still had tights on and was a bit sweaty, but she needed a beer.

There was some poetry reading in the corner.

She stood up and walked to the bar. A young man stood behind her and asked:

"Do you want me to help you carry it?"

"Yeah."

He asked her if she liked poetry. She thought of Pia. She thought of her ceiling, of Hugo, she smiled and said, *"Sure."*

"If you wish, come over later…I am Dean."

"Nikki."

"Nikki with a beautiful smile."

She spilled the beer and said, *"Shit!"* he said:

"See you later."

That evening, when he asked her *'where she had been hiding all this time'* she told him she worked at the Greek restaurant five days a week, she cleaned a wealthy man's kitchen and dining room three times a week and she attended the dance academy and danced the rest of the time.

But they managed to catch up. He waited for her after she finished work a few days after he met her. He waited till eleven thirty that evening and almost left, but when he saw several people leaving through the back door, he stayed longer. She came out with a young girl and he called her name. She smiled when she saw him. He said:

"I really wasn't waiting for you, but someone else. They didn't come, how about you and I have a late drink?"

Dean was an introvert: a quiet thinker, a wise young man who questioned everything. He was deep and way beyond his age. She learned that he lost his father and that this event made him mature quickly, as he wanted to look after his mother and his younger brother. Not that he had to look after them financially, obviously, Nikki quickly understood that his background was one of wealth and privilege, but he wanted to be the man in the family.

Bobby was his best friend and when Bobby's mother died they adopted him. Dean had a younger brother Andrew, a melancholic but spoilt soul who was at his highest when receiving material rewards: anything from bicycles when little to Porches much later, but in between, Mother had regularly rewarded his rare enthusiasm for life with different extravagant gifts. He was always in some sort of search for meaning, any meaning, as if his young life were absolutely devoid of any such thing. It was reinforced and emphasised by his father's leaving. He just, kind of, shrank in, his light dimmed and his speech became erratic or non-existent. Their mother, according to Dean, was much more preoccupied with Andrew who stood, in her books, as *'the sensitive one'*; nevertheless, Dean believed that he was the protector of the entire family since Dad's passing; when saying *'the entire family'*, Bobby was included as well, regardless of Bobby's unwillingness to be controlled, told or *'looked after'*. Bobby was strong-willed, quick minded with tongue never in check.

Nikki learned all those details on their first date.

A date was agreed on the third of their *'chance'* encounters: the first one in the same pub, the other right in front of the back door when Nikki ended her shift, and the third one again, at exactly the same corner.

Nikki said:

256

"You again."

"Oh, yeah. Funny, hey?"

"What are you doing here?"

"Fancy a drink?"

"Sure."

When they parted ways, Dean said:

"I'll wait for you here tomorrow, yeah?"

She just nodded her head.

It was a strange feeling for Nikki. No one had ever waited for her after school, or in front of any other place, behind any spot or in any corner. She felt unattractive and unwanted for the major part of her life. Here was a young man, with fine manners, with a knack for poetry, quite good looking, wanting to see her again.

"Strange things happen in this bloody city!" she muttered but couldn't suppress a little smile of contentment.

When she asked Caesar what he thought about the *'situation'*, he said:

"Stop thinking, you silly girl. Just stop thinking and have some fun. No one ever taught you to have some fun? Thinking, thinking all the time. Hey, relax and go with the flow."

"Go with the flow", resonated in Nikki's head and after some pondering she understood that her studying wouldn't suffer if she were to meet him again. As time passed she understood that her studying was enhanced by this friendship.

Prior to Christmas he invited her over. He said, *'Bring nothing'* when she asked about it. No one was in the living room when they entered. The strong smell of quinces prevailed; it brought back memories. She shook her head; she didn't want such memories. She wasn't Veronika any longer; that was someone else's name and life. A tall young man walked in later. He said something, but Dean said:

"Meet Nikki. Nikki, Andrew, my brother."

Soon he left the room.

She heard loud music and Dean said:

"That's Bobby. Everything about him is loud." He yelled, *"Turn it down, Bobby!"*

And then a woman walked in. She was tall and slender, with piercing blue eyes, small pug nose and very thin lips. Her eyelids were on half-mast and she just lifted her eyebrows when she looked at Dean.

"Mum, this is Nikki."

"Fine." She said and went out. Dean tried to say something but Nikki said:

"Frau Elsa, the woman who gave birth to Veronika Truba had that aura. Don't worry, say nothing, Nikki Barlow needs no explanation."

They moved to Dean's room where he read Nikki some poetry while drinking good wine. She met Bobby, too. He ran into Dean's room without knocking on his door or anything, he just burst into the room and started to swear and accuse randomly, then he looked and Nikki with a blank expression and said:

"Andy isn't here?"

"Does she look like Andy?"

"She looks like a piece of shit!"

"Bugger off, close the door" then he turned to Nikki and said:

"Crazy family, hey?"

"Hmm. I had a crazier one, believe me. I have a brother who passed away and my heart was broken for good. When he passed away I understood there was nothing to tie me anymore to my, so called, family, to my town…so, I left."

"I can't leave."

"Why?"

"I look after my family."

"Successfully?"

"Listen to this one, it's called 'When Dawned'. Listen attentively, I want your feedback."

Life went well so far and Nikki was settling in, then Dean cheated on her and broke her heart. She learned it in the most blatant way. Unannounced, she came to the poetry evening he attended every second Friday. More often than not she couldn't make it as her school commitments prevented her, but on that particular Friday she finished much earlier, took the tube and headed for the pub. She saw him kissing a girl. She ran out breathless. She sat on the pavement and cried.

She took a taxi home and called Caesar.

"This is not Victorian England, Nikki. He has the right to kiss other girls. You want an exclusive relationship? There is no such thing as an exclusive relationship. Everybody's cheating. You just pretend that you have never seen it. If he hasn't seen you, then all's well. Don't tell him anything and all will be fine, you silly girl. You still believe in fairy-tales?"

"You are an idiot and a pervert!" Said Nikki and slammed the phone. She cried herself to sleep.

The only person she ever missed was Pia. She would understand her, only Pia would. But Pia told her not to stay in contact. Pia never wanted anything to do with any member of the Truba family. That was partly the reason why Nikki had changed her name; she wasn't Truba anymore. But she never wanted to compromise Pia's peace or cross her wishes. She missed Pia so much and feared that she would never meet her again. That hurt as much as Dean's infidelity did. She hated Caesar, too. This time she really thought him to be a pervert and a sick mind. He lived with the old man, he lived of his money, yet had, a so-called boyfriend in Rome, he went to crazy parties, full of perverts and drugs…oh, she hated him passionately.

But on the following evening Caesar came with sausage-rolls and a bottle of wine. He sang:

"Angry-hungry, angry-hungry, angry-hungry, la-la-la!"

When she told him again about Dean kissing a girl, he said:

"I see, my poor girl. Your current diagnoses would be: an incurable case of unrealistic expectations about love. You are in love! Oh, how horrible, Nikki. You shouldn't let yourself into that trap, or…crap. Love is not real. It just happens in one's head and brings a horrible, almost incurable disease. We live

in times and places where love is not needed. Not that kind of love. Have a good time, have good sex, but be level-headed."

"Stop talking crap, your mind is twisted. Sit, eat and drink, shut up that hole that produces a river of liquid crap; your mouth stinks."

"Nikki, that's what I call a friend! Good girl, get angry, not emotional."

"But only last week, you creep, you said that you loved me."

"Yes, I do. And, I always will. But there's a difference, I never wanted to get into your pants. That's why we love each other, you don't care with whom I sleep, I couldn't care less about your lovers… we love each other for who we are and we don't expect anything from each other… plus, we don't attempt to change or alter each other… that, for me, is genuine love: caring for someone without expectations and letting them be!"

"OK. Stop now as all this is too much for me."

"Cure yourself from stupidity as quick as you can."

But that wasn't what Nikki wanted or needed. She needed and wanted Dean's love, the kind of love Tristan had for Isolde, perhaps…

"If anyone calls, I am not at home, OK?" she said to her roommate. She left work earlier for several days, lying about school commitments; she left school earlier, lying about doctor's appointments. She didn't know if he waited or if he had forgotten about her and enjoyed his new relationship.

But on the fourth evening he met her in front of her building. She was carrying two heavy bags and he approached from behind and said:

"Let me carry them for you."

"Go away."

"What crime have I committed this time?"

"The crime of kissing a girl on Friday the 27th, in the pub, I saw you through the window and never came in."

"Oh!"

"Oh!"

"Sorry."

"Go to hell."

"But I care about you."

"Obviously not enough."

"More than you think."

"Bugger off."

"I never cared about that girl."

"For you kissing a girl means nothing?"

"I probably had too much to drink."

"So we can blame it on drinking every time."

"You can forgive me once, can't you?"

"No."

"Too much pride?"

"Not too much pride, but too much hurt."

"You really care about me, don't you?"

"More than you have ever cared about me."

"How do you know that?"

"I never went around kissing other men, you did that; I can't trust you."

"I never knew you cared about me that much?"

"What did you want from me, to put it on a billboard?"

"What if I say it will never happen again?"

"What if I don't trust you?"

"What if you try to build your trust?"

"I am tired, good night."

"I'll call you."

"Call that girl, it's still early, she might be waiting for your call."

"I won't stop calling you."

"Selfish, spoilt brat!" she murmured as she climbed the stairs.

"What did you just say?"

"I just said that you are a bloody selfish, spoilt brat! You think just because you are wealthy and your mother happens to be a so-called upper-class-bitch that you are better than I am. Well you are not! You are just a selfish bastard. Burn in hell!"

But she missed him the same way Gregor missed Pia every time she walked away.

She never wanted to think about Gregor… or Dean.

She moved out, changed her address and had a haircut.

***

Caesar picked her up and took her to a pub; they were hungry. There was a group of ten people, loud, sort of arguing, or rather mocking someone.

Dean stood up and walked to their table.

It was exactly seven months since she changed her address and had her hair cut.

He said:

"You've changed your hairstyle. It suits you."

"This is Caesar, my friend. Caesar, Dean."

"Oh!" a sigh escaped from Caesar's lips.

"You've changed your address, too? I thought you went back home."

"Where would that be?" asked Caesar then started to pull apart the bread."

"How could I have gone when I haven't graduated? I just moved, closer to Caesar."

"Oh, I see." Said Dean, ready to go back to his mates, but Caesar added:

"You see nothing, you are blind."

"What?"

"Nothing!"

"You are insinuating…"

"Look, my pretty friend, I am not insinuating, or anything, I am just talking as I do all the time. You know, one of those who makes remarks, talks to himself and blah, blah, blah…"

Dean left their table but when they were about to leave he came again and handed Nikki a paper, some sort of a magazine, very cheap, bad printing. He said:

"Whenever you have time, take a look."

When she switched on the lamp on her bedside table she took the magazine out. On page 32 there was a poem titled *'Nikki's Leaving'*; she read it several times not knowing what she was feeling.

Underneath he wrote in his unsteady handwriting, *'Call me sometime'*.

And she thought, *'Probably, I will'*, then she put the magazine down and switched off the lamp.

"Nikki left her home,
Nikki never smiled,
Never liked a crowd,
Never cried aloud,
Never confided in anyone
'Tired and pissed off'...
...now:
Nikki's leaving
Nikki's left
Nikki's lost."

Prior to giving herself to the velvety embrace of sleep she said to herself:

'Nikki's lost: she hates this constant rain, this greedy city, she is all alone, she doesn't have friends and occasionally, she passionately hates Caesar, the only creature who pays attention...' then sleep took over the chatter of her mind and her little heart.

Just a few verses were enough to bring her back to him. She reasoned that he hadn't written it intentionally, for that purpose alone, as how could he ever know that she would read the poem?

Caesar said:

"Believe in what you wanna believe. Have fun, Nikki. Don't take him seriously. Have fun! And, don't forget: cheat on him whenever the occasion comes up, you don't belong to anyone but yourself."

But she wanted to *'take him seriously'*, only this time she knew better the rules of this silly game called love, or, whatever it was called.

Painfully, there was not much love for Nikki that came from that relationship, or to be more precise – from the entire family. Somehow they were sophisticatedly hostile, the mother was some sort of a mute-divine-sufferer that everyone tiptoed around. She regularly ignored Nikki and pretended not to understand a word that was coming from her mouth; she looked at her as one would look at an exotic and rare insect – with a touch of fear and a heavy dose of disgust. It never, ever occurred to Nikki that she was a pretty girl, talented and committed. The quality that came out as the first to be displayed was – straightforwardness which always labelled her as a *'weird'* person. She would say things that no one else wouldn't dream of saying loudly in their bravest dreams. But she did. She started with such practise long ago, under the roof of her virtuous but, sadly, ex-mother Elsa, just to irritate and annoy her as a punishment for Elsa's petty, but often nasty ways, easily recognised by thoughtful Nikki, back then when she used to be someone else, responsive to the name – Veronika.

Then, there was that redhead boy, the orphan, full of wit but never short of insults to what, seemingly, no one ever responded in any other way but – smiling benevolently. He was quick in his movements, his mind was quick and his tongue always caught up with the quickness of his limbs and his mind. Even though he smelled like a bag full of weed, the fact that he smoked never slowed him down. If he went to see any kind of doctor, they would diagnose him with attention deficiency disorder, or any of those disorders of modern times that helps doctors to sell drugs. Nikki remembered in her youth that witty and quick-minded kids were awarded, being the most creative ones. She was convinced that there was a conspiracy in this country that aimed to destroy kids' creativity: *'Be quiet!'*, *'Be polite!'*, *'Don't jump!'*, *'Don't say that!'* – way too many *'Don'ts'* caging young souls.

Not only he smoked weed, they all did, including Nikki.

There was that other brother, Andrew, Andy as they called him. He was hellishly good looking, but melancholic, a real spoilt brat as nothing was ever good enough for him. He was indifferent to anything and couldn't care less if an invasion of aliens were about to happen. He would keep his eyes half-mast and gently rock his head. Nikki had heard that he was a *'venom for girls'*, about which statement she had mixed feelings. Yes, when it come to his looks she could easily understand that girls would lose their heads for him, but what exactly was attractive about his attitude and unconcern for fellow humans, that she could not grasp. He reminded her, often, of her ex-brother Gregor who believed himself to be God's gift to humanity.

Whenever she had thoughts about any member of her ex-Truba-tribe, she would discard them with quick discomfort, covered with a layer of barely noticeable anger.

Andy would come and go and no one was ever entitled to ask anything about his whereabouts, including his mother, who was to common knowledge, the most entitled one when it came to his personal life. It was so obvious that he was the *'darling'* of the family, which only added to his inborn arrogance.

And there was Dean, a poet, a brave soul who *'took care of the family since father passed away.'* Nikki never learned what his father did but knew that he left a hefty inheritance, leaving the family without worries about their future. Their mother, apparently, was from a noble background, a wealthy woman herself; all that measured up to establish and cement their stance towards *'Nikki and her kind'*. Of course they loathed migrants, they loathed the poor regardless of where they came from. Dean had the privilege of being a poet, hence associating with artists, poets, writers… God forbid socialists, but he had the right to visit pubs and mingle with commoners. Andrew never had such a privilege after his heart was broken by a migrant's daughter, and his nose by her father or one of his Italian thugs.

Dean smoked marijuana the least; he liked his booze, and the problem would arise when he had one too many, then he would get cosy with girls he knew who had fancied him for a while. He would pay compliments only when tipsy, he would advance only when alcohol stripped him of any inhibitions, family pride or sense of fidelity. And that would infuriate Nikki. He liked her infuriated, for that fed his ego and added a different dimension to his emotionally average life.

They rode on this rollercoaster for several years and both were left exhausted and with less faith in love and respect in general.

***

In early July of 1991 Nikki Barlow graduated from the London Academy of Dance and the name, Nikki Barlow, was inscribed on her diploma. Just several weeks prior to her graduation she said her final *'good-bye'* to Dean Bloxham, who left a legacy of disorientated love in her heart. She made the final cut with the precision of an absolutely skilled surgeon, unshakable cut, and the wound in her heart sealed by a scab never bled, but the scab got hard and healed instantly in her determined mind.

That was a good year for Nikki. She had plenty of work, she found a new place and never thought about her past. The only person she thought about on a daily basis was Hugo, but she thought of him as one would about the dearest pet one had lost; she never thought about him as her brother form her former life, but rather as some kind alien that graced her inner life continuously.

She developed a rare skill of escaping the reality of the past by bringing the present or more art and fantasy into her daily life. She lived some sort of parallel life, as she divided it into *'things that have to be done'* and *'the life I live just for Nikki.'* Hugo belonged to both as his kind eyes followed wherever she went, whatever she did.

Nowadays she was only called by the name Nikki Barlow and she had completely forgotten that some time ago, let's say, a long time ago, she was called Veronika Truba. The flood of people as silt carried by a filthy river floated on the banks of London; people from the country of her birth, the people she never wanted to meet, to know or acknowledge. She never, ever wanted to speak this language again, to reveal her origins or to associate with them. They brought trouble in their souls and there was nothing that could tie her to such a phenomenon, she was Nikki Barlow, a dancer, a free spirit, a Londoner.

Then, in the same year, 1991, in late December, she heard someone's voice calling her, *'Nikki, Nikki!'* She knew that voice, turned back and saw Dean across the road standing with a tall woman dressed in black. She had long, long black silky hair and such regular features that from the distance Nikki thought she was the most beautiful woman she had ever seen. *'Except Pia. Pia! Was that Pia standing next to Dean? Can't be!'* she discarded such a thought and waved to Dean, he said:

"Wait up!" and hurried across the road, the pretty woman followed, stretching her long legs in the same intervals as Dean stretched his.

"Are you well?"

"Sure."

The two women looked into each other's eyes without saying a word. Dean said:

"Nikki, Pia's my mentor. I am studying creative writing. Pia – Nikki."

The two women stood motionless, Dean continued:

"Always nice to see you."

"Your phrases, they are so original."

"There's a reading tonight, pop in."

"Not too sure."

"See you some other time."

"Yeah."

Nikki turned her back and started to walk, Pia's eyes haunted her while she was slowly walking as if she were walking through a dream. She heard a voice again. It called:

"Lonnie, Lonnie, wait up!"

Pia ran to her and the two women embraced. One cried. The other one who thought that she had died long ago – Lonnie, cried. Pia whispered:

"I missed you so much."

Lonnie kept on crying, her tears were timid as if it were shameful to admit that she missed her friend, her country and her own language. But she would never admit, not even to her deepest self, that apart from missing her home, she missed her brother, father and her mother Elsa.

***

Pia's arrival in London was much different to Veronika's. She didn't come with a tiny piece of paper with a name of a person she never knew on it. She came with recommendations from the highest places and found a job just a week after her arrival.

It was the end of summer 1989, the day was cold as any winter day on the Adriatic coast, but she knew London weather well.

When she landed at Heathrow there were two people waiting for her. One was a driver and the other was a personal assistant to the consul general. She was driven to an apartment given to her to use *'until she settled in'*, which might as well have been – indefinitely. A luxury apartment with the best view and well connected neighbours.

For eight months she taught English as a second language in a private institute; after that period a new position was offered and yet again, she had the same position she had prior to coming to London – teaching creative writing at university.

In 1991 Dean Bloxham met Pia at university. She was his mentor and soon they developed a good understanding through literature and poetry. She had never really been a social person; never really cared too much about meeting new people, but whenever Dean would invite her to poetry evenings, she would attend. She had published a book of poems that same year and was working on the translation of her earlier works. Dean offered to help.

When she said, *'Thanks'*, Dean commented, *'Who wouldn't help you?'*. Pia flagged him with a red flag. She was immune to men's flattering comments or their wild gaze, she handled men as a strong and sophisticated trainer would control and tame wild animals. She was superior in any relationship between woman and man. She was always superior because she didn't care. She never wanted a *'proper relationship'*, she never wanted to belong to someone, never wanted to be caged or blackmailed by emotions, her mind was brilliant, especially when she was alone and in charge of it and likewise of her decisions. She never asked but demanded, in a very placid tone, with a very indifferent attitude, as she knew that, in the end, she could do it alone, she could perform, she could deliver, she was independent and wanted to stay independent by any means: financially, mentally and emotionally.

No, she wasn't cold, on the contrary: she was warm and kind but she wanted to keep that warmth and kindness to herself, for her poetry, for her Muse and her Sapphire. Those were the only categories that Pia wanted to be shared with. She liked friendship with men but found them to be overwhelming, overprotective, too keen, or – not reliable, having *'an agenda'*.

The first meaningful friendship she had struck was with Timothy Wild, a man she met through her friend Theodor Lukas. It was after Theodor's concert that he introduced her to composer Wild. Wild was visibly unnerved when he shook hands with Pia, later he said it was the first time he had ever been absolutely speechless. He stood next to the silent Pia and felt as if he had fallen under a spell, the one that locks the tongue indefinitely. He rubbed his temple in an attempt to open that hidden cord from where, usually, his ideas and words flew effortlessly, but to no avail. He cleared his throat, but it was still croaky and harsh, and words couldn't get out with ease.

Lukas said:

"Time to eat, let's have a bite."

And, yes, they had dinner, a dinner that was the sweetest dinner for Timothy Wild, but it was heavily spiced with all sorts of unfamiliar emotions and his most peculiar behaviour: he over-salted every dish, he poured wine into a coffee cup, his fork fell on the floor and he decided to get drunk in an attempt to calm something that controlled his voice, movements and thoughts – unwillingly. Yet, Miss Pia sat down all evening, with a calm, yet indifferent expression, ever polite, emotionally unavailable, she smiled at Lukas's jokes and stories but commented on almost none of them; she ate slowly and refused to drink wine. Often she would look into some ornament in the room and stayed silent. Her eyes were silent too. She never talked about herself that evening, only Lukas said to Timothy that Pia was *'a very talented poetess and a fine writer'*, to which Pia gently shook her head as if she wanted to deny the overstatement.

After that dinner Timothy Wild couldn't stop thinking about Pia. At moments it annoyed him even angered him – *'Why would she take so much space in my head?'*; he would discard thoughts about her, but unwillingly his mind went back to the object of his admiration. He spent several weeks in that sweet agony and when he understood that thinking about her *'won't simply fade away'* he decided to invite Lukas to dinner saying, *'Well, it's my turn now.'*

When Lukas had agreed, Wild said:

"Invite Pia, the poetess."

He prepared himself for that dinner and rehearsed in front of the mirror. He couldn't believe it; he couldn't understand what had happened to his steadiness, his spontaneity and his skill as a good orator.

The first time he met her he was wearing a dark suit, so he decided to dress in a smart but casual style; he knew he'd look presentable; his hair needed a haircut, yes, he went to his barber to have his hair cut and for a shave, so that he could look even younger, more appealing, sexier. He reserved a table a week earlier, he did everything right to the miniscule detail, yet when he arrived he had to put his hands in the pockets of his jersey for they were trembling like young leaves in a gentle spring wind. He couldn't stop his mind; whenever he thought of Pia he thought of sex; that angered him too, for that wasn't what he wanted from Pia. He didn't really want anything specific, he wanted to sit next to her and listen to how she breathed slowly through her nose, never through her mouth, which he noticed the first time they met. Her mouth was closed, almost all the time; only sometimes she would stretch her lips into a gentle smile and swing her head towards the left shoulder. He thought that here was something mystical, eternal, unearthly about Pia; he thought there was something about her that he was always hoping he might find one day in a real woman.

Thanks to Lukas the evening was flawless as his wit predominated. If it were for Pia, they would probably eat in utter silence, and if it were for Wild he would stutter and perform the most unusual rituals with falling forks and turning glasses over... but Lukas saved the evening. What Wild did not know was that Lukas was well aware of his clumsiness, the redness of his cheeks and illogicality of his sentences.

Nevertheless, he didn't learn anything new about Pia except that she was a lecturer and she put a full-stop after that sentence as if she wanted to say, '... *and that's all there is to it!*'

But she played tennis!

She accepted his invitation and gave him her number. When he dialled the number a week after that dinner, he had prepared a casual speech. She answered:

"Pia."

"Pia, Timothy. Remember Timothy..."

"I do remember. How are you Timothy?"

"You said you'd like to... you'd like to... umm..."

"Play a match of tennis, right?"

"Oh, yes, yes, you are quite right, a game of tennis."

Then there was a silence. Nothing from her side, nothing came out of is mouth. Silence prevailed. Then she asked:

"Are you still there, Timothy?"

"Yes, yes. Just thinking... was thinking about a day... what would be the best day for you?"

"Saturday."

"Coming Saturday?"

"What time?"

"Oh, um... um..." went Timothy not knowing what time and if the tennis court would be available. Then he said:

"We can visit my sister, she has a tennis court... I mean, if you... you wish."

"Yes, sounds good."

Then she said nothing and he stuttered in his mind, and the mind's stutter threatened to pour down into his mouth and play carelessly with his tongue.

After a longer silence she asked again:

"Timothy, are you still there?"

She couldn't help but laugh quietly, it wasn't anything new to her, but she never knew how to help someone in such trouble.

Timothy said:

"Well, you can call me Tim, no one really calls me Timothy... I mean, except my mother."

Silence from her side, as she was expecting him to tell her the details: what time, where and how to get to his sister's place.

"I suppose, you don't mind, if my sister and her husband join us for the game?"

He made it up on the spot believing that, if only they wanted or had time to join them, he would be at much more ease than if he had to face Pia all alone.

"That'd be great."

"You want me to pick you up?"

"Sure. Take a pen and write down my address."

"Saturday 9 a.m.; is that too early for you?"

"No, I get up early."

Ant that was how it all started: they played tennis in pairs almost every Saturday and had brunch after the match. Tim's sister and brother-in-law helped to create a friendly and relaxed atmosphere, and he went back to his old self: easy-going and effortless attitude, which contributed to Pia's changed attitude. She was more relaxed, though she never talked more. She would just sit and listen, often loll in her chair, legs crossed, eyes closed and a gentle, almost mysterious smile on her face. Tim loved her face, thin and sculpted to perfection. He loved her dark, silky hair and her green eyes, but what he feared was that unavailability that was so obvious from the first day.

Yes, she was polite, kind and a good listener, but somehow, he felt that she was emotionally unengaged and almost – vacant.

After Saturday mornings, evenings followed: dinners and theatres; she attended concerts with him and was at complete ease while holding his hand, but still, he felt that the major part of Pia belonged to the unknown.

He read her poetry, her essays and short stories; he tried to get to know her through her dark poetry but every time he thought that he knew her, at least, a little bit better, a new poem would come and reveal something new, often something disturbing, dark, almost dangerous as if there was some irreparable mistake or loss, some cry hidden on the following page that hadn't been written yet. The more he knew Pia, the more he feared that he would never really get to know her, he feared that she was just a short paragraph added to the book of his own history.

It had been almost a year since he started dating Pia; they were sitting in a café, she had a lunch break; he said:

"I fear you Pia. Often I fear you."

"Why?"

"Sometimes you are so distant, unavailable."

"I am. I always am."

"Why so?"

"I am distant. I told you not to take me too seriously. I told you never to let me know that you need me or miss me. It wasn't a joke. I don't miss people."

"What's wrong then?"

"Wrong?"

"Yeah, I think something went wrong, sometime in your life."

"Nothing went wrong. I don't need people. I am happiest when I am alone."

"But, what am I to you, Pia?"

"A friend."

"A friend? Nothing more than a friend?"

"No."

"We've been together a year, and yet, to you I am no more than a friend."

"Don't get agitated."

"How could I not get agitated? I love you Pia, and you are telling me that there's nothing more between us than friendship."

273

She was stirring the rest of her coffee with a small spoon. He stopped her hand and said:

"Look at me! Look into my eyes. Tell me now that there's nothing else between us but plain friendship."

"Don't insist!"

"What do you mean by – don't insist! You don't love me, do you?"

She shook her head barely visibly and he felt as if a sharp knife was thrust into his heart.

"Say it!"

She looked at the table. Her hands were resting on the table, her head rocking slowly, her silky hair was waving as if saying a silent *'good-bye'* to the man who sat next to her and in utter disbelief gazed at her waving hair.

He put a finger under her chin and said quietly, lifting her head up:

"Say it, please, verbalise it, Pia."

"You know that."

"What do I know? I think you have a problem."

"I never asked you to love me."

"You never asked? Do you think that love has to be asked for? Wasn't all I have done enough for you, for us? And you want to say that you have never asked for it? Is that what you are saying?"

She nodded her head.

"What do you want me to do? Do you want me to go away? To disappear from your life? Do you want me to stop loving you?"

"I don't want anything, Tim. I never asked you to love me."

"You shouldn't ask. Love happens, Pia. How did you see our relationship? What was I to you? A friend?"

"I don't fall in love... as, I don't need love."

"You don't need love?"

Slightly she lifted her left shoulder up and bit her lip.

"What the hell is wrong with you, Pia?"

"Nothing's wrong with me. I don't need people. If you walked away now, it wouldn't be a disaster; I wouldn't be upset or unhappy. Tim, don't get upset, please, but I simply don't have those feelings..."

"... for me? It's me! Isn't it?"
"No. It's me."

He stood up and walked away. She sat there overwhelmed with feelings of relief. She liked him in her own way, but she couldn't share Pia. No, she couldn't share Pia with anyone.

The next morning Tim called to ask her if she wanted to talk about it again. He asked if she was sure about her feelings, all she said to a rather confused man was:

"I never needed a lasting friendship, everything is so transient."
"It wasn't a friendship, there was more to it."
"Don't get upset."
"You can't handle feelings!"
"No, it's not about that. Just... I don't feel like sharing right now."
"Have you ever shared anything with anyone?"
"Please, don't get upset. It is late and cold, I am off to bed. Good night."

***

Tim knew Theodor Lukas was a childhood friend of Pia's father, when he asked about Pia's life, Theodor said:

"I can't help you, my friend. All I can say is that she had lost her mother quite young under difficult circumstances. But, I don't have the right to talk about her life, move on, I don't know much about it, I don't know anything at all. You'll get over her."

"I'll get over her. Is that all there is left to say?"

Lukas swiftly changed the subject:

"Have you heard the rumours, apparently, Placido is coming to London. Ring Teresa Callo and ask her, she'd be the first to know if it's just a rumour or if there's more to it."

275

For the entire thirty-six years of his life, Tim hadn't met a woman that he liked more than Pia, but on the other hand, he had never met a woman with such little need for sharing. She shared barely anything: she was locked in her thoughts, probably past, or even projected into some future, but surely, their states of being present at the same time in the same place were disharmonious. He couldn't even say she was cold, as he had met cold women; she was simply self-sufficient while polite; her expression always the same, a real enigma for an easy-going person as Tim was. While her eyes were always placid and calm, they never gave any sign of love or compassion. Their last conversation was a sudden shock for Tim, as Pia's eyes never gave any sign of a farewell.

How to get over Pia? He buried himself in work, he locked himself into his self, he barely walked out of his music room and decided not to read poetry ever again; he rendered himself to a wholly undesirable life. One thing he regretted – they had never come to know each other, and that meant he was touched by mystery to which he didn't respond in any acceptable way. His solitude deepened and started to weary him unspeakably.

Approximately three months after their last conversation Tim met Pia at Lukas' dinner-party.

He came quite late; no one was expecting him any longer. Pia had no knowledge that he was invited; as a matter of fact – she had forgotten him.

It was a commotion that awakened her from her introverted state of being. Lucas told Caesar to *'materialise a chair'* and Caesar became agitated, his voice pitched while trying to explain that all chairs were taken at the beginning of the evening his excitement escalated into hysteria; he knelt on the floor and started to cry. Lukas turned his back on him pretending not to be aware of his silliness; Pia squatted next to Caesar who was dressed all in greenish yellow and looked like a sad, bitter lemon with human characteristics and emotions.

"What now?"

"He relies on me for everything and if I can't deliver in an instant, he ac- cuses me with his indifferent look, or with words in his mouth that I dislike; he

wants me to be perfect but how can I? How can I be perfect twenty-four-seven? I can't bare it any longer. I want to go home; he can find someone else to try to please him all the time. A selfish, spoilt brat!"

Bitterly, he cried the tears of under-appreciation from his lover. Pia held her handkerchief while kneeling next to Caesar.

"Stop being a drama queen!" Lukas's voice ordered from a distance. Caesar started to cry even more bitterly.

"Stop playing the role of a victim. You are not irreplaceable, don't you know that?"

"Oh! You old bastard! I am not irreplaceable, but neither are you! I already have a boyfriend, young and talented..."

"...but penniless..."

"I don't need your money..."

"...and pure love ties you to me!"

"Off I go! I can't stand such a life anymore. You are a selfish old bastard."

"I heard that earlier. You can go, I won't stop you."

Then amongst all this drama, a much more sober voice changed the atmosphere:

"I don't need a chair. I apologise for being so late. I can share my chair with Pia."

Pia looked at Tim and said:

"Sure!"

Lukas came closer, extended his hand to, still sobbing, Caesar, who took his hand while involuntarily looking in his eyes, then stood up and found himself in Lukas's embrace, and sobbed, a little bit more. Lukas pressed him onto his chest and patted his back, as one would do with a child in distress.

They all went back to the opulent table that now had a new member: Timothy Wild.

Pia noticed there was something different about Tim. He looked thinner; the dark circles around his eyes made him look worn out. When she asked him if he was *'all right'*, he said:

"Thank you, Pia. I lead the most splendid life. Everything's roses. I am so inspired by daily events and people that I can't stop admiring life. Often I feel

as if I were chosen by some maleficent and sinful being to prove himself wrong, which means, he showers and tortures me with splendid ideas."

She understood: he came led by the desire to confess something. And his confession continued:

"I met a fantastic woman. She possessed all the qualities one can desire in a woman: beautiful, wise and talented. Oh, how lucky I was. But, alas, she was born without a human heart. Can you believe that? What a mistake made by God as he tried to create perfection. The mistake was the worst of its kind as it was unseen! A Dark Queen! Do you know a woman like that Pia?

Deep silence took possession of the room they were sitting in, and under cover of that silence she took the advantage of lacking empathy for men and kept on insisting on silence. He repeated his last question but Pia was somewhere else. It was Caesar's turn to return a favour:

"Let's dance, Pia." He took her hand and led her to the middle of the spacious dining room that had an entrance to the garden. The door was opened and Pia felt an instant relief.

Caesar said:

"You are gorgeous, Pia. I admire you. If I were a woman I would kill for you looks and your attitude. You go, sister, give them a hard time! Give them hell as they deserve it!"

Pia never wanted to give a hard time to anyone, Pia wanted to be Pia, to be more often than not, left alone to create, to communicate with the forces beyond her understanding in an attempt to touch love again, the love that was taken away from her unscrupulously, not by fate, but by one pair, the pair who claimed they both loved Sapphire, the pair that destroyed her in the end.

She shook her head to get rid of such thoughts, the truth that she learned not long ago, when Luna Averna was a crown witness in the last case of the *'utter violence and unseen vandalism.'*

For Pia that evening ended in unease as Tim begged her to give him another chance; it was the wine to blame, confidently presenting his most hidden thoughts and feelings. She politely declined the unexpected offer, but it seemed to her that it never reached his intoxicated mind. She left in secrecy, without saying a word; she just kissed Caesar's cheek and vanished into a chilly morning. She didn't drive home but walked. Her head was hot from the heated atmosphere; her heart was cold.

She missed her grandmother.

Prior to her leaving, Granny Sava told her:

"Go, my child, go! Heavy times will fall upon this country once again. So much hatred, it looks as if in this country wars have never stopped as the engine of humanity here was stoked by the wrong fuel. Go, you have a far too fine and sensitive soul for the future that is awaiting us. Our ancestors had left many times, some had seemingly found a better life, some never did, like Nikola. He gave his life to science, yet, he had received nothing in return: he was robbed and unappreciated in that vile country. He died without friends, money or deserved recognition. Such a genius, yet this world stayed speechless. Word that he was possibly murdered came after his death; they used him unscrupulously and when everything was taken they got rid of him. I'll pray for you, I'll pray for your brighter days, I'll look after your mother's grave; I'll see it has fresh flowers always."

She shook that thought and ran towards her building, as she had the feeling that someone was walking behind her.

It was just her past, always disguised in different forms, shapes and shadows.

***

She always loved Veronika and never blamed her for anything that had happened on that night, she just happened to be his sister. She never even liked him, she warned Pia about his ways.

Several days upon her arrival, she telephoned Theodor Lukas. When he heard Pia's voice, he was delighted and organised a car to pick her up at once. She arrived approximately at dinnertime; he was standing at the open door in

279

his bright red suit, barefoot even though it was cold. She almost ran towards him as she used to when she was little, she always liked uncle Theo; he used to bring her presents from London.

He pressed her tight onto his chest and said:

"Voilà! My gorgeous, gorgeous girl – welcome!"

She met his lover: a much younger, skinny, Italian lad with an attitude. She didn't know whether to like or dislike him, so she stayed neutral towards him for most of the evening. He tried to strike up a conversation a few times, but she mainly ignored his comments without any expression in her eyes. Lukas had never been bothered by others' relationships or courtesy, he had never even noticed that other people related to one another – if it wasn't about him, nothing ever counted as if it had never existed.

But what led Pia to soften towards Caesar was as follows:

She asked Theo about Veronika as she had given her his address. Theo looked at her and said:

"Doesn't ring a bell."

"Three years ago, remember, I called you and told you a young girl would come with my letter of recommendation to your door, Veronika, I told you to help her for the first several weeks. Don't you remember?"

"Vaguely. I remember our conversation, not the letter, but, yes, you have mentioned someone was coming ... to the concert ... or something ... I don't remember anymore."

"You never met Veronika? No one came claiming to be my friend?"

"As long as my memory goes – no! I haven't had any strangers, but if she was the one you had sent, I would have most probably done something ... something that you asked."

Pia was puzzled, *'Why wouldn't she come and ask for help?'* But, obviously, if she was there, he would remember as he never opened his door to people from his old country.

'Troublemakers and tramps!' as he would say.

The more she saw Caesar, the more she believed he was a slimy, dishonest man. She didn't like his manner, his loud reading and mocking of the finest verses; she didn't like his voice, but she really didn't care as long as Theo was *'in a quite bearable and sometimes harmonious little relationship.'*

Almost a year had passed when Caesar came near her whilst she was standing on the patio drinking her cocktail. There were too many people in the house and whenever possible Pia avoided the crowd.

Caesar asked:

"Are you still searching for your little friend?"

"My little friend?"

"The girl that was to knock on Theo's door three or four years ago?"

Pia lifted her eyebrow.

"Actually, she knocked, I opened the door and let her in."

"You are talking about?"

"Your friend Veronika, who is actually Nikki, Nikki Barlow, my little cousin."

He told her about Veronika, claiming that he didn't know where she had moved, apparently closer to her boyfriend, and the boyfriend Caesar never met, nor did he know his name.

As a personal revenge towards Pia's coldness, superiority and inborn snobbishness he kept to himself the information about Nikki's work, and never told Nikki a single word about Pia, believing that Pia had never had the intention of helping her settle in London, as he knew too well that Theo never helped anyone: at least no one from that country. In all honesty: Theo never helped him either, he just kept him as some sort of sex slave knowing all of Caesar's troubles and secrets. Caesar liked his cousin Nikki too much and wanted to protect her from such people.

'What on earth would my Nikki have in common with this perfectly cold and unapproachable bitch?'

But to Pia that information was worth pure gold, as she knew that Veronika was in the same city. She knew she'd find her if she only searched properly or tirelessly. She had never given up, but providence crossed their path the day she went out on a lunch-break with Dean Bloxham. At that time Pia didn't know how important Dean was to Veronika, nor that Dean's younger brother Andrew was reading her poem every day. He walked in the rhythm of Pia's poem and dreamed of the poetess, seeing her eyes and listening to her whispers, as there was something in his soul that was touched and disturbed by this poem. Young Andrew Bloxham never knew who wrote these, to his heart dearest words, but only when he met Pia on that random, but for him fateful evening, did he come face to face with the mind that tortured his soul even before they had met.

When Pia published yet another collection of poetry; Dean was present at the modest book launch. He adored Pia, but perhaps it was because she was his mentor and a real erudite, because she wrote with such passion and skill or, simply and blatantly, because she was breathtakingly beautiful and sexy.

But, what difference would the conclusion make? She gave him the collection and early in the morning, when he came back home, he ripped out one page from the book:

Longing - the title under which words flowed.

He slept in; the sun high in the sky woke him up. He wasn't sober yet, but he had remembered Pia's little book. What he hadn't remembered was the page torn out of it.

That leaf was missing from his table just as it was missing from his memory. In the morning Andrew walked into his room in search for his car keys and had found a torn-out page next to the keys. He read it, folded it twice in half and put it into his back pocket. While having his breakfast in a café down the road, he took the leaf out and read the poem, with its torn off title, over and over. He was almost possessed by the words.

I am who I am
A petal torn off your bud
You are who you are
A thorn in my heart
And you are not

DETHRONED

Without me
No breath; no blood
Without you
And when I walk I walk your walk
And when I dream I dream your dream
Dreamed by you
Before you met me
And who am I
But a bud-less petal
And who are you but my voice in the dark
Call me
Call me
Dethroned from love
Call me
Call me
And I shall come.

The poem spoke directly to Andrew's heart, he knew that the poetess longed for her lost love, but he never knew this *'love poem'* hadn't been written to her lost lover. He read it over and over and chewed his food in its rhythm; the wind rose up out of nowhere, it blew across his table, lifted the leaf up and started to play with it. It carried the dancing leaf across the road while Andrew tried to fetch it; a car nearly hit him in the middle of the road; he ran and ran after it, but all of a sudden he stopped and gave up the chase – he knew the poem off by heart. He stood in the middle of the road reciting it out loud and at that moment it seemed to him not only that all the traffic had stopped but also that the words had ceased to exist.

Meeting Pia

It was the end of September 1992, Andrew was reluctant to take Dean downtown to one of his poetry evenings: Dean was ill; he was coughing yet he was determined to go no matter what. Andrew always held that Dean inherited father's intellect, wit, his way with women and his stubbornness.

In Andrew's opinion the place was some *'dark hole'* where he, really didn't want to find himself for an entire evening, but seeing Dean lighting up a cigarette and grabbing a pint of cold beer he decided to stay. Andrew was always level-headed. Dean had been in love, at least five times, but Andrew, really liked only one girl – Apollonia Something, as he couldn't remember her Italian surname, but the feelings he had for her stuck with him all those years, as they were never repeated again regardless of how many young and pretty girls he had courted. His girl had to be pretty, he wouldn't settle for less than a *'real beauty'*.

He was introduced to an absolutely beautiful girl that evening, but he was in a bad mood, not talkative at all: he sat in a dark corner and listened to amateur poets trying to sound like anything from Yeats to T.S. Eliot, so pretentious and grandiose. There were a few moderns, purely vulgar; Andrew was bored to bits. His brother read his poem, and he liked it best not only because it was his brother's poem, Dean had a way with words, yes he did.

The pretty woman came up and read a poem. The poem Andrew knew off by heart. She renamed it. She took his breath away. When she finished she sat down without any interest in any conversation – with anyone.

***

Only after three dates he knew he loved Pia. He was only seventeen when he loved Apollonia, but age doesn't define love and love has never been age exclusive. But that feeling never came back until he met Pia.

Andrew always knew how to play a game of being sovereign master of his emotions, his movements and words. Measured and quiet. Not like Dean, nothing like him! He met a woman that was a master of her emotions, of her movements and her few words. He met someone who matched him this time, but his art of strict control and an unconquerable heart started to lose its strength in the shadow of her powerful quietness and self-sufficiency. He made a *'mistake'*, the one that he promised himself he would never ever repeat – he fell in love with beautiful Pia the moment he saw her, he admitted it to himself on their third meeting. But he played it cool, as she told him:

"Never take me seriously. I am not a woman who will stay; I never stayed and never will. I don't love as I am not gifted in that field, but we can stay friends as long as we both wish to."

He never wanted to love her. He wanted to be friends, why not and who wouldn't want to?

His heart beat in a different rhythm, one he stifled from the beginning. He kept on loving mysterious and elusive Pia without words or expressing his needs. He played as if he never had any needs, as if he were with her by chance, by mutual agreement, out of boredom or plainly for fun.

But he was played the way he never believed he would be played. Not out of malice, not out of wickedness, but out of habit. She didn't know any other way to relate to any man. She was silent, distant, yet a perfect woman who without any demand received what was needed in any moment. She lived for herself only, without being purposely selfish, she lived for her poetry and her selfhood. Men what were they to Pia? Some were seen as friends, others were seen as *'just men'* and yet others as people that passed through her life.

No special poem, just words in a book crowded with lower-case letters.

It was a year of hell for Andrew as he had decided to *'keep Pia at any cost'*, believing that the *'neutral game'* would be the perfect one, as she appeared to like people who gave her freedom and space. He gave her as much as she wanted, she would disappear, go absent for days or weeks, he stayed in his room with hands in his pockets. Not a telephone call! His resentment would build up to the maximum and cause all sorts of unacceptable behaviour; often Dean, Bobby, or his mother were victims of his *'uncommon outbursts'*. She would never say, nor would she explain where she was and why she had never come to visit. She gave explanations to no one, ever; she just lived as if the universe had been created for her.

He hated himself for thinking of her twenty-four hours a day; he couldn't sleep nor eat on some days. He hated himself when he started to spy on her; waiting hidden behind his car, several hundred meters from her building or university; he would follow her but never found out why she went to certain places always alone, yes, always alone and pensive. He had never found out. Then she would come along, to say a few words, to offer a faint smile; her hands were cold but her eyes shone with a strange shine, her words sounded as if they came from distant cultures or souls, from a distant land, not only land, but another planet. He could never figure out on which planet Pia lived; he asked her about the origin of her poetry and she would always point out with her index finger to her heart.

"The soul, or the heart?" he asked.

"Isn't it the same?"

"It comes from your soul?"

"Most probably."

"And what is in your heart, Pia?"

She would just smile never ready to prattle on such uncertainty.

When she was distant he tried to show some affection but it made her even more withdrawn; when he applied her own tactic something terrible cried inside of him, some part of him that he didn't know how to help. Whatever he did she remained the same: with a faint smile, and, sort of, distant look in her eyes, she wasn't his; she never belonged to anyone.

He would worry himself sick when she wasn't around for a few days, he would drive his car in the hope of running into her, he would read her poems, in an attempt to penetrate into her brain or heart or even soul… but all in vain. He was never closer to Pia, she was never more indifferent and he had never betrayed himself to such an extent. He was like a stranger to himself, not knowing why he entered this train which was taking him to a deserted land.

Even though he had never been the most affectionate person, his brother, friends and him mother noticed that he was suffering. Only Dean knew the real name of his malady, but mother, nevertheless, suspected that Pia was the cause of his melancholic, yet distant, ways. The more Andrew suffered, the more his mother showered him with materialistic things as if they were a real substitute for suffering.

Towards the end of their relationship her vocabulary steadily marched in the phrase, *'even when I go... '* he knew he was about to lose her soon. He never anticipated what would be the cause: her neurotic nature, her solitude or even, a new man, but he knew it was inevitable; the end was nearing.

Other than Dean, no one liked her. Mother never even liked the sound of her name, he knew it, Bobby's friend Marshall's words *'suicidal material'* made Andrew kick him out of his house. Was there another man? She would tell him, not because of some rare honesty, but out of indifference, she would tell him just because it was so.

One day she called and said she was leaving, the same day, for some place on the planet, far away, in the forgotten country of Australia. She said she was going to Sydney. No one commented, Andrew smiled and cried inside at the same moment. At the same moment he was alert and he died, at the same moment he cleared his throat and it sounded like agreement, sounded like, *'Hmm'*. One might think it meant, *'All right, go! Fine decision, fine!'*

It meant something else to him. It meant instant death. The dead person walked down the road and went into his room. He wasn't Andrew Bloxham any longer. He looked at Dean who used to be his brother, the man who introduced Pia to him, he looked at his mother who was, as always at this time of day, arranging flowers in the vase and he said:

"I am going to read, please don't disturb me, I won't eat today."

His mother and Dean exchanged quick glances while he opened the door to escape into his nothingness. In that nothingness he remembered asking her for friendship, a lasting friendship... but her last words full of wonderment were, *'A lasting friendship? Even when I go?'*

He concluded that he never knew her, not only as a person, but he knew nothing about her background: where she came from, who her ancestors were, what kind of work she was doing apart from writing poems overflowing with unique sadness and longing. He knew nothing about her, and his pride prevented him from asking Dean anything about her, he only said, *'Yeah, off to Australia she's gone. Good luck, I really don't mind.'*

After her leaving, a long stretch of silence covered Andrew's existence.

In Pia's book of memory his name was taken down as if it had never been written there in the first place. She never wanted to carry too many words and names with her. She knew how to let go instantly, how to never look back, she never even knew who Gregor Truba was, more for the reason that her best friend had forgotten the place she came from, she had forgotten that she had been called Truba once upon a time. Her best friend's name was Nikki Barlow. And Nikki Barlow was the only person who knew why Pia Odak went to Australia. Only Nikki Barlow knew her plans and gave her support.

A week before Pia bid farewell to Andrew Bloxham she had lunch with Nikki to tell her the rest of the story about Nicholas O'B.

Nikki was there when they met. She was there with fingers crossed wishing that this story whose beginning she witnessed, would have a liberating and quick end. While Pia was recounting her epilogue Nikki was biting her lower lip the whole time.

Meeting Nicholas

For Nicholas it was a long day.

Perhaps the longest one in the history of his adventures. Yes, Nicholas was a born adventurer with long hair whose each and every strand carried the sand from different, distant shores. His hair was sandy-blond with letters attached to each strand of his hair; the letters carried a name: the name of a woman he claimed he loved.

Had Nicholas ever really loved?

Ever? Anyone?

We'll see, as the story unravels, through the story that had started some time ago and was initially told by no one else but Nicholas's disappointed mother; we'll eventually come closer to the truth. Nicholas's mothers' disappointment led her to do two things: write poetry and enjoy alcohol without restriction or shame. She loved both of these activities with almost equal vigour, but more than a few times it was witnessed that the needle tipped towards the latter.

Blaming oneself can't bring any good, it can lead towards writing poetry and writing poetry could easily touch a soul's deepest secrets... all of it could be a suitable vehicle for travelling to AA meetings... and right there, at AA meetings they all met. Nicholas's mother was a woman with porcelain skin and an insecure smile, trembling fingers and big brown glassy eyes. She was humble and unappreciated with unfulfilled ambitions. Disappointment sat between her eyes, right there in those two vertical lines where eyebrows outlined their journey. She was coughing and crying inwardly while there was a smile on her transparent face.

She came with a *'Boy'*. The *'Boy'* was in his early thirties, with a cheeky grin and a direct, shameless gaze he could have been likable, loveable to a weak or capricious woman, for both liked such types of *'boys'*. He was a lean man, but his leanness didn't rule out strength: the strength of youth aware of its worthy appearance.

Naturally, anyone's first thought would be that she had accompanied her *'troubled Boy'* to the meeting, but fairly soon it was understood that quite the opposite was the case – Nicholas was the one who brought the lady with him and she was in need of urgent help.

That was where they all met on that, partly filled-with-shame partly proud, day: Nicholas and his mother were sitting next to each other, next to him Nikki was seated with her friend Caesar. After several attempts she managed to persuade him to seek help. He would never ever admit to any living soul that he had a problem with alcohol, no one including himself, which excluded Nikki as she had *'an eagle's eye'*. She read him like an open book: '*After all we don't carry the same surname in vain'*.

He was sulky as a child whose wish wasn't instantly met with delight. Caesar started *'experimenting'* with alcohol at the age of thirteen and that experiment led to yet another one – experimenting with *Mary Jane*, which much later his family understood the reference to, when he talked to his neighbour and brother in crime. For an entire year *Mary Jane* was mistaken for the neighbour's youngest daughter. Alas, it took them a year to discover the truth while Caesar was unrestrictedly experimenting with both – alcohol and marijuana.

Caesar was born to the wrong father, with faulty genes and a restless soul. His steadiness, the finest ingredient of his character, was passed by nature, by God or whoever it was decided which genes Caesar was going to collect. His restless soul and faulty genes attracted events which he selectively collected as one collects little butterflies for a future herbarium of deviant behaviour. No one ever blamed him for his wrong choices for which he paid the price, poor soul; he never asked for such a set of parents. Quite frankly, who would willingly, gladly, ask for such kind of people to take care of them while little? Well, that epiphany occurred to his parents when they discovered *'who'* that much-talked-about *Mary Jane* was. Guilt had found solace in their soul. Guilt was their holiness. For the first time in their life they experienced the urge to do something what would be classified as a *'super-human deed'*, in an attempt to help their son and ease the shame that fell upon the family. Caesar's mother started to read books about holy people and to invite the spirit of Mother Theresa to enter her darkened and frightened soul. They almost succeeded in their attempt *'to cast the devil out'* when he, Caesar, came out and told them an even more horrifying truth – he was gay. In the 1980s one couldn't say that to a plain Italian father or mother. Juvenile alcoholism was a far more acceptable illness than gayness, or whatever they called that horrible, horrible incurable illness that cast a dark shadow upon their family for generations to come.

By the time they sat next to Nicholas and his mother, Caesar and Nikki had become best friends, almost a brother and sister, after all, Caesar invited her into his family, the Barlows. They were holding hands moist with sweat; there was one more person missing, the one that wasn't in need of any such of help, but promised to come as a support for Nikki. Tricky as it could be: Caesar needed Nikki as a support person, while Nikki needed Pia to be her support, as she anticipated that images of her late brother Hugo might hover over the hall full of misfortunate spirits.

Pia was late. Only ten minutes. The hall was full, Nikki waved and Pia hurried with her little smile and a pile of books under her arm.

She sat next to the woman who smiled at her:

"I am Ffiona."

Then she started to retell her story to the panting Pia pointing her finger at the man that Pia looked at, as if mesmerised. It was the first time in her young life full of potential suitors and admirers that Pia looked at someone in disbelief. That she looked at someone and lost her cool. That she looked at a man and her heart skipped. She knit her brows and banished those thoughts, but the feelings stayed. Nicholas was looking at Pia as a child would look at the best candy he had ever seen. He licked his lips, he showed his teeth; he bit his lower lip full and red as a ripe cherry. Pia gasped for air, Nikki leaned over, someone said:

"My name is Rob and I am an alcoholic."

Ffiona leaned her head towards Pia and Nikki, and opened her heart telling them story one would tell their best friend:

"*This is my Boy... he just came back from Andalusia. You can ask me, 'What was he doing there?' Well...* " she shrugged her shoulders, "*... he chased a woman down there, the woman he claimed he loved, and wanted to take his own life when he came back to Dublin.*"

"*Wanted to take his own life?* " Nikki repeated.

"*No, not because of the woman but because of – emptiness.*"

"*Oh, because of emptiness!*" said Nikki again.

"*He used to write letters to yet another woman, a fellow-writer he had met down in Andalusia, but alas, the woman, the fellow-writer, never really answered any of his letters, which only aggravated his feeling of emptiness. The emptiness he tried to fill with weird activities and engagements, with dangerous associations and seedy characters. The precise reason, according to my findings, why the fellow-writer had never written back to him, was that she, herself, grew tired of sending love letters to two wrong men... the letters that had never been answered, so she said to Nicholas that she didn't need yet another loser to write to. Listen love, while Ffiona was trying to save his sanity, her marbles had spilt all over the neighbourhood's local pubs as she: a) visited them all in an attempt to find her misfortunate and full of sins son, and drag him home, and b) exhausted of unfruitful excursions she would sit and order a simple pint of Guinness. Well, that's how my story really started – with a simple pint of Guinness. I started my journey with a new habit of living in the present like meek animals do. I don't have to go (nor do I feel obliged to) into the details of how one progresses from that simple pint into more successful liquid-adventures, for we all know similar stories, every family nurtures or hides, at least, one of them. Absolutely, thoroughly, I was free of knowledge of the written word. In simple words – I had never read a book, for I was a simple woman, from a simple background where people would rather spend wisely their hard-earned money on Friday evening entertainment than on printed letters. What possible entertainment could that bring? But Friday evenings certainly were full of surprises and excitement. Look, my son is an educated man, bastard though, but an educated bastard.*"

Thunder-like laughter erupted from his seat; Nicholas leaned over, extended his big hand to Pia and said:

"Nicholas the Horrible! That'd be me."

"Pia." She said quietly and shook his hand. He looked at her eyes as if he were expecting some miracle to happen –as if a little leprechaun would appear and start dancing on the floor.

When the voice from the back, in all honesty, announced:

"My name is Terence and I am an alcoholic", someone tapped Nicholas on his shoulder and said:

"Sir, quiet, please, you'll have your chance."

"I don't need my chance, I'll take my chance when I'm out of this building."

He looked at Pia, again, into her green eyes, and they were not steady as usual; she looked away as Nicholas asked:

"So, Pia, you are an alcoholic?"

She stayed quiet.

When they were about to leave, he approached:

"You are not an alcoholic but a 'saviour'. How does that work for you?"

"It works well."

"It works miracles as they would say, yeah?"

"No, it doesn't work miracles, it just works well."

"We should practise together, Pia."

"Practice what?"

"Sainthood. Salvation. Compassion and hope. For others' sake."

"Let's go, you devil's son." said Ffiona.

"Good-bye and see you next time."

"I don't want to wait till the next time. Pretty Pia, how about I see you tomorrow, we are not officially alcoholics, so we can have a drink together."

He licked his lips and scratched his freckled nose, Pia hurried, Nikki swung her head and Caesar commented, *"Jerk or fag?"* Nicholas replied loudly, *"Jerk yes, fag – no way!"*

"Is there anything wrong with being a fag?"

"You know that better than I do, you know it, my love!"

Ffiona pulled Nicholas to the other side of the road while he whistled and yelled:

"I'll find you, Pia. Don't worry, sweetie, I'll find you!"

Caesar was fuming, said several times, *"What a jerk, what a jerk, what a fag!"* Nikki said, *"Let it go and breathe, breathe, breathe…"*

As usual, Pia said nothing.

She couldn't figure out *'What it was about that man that made her feel angry?'* Yes, it was the emotion – anger, and so rarely would she be angry. She thought that it would be best to forget him but she didn't succeed in such a simple task. Her mind kept on returning to the image of the man who wasn't *'worthy of any attention'*. And, maybe he wasn't worthy of attention, but her attention was mightily grabbed and undivided.

*** *

Late that afternoon she decided to call her Granny; she needed her soothing voice. Her country was decomposing as a dead corpse does, it stank from all six sides, Pia hated to talk politics knowing that the guilt was equally divided among the three butchers, orchestrated and led by far-away masters. Yes, equally. If she voiced that, she would be called horrible names, those people knew how to offend, how to be vulgar and cruel, without a hint of tolerance for someone's personal view or opinion. Granny Sava said that times were difficult; she said she was glad Pia wasn't home during civil unrest and anarchy of making new history and barbaric destruction of anything that was built in the past hundred years. Granny Sava was a woman of few words, fewer when times were difficult. Pia read through her sentences. She learned that her father was quite engaged politically, as the current political milieu was one of extreme and dishonest bastards. She knew how difficult he could be at times, capricious and partial. He always saw what he wanted to see, a partial truth and the truth that could be to his advantage. She dismissed thoughts of her father, he never sweated a day; if *'the new democracy'* was galloping he was to be the lead chevalier.

Granny told her that common sense was killed and men from the mountains came to the cities, men that never understood urban life, read books or had any decency. She said:

"Regardless of how much I miss you I am advising you to stay as long as possible. It would be selfish of me to tell you to come and visit, as there is nothing good to see here. I might travel to London, I was thinking about it since you mentioned it in our last conversation. I haven't been to London for more than ten years; I would love to see the place where you live and the university where you lecture. My sweet Pia, you've always been my pride. Granddad sends his regards, he is trying to convince me to go and see you rather than you coming over here."

Pia's grandmother never came; Pia came to her funeral and learned the truth there. She was killed while crossing the road.

When they'd finished the conversation she had already made up her mind. The next day she took her handbag and the cane she carried only on rare occasions. She felt frail on that day; maybe out of excitement that she was going to see Pia after several years of absence.

She walked slowly; she waddled in a way, into a travel agency. She booked the ticket and with trembling fingers paid the fare. She thought her trembling to be silly, but doesn't travelling bring excitement? Especially for someone who hadn't travelled for a number of years? Plus quite far; then, all alone. But the decision was worthy of effort: she missed Pia so much and never really verbalised the extent of the pain that her absence had created in her old soul.

The road wasn't busy at this time of day, the sun was setting down behind the tallest building, there were a few pinkish clouds that diminished its brightness; she waited for the light to change and she didn't hear anything, she just felt a rush of air approaching, like a strong wind with its power concentrated in a single spot. She didn't turn this time, the bullet struck her back at the height of her heart, then she turned as if a mighty hand grabbed her and turned her around, she faced the silent invisible sniper and the second blow hit the middle of her chest, she knelt, and the third blow blew off her head. Her bag fell open and the ticket fell out, the little bottle of small white pills rolled out, a little mirror and an old brown leather wallet twisted on the road resembling a baby-beaver. Silence fell upon the road, the traffic stopped and a few passers-by stopped in disbelief; a loud shout from an uncertain direction broke the silence:

"Bloody communists! We'll get you all one by one!"

Someone yelled:

"This lady... she is Doctor Odak's wife. Call an ambulance!"

"Call an undertaker she doesn't need an ambulance anymore."

The telephone rang in the quiet house of Doctor Jure Odak. He was annoyed by the constant buzzing, but then he remembered that his wife went to the travel agency to book a ticket. It took some time for him to get up and walk to the table where the telephone rang incessantly.

He said:

"Doctor Odak speaking."

When he heard the news he fell on his knees. Lately he had become soft and emotional like a child again, when he would think about Pia, his eyes would water. He fell on his knees and started to cry like a lost little child, repeating:

"Sava, Sava..."

The person who informed Pia about her grandmother's death was her uncle Boris. The telephone rang, just a day after she talked to her Granny. Pia thought Granny was calling to tell her about travel plans. Cheerfully she answered but as soon as he said, *'Pia, uncle Boris here...'* she knew something went horribly wrong, he would never call her in London for any other reason but one that could be very disturbing.

Disturbing indeed: when she heard the news, she put the receiver down, she knelt on the floor with her forehead touching the floor-boards and trembling hands holding her heart that raced so fast as if it wanted to race back to her home-town and beat in her Granny's chest. After many, many years Pia Odak cried.

When they buried her mother, out of shock and wrongly embedded guilt, she couldn't cry but stood frozen. This time tears poured out as if the water broke a thousand-year-old steel water gate, and was running and running seemingly without any possibility to stop in a predictive future.

When she walked out of the airport her uncles were waiting for her, her father was *'too busy to come'*, to which Pia answered that he was *'always too busy for anything but himself, let's skip the nonsense and take me to Granddad, I don't want to go home.'*

She looked at the familiar streets with the eyes of a stranger: it wasn't her home anymore, the town where she was born and grew up; the horrible place where they killed her grandmother. She despised the whole town, its people; the country… war was made by beasts, fed by beasts and maintained by beasts in the name of humanity – what a bizarre world she lived in!

***

The funeral and the service were to be held the next day. Her grandfather wasn't well. She picked the little fragments of their lives quickly: her uncle Ivan was forced into retirement; a new government with new people imported from rural parts of the country was established, locals were removed from important civil services, songs were sung on the streets loudly all night long, they called people out to cut the throats of communists or those who dared to think differently.

Her father denied his mother's side of the family publicly to the shame of the rest of the family. Boris was neutral but kept his position and reputation intact, while Ivan saw the times as *'evil, perverse and soulless'*.

Simon Odak left his job as a theatre director and climbed up the ladder, he became a highly ranked military officer, with a ridiculously pompous uniform and an excessive ambition. The uniform was décor, a statement, a new identity that screamed, *'Yes, I am on the right side, I am one of you!'*

Uncle Ivan took his retirement with a pinch of salt characterising the current times as *'madness that will wear itself out sooner or later'*, and dedicated himself to reading and looking after his aging parents, while uncle Boris continued his practice defending all sorts of *'new criminals'* for old criminals who were in prison, including murderers – were pardoned and let off. The majority of them were sent to war with their hearts full of hatred and resentment towards the old government as if the government itself were to be blamed for someone's sadistic nature.

Pia never asked, on any occasion, or any person – *'What happened to Gregor Truba?'*

She pretended that she had never known him. Never!

That evening, when she arrived she went to visit Nonna Oriana. She was much quieter than ever before, she somehow looked much older than Pia would have imagined her to be. She shrugged her shoulders when Pia told her about the horrible death Granny had suffered; she said:

"I've lived long enough, but this madness is something unbelievable. People are so destructive, so full of hatred. I am so glad, Pia, that you live in London. Stay there."

She said she would not attend the funeral. She feared going to the Orthodox cemetery; Pia didn't blame her. Her father didn't come to the funeral either; Pia didn't blame him, even though the whole family couldn't believe that he didn't attend his mother's funeral. Pia didn't blame anyone. She pitied them – all.

She couldn't wait to go back to London, even constantly-mood-changing Caesar and music-and-bum-obsessed Theodor looked like balanced guys compared to the people she met here.

After the funeral, the small family affair, she asked to be left alone. She talked to her Granny for a while, then she crossed the road and entered the Italian part of the cemetery. Her mother, her Sapphire was buried there.

"Sapphire, how can I love when all I have ever loved lies here? I wish I could be with you. People are so difficult to understand and to relate to. Even

my own father is a brainless, obedient, power and recognition hungry monster. Mum, I hate them all, sorry mum; I hate them all. I wished for a better world, the perfect one you and I had created. I would write silly little words and you would paint beautiful pictures, you are my soul and I don't know where to go without you. You shouldn't have left me like a candle in the wind, like a leaf carried by the wind! Yes, there is reproach in my words, I don't think you were selfish, I sincerely don't think you were, but I wish you could have taken me with you. And now, there is no more my second-dearest-person, my Granny Sava, what am I to do? To hang around with a moody gay-friend Theodor and his entourage? Or to monitor the often lost and angry Veronika who calls herself Nikki? Or to sleep with men I don't care about? To believe in love that I have never experienced? To bury myself into books and get all kinds of degrees and PhDs and who-knows-what? To educate predominantly disinterested kids? Or, to have my own kids for the sake of my own sanity? Sapphire, I miss you endlessly. I see you in the morning mist, in London's river of ever changing faces, I often find you among the long sentences on various pages or, I visit galleries just to feel your breath on my nape. Sapphire, I shall leave this town now and I will probably never come back here – why and to whom? I shall carry you within me wherever I go, and we'll talk as we always did. I love you, Sapphire."

She hugged the tombstone, she looked at the picture of a young woman, a beautiful young woman who looked like Pia herself, she kissed the photo, wiped off a tear, stood up and in a brisk walk she left the cemetery.

She refused to see her father; early in the morning she went again to the Bonifacio's house and stayed only fifteen minutes, long enough to kiss them good-bye. This time for good.

Nonna Oriana was much quieter than she usually was. *Nonno* said, '*Go, Pia, go, those bastards will destroy any decency, people are like sheep, they just follow, but mark my words, they'll understand it all in twenty years' time, but it'll be too late. We will be left with nothing. Nothing, Pia, nothing! These are worse than communists; believe me. Mark my words, people will wake up in twenty years' time when they are robbed of everything, of any right, even the right to their own life.'*

When she sat on the plane she felt relieved.

But the melancholy in her soul just deepened.

She remembered the last words Granny told her before leaving:

"You are going to a foreign land where you don't have brothers. Nikola left, and he had never found anything that he couldn't have found here, except his God-given mission that had to be accomplished. His soul was unsettled and empty in that land, he was cheated and lied to: they took advantage of him, he knew it, but he adhered to his mission. He had faith. You have a similar sensibility to his, retrospective and wise you are but a solitary soul, don't let the wedges of darkness be driven into your conscience thus separating you from your source. Don't let agitation or any sort of disharmony break down the protection that has always been sustained as our family and friends alike expressed true brotherhood to one another. Don't let self-doubt or fear widen the gap between you and God."

She smiled.

"OK. London. Let it be London."

For Pia Odak there was no more home.

***

Nikki was waiting for her at Heathrow. She drove back home in silence; she knew that Pia's dearest person had passed away but didn't know the details. Actually, no one knew the details, except the two people who congratulated each other after *'the task'* was completed: the sniper and his mentor.

The coldness of London sneaked into her heart.

Who would care, anywhere, that she had lost her grandmother? Yes, Nikki did, but she felt alone, and that was a rare feeling in Pia's life. The most unlikely question she imposed:

300

"Would you care to stay over tonight?"
"Sure."

Everything passed in silence: the drive without a word, Nikki parked and took Pia's bag into her apartment, she unlocked the door as she had her key, they walked in and Pia just threw herself on the sofa. She looked at the switched-off television set as if there were someone who was going to tell her a story. A story that might cheer her up. She didn't believe that any story would cheer her up, but when Nikki pressed the button on the answering machine, the messages played: Andrew said, *'Pia, Andy'*, a colleague asked if she was back, then, *'Pia, Andy again...'*, Theodor expressed his concern, the most unlikely gesture that Nikki would ever expect from such a poof, some other voices and names, once again Andrew said, *'Hope you are well'*, and the last voice in a heavy accent teasingly said:

"Beautiful Pia, how about a drink? We are clean and beautiful; we fear nothing. Call me any time. I'll leave anything I'm engaged with if I hear your voice. Drink's on me."

A little smile slipped from the corner of Pia's lips.

"What a creep!" said Nikki.

"A creep? Why a creep?"

"He drank you up with his eyes, he drooled like a dog; he is an idiot. A real creep."

"No, I would not agree this time, Nikki. He is an act. A charmer. He performed for us while having a good time. His life is like a big performance, a theatre, he is a director, a dramatist, a main protagonist, and then any character he chooses to be at any given moment."

"Is that appealing, appalling, or... what?"

"I don't know. I really don't know, nor do I care."

All of a sudden Nikki asked:

"You never saw... Him, back there?"

"No."

"You never loved him?"

"I never loved anyone, Nikki."

"Sometimes I pity you, sometimes I envy you."

"No need for either, Nikki."

"What is it like to be so perfectly disinterested, so utterly indifferent and authentically yourself? I lose my cool so easily; I fall in love with idiots at the drop of a hat. I always admired your coolness."

"Nikki, there is no coolness, only malady is there. I am not able to love anyone. I loved my mother when I was a child and I lost her. Then I stopped loving as if love were a sin, a prelude to disaster, an unsettling dream or Neverland. I loved my grandmother and she was killed, Nikki. She was killed like a fly. A cunning beast shot her from the back, an old woman, what human would do that? To kill an old woman that was walking down the street? A nameless man killed, to him, a nameless woman. Otherwise, who would harm my grandmother: such a goodhearted, and almost invisible, soul. She was so modest and quiet; she helped whenever help was needed. As a doctor's wife and a priest's daughter she understood humans and loved them without discrimination. Do you remember how gentle and kind she was to Hugo from the first time she met him? She used to call him 'Little Angel' because she meant it."

Pia's eyes became glossy; Nikki hugged her and said:

"You loved your mother and I loved my Hugo, no one can replace those sincere and holy loves that we've lost. You loved your granny too, but I never loved anyone other than Hugo. I sleep around with good-looking guys only because no one wanted to be my boyfriend back home. Do you know why? Because my mother spoke ill of me. She told neighbours and teachers, and kids alike, that I was disobedient and impossible to handle, that I was a wicked child. Kids stayed away from me. That was my mother. What memories will I ever carry with me when she passes away? I have let them all go. I have changed my name. I won't remember them, nor talk about them ever. Right now my father is probably studying 'Mein Kampf' with references given by our family's favourite friend, the Holy Father Marag. Or he has been studying it for years, a hard copy brought by my grandfather straight from the source."

The telephone interrupted their conversation.

"Pia?"

"Yes."

"I left messages, and you are playing cool. I love you being cool. I love your cool, little heartless heart. Where have you been?"

"Too busy lately."

"A drink tomorrow?"

"No. Thanks, but no."

"Someone's with you."

"Yes."

"Tell him I hate him and I envy him, OK?"

"I certainly shall."

"See you tomorrow, Pia."

Nikki lifted her eyebrows and said:

"The Irish bastard?"

"Yep."

"The new candidate who thinks that he'd be the one to conquer the unconquerable fortress."

"Go to bed now, Nikki."

Why was she thinking of that man? She couldn't answer that question. Probably, because he was more annoying than would be considered acceptable. She strongly disliked all the words that came from his mouth, she disliked the look in his eyes while observing her, even the tone of his voice she disliked, but yet, there was something likable about Nicholas. What was it? She couldn't put her finger on it. Did he take her back in time when she just started to trust Gregor Truba and utterly liked that new feeling? But Nicholas, it was obvious, was such an untrustworthy creature, every pore of his emitted – liar, liar, liar.

All but liar he was. He never lied, at least, not purposely, not consciously; he told his truth with brutal honesty and because of it he always left the impression that he lied or, at least, exaggerated.

But he never did. He was a shameless man who enjoyed seeing confusion and disbelief on people's faces.

***

On the third day she went back to work. On her way out a wolf-whistle almost drew her attention, but when he called out her name she turned around. He was leaning against a rail, smoking. She said:

"Hi, I am in a hurry."

"No, you are not. No one's waiting for you Pia, let's have a drink."

He took her hand and led her into his car. He sang a song with his ever-present smile.

"Where are you taking me?"

"To the most horrible place. Somewhere I can torture you, you can't even imagine what I will do to you."

"You are not funny."

"I am taking you to the pub, OK?"

And he did. He took her to the pub where they sat in the corner; he put his hand on hers and said:

"Relax, I am just a barking dog, I don't bite."

He brought two pints to the table.

"Listen!" he said.

"You remind me of someone…

I met her on the long sandy beach of Cadiz in Andalusia. She was sitting there all alone, all day long. Writing love letters every day addressed to two wrong men, as she told me, a few summers ago. She told me of the aches in her soul which were reflected onto her face and her body, she told me she had a strange instinct of choosing a wrong, sometimes troubled man… and I hoped, back then, that I could be that choice easily, for I was a wrong man for any woman, and troubled as no man on this earth could have been troubled, ever. So, I believed back then, that I was the right one for her, and told her so one starry night while I lent her my sympathetic ear to absorb her pains and to take them into my inner chambers allowing them to become the prisoners of my secret wishes.

DETHRONED

I was more than a troubled man back then; I was an alcoholic who was never aware of the seriousness and the extent of his own troubles, simply called alcoholism.

I am a writer who had published only two novels even though I had almost written seven but never finished them for I had never had steady concentration nor did I have the discipline to continue with almost anything I commenced. All I could commit to was to chase loose women wherever their whims used to take me. The latest one took me down to Andalusia with her swift steps and a promise to teach me the art of perfect lovemaking. It was all that mattered – lovemaking, drinking and dancing, for I thought it would heal my troubled soul and it somehow could build a great exciting novel, to beat the words and curses of those bastards who said that I was written off as a writer and as a man. The word 'honesty' was never sewn onto the epaulettes of my ancestors' garments. Consequently, neither onto mine. A plain bastard, that's what I was – but became aware of it, only lately.

I despised honest women, mocking their boring lives, always searching for something shameful to be disclosed about them, only if I could succeed in finding it.

I was born as Nicholas Jonathan O'Brien in 1971. Dublin. When I was born my father ran away, for my mother's father was approaching his flat with a long sharp green piece of broken glass to slit his throat. I met my supposed father 28 years later on his deathbed, and he said he never knew I was his son. He said I did not look like him, but I told him I drank like him, so we laughed together for the first and last time, ever. This is the only recollection of my father Joseph... I never bore his last name, never wanted to.

My grandfather on my mother's side, who never slit Joseph's throat, kicked me, and my mum out of his house on the very same day she took me home from the hospital. I was not welcomed; I was a real bastard. On that day I started to cry so heavily and loudly that my mother was forced to move out of town, but she said that I was lucky for I cried so much, and because of it my eye-lashes grew thick and long, and you know, such thick and long eye-lashes could only be found in folk stories. She told and retold the same story to anyone who was willing to listen to such nonsense without protesting. Someone told me, when I was a child, that it would be good to piss a lot, maybe my penis would grow long and thick. Solely for that purpose I started to drink enormous quantities of water (and beer later) hoping that those words were blessings, which would come true only if I followed them religiously. Which I did! Waiting for my penis to grow thick and long I developed a huge pit in my stomach, where later, I could have stored half the stock from the bottle shop around the corner, where my mother used to work at that time. She changed her job easily and frequently, but she had always worked in bottle shops or local pubs. Her nickname was 'Luv' for that's how she called each and every person she ever met. As Luv was only sixteen when she had me, she never knew what to do with a crying child but to yell at him, so she became a champion at yelling and if only there was some championship in the world in that regard, she would be the one to win the prize year after year, and her name would be written in the Guinness's thick book. She could have been crowned as yelling queen, all thanks to my constant loud crying, and her disappointment in the world so early in her life. She was so bitter that all the dogs in the neighbourhood would run away as soon as they smelled her approaching. Paradoxically, she called people 'Luv' not out of 'luv', only because she learned that name from her mother. Plain as this, kindness and empathy did not play any role in it. Did I mention that I was the only one she never called 'Luv'? Bastard, she called me, she yelled,

"Stop crying you bloody bastard!"

I liked to be a bastard, for I thought that was what made her angry; as I could not get her love I always provoked the opposite. It was a mean but easy game I learned to enjoy very early on in life.

When I was about seven years old I started to hear music. Out of nowhere. Just gentle, beautiful sounds produced by leaves trembling in the breeze, or music of a distant river, wings flapping above my head as birds were gliding gracefully, the crickets' song, a gentle buzzing of bees and the marching song of a colony of ants... Endless songs and melodies.

Then, those songs were transformed into plain words, and I would hear the most beautiful conversations between two birches or an intense argument between two or three crows, sometimes pigeons; the wind had the voice of an icy lord and talked to me in an ordering manner; the seasons had different voices and all of them had messages for me. That was why I never liked being around my mother, for her voice would overtake all the others, and it was harsh and deep as if it were coming from the underground, from some dark otherworldly princess.

As I couldn't afford a guitar, I had stolen my first one. I needed an instrument to convey this music, and a vehicle for my words.

I don't even know if 'stealing' was the right word. I came into the music shop and Fat Liam was there, eating his sandwich. Asked him if he wanted a beer to which he replied by hysterically nodding his head. I told him 'get a six-pack', gave him some change and he went out to get a six-pack. I took a guitar and carried it out. Liam stared at me with the six-pack in his hand and I said, "What? What are you staring at? I'll break your nose if you don't mind your own business, you've got your beers."

He feared me. Most of the boys did. Even when they were in a larger group, they feared me, I was known for my fierce character and quick fists. And I was unforgiving; they knew I would get them one by one sooner or later if they ever tried...anything. So they never did. My reputation grew steadily day-by-day, year-by-year."

"Why are you telling me your story?"

"Because you'd like to know, wouldn't you?"

"Not really, Nicholas, not really. Plus, this story doesn't sound very convincing. Is it a novel that you are writing?"

"Yes, dear Pia, it is my novel, and you are going to be the main character."

"Hmm...I have a different view of my future engagements."

"Let's make love, that'd be the best way to start out novel."

"Now it is our novel, is it?"

"Well, if I am going to include you and make you the main character, then yes. It is going to be 'our novel'. We can call it 'Beautiful Mysterious Pia and the Beasty Beast'...or something like that."

"The Beasty Beast?"

"Well, you can contribute, I value each and every one of your pauses, commas or question marks – you know that."

"Do I?"

"Of course you do. You know that men search for you if you don't turn up; you know we spy on you if we don't know where you work or live; you know that men are intrigued, they care about your pauses, commas and question marks. You know all of that, yet you pretend you don't have a clue."

"What's your intention?"

"To make you the main character of my upcoming novel."

"When did you start it?"

"At the AA. Alcoholics Anonymous. What a splendid opening. Listen: I met her at Alcoholics Anonymous, she came in and the place ceased to exist as people stopped to breathe, all of that merry audience fell under her spell, just Nicholas O'B choked and coughed as smoke from the latest cigarette was still slowly pouring down his Adam's apple. How about that?"

"An absolute hit."

"Just wait till it hits bookstores!"

"Nicholas, you are charming, but you are a waste of time."

"Am I?"

Pia nodded her head, sipped her beer and couldn't help but show a little smile.

"That's a good sign."

He said, grabbed her hand and planted a wet kiss onto it.

"I like you that much, that if I had another beer I would ask you to marry me, yes, to marry me, the man who said he would never get married even if he lived another hundred years, Pia... Pia what?"

"Odak."

"Wow! Pia Odak, it sounds so mighty – Pia O'Dak. So, Pia O'Dak would you like to be the most prominent, the most important character in my new novel which I have commenced right now?"

"No, thanks. Pia O'Dak has to go. She has to meet some people and she is a little bit late."

"What people? The alcoholic queer? Please, don't let me down because of one simpleton, let's get sloshed and continue writing our novel with a new opening. Let's title it: In Nicholas's bedroom."

"I'll call this chapter - Pia's Leaving."

"Don't you forget that this will be just a chapter, a simple insignificant chapter of a Long Book of Loving and Longing. You can leave now, Pia, and console your pathetic, little queer friend and I'll stay with another beer waiting for another protagonist to fill the gaps and the cracks. But tomorrow, I shall wait for you with a prelude written, for a new chapter."

'What character!' Pia said to herself and hurried to catch a cab.

When she came to her car Andrew was crossing the road. He gave her a quick kiss as she offered her cheek.

"What are you doing here?"

"Went to buy some records."

He waited more than an hour before she appeared, but he never told her that.

"I haven't seen you for a week."

"Yeah." It was all she said. He sighed; she sat in her car and said:

"Speak soon."

"I'll call you in the evening."

She honked and let herself into the madness of the London traffic. Andrew bit his lip but it didn't do a thing to his anger. It just grew deeper, it sat on his tongue and pulled it backwards into his throat: choking the life out of him.

When he walked through the door the strong smell of quinces over-whelmed his sense. Mother was always mindful of beautiful smells, that's why she always had fresh flowers in her vases and fresh quinces on the table. His mother said:

"You look pale, Andy. Is everything all right, son?"

"Why wouldn't it be?"

"Here, pour some Moët for both of us." She said while taking out two crystal glasses from a cabinet.

He sat at the table and remembered the day his dad passed away. He didn't cry on that day, but those quinces always reminded him of something unpleasant coming.

"Cheers! And cheer up Andy, cheer up!"

Andy smiled only with one corner of his lips as a disappointed, or bitter, person would.

That evening he came over, Pia was reading while Nikki was preparing dinner. He sat next to Pia and after a short time he said:

"Is everything fine?"

"It has never been – just fine. It is so British 'just fine'. I see things differently than you do. Things are not fine."

"What bothers you?"

"Please, Andy, don't you start again with the 'what-bothers-you' conversation. There's nothing that really bothers me, it's just life in general that isn't kind to people. Things like war, like killing innocent people, my Granny... all sorts of things can be wrong. I am reading a book in an attempt to skip reality. I peep into some other realities that serve not only as a means of escape, but as some sort of consolation when I witness more morbid forms of existence. Does that answer your question?"

"No. Are you seeing someone else?"

Nikki quickly left the room. Pia put down her book and took off her reading glasses.

She gave him a long peaceful look and after a short silence she asked:

"What do you think?"

"I am asking you, I don't know."

"No. I had a drink yesterday with someone, but I'm not seeing any other man. Is that what you wanted to hear? Is it that you are asking me to justify my breathing? What is it exactly that you want from me? Put it in plain language."

"Sorry."

"Sorry. That's again, so British. Just 'sorry', that would do."

"What do you want me to say? That I am not sorry?"

"Yes. Don't be sorry, but think prior to saying something you might regret."

"Are we going out?"

"I have to finish an essay. You better go now, I'll call you tomorrow."

He left angrier than he was when he came over. He couldn't read her; he couldn't get any warmth from that woman. She was perfectly self-sufficient, never missed anyone, anything, never asked for anything. He noticed, when he stood up she just sank deeper into the couch and adjusted the pillow behind her back.

That evening, for the first time he talked with Dean about Pia. Dean knew her better, or it just seemed so.

"Don't make a mistake and fall in love with Pia." Dean warned him.

"Oh, no, no. Don't be silly… it is just that I can't understand her sometimes. Should be just a matter of a different culture… I'd say…"

"Or, she is freakishly unattached, unavailable by all means. Don't get attached, keep it casual…"

"…as I do."

Everyone knew Pia didn't belong to anyone. She belonged to herself. What bothered him the most was the fact that she was happy with that. She never looked for anyone or complained in any way. Yes, she was frustrated, often worried, but she didn't need others to soothe her soul in any regard. He didn't know anything about her inner life, about her past or future plans. His name hadn't been written in her future books or poems, he knew that and there was no way to change it, to please her in an attempt to open her book and let the light shine onto her pages. They were obscure and hidden. At least to him, Andrew Bloxham.

Nikki's high-pitched voice snapped her out of her thoughts:

"Shit, shit, shit! I am running late!"

"Where to?"

"Caesar's waiting. Meeting's today."

"Don't even bother asking me to accompany you today."

Nikki took off her apron, ran through her hair with quick fingers and said:

"Veggies are in the oven, give them another ten and take them out. I got to run."

Off she went leaving Pia seated on the couch with a book in her hands and a look of indifference in her eyes.

When she was alone the telephone rang. Nicholas asked:

"Has he gone?"

"Yes, he has."

"Fancy some company?"

"Aren't you going to the meeting?"

"We had a fight. Nothing new. She can go by herself, anyway, she'll find your poof-friend and the tall girl."

"Nikki."

"Whatever."

"Whatever."

"Hey, hey, don't you shut me down. How about a drink?"

"I don't feel like…"

"When you get out you'll feel like it. Please."

Silence.

"Pia? I said, please."

Silence.

"So, you don't even wanna answer? Like, answering with silence, what an attitude."

"Give me half an hour."

"Half eight."

"Half eight"

DETHRONED

Nicholas O'Brien licked his lips and rubbed his hands. Pia. Yes, he liked this woman, it wasn't only that he was capricious and keen to get into her bed; he genuinely liked Pia *O'Dak*.

***

"That lanky bloke, is he some sort of a boyfriend?"

"Is this an interview?"

"No, just asking questions and expecting you to answer to your best knowledge and full honesty."

"Nothing to say."

"I told you my story."

"You made up your story."

"Yes, I did. Now's your turn to make up your story."

"I don't make up stories."

"Then tell me the plain truth."

"I don't know what that would be."

"Never mind. Let's talk about our future. How about I take you down to Andalusia where we can look at the starry night, listen to the cicadas and drink some local homemade wine, you could write poetry and I could tailor my new novel according to your moods, your eyes and physical beauty. Let me take you, Pia. London is rainy, boring, it drains one's soul… let's go where people play Flamenco guitars, where they drink fantastic wine, dance and celebrate life and love. Let me take you Pia O'Dak to the most beautiful places where I haven't taken anyone before."

"Inviting, tempting, but…no!"

"Oh, my heartless little bitch, what can I do, or promise that would melt that ice from your little, one-square-millimetre-surface heart? Do you want me to sing, play, dance, recite, take off my clothes, cry, beat someone, cut my veins…what do you want me to do in order to please you, in order to change your heart?"

"Stop acting out!"

313

"What then? You want a boring friend? A boring situation? Go, go and call your lanky bloke, he seems to be all proper and utterly tedious, you can sit next to him and read your hard-cover book and feel safe, predictable and lifeless."

"I can't follow, you give me a headache, too much information, it looks as if you had ADD when you were a child?"

"Yeah, medications never worked. But alcohol did, and it made me even crazier than Ffiona had ever been. That's how I can handle her; I am more knowledgeable on the subject than any of those teachers-preachers at AA.

"You were a drunkard, you said that."

"Yes, thanks! I was, once upon a time. I am, a so-called, recovered alcoholic, how about that? Does that bother you at all?"

"Not in the slightest."

"Thank you, then. We can continue now with making plans for our honeymoon. I have been offered an opportunity of a lifetime to go to Australia and work with Aboriginal people. I was keen to go, but then, I have met you and promised myself that I will only go with you as a trophy in my hand. That's what I am working on right now: How to take my trophy into far-away Australia, the land of crocodiles, koalas and cockroaches."

"You are crazy, Nicholas..."

"Thank you, I know I am. But you have to admit that you have never had such a good time with any of your lanky boys that drive expensive cars, have you?"

"Now you've got it all wrong."

"No, no, I haven't. I know exactly what I am talking about, you know it as well, but let's talk about our bright future, about the Australian landscape where swarms of huge and frightening flying adders blacken the ever-blue clear sky. See us as pioneers, as adventurers in immense savannahs and tundras, or whatever they call those vast open spaces that only the sky and crocodiles walk but never a human being, except for the Aboriginals, who have banned people from ever crossing their land."

"ADD in its full splendour."

"No, this madness is called love, my imagination runs wild when I am in love, my ideas never run short of a grandiose glow... Pia, Pia, Pia... let's run away together. You are my ADD, without you my mind is boring, a stale swamp... and when it comes to, the so-called ADD, it is all made up believe me. I was a brilliant child with brilliant ideas bursting under my skull, singing beautiful songs, talking languages and entertaining the entire class; in my days it used to be called creativity, imagination and wonderment, today, they sell drugs to gifted kids, as if we don't need creative and clever people but only obedient brainwashed machines. If you prefer to label me – call me 'ADD Nicholas' and join the mass of misinformed or frightened people. Yes, frightened in expressing their treasure, as they fear it can be stolen or forbidden. There are so many made-up mental 'illnesses' and 'disorders' in order to make us dependent on drugs, doctors and experts... that's all bullshit, as the bigger plan is to drug the nation and turn us all into zombies. Look how many zombie-stories 'writers' write nowadays. Everyone's a writer today as they create their zombies, vampires, wizards, lizards, bloody kooks... What? Funny?"

"So funny you give me a headache."

"That's good, very good, I arouse all sorts of feelings in your heart. I am able to warm your heart to mess with your head, and of course, in the end – to mess with your unholy heart."

Last Day in London
(Late Autumn 1993)

"A voyage
An urge to say good-bye
A lie
...and to the lie
A cry
For some form of a life
A truth
The unquenchable thirst
Loving or longing
The sadness of belonging
A voyage
My voyage to eternity
...at last,
Closer to your breath
At least,
Oh, sweet, sweet never-ending past." (Gemstone, London 1993)

That was the last of Pia's poems written in London.

It was a coldish day. Her bags were packed. She sealed two envelopes: one was addressed to *Sir Theodor Lukas*, the second one to *Miss Nikki Barlow*.

She put her light coat on and telephoned Andrew:

"I have to see you, now."

"I haven't heard from you in eleven days."

"I know. May I see you in a short time?"

"Yes. When?"

"I'll come to Forest Hill Road in ten minutes, can you make it?"

"You wanna see me on the road?"

"Yes, if possible."

DETHRONED

"I'll be there in ten, see you then."

She walked an uncertain walk.

Met him without any smile or a sign of warmth.

He almost hugged her but restrained himself not knowing exactly why, he just thought of it to be wrong.

She said:

"Today at 11 o'clock I am departing."

"Where to?" Andrew asked, almost choking on those two words.

"To Australia."

"Hmm." Andrew said, as he couldn't manage any words, he feared that words would betray him or liquefy on his face.

He said nothing more but just gazed into her back getting smaller and smaller down The Forest Hill Road.

She expressed a wish not to be accompanied to the airport, as she never liked *'public displays of affection'*.

He stood there like a frozen, heartless creature himself, unable to move or to say anything while the image of his beloved Pia got smaller and smaller and it eventually disappeared on the winding Forest Hill Road.

Slowly he walked back home and closed the door of his odourless, sad room.

***

On that day, in Nikki's letter box there was actually a letter, a real letter not just advertising junk. She turned around and shoved it into her bag. She climbed the stairs, unlocked the door and yelled:

"Nikki's home!"

No one replied. While pouring herself a glass of milk she remembered the letter, opened it up and stared into it with her mouth wide open.

The letter was from Pia. A few words and a poem.

"By the time you read it, I will already be on the flight to Australia. Nikki, I'll miss you very, very much. I fear I won't see you ever again. This is my last poem. Please, take care and keep Hugo's photo on your fridge forever! Pia."

Nikki sat down and in one go drained the glass of cold milk. She said to herself:

"Bugger! I don't need milk, I need a stiff drink!" and poured herself a glass of cheap whiskey. Almost a full glass.

Nothing was written there: why, how long and with whom she went to Australia. No address, no explanation.

She never mentioned anything about it – ever!

'It couldn't be that Pia left for good! No, she only went to visit… or, for a holiday, or some other reason… but she'll be back.'

Nikki thought, *'I couldn't bear it here without Pia, I couldn't bear the thought of not seeing her in a short while.'*

Her heart was filled with hope and dread at the same time.

***

The second letter addressed to Theodor Lukas reached him three days after she wrote it. Caesar said:

"Oh, by the way, there is a letter for you…"

"A letter? For me?"

"A letter for you, you wonder – who on Earth would write to an old man? Well, obviously there's someone who would. Do you owe something to some-one?"

Caesar said it in a voice full of accusation and reproach; hatred almost rang in the melody of his voice.

Theodor Lukas put the letter on the side table and didn't pay attention to it any more. Curiosity killed the cat, and what a cat Caesar was! – he took a paper knife and opened the letter. Then sat next to Lukas and in his theatrical manner started to read:

"Dear Theo, my sweet pumpkin! I am off to somewhere else: far away from our hometown, from my family and those ghastly events that are filling the headlines, equally in the local press and the world papers. The headlines that evoke dread in the citizens of this town and encourage their mighty and daily exercised hatred for anyone who comes from such a land. Maybe they are right, I don't know; don't even want to contemplate who's right who's wrong. I suppose we are all right and wrong at the same time. At the moment I feel as if I don't belong anywhere, hence I let myself into a very strange adventure. Let's see what it would make of me, at least my curiosity has been tickled. Stay well, and be aware of people and events around you – read between the lines. Pia."

With an utter expression of annoyance he read the letter, and then he repeated twice mimicking Pia's voice and accent, *"Stay well, and be aware of people and events around you – read between the lines."*

"And, that's me, if you didn't get it. It is me that you have to be aware of, and the events that I create around you. Oh, my poor sweet pumpkin, oh, my old greedy pervert, be aware of Caesar, he is a queer, an alcoholic and a druggie. He lies and steals from you because he's never paid as he was promised he would be. Yes, Caesar was cheated in so many ways, so he steals your money and possessions and sells your jewellery, didn't you know that? Caesar is a queer and you are a sweet pumpkin. And what is she? She is a bloody cold bitch, heartless and without a soul and human warmth. That's who your, much-concerned-for-your-wellbeing friend is."

"Enough now!"

"I can carry on, I know more than you ever knew…"

"I said – enough now!"

He said it in such a high-pitched voice that it almost sounded like a hysterical scream, Caesar backed off, Theodor took the letter, ripped it into pieces, let the pieces fall down into the garden and then he said:

"Clean it up!"

Caesar took a small vacuum cleaner and sucked the papers in, saying:

319

"Good-bye Pia, you shall be forgotten in ten seconds, that's all Mr Lukas needs to discard people. Voilà!"

Lukas took the papers, glasses and said:

"Make me a cup of coffee and don't bother me for the rest of the day."

"Certainly Captain!!!"

"I am so glad that you are aware of who is the Captain of this luxurious yacht."

When Caesar came to the kitchen, the cup that he reached for fell out of his trembling hand. His eyes filled with tears and he sat on the floor and started to cry as a child who was wrongly accused.

Theodor heard him crying, he slowly got out of his comfortable chair, he muttered, *'Here we go again'*, waddled into the kitchen, knelt down, hugged crying Caesar and said:

"Come here, give daddy a big hug."

Caesar buried his head into Theodor's chest and cried bitterly, while Theodor was telling him soothing words and repeating, *"You are the Captain sweetheart, you know that, you are the Captain, my sweet boy."*

And the sobs eventually stopped and somehow, as if by magic, they turned into laughter; they sat on the kitchen floor laughing like kids while the velvety baritone voice reached the crescendo.

"I am so happy that she has gone." Said Caesar, to which Theodor replied, *"Don't be a mean little boy."*

"I never liked her."

"I know, I know sweetie, don't worry about her anymore."

"Just us!"

"Just us – forever."

***

No one really knew where exactly she had gone, how long she would stay or with whom she had gone.

Pia never explained her decisions in details to anyone.

She just packed her bags and left.

DETHRONED

It was strange that she even said her final *'Good-bye'* to the heartbroken Andrew; it was strange that she had written those two letters.

As her grandmother was no more, she didn't feel obliged or willing to advise anyone back home about her whereabouts.

'Could be', she thought *'that no one remembers Pia Odak anymore. Not even my own father who became a famous man-at-arms.'*
Yes, fame at any cost for Simon Odak – that ex, average theatre director.

This last thought, while still in London, brought her a strange sense of relief.

Anyhow, whatever she wanted to take with her could have been carried easily – in her illimitable mind and in her, secretly humble, heart.

Not too much to start again, seemingly, but not too little either, as no one knew it as well as she did – what she was in possession of.

III

Brothers in Arms

(1985-1995)

Death of the Party

Gregor left the restaurant running. The purple leaf of paper he handed over to Ivan Odak, the district attorney, and since then he couldn't stop running as if a pack of wild wolves were running after him. It was almost the same, as he knew that Ivan Odak or his brother Boris, would run after him, not that they would use their legs but their long arms of the law, he knew, extended endlessly.

Anger blinded him.

Anger, like madness, would lead his feet: he was carried to the house where he spent, only one night not long ago. That night he was intoxicated and exhausted by Pia's countless rejections. He ran led by a single thought.

***

Twenty minutes past midnight Ivan Odak called the house of Milan Lucic, chief of the local police and told him:

"Send your men to the house of Luna Bonifacio. I expect a young man to arrive there very soon with the intention to harm her. But listen, don't intervene immediately, wait, I need proof, at least one broken bone, this fella has to be put away for a very long time."

***

When Gregor reached Luna's house he wasn't aware of anything: there were two police cars parked in the street. The lights in the house were off and the lights in Luna's bedroom were off; *'The Princess has fallen asleep, not for too long,'* thought Gregor Truba climbing up her balcony. The heavy door with the double-glazed windows was locked. He took off his jumper, rolled it around his forearm and smashed the windows. As if possessed by madness given to him by some unseen force, he smashed them several more times; his arms were bleeding; Luna switched on a side lamp still sleepy and unaware what was happening. He hopped onto her bed and started to bash her head against the wooden headboard. She screamed in terror, but he said nothing, just kept on with this rocking motion, in the semi-darkness of the room led by absolute darkness of his inner prison, graced by blind rage and hatred.

He didn't even know whether he wanted to punish her for her evil ways or to kill her on that mad evening, but while he was blindly adhering to his mission, the lights went on and he heard voices; even before he understood what was going on, two men were pulling him apart from his victim, then he felt a dull kick to his head and fell down on Luna's sweet-smelling bed of blood and roses, like a sack of potatoes.

Luna couldn't breathe, she cried and screamed and gasped for air absolutely unaware of what had happened just then. Later she said she thought it was just a burglar, never admitting that she knew Gregor Truba *'that well'*.

He was taken into custody for the second time in his life, but this time he knew that the Odak family and his beloved Pia weren't on his side. No one there to help him.

Alone and cold as a naked gun.

He was about to learn what it really meant to make enemies with the Odaks.

***

Back in the restaurant guests disappeared like cockroaches when the light illuminates a darkened kitchen full of crumbs and leftovers. The first one to run away was Pia, and all of a sudden everyone had to go. Not even an excuse was prepared or needed; they just left.

Only Ivan Odak was standing there with his erect back and his feet apart talking on the phone, giving instructions in his always calm, but unwavering, voice.

The last sentence he said was:

"Yes, he is the son of that politically problematic worm who pretends to be a light-hearted lad, behind whose ideas the clerical mind of that priest stands,

and his father-in-law, a naturalised German. Early Monday morning you'll receive an indictment, we'll keep him in until the verdict's passed, he is a dangerous criminal and a right-winged extremist."

For breaking into her house and beating up Luna Bonifacio, Gregor Truba wasn't labelled as a roughneck or hooligan, but as *'his father's son'*, Truba was treated as a *'dangerous criminal and a right-winged extremist.'*

He knew in that cell, that it was the very last time he had seen Pia Odak, the love of his life. That was the real reason he cried, not because he was badly beaten and was bleeding from his arse, not even because he knew they would keep him in as long as they wanted. He cried because he knew Pia would never forgive him, not with her already hardened heart. He cried knowing he would never ever call her number again, he would never ever hold her hand.

The dream was over.

New pages were to be written but all the letters that he was aware of were confused letters written on the cell wall: letters of longing or letters of hate, originated and engraved by disturbed minds.

The next morning a short man came in. He had a briefcase in his hand and talked in a high-pitched voice to a guard. When he came he said:

"Gregor Truba, I am your lawyer assigned by duty of court. My name is Goran Valic, call me Goran, let's skip formalities and courtesy, but tell me, what have you done?"

"I bashed Luna Bonifacio at midnight."

"Very poetic, indeed. OK, how did it happen? Do you know her personally or you randomly picked the house? Tell me as much as you remember?"

When Gregor told him his story, Goran said:

"What about the officers? You started a fight with them too? You broke one officer's nose, didn't you?"

"No. They came in and someone hit me on the head, I fell down and woke up here."

"Of course, of course…"

325

"You don't believe me?"

"Sure I do. You are saying that she had written a letter to Pia, or whatever her name is, and you came in to talk to her about it, then you lost the plot and gave her some shaking, is that correct?"

"Yes."

"What about the cop's broken nose and Luna's broken ribs?"

"Broken ribs? I just shook her. I know nothing about a cop's broken nose. I didn't even see them. I think the two of them held my hands behind my back while someone hit me on the head, then I blacked out."

"You are Anton Truba's son, aren't you?"

"What has he got to do with it? He doesn't even know those people?"

"I wouldn't say so."

"What do you mean by that?"

"How often does that priest come to your house? What is his name...uh...?"

"Friar Marag?"

"Oh, yes, Friar Marag. That fellow."

"He is a family friend. I don't even know him well."

"But he was the first one this morning to come to ask about you. Still he is waiting for a pass, I am not sure whether he'll get it or not, as you are considered to be a political prisoner."

"Political? To bash Luna Bonifacio is a political issue?"

"I think there are some other things you carry on your conscience."

"You are insane."

"Well, could as well be that I am, but that's how it is, my friend."

"Bashing that bitch is a political issue. Or is it a set up that they can hold me in for as long as they want to? Does that have much more to do with my father than with me? I told you all my sins – I bashed the bitch as there is no other word for this woman."

"OK, OK, you've slept with her, now you call her a bitch."

"How do you know that I've slept with her? Who told you that?"

"I am your lawyer, I have to know. You'd better tell me everything if you want my help... if you wish to leave this hole ever?"

"How can I trust you? I don't trust you."

"Then you are in even more trouble if you don't trust me."

"I want to see my family. I want to find a lawyer of my choice. Can't I see my friends or my family members?"

"You can probably see your mother. No one else at this moment."

"What have I done wrong?"

"You nearly killed a woman, isn't that enough?"

Gregor threw himself on the bunk bed and buried his head into his big hands. He wept without tears. Goran, his disinterested lawyer, left the cell and through the metal bars said:

"Make it easier for yourself. I'll see that someone gets a visitor's pass soon."

The silliest thought crossed his confused mind, *'Maybe Pia would come as she did before...'* even then he knew that this fallacy wouldn't serve him. He knew that he had to do something – but what, he didn't know as it looked like the darkest clouds filled this cell and were about to penetrate his mind and eat his heart. Fear was as cold as the cell itself. The future was all in dots, but the dots were disconnected. That morning he vomited three times, he cried and screamed a few times but no one came. Silence here was different, it was spooky – when it talked its language he couldn't understand, it talked in unknown and unrhymed syllables.

The most frightening thing for Gregor Truba was the fact that the story itself was changed and no one understood his language. They kept on adding to the story naming people he had never heard of before.

Again, as that time before, two investigators came in. He asked for his lawyer but as he wasn't available at that moment, they proceeded with their interrogation. They said things that had never happened and when he said he never remembered the events in that order, he was told it was because of his drug use. They called him a druggie and told him druggies tended to forget and often showed confusion and forgetfulness. He wanted his mother but she wasn't let in that day. She came the next morning accompanied by her husband and Friar Marag. They let mother Elsa in and the two men were refused entry.

The first thing she said wasn't the smartest:

"I told you this woman, sooner or later, would cost you dearly."

"Don't say that. Can't you just hug me? I am lost."

She hugged him as if she was hugging her only child. Yes, he was the only child that she really loved. Poor late Hugo was more a burden than a joy, while Veronika was an unsolved riddle, who brought more trouble than anyone else ever brought to her seemingly peaceful life. Gregor was her first-born son, her pride and her heartache. She always feared for him, because in that crazy land where she willingly came to live, anything could happen to her son who deserved much better: a better country to live in and a better life. She should have taken him to Germany and raised him up there, she thought that he might have become a modern era Beethoven or some other incredibly gifted and successful personality, but in this hell-hole they just threw him in jail because he fell in love with the wrong girl. That was what she was thinking while she ruffled his long blond hair.

"We've organised a lawyer, your granddad will pay for the fees, don't you worry, they can't punish you for what you haven't done. Friar Marag will support you by all means."

"I don't need his help, Mum."

"He'll speak to you from a spiritual side of life. You know, my son, God never gives us more than we can bear, let him help you as God sends help to those in need. No one knows you better than he does; no one wishes you better than he does.

"If you say so Mum, but you know that I rely on common sense more than on God."

"You see where you have ended up with your common sense? If you had trusted what Friar Marag had to say, you would be in a different situation now. And that woman, she is the devil's daughter, it was all her fault from the first day she walked into our house. It was her fault that Hugo was run over, if it weren't for her he would still be with us. She has a horrible influence on your sister, she was supplying her with marijuana – you don't think that I wasn't

aware what they were smoking? Yet, she can get away with all her evil deeds because her family rules this town. What a misfortune, what a heartache, just because we are honest, God-fearing people we have always been punished."

"Say no more, Mum. Calm down, please calm down!"

"They'll pay for that, sooner or later they'll pay for that, believe me son, we'll win."

She whispered into his ear as if she knew something he didn't.

***

The next day they let Friar Marag in. He came with an almost solemn expression: lips tight, chin up, eyes half-closed and fingers interlocked resting on his chest. The guard showed him in, and the priest sat down without a word. For some time his eyes just rested on Gregor's worried face but he didn't talk, he closed his eyes and started to pray quietly. Unease – that was what Gregor felt in his belly. When the priest opened his eyes, he wiped off the corners of his lips with his index finger and thumb.

"The Devil's work is to make us worthless sinners, condemned forever, you are our Father's son."

"Friar Marag, thank you for coming, but please, do not talk of the devil, as I don't believe in the devil, nor do I believe in God, it is like believing in a fairy-tale."

"You don't believe in anything, son. And that is what they taught you in their schools. Denying God is denying life that had created you. You ought to understand that you haven't done anything evil, your evil is relative as it consists of such acts as can be forgiven because they were committed by a son of God who would do better if he knew better. How could you ever have known that those people were so cunning and evil as to set you up? They had absolute determination to destroy your father over and over, but he recognised and understood how they tried to break down this beautiful country of our ancestors, our land, which prior to their infiltration, was led by a good government that believed in God. Our government and its representatives in the past were chosen through a democratic process in which representatives were chosen by

our own people and brought to their seats, to the position of authority and responsibility. Our Lord, Jesus Christ, in every age delivered the mandate – 'Choose ye this day whom ye will serve.' Son, choose this day whom you will serve, understand what your father had been through to save us, and accept what your heavenly Father assigned for you and for our people."

"I am not stupid, I know what Dad is all about, but I've grown up with all sorts of friends, do I really care? Why would I prefer one friend over another just because of their nationality or their religion?"

"Because they have always hated us! Your grandfather left the country because of that, your father fought against them, they wanted to rule, change our past and history. It is our land, a land of our ancestors. How many people have had to leave because of them?"

"Who are 'they' in your view? Who's the enemy?"

"Kids were indoctrinated in their schools. There was no more religious education in schools and they filled young heads and hearts with ungodly ideas. This country is moaning and crying under their weight."

"Weren't 'they' created by God as well?"

"That's another question, my dear son. Let's leave it there. I'll see what can be done to help you in both regards: how to end this horrible injustice that has befallen you, and how to care for your soul right now in this ungodly place."

"And you are saying that such a responsibility is yours, to look after my soul?"

"I am not concerned with the tempter, I am concerned with God."

"Send me a lawyer. I believe in a good lawyer."

"Let us pray; prayer will awake much needed hope in your heart."

Before leaving Friar Marag prayed again, then he left with the same solemn aura around his erect, almost gracious, figure.

Gregor sat on his mattress thinking about this unusual visit: *'What did he really want?'* After a while he concluded, *'Nothing really, he was just a close family friend, and a priest ready to help a person in need.'*

Quickly, he understood that he needed as much help and support as possible in this awful, awful situation, hence the priest's visits became more frequent; their discussions deepened and widened. Gregor learned more about his grandfathers on both sides of the family. He learned about their struggles and their sacrifices.

His lawyer was quite a reputable lawyer, one that mostly dealt with political prisoners and criminal offenders.

When he handed him the indictment Gregor's eyes popped out as if he were whacked with the ogre's fist right in the middle of his belly.

"What?" was all he managed to say, but his lawyer calmed him down, explaining and promising things that Gregor couldn't understand at that moment, anyway.

His eyes went over and over the parts of several sentences:

Hooliganism, trespassing, burglary, obstructing police officers on duty, grievous bodily harm and attempted murder with premeditation.

Further down it said that he was *'a repeat offender and an enemy of the State.'*

"Who? Me? Gregor Truba? This is ridiculous! Unreal!"

Ridiculous it may have been, but unreal – it wasn't. It was very real, well written on several sheets of paper, stapled neatly in the corner with a light blue staple. Written and signed by the district attorney, the omnipotent Mr Ivan Odak, Doctor of Law. His fate was sealed; he knew it the moment he handed Mr Odak that purple piece of paper signed by the virtuous Ms Luna Averna Bonifacio, on the eve of his dearest niece's graduation party.

'I wish I had killed her!' the most intimate, but disturbing, thought surfaced to his awareness, and produced so much anger – he scrunched the papers first, then flattened them straight and again scrunched them then started to rip them in smaller and smaller pieces, screaming, *"damn bastards, damn bastards!"*

Since then, the pillar of his strength and the anchor for his undulating soul became none other than the enlightened Friar Marag, who visited readily and regularly, as any religious guardian who deeply cared for his holy herd, would.

He taught him a different history of his country, the one that hadn't been taught in *'their schools'* where *'traitors and tyrants became heroes and liberators'*. Gregor just listened, often in disbelief, as that *truth* was simply in total opposition to everything he had ever known. He learned how Friar Marag almost saved his father's life, how their friendship grew stronger, and history was re-written in that tiny cell of his in a matter of several weeks of Friar Marag's passionate and dedicated tutoring.

A new mind of young Gregor Truba was taking shape: a mind – mindboggling indeed!

Friar Marag's holy mission was to *'awaken Gregor's sleepy soul and potential'*. And he, the holy Marag, dedicated his own soul to this mission unreservedly.

Imprisoned Gregor didn't know where his soul had gone at the time, but he couldn't care less as he had a support and a guide, God knew, any God knew that he was ready to give his soul to any of them in an attempt to ease his pain.

One sentence Gregor's father, mother, Friar Marag and his grandfather kept on repeating each time when they left, *'Do not worry, whatever has happened won't last forever, our time has come.'*

And that mantra made a wide path in his brain, the path that led him into blind fate: *Our time has come!*

With such knowledge he imagined daily, over and over, all sorts of bestialities he would perform in Luna's honour; he dreamed about her, he spoke to her in his angriest voice, he insulted her countless times and spat in her mouth.

'If our time has come, she is going to be the first one I shall announce the dawn of the new era to'; he would entertain his mind with such thoughts and his heart skipped every time when he thought about the details of his revenge.

'*Revenge, sweet Revenge*' – he inscribed it on a piece of the dirty wall above his bed as one would the words of the sweetest prayer.

Many in the Truba family wanted *Revenge* for different reasons with emotions differently shaped and shadowed: Anton Truba dreamed of avenging his losses in the previous war and his imprisonments; Elsa Truba dreamed of avenging her '*fate among barbarians that had infiltrated her life and she had to endure them*', Gregor's list of revenge steadily grew day by day, while Veronika Truba dreamed of the ultimate revenge – leave them all behind without a word: change her name in absolute hope that it would change her destiny.

Crime and Punishment

Then, in the courtroom, witnesses took stand one by one, day after day. People Gregor knew, and some others that he had never met.

Luna told her story claiming that she *'Barely knew the man who attacked her.'* She said:

"That same year he came to my Gallery and wanted to purchase a chain. He bought it; he was quiet and polite, paid the price without any complaint. I don't recall that I had met him ever again."

Luna's letter ended up in Ivan Odak's hand on that evening and it had never been brought to the light of day; it had disappeared and no one knew about it, even if anyone knew about the letter, no one would ever admit having any knowledge of it.

"I have a police document... on the 22ⁿᵈ of May, this year, Gregor Truba, apparently walked into your Gallery and trashed it. Don't you remember this event or him on that occasion?"

"No. I wouldn't recognize the person who did it. Yes, someone walked in and trashed the Gallery, but I don't know who the person was, and wouldn't recognise that person. One thing I know for sure is, that the young man who came into the Gallery was short and stubby, with short dark hair."

"Do you have any recollection of Mr Truba coming to your house and spending the night with you?"

"This is beyond ridiculous."

"Does that imply that you don't have any recollection?"

"It does. I have never met that man apart from selling to him a chain in my Gallery. I have never met him again, and no, he had never come to my home."

The district attorney suggested another witness: Antonio Lanza, a local resident who occasionally lived in Italy as his job directed.

"Mr Lanza, what would be your knowledge about, the so-called friendship between Ms Bonifacio and Mr Truba?"

"Well, Ms Bonifacio is a life-long friend of mine and my confidante. One evening she called me and asked for my presence. I came over and she complained about a certain young man following her. She said he was a rather tall and blond man, always on his motorbike and she feared that he might, in some way, hurt her. As we all know, and could easily witness right now, Ms Bonifacio has always been an extremely beautiful woman and many men lusted after her. It has been no secret; I know that a few men attempted to do silly things to attract her attention. On the other hand, she is an extremely honest woman, a philanthropist, a friend to many exemplary men and women in our society. She is kind, helpful and inspiring in many ways. If I have to talk about her character, I could mention only good deeds that embellish this worthy woman. But she told me that she was in a, sort of, altered state of anxiety, as that young man was following her often on his bike. As I have always been fond of my dear friend I, sort of, worried about what might happen to her, so I monitored her house for several evenings without her knowledge. I saw that young man coming, taking photos of the house, particularly the window and the balcony, and when I saw him climbing the balcony I was ready to call police, but then, he jumped down and I didn't see him for several days. I assumed that he had never returned, as Ms Bonifacio didn't complain again. After that, I had to go to Trento as my business is based in Trento."

Fumes came out of Gregor's nostrils, his lawyer kept his hand on Gregor's while telling him something under his breath.

The guests from the party mentioned that Gregor's role at the party was to entertain, that he was *'just a musician who happened to be there'*, no one really knew him; he never had a close relationship with any member of the Odak or the Bonifacio family, particularly with Pia. He was called to entertain together with several other musicians and the catering staff.

There were witnesses who *'Knew young Truba was obsessed with Ms Bonifacio'* or *'He would often comment on her beauty.'*

Pia Odak wasn't mentioned; she was never called to be a witness in the case.

For Gregor Truba there were no witnesses, on one to confirm his whereabouts, his intentions to talk about his virtuous character. No, there was only evidence that *'He was briefly jailed for disturbing public order whilst drunk, singing prohibited Nazi songs and saluting with the Nazi salutation.'*

There was another witness who talked about *'Ms Bonifacio's worthy character, and an exemplary behaviour as an outstanding member of our society.'*

Mr Leo Maretti, mayor of the town. He kept going on and on, listing all her achievements as a *'Tireless charity organiser, a donor of her own art, and an avid supporter of young artists in the region.'*

The Truba family, minus disillusioned Veronika Truba, were seated tightly together, accompanied by Friar Marag and Elsa's father. They sat there with sealed lips and a few prayers. A row behind them, Gregor's friends were seated, many of them: all dressed up and combed for the sake of mocking the case and the court. At that time Elsa Truba didn't know that her daughter Veronika had already left in an attempt to forget them all, to change the history of her family by changing her family name and her location. At that moment all that Elsa Truba wished was that her son had downright harmed that woman! Her lies made Elsa sick in the stomach and sick in her head; she dreamed of sweet revenge as well, she dreamed of the times her father and Friar Marag had promised would come, not long ago.

When mayor Maretti finished his fine speech portraying Ms Bonifacio as *'The most virtuous and generous woman'* the men behind the Truba family started to clap their hands and stamp their feet.

"Quiet! Quiet in the courtroom!"
Three men got up and walked to the door, on leaving, one yelled:
"Everybody knows what a fine hooker she is! For the selected elite!" they left in a hurry and once again applause erupted and echoed from one corner of the courtroom to another. Luna had a fine little smile on her pretty face she knew why people didn't like her, they were just common people; the kind she

would never even look at. She looked at mayor Maretti and barely noticeably winked with her left eye. She looked composed but innocent. As she always looked: composed and innocent.

Elsa cried when Gregor stood up. His pants were falling down, he had lost weight; his hair was too long and unwashed, his face grey. The long fingers which trembled when he played his guitar or the piano, were trembling without control. He was shaking and she couldn't bear looking at him. She buried her face into a scarf she was holding in her lap while her husband put the palm of his hand protectively on her upper back. Friar Marag moved his lips barely noticeably, but his eyes stood on Anton's protective hand: on his wedding band and the prominent veins running down towards his strong fingers.

As the sobs became louder, the crowd turned their heads, Gregor turned and yelled, *'Mum please, Mum!'* a commotion took over and a loud murmur filled the room. The judge's voice overtook the murmur:
"Quiet! Quiet in the courtroom!"

"I met Ms Luna Bonifacio several days after I had purchased a necklace for my girlfriend Pia Odak, at her Gallery. It was the third time that I'd met her, but this was rather a chance meeting, or she made it to look that way. She followed me that late afternoon and entered the pub after I walked in. She sat next to me and asked if I wanted to buy her a drink, which I did. We drank and talked, and she asked me what Pia had that she didn't. I told her that I loved Pia and what Pia had was youth and quiet sincerity as opposed to Ms Bonifacio. I have never been interested in older women, I loved my girlfriend and would never cheat on her, but Ms Bonifacio kept ordering more liquor and we started to laugh together... I can't recall our conversation, but there is still that flavour of dirty talking from her side. I don't remember how I had ended up in her bedroom... I just woke up in the morning... she told me to forget her and never to mention what had happened as no one would ever even believe me."

He kept on talking, Luna kept on smiling as if he was telling the sweetest fairy-tale; mayor Maretti was laughing loudly; some people clapped and laughed forcefully; Luna changed the position of her legs several times, smoothing her hair and twitching one of her shoulders.

When she was asked to comment on his statement, she said:

"There is nothing to add. This young man has a wild imagination. I have never in my entire life entered any pub, I dine in fine restaurants and associate with fine people of the appropriate age."

No one was there to confirm his story. The pub owner said he hadn't been in the pub on that particular day; the staff never noticed such an unlikely couple. No one saw them together in the city or in any place that Gregor claimed they could have been seen together.

That was the first and the only time that the name Pia Odak was mentioned but dismissed as if it had never appeared before the judge, the prosecution and the defence.

***

The case dragged on for several months, but after the first hearing when distressed Elsa came back home, she didn't even notice the house was empty. Her heart was empty and there were no other people or events that could fill that emptiness caused by her son's imprisonment.

She took several pills and went to bed. The next morning her father woke her up, she felt exhausted and heart-broken. There at the kitchen table three men were sitting: Anton, Friar Marag and her father. She prepared another pot of coffee, never noticing that the day dawned in its full splendour. If she had only looked through the window, she would have witnessed the most beautiful colours painted into the window-frame, the picture that captured her heart when they first moved into the house. She opened the window to let fresh air in, for she felt as if she were going to suffocate, but her father said:

"Close this window, Elsa, come over and sit with us. Even those walls have ears."

When Elsa sat down, he said:

"I've brought thirty thousand German Marks. All collected from our people in Germany. We have enough money for Gregor's defence, but mainly the money is for our case, for what we have been preparing for decades. Our time has come. People are strong and prepared, money has been coming from all parts of the world: Australia, Argentina, Canada, Germany... we are strong and we are many. Elsa, endure this injustice, their days are numbered. This country is going to be broken as a glass-ball just wait and fill your heart with strong emotions: hatred for the enemy and happiness for our future."

As paradox has it hatred and happiness were chanted and planted in their hearts. When Elsa Truba found a note on Veronika's empty bed, that hatred and happiness made her absolutely indifferent. It read:

"I don't belong to this family: My father loved his country, Gregor loved his image in the mirror, you have an inexhaustible love for your Friar and there is no more Hugo. You won't see me ever again."

She didn't even sign the note, as from that moment she knew she was going to be someone else. She didn't know she was going to be Nikki Barlow, but surely she knew that, somehow, the address Pia gave her would secure a new beginning. And a new beginning asked for a new name.

Elsa took the note and put it on the table, the three men read the note, passing it around the table. Their reactions were different yet similar. Her father said:

"Sure I love my country. It is the responsibility of every man to love his fatherland. What is she implying? Is she accusing me of something? I have done things right! I did everything for my country, and that means that I have done everything for my family. Veronika, Veronika, she was always a problem child. She's gone somewhere for a few days, she'll be back before dusk. Where on earth could she have gone? As if we don't have enough trouble with this

theatre assigned to Gregor. As if we don't have a lot on our plate as it is, organising people and money for upcoming changes. Deal with that Elsa, you know where she could have wandered off."

Veronika's grandfather said:

"You were unlucky, Elsa. Poor Hugo was born with a defect and his life ended the way it was expected. Veronika was always a very wicked girl. This is only one of her wicked games. She is not the centre of attention, but Gregor is. I think she just wanted to draw attention. She'll be back, don't you worry! Poor Elsa, my poor girl as if you don't have enough trouble. Veronika's a real troublemaker."

Friar Marag was arranging some breadcrumbs on the tablecloth. He cleared his throat, laid his hand onto Elsa's, gathered all possible compassion he had ever mustered to present in his placid eyes and said:

"Led astray by bad, evil people… There is a difference between relative good and evil and absolute good and absolute evil. One becomes like the people one associates with. Elsa, you couldn't have done more than you have. Only God is the witness to your goodness and kindness towards that child, but there were the ravages of darkness working together to tear your family apart. You know, Elsa, we know, who they were, who they are."

From the concerns about Veronika, swiftly they changed the topic: counting money, talking strategies and code-names… they had even bigger duties and obligations than Gregor's case, they needed to organise a meeting for fifty citizens called by those code-names, to attend. While they talked Friar Marag leaned his head, with closed eyes, against the headrest of his armchair and listened attentively, sporadically nodding his head barely noticeably. He had already given all his instructions to Anton Truba; after all he was just a clergyman, not a strategist, not a soldier.

The Verdict

Elsa saw him and her tears started to run as a wild uncontrolled river: her first-born child, her God of Love, Beauty and Pride was standing with his pants hanging off his bottom as he had been starved for months. He was unshaven, even though his facial hair was light, a short beard made him look even thinner – sunken cheeks, protruding cheekbones.

She never listened to what the public prosecutor was reading in his long litany of words, she couldn't understand what Gregor's lawyer was reading and numbering, she just held with her right hand Anton's hand, and with her left Friar Marag's.

When the judge read the verdict, a long, loud *'Boo'* echoed, not only through the courtroom, but it escaped through the corridors, out on the streets and people stopped as if paralysed.

Paralysed was Elsa Truba when she saw her son, her Wothan, just stood there unable to speak or to move. Even her eyes stood frozen, she just dug deeper into Anton's and Marag's palms and looked as if about to sing a song.

They walked her out of the courtroom; she never glanced towards her son, they sat her in a car where she started to sing, and much later to cry.

Gregor Truba was *'Sentenced with no parole'* some saw it as *'Justice has been served'* whilst the outraged crowd chanted in front of the courthouse: *'Injustice! Unseen injustice!'*

Give or take: they were both right!
Gregor Truba was sentenced to serve six years in prison. Yes, he nearly killed Luna Bonifacio, he came with premeditation, his visits to her home became more frequent prior to his final act; he had been sentenced before for

'violence and extreme nationalism'; he didn't show any remorse and his version of the story proved to be a *'blatant lie'*. On that night, Gregor Truba, came to the house of Luna Bonifacio with a single intent – to kill her.

His lawyer said they would appeal, as that was outrageous; Luna Bonifacio walked out with her signature little smile on her, still, very pretty and untroubled face: justice has just been served!

The heavy doors had closed, one more case was finished and the Odak Empire stayed intact. Justice has many faces, many chapters; it can be looked at from very many sides and angles.

Gregor Truba was led into his cell with the feeling of nausea in the pit of his stomach; he walked with only one thought in his head: *'I'll clear my name. I'll avenge my family.'*

The determination to overthrow this government, to destroy this country was never as strong for Anton Truba as on that bitter day: when a son paid for his father's sins. That's what he, at least, thought. He thought that the whole process was assembled to hit him where he was the most vulnerable. He never thought that his son had done anything wrong, he knew that the Odaks were after him, and even that girl was planted to act as if she were in love with Gregor. After all, she wasn't pretty, she was tall and skinny, arrogant and unsympathetic; why would his son ever fancy a girl like her? No, those were the Odak's workings behind the scenes in order to punish and silence him. He was ready to hate more, to dream and act on yet a more profound way of destroying them. He had a strong likeminded group, he had Marag and the church behind him, emigrants from all over the world; he knew that in just a few years the roles would be reversed. He knew that in his heart; he knew that revenge would be sweet and the final victory absolute and everlasting.

***

DETHRONED

It took Elsa three months to understand what had happened to her, and to her beloved son. It took only several minutes for Friar Marag to organise a visit to see the young man. He knew that he could have all of his wounded soul right now, and he wouldn't waste a second to grab this, rare but ripe, opportunity.

He smiled a little wry smile, like Luna did when she walked slowly, on her high heels, out of the building with her head held high.

Only Pia, who gave Veronika the address of her family friend in London, not too long ago, dreamed the same dream Veronika did – to run away, to run away far, and if possible – forever.

"Via Roma"
(1986-1990)
Prison Time

Prison time was schooling time: a fine academy, where Gregor learned about things he never dreamed he would. It was a grooming and rerouting time, like the making of a fine map of his future destinations and involvements. The headmaster, though not from within the walls, was his mother's beloved friend. He knew everything: all the sins humans invented or were tempted into, he knew the scriptures off by heart, he knew prayers and curses, he had a vast knowledge of history: distant history of the world, of their land, a not-so-distant history of their ancestors. He knew about the wars: the First one, the Second, the post-war era… he knew, literally everything. He had an exceptional knowledge of philosophy and religion; he spoke of fate in general, and of Gregor's fate in particular, then he spoke of the reasons to endure. He understood physical, mental and emotional pain; he told him stories about his own father, then about Gregor's father – how he suffered during WW2, and how that suffering continued into present times. He knew why his grandfather left the country and started a new life in Germany from scratch; he learned about people, their people, that fought against those rotten red devils; he heard stories he had never heard of before, or they were somehow different, but as they were coming from Friar Marag's lips they sounded, this time, authentic, believable, and somehow, inspiring and soothing to his, by absolute injustice, wounded soul.

He 'opened his eyes' so that Gregor might understand and remember all the horrible things he experienced throughout his childhood and youth due to the faulty regime. Gregor went through total rewiring, deleting of the old and implementing the new material: the one that the Friar needed for his new order. The Friar opened Gregor's eyes and he understood who his friends really were, he understood why some were worthless as worms in an apple tree. He taught him about pride: national pride, pride in one's family, nation and pride in one's physical appearance. About superiority and being chosen.

"Not many were chosen, but you were! Look at you! You are our pride, not just your family's pride, but you represent our nation: the land of beauty but of constant suffering, and injustice as well, that moans under the yoke of the devil. People are waking up, you are going to be just as your father was in the previous war: fearless, fierce and invincible. We are many and our time has come."

Gregor still couldn't understand when that time was coming to their shores, but his heart was full of hope that one day he would be able to avenge the injustice: to jump through Luna's window in the middle of the night and rape her till she dies. That was his dream, but the list never stopped there: under Luna's name, the Odak family members were listed one by one in the order of their importance and relation to Gregor's own life. Gregor never hated the country; his hatred was ignited by Luna Bonifacio's perverted heart and would be extinguished only when he witnessed despair and misery of the last Odak.

Was Pia Odak on his list?

The woman he loved at times *'more than he loved himself'*, as he used to think.

He wasn't sure. He just put her image out of his prison cell, wiped off her name, her smile and her poems from the memory of his inner library.

He left it to chance, as he believed that chance would bring them together again, at least for a short, unexpected encounter. Till then, he decided he would not dwell on Pia Odak in this hole that made his heart full of poison and his mind embodied by the Friar's view of life, love, revenge and hate. Somehow, he was still under the impression that he was seeing through the Friar's eyes; that the Friar was the one who was speaking when Gregor spoke.

He didn't know what had happened to Gregor Truba, the musician, Gregor – the easy-going and fun loving tall, blond maverick, irresponsible, but likable, a next-door helpful hand whenever needed. He never dreamed his father's dreams, he never wanted his mother's friends – how had he found himself to be so much like them in his early twenties? It was too early to look in a mirror and to see Father's bitterness staring back into his eyes. But bitterness was all that was left to him.

***

Dido Baretta was a liar, cheater, small thief, womaniser and a cheap gigolo. All of his life he lived at other people's expense: when his father died his mother had several men that looked after her and young Dido. Each man would leave when he understood that Dido cleaned out his pockets, or that Dido's mum was with him only for one reason – to get by. Some stayed shorter, some a bit longer, but when Dido grew to be a teenager, real troubles started. He was of exceptionally good looks that helped him to charm a woman of any age: he looked like a very mature young man, or a child in a man's body; he was so eloquent and skilled with convincing lies that it needed years for someone to really understand who Dido was. With his puppy-like eyes and soft, mellow voice he would charm women and men alike, and often a husband would fall in love with this charming fellow never aware that his wife had an affair with his *'best pal'*. Dido never had a conscience: he stole from his mother, his friends, the church altar, in shops and petrol stations… all small thefts, as he never had a bigger opportunity to prove that he was *'better than just a petty thief'*. With ease he would break into friends' houses or cars, with the same ease with which he broke women's hearts: he couldn't care less. He would befriend people only to gain trust, information or to seduce a new friend's wife, or sister, or even – mother. He gambled but never drank; at first glance he was a real gentleman: dressed as the most dapper man would dress, his almost black hair slicked backwards, a white laced handkerchief in the lapel, decent but expensive perfume on his sideburns and wrists, an expensive watch and shoes made of the softest, finest Italian leather. Softly spoken, quick to show surprise or excite-ment as a part of his well-rehearsed act, friendly and easy-going. When caught in any misdeed he never argued or explained anything; he would look his victim in the eye and say in the saddest voice:

"I never wanted to hurt you."

But he did. He never cared about people or their emotions, all he cared about was how to gain any kind of interest from others: material interest or sexual pleasure. His statement, *'I never wanted to hurt you'* made him feel superior, gave him a feeling of his own naïveté and goodness buried under his expensive suit and the intent he couldn't resist – to get what was never meant to be his. With age and experience his repertoire and appetites expanded, and from a petty thief he built up his *curriculum vitae* to read: a racketeer, a beater and a debt collector (of often non-existent debts). Yes, someone would call him to do the job for them; to collect their debts and he would knock on the door with a pal, a thug, and deprive them of anything valuable if they didn't have the money to settle a rather suspicious debt.

The only woman he sincerely liked but never managed to sleep with was Luna Bonifacio. She plainly told him that *'regardless of his good looks, he was a little nobody'*, and Luna never slept with a *'nobody'*. When it came to Gregor, not that she slept with him because he was somebody important or worthy of her attention, no, she slept with him because he loved Pia. Yes, that was a good enough reason to let him into her perfumed and famed *boudoir*.

In and out of jail he went in the past ten years. Never too long as he was a valuable asset to the police as well: he shared information about others without any hesitation or conscience. Again, as long as it served him he would co-operate with the Devil himself.

When Gregor heard a loud noise he put his book down. They threw Dido in through the door and threw his few belongings in and locked the door.

"Motherfuck... Oh, I never swear. A gentleman never swears, but those imbeciles!"

He looked at Gregor and said:

"Aren't you that guy with the guitar, the band... whatever it might be called?"

"Yep. I was that guy."

"I followed your case. They got you! You messed with Odak family, what was it exactly?"

Gregor didn't know who Dido was, hence he told him a tailored story; he narrated his story in only four sentences. Then Dido said:

"They won't last forever. Nowadays an honest person can't even buy a new car, let alone a Mercedes that we used to drive a few seasons back. You know, the economy is declining, I used to by a new Merc every season, people had more; if things go wrong I'll cross the border. What about you and your guitar? Could you ever live of it? You musicians are a weird sort. Who's your father, remind me?"

"Ah, no one important."

"I know that he isn't an important man, otherwise you wouldn't end up in this hole, but remind me, I think that I've read something about your background... something like... your father, or someone in your family, apart from you, made some headlines."

"Anton Truba. He was famous for being an extreme right-wing rebel all his life, in his youth and his mature age alike. I don't know much about it, but the more time I spend here, the more I am aware of his 'achievements' from inmates. Seems that he has been well known."

"Interesting, interesting... Yes, like conspiring against the current regime and the state bullshit and another bullshit. I think I know now. Isn't your mother that pretty German woman... don't take me wrong, you got those looks from somewhere, didn't you?"

***

The next morning Dido introduced Gregor to Tonchy Bedak, accused of murdering a local man. He dug his dagger into the man's chest during a game of poker, not that the man was cheating only, but he was a Gypsy man, and there could not be a worse nightmare for a poker-player of his reputation and temperament – than the bastard cheating on him, and the bastard being a plain, stupid local gypsy who was supposed to be *'smaller than a worm'*. But no! The Gypsy was a tall man, with broad shoulders and a fantastic skill for both – playing the game and cheating. He was fierce and direct in his speech and action while Tonchy asked for obedience from anyone he came in contact with. When not obeyed, his temperament was uncontrollable – the lid would blow up and the consequences were dire. It was the second time that he dug his dagger into someone's chest, but the first time the man survived and changed the story to the extent that wasn't believable even to him. But he did change it. The second time they caught Bedak in the act, was when one of the players saw it as a powerful moment for revenge: he called the police, and they were waiting for his call. On that night Bedak was set-up not for murder but for a large sum of money that he had robbed from a local bank. The money was hidden in his house, but when police searched the house it was never found. The money was given to a friar, never named, who deposited it in the account of a man who had German citizenship.

Bedak had two personalities: One personality showed a quiet, introverted man who ate his lunch all alone, never talking to anyone. When this personality dominated he appeared mysterious and dangerous, the signals were flashing: back off! The other personality showed a fierce, shrewish man easily exasperated and uncontrollable. He never feared anyone, and when that personality dominated, inmates and guards alike feared him even more than when he was quiet and unreadable. Sometimes eight guards were needed to control him, to calm him down, to lay him down on the ground – but they never beat Tonchy Bedak! They feared him too much.

He took Gregor under his wing; he asked him to sing for him and, in a very mysterious way a guitar appeared in Gregor's cell that he could play and entertain some inmates and guards. That brought him a new nickname – The Boss as all agreed that he would shame Bruce Springsteen if they were put together on stage. Having a guitar made life a little bit more bearable.

When he was alone his mind often wandered off to the past and visited the days when he was carefree, plucking his guitar for his beloved Hugo who would clap and cheer, then Gregor would tickle him until he cried of laughter.

Often Gregor was woken up in a cold sweat screaming, *'Don't go Hugo, don't fade away'* spreading his arms wide in an attempt to hang onto this faint figure that had escaped from his dream and flew off into a freedom where Gregor didn't belong. Yes, Hugo would come into his dreams, with his little tongue hanging, his mischievous smile and he talked to him:

"Gogol, don't hurt anyone, you are a good brother. Gogol loves Yugo and he loves Lonnie, and Gogol loves beautiful Pia… stay a good brother Gogol, don't hurt anyone, it is not your dream…'

When Hugo would disappear, then the real nightmare started. So many buzzing questions in his head, they never found a truthful answer: *'What was the truth?', 'Was his previous life just a dream?', 'Was it fine and rosy?', 'Was it really horrible as everyone here wanted to convince him?'*

In one of his dreams Hugo said:

"Don't forget Lonnie, Lonnie's lonely and sad sometimes. Then I come in her dreams too, and Lonnie's happy. She keeps Yugo's photo on her fridge, she talks to Yugo in the daytime and Yugo visits Lonnie in her sleep, just as Yugo visits Gogol in his dreams.'

On the next visit, when mother Elsa shed her last tear, Gregor asked:

"Why hasn't she ever come to visit? She's never asked about me, has she? Is she that ashamed of me that she never wants to see me again? I know she can be moody, even lost at times, but two years have passed, and she's never come to see me. Is it true that she has never asked about me? She was angry believing that it was my fault; that I didn't look after him properly on that day. Is that the reason that she's never asked about her other brother? Or, was Hugo her only brother in her heart?"

But he never heard the truth about his sister. He never heard that she had left without a simple *'Good-bye'* that she believed – no one deserved! No one from the Truba family, led by a wise pastor.

Elsa said:

"You know we all tried our best. She was the way she was – no one could ever help her. Even the Friar said that she was one of those who denounce goodness and light of our Lord Jesus Christ. Say no more, please, forget her! If she needs not a single one of us why would you want her to come? Only trouble she would bring to you, just more trouble."
"Is she all right?"
"Don't worry about her. Yes, she is all right because that is all she cares about – looking after her own needs."
"Does she have any friends?" he asked, his voice still trembling.
"Look what I've brought you, a nice jumper. Your Grandma knitted it for you. Focus on those who love you, my son."

Gregor knew that on the day they lost Hugo he lost a big part of his heart, when he was jailed he lost another part of his heart; Veronika never came to see him, he didn't know which part of his heart had died because of that, but one thing he knew for sure– in his young chest a bitter and withered away heart was beating, the heart of an old man left to his own sad destiny. He stopped believing that the day of his freedom would ever come. Freedom looked like a poster on an exotic beach, far away, on some island to which he had never known the way.

With such a heart – broken and partial, he couldn't find any positive emotion any longer, he became so similar to the two men that he initially feared a little bit later despised, but he had grown to be similar to these future national heroes: Dido Baretta and Tonchy Bedak.

In the beginning of the nineties *'good news'* reached them every day: the end was nearing, *'the end of darkness', 'the end of living in a dungeon of a socialist country',* even though he still couldn't believe all he was served with; he knew that he had to take a side, and he knew which side would be his: the same side his father had chosen some fifty years ago.

They were waiting every day for the news, anxious and full of hope that the *'nightmare would soon end'.*

It did!

'Or was it just the beginning of it?' to that question, Gregor Truba, had never had a definite answer, back then, towards the end of the 1990.

His brothers in prison became his brothers in arms. He couldn't say at that moment what would be the consequences of his chosen path, or if there would be any consequences but ever-lasting pride and happiness.

And *'everlasting pride and happiness'* had some untrue ring to it, like a mocking echo that rang inside his head, while his heart remained silent. His mind was poisoned by hatred and revenge, but there was nothing in his heart. Nothing! But, it is the flame of one's heart, not a sense of self-righteousness, which would deliver the world.

On his last visit, even though, neither Gregor nor Friar Marag knew it would be the last one, the latter said to his protégé:

"When God created man he gave him the power to choose. My son, He speaks loudly to our nation right now. Be prepared, be prepared to choose and to lead. My eyes and prayers follow you wherever you go."

As a clergyman he knew that God had given man power, and he was well aware that God had placed him between this power and the individuals, that he could reserve them or bend those powers and secret mysteries the way it served him, suppressed for decades, ideas and ideals.

***

Amnesty for all!

The criminals were let off: small thieves and the bigger calibre of criminals, fraudsters, political prisoners, rapists and murderers. They were all let out. Amnesty for all. And the new army of Brothers in Arms was formed. Thousands of people: grateful, thirsty for revenge and bloody missions, sang loud songs, so loud that the near-by mountains shook, the streets of towns cracked, drunk with freedom and alcohol they sang their songs with full lungs and extreme pride. It wasn't only national pride; it was their private pride, the pride of the Brothers in Arms.

Gregor Truba sang with them loudly, as singing was the best way he could express himself at any time.

New times were ahead of him. He was a free man, in a land that had to be freed, his own land, therefore he proudly sang songs which were forbidden for his father to sing only ten years before. He sang loudly; he sang proudly!

When he crossed the threshold mother Elsa fell onto her knees, hugged his calves and through the tears she said:

"We won! We have already won!"

Friar Marag said:

"We are many."

Gregor's father Anton said nothing. He just smiled, his time had come; he knew it would come, but his biggest pride was – his son by his side.

There were three of them: Baretta, Bedak and Truba, the three prison heroes in a new uniform, shiny shoes and little berets walking with their heads lifted high and with a new feeling of belonging to the new Brotherhood.

"Where's Veronika?"

"We haven't heard from her since you went to prison."

"Do you know where she has gone?"

"London, apparently. Might not be true, but our neighbour's son said so. She never called anyone, she never asked about you."

He would never ask for Pia's whereabouts. Never! He believed that his heart was dead for her and lived for his country, what was deep down he never wanted to know, if something, anything, was buried there he wanted to let it sleep. Yes, forever!

***

The new government set up a new administration, new judiciary, new police force and army.

'What happened to the Odak brothers?' he wondered.

Dr Ivan Odak, a public Prosecutor, the man who issued Gregor's indictment was sent to early retirement. His brother, Gregor's first lawyer appointed by his, at that time girlfriend Pia, kept his position as a lawyer but wasn't in such a demand as before, while the third Odak brother, Simon Odak, the former theatre director, was very ambitious in an entirely different field – politics and the army. Outspoken, he elbowed his way into a new role that no one knew he had in him.

Their father, the old Doctor Jure Odak wasn't seen in public as far as Gregor heard.

Their mother, Sava Odak, was of Serbian background, everyone knew it. The Odak brothers were not of pure blood.

He never asked about Pia. Why should he? His mother was right; on the first day he saw Pia, mother Elsa said that she would bring only trouble. She brought only trouble: Hugo was hit by a car on that day because Gregor only had eyes for Pia; he bashed this woman, Luna, because of Pia, and his sister wandered off, somewhere, who-knows-where, and he believed his mother's words that Pia was responsible for all of those misfortunes. She brought disaster to him and his family.

But that other woman!

She was on his mind.

She had been on his mind every day for the last five years.

Luna Averna Bonifacio.

'Was her Gallery still intact?' he asked himself.

'Dido said Luna was the only woman he never had, didn't he?' his thoughts continued, then he commented loudly:

"Arrogant, selfish bitch." He slowly accentuated each word, there was a little smile on his face, then he said loudly again:

DETHRONED

"Time has come. Pay back time."

It was a warm Saturday evening; Gregor was sitting in a tavern with his, now best, pals Dido Baretta and Tonchy Bedak. Gregor played his guitar and some other young men joined in. They drank a lot. As they were in their uniforms, everywhere they went they were given free drinks. Half-drunk Gregor said to his drunken brother:

"In your words, Dido: 'The only woman I sincerely liked but never managed to sleep with was Luna Bonifacio. She plainly told me that regardless of my good looks, I was a little nobody, and Luna never slept with a nobody.' Do you remember?"

"I remember, that bird turned me down a number of times. She behaved as if the sun shone out of her bum."

"Do you wanna have a go?"

"What are you saying?"

"Let's go and have fun at Luna's. I ended up in jail because she had forgotten that I banged her. I wanna see if her memory has improved."

They laughed; all three hugged each other and drained their glasses. On their way they sang loudly, applauded by passers-by.

They stopped at two or three more pubs, gobbled up more food and drinks and headed the way Greor led them.

***

Nightfall was sudden but soft as the air was soft in that season. There was a strong smell of bay leaves in the air and Gregor felt again as if this was home; he felt carefree and secure the way he felt when he went back home after his lectures or rehearsals, knowing that mother Elsa had baked her thick brown German bread. He felt at such ease like a young boy felt when he went on his third date: without jitters, but just accompanied by sweet anticipation. That was his definition of home: security and that sweet, ever-present anticipation.

The song they sang was a love ballad written by a sad young man to the woman who turned him down for the sake of a golden ring from an old man. When Gregor sang that song the golden chain came to his mind, the chain with a pendant that he designed... the chain and the pendant that the finest artist made. The artisan who owned the renowned gallery – the *Luna Gallery*.

Because of this thought or, of his drunkenness, he felt dizzy; he stopped in the corner of the street, leaned against some fence and vomited. The two brothers laughed and cheered. All of a sudden he felt like crying, but he commenced a new song instead.

Loudly, he started:

"These mist-covered mountains
Are home now for me
But my home is the lowlands
And always will be..."

***

From a distance Luna Bonifacio heard a song sung by drunken soldiers. She stood up and closed the balcony door. She closed the window, sat down and resumed reading a book. Finally, she had managed to publish a book of poetry and her fine art. The book was her latest accomplishment, the task she had always wanted to undertake but never managed for a variety of reasons. Now that the book was published, with her face on it and a short biography, she examined it, once again, with a very critical eye. The photograph was air-brushed and all her wrinkles were carefully erased. There was no smile on her face and it took her exactly three months to decide whether her image in the photograph should be serious and poised or, should she be smiling only with the corners of her lips. The longer she looked at the photo the more uncertain she was. But finally several friends and the publisher convinced her that *'The serious and poised look was more Luna-like'.*

The doorbell rang. She looked at the wall-clock: it was 10:45 pm. Highly unusual time for a visitor. She tiptoed to the door and through the peephole she saw two uniformed men. She opened the door. The younger said:

"Luna Bonifacio?"

"Yes!" there was wariness in her voice.

"Mr Dido Baretta." And he took off his beret.

"Of course." She said showing a small, insecure, smile. She didn't know if she should show them in, but while thinking such thoughts, they heard glass breaking and she saw another uniformed man breaking in through the balcony door. Her heart skipped a beat but a gentle smile on Baretta's face gave her a little comfort. After all, she had known him for a long time and he wouldn't hurt her.

'Why would he? I never wronged him!'

The other man standing next to Baretta had no expression on his face, only his eyes looked to Luna so hazy as if he were very much drunk... or doped for that matter. The one who entered through the broken balcony door took off his beret and started the well-known song, the one that played on Luna's recorder when he entered her Gallery:

"... nono sono ancora diventato matto
qualcosa farò ma adesso no
Luna!
Luna non mostri solamente la tua parte migliore
Stai benissimo da sola sai cos' è l'amore..."

She looked at him and said in disbelief:

"Gregor?"

"Oh, you know me?"

"Of course I know you."

"What do you know about me?"

In that moment it looked as if Luna had lost her cool, her left eye twitched, her breathing was a bit faster, but all of a sudden she took control of her breathing, she straightened her back and gave a different, but still friendly, tone to her voice:

"Why don't we all sit down, I can bring something to drink and to nibble… would that be OK at this hour?"

"We are not in a rush, Luna. You decide what we'll do. It is your house, we are just guests." Said Gregor and took Luna's book into his hands.

"Uninvited guests, I'd say. But I think you don't mind, do you?" asked Baretta, while Bedak sat there and appeared quite annoyed with the slow development of the unfolding story.

"You published a book?"

"Well, yes I have."

"Poetry, hey?"

"Poetry, yes."

"Sit down and read to us, beautiful Luna."

"Can I bring something to drink or…"

"No. We've drunk enough, isn't it so brothers? I fear, Luna, that you might sneak into your bedroom and use your telephone, as I remember that you keep a telephone next to your bed, don't you? No, no, no need to talk, just listen for a while. You might ring someone, but not that great friend of yours whatever-his-name-was, as he lost his position as mayor. Italian bastard, he can't be a mayor in our city nowadays. So, who else would Luna Bonifacio call in such a situation. Someone from the Odak family? Lawyers, judges and public prosecutors? I heard some of them have retired; some are very small fish now, insignificant people, or as you would say – insignificant nobodies. Times have changed. And people, too; we do change as well, don't we? Yes, we do! All of us except you! I was a musician, now I am a soldier. I was a prisoner, now I am a soldier. You were a beautiful woman, and, good on you; you've managed to remain a beautiful woman. You were a liar and you've stayed a liar. Just one thing about you I am not sure right now: you loved men, is it that you still love men? You loved powerful men, didn't you? Men in uniform, are they powerful men? Powerful enough for you?"

"Gregor, please…"

"Please. Luna said please. Is it with a capital 'P' or, are we still lower-case people for you?"

"What is it exactly that you want from me now?"

"You are a brave woman. You were always brave."

"... and arrogant..." said Baretta under his voice.

"Arrogant or proud? What would you say, brother?"

"I'd say... maybe... a bit of both. Let me think: arrogant or proud... proud or arrogant? Yeah, both, but it leans more towards arrogant. I like proud women, sensibly proud. Being overly proud leads to arrogance, isn't that so Boss?" asked Baretta while Bedak stood up and looked out through the broken glass on the balcony door. He said:

"Look, there is a full moon."

"La Luna piena." Said Gregor.

Luna sat on the couch and said:

"You wanna set the record straight, I see." Her voice gave her out. Fear coloured her dark green eyes, but she appeared calm and meek as a lamb destined for slaughter.

"Oh, dear Luna, do not fear: I am not keen on you now that I see your memory has been refreshed. You see this guy? He looks so disinterested and bored. Yep! He is. Bedak doesn't like older women. What are you now – fifty? Still beautiful but, for him if a chick is older than sixteen it doesn't work at all; it doesn't excite him. The only one who has always been interested in you is this bloke – an old acquaintance of yours, the guy you'd always turn down saying he wasn't really someone worthy of your attention. He can play with you Luna, while Bedak, most probably, watches the telly and, I can just sit and doze off, or watch the spectacle... I don't guarantee I won't join in your games, when I think better of you, you were an amazing animal in bed. Take off your clothes, Luna. And while you are talking off your clothes, I shall read to you a poem that you have published in your collection, only the poem is stolen. It was written by your niece, how did you get it? Never mind, I'll just read and you start with taking off your stockings."

The two other men didn't say a word: Bedak was occupied with his finger-nails, cleaning the dirt underneath with a toothpick which was earlier in his mouth, while Baretta had a friendly smile on his, drunken but calm, face. He looked at Luna lifted both his eyebrows up and lifted one shoulder up, then he said:

"Oops!"

Luna turned to Gregor and said:

"I am an old woman, Gregor, I could almost be your mother."

"Oh, God forbid! You are not an old woman: you look like a young wom-an, you dress like a young woman, you write like a young woman and you have the sexual appetite of a young woman. What is written on your birth certificate doesn't concern anyone, particularly you, you never cared about it. Come Snow White, come over here."

She came closer and he said:

"Bring out the finest whiskey you have, we haven't had a drink yet."

When she took out a bottle of whiskey, Gregor said:

"Get out the other one too, one won't do!"

Gregor stood up and went through Luna's CD collection, then he said:

"That's the one you like 'Luna Mezz'o Mare' don't you? Hmm, let see this one, Dean Martin sings. Let's hear it and enjoy!"

Then he put the CD on and turned the volume up, full blast! He closed the windows, even the bathroom window, then he drew the heavy curtains together and smacked his lips:

"Mr Baretta, the opening act would be yours."

***

When Simon Odak rang the bell no one answered. He rang again, but there was only silence. He saw that *Luna Gallery* was still closed at eleven and he tried to contact her. When he couldn't reach her, he decided to pay her a visit – she might have been ill, or something, because she was never ten minutes late, let alone three hours.

Since Pia left he made their *'friendship'* open. Now that Luna was approaching her fifties, he would rather have younger girls around him, but he couldn't write her off or deny that he loved her over the years. Plus, there was so much history between them, so many uncountable misdeeds; so many secrets they shared and covered up for each other, they practically owed each other's soul. He gave her Gemma's unpublished poetry, her paintings; he even gave her permission to take some of Pia's hidden papers and scribbles after Pia left for London.

When the silence continued after the third buzz, out of his wallet he took a key and opened the door. He found her in the living room lying on the floor in the position of a foetus, with hands covering her face and hair messed up; it even looked as if some strands of her hair were pulled out. He came closer and called out her name, but she remained in the same position, appearing to be dead, as there was no sign that she was breathing at all. Quickly, he took off his jacket, knelt next to Luna and whispered her name into her ear. He grabbed her wrist and felt a faint pulsation.

At that moment he felt nothing. Absolutely nothing.

He called the police and the ambulance, then he brought some water and tried to make Luna sip it. She was naked and it was blatantly obvious what had happened to her. He covered her naked body and poured some water over her wrists and her forehead. He whispered into her ear:

"He'll pay for this, I swear to you whoever has done it will pay for it!"

Luna said nothing; still she appeared to be nothing but – dead.

***

On the third day, she opened her eyes and looked at the strange Hospital room. Slowly, her memory started telling her the story exactly as it happened and she screamed as only a beast would; nurses rushed to her side, but couldn't calm her down until they gave her intravenous morphine, as she cried and cried and cried, they thought of the pains, but she cried of terror when she relived her latest memories. She tried to touch her face to assure herself that all was still

361

there – eyes, nose, lips and ears, but when she lifted her arms, the sharp pain prevented her arms from reaching the face. Her right hand and fingers were bandaged and bandaged was her thumb on the left hand. She felt a sharp pain in her lower back too, but then the morphine threw a soft blanket over her and she lost her memory again and sank into that velvety darkness.

The nurse made a call to Mr Simon Odak advising him that Luna had regained consciousness. He rushed to the hospital, all he wanted was that Luna confirm his name, he wanted to hear his name coming from Luna's lips, even though he knew that no one else would do it, especially in such a sadistic way.

She was fast asleep when he came in. The doctor told him, because of the morphine she would sleep for several hours. He asked the nurse if she had heard Luna talking, did she manage to say anything, any name… or whether she called him. But – no! Luna said nothing. She just screamed and cried hysterically, then she injected her according to doctor's directions.

He stayed a little bit longer but she did not wake up from her velvety darkness. He took her fingers and kissed the tip of each, even those that were bandaged. The doctor, an old friend of his and Luna's, told him it looked as if her knuckles had been smashed with a hammer, or something heavy, dull. He was advised that her insides were ripped, and it took him seven hours to completely stitch her up. He said, Luna's aging parents came unable to speak, unable to understand what had happened. Her father, Ernesto Bonifacio, said they should have left for Italy long ago, and mother just cried and fainted after a while.

Simon scratched his head thinking about Gregor Truba and about the way in which he would be able to find out what exactly had happened. He needed witnesses. He swore to himself he would turn around every stone in order to find them. There must have been some witnesses as there is no such a thing as a perfect crime.

As he was quickly climbing up the ladder he was gaining a reputation, he was gaining new friends and strengthening the grip on his old foes. He was never aware that he was losing grip of his family ties. He hadn't heard from his daughter in over a year, his father never approved of his military achievements, his brothers were not supportive nor did they discuss his position. He thought, *'it is so common that jealousy rips a family apart'*; he wasn't sad, or bitter, all he wanted was approval, if his family wasn't going to give him the long lusted-after approval, his friends would. It was the right and ripe situation to excel, to show everyone what he was made of. He knew that there would be no one standing in his way to power and importance: his country was calling him and he would respond by giving himself to his fatherland without any sentiment, without a second thought; war trumpets were playing in his inner chambers. He felt invincible; his time had come!

***

Gregor Truba slept for three days, in a heavy sleep without dreams, without wakening to his mother Elsa's numerous attempts to wake him and convince him to get up and have some food. Delirious, he would say:

"Just let me sleep, let me sleep a little longer..." and he would doze off resuming his heaving snoring. He slept for three dreamless nights and three dreamless days, and on the fourth day he was awakened by a sharp pain in his bottomless stomach, he called out:

"Mother! Mother! Your boy is hungry! Is there anything in this house to eat, otherwise I'll eat the plants or the blankets..."

Elsa hurried into his room, red in the face she said:

"Thank Heavens! You've slept for three days without awakening. I came in numerous times just to check whether you were still breathing. If it weren't for hunger you'd sleep another day or two. What happened?!"

"Oh, nothing happened, Mother, we just celebrated, I feel like a free man again, everyone wanted a piece of me."

"Including Ivo."

"What's with Ivo?"

"He came over twice, asked me to let you know he passed by."

"I'll sort it out. All I want now is a good meal, and who better to fix my meal than my beloved Elsa. Hurry up, schnell, schnell!"

She brought food to his bed while he was eating she massaged his neck and shoulders.

"I love your hands, I missed you so much."

"Now that we have our own country we won't live in fear any more. We just have to fight to the end but the end is on the horizon, it is dawning. You are my hero, my son."

The doorbell rang. She opened the door and there were two men standing in front of Elsa. One had a long black robe and she greeted him with a wide smile, *"Come in; come in Friar"*, while to the other man she said:

"Finally he has woken up, go to his room, Ivo."

She led the Friar to the living room while Ivo proceeded into Gregor's room.

"Sit down, man."

"I came to warn you."

"... of what?"

"You have changed, Gregor."

"If you went to jail, pussy, for five years, wouldn't you change? Not a bit? What's the problem?"

"There are rumours..."

"Look, if you wanna talk rumours, you can nicely get up and kiss my arse before leaving."

"I am leaving the country. I just wanted to say good-bye and warn you for the sake of old days."

"Yet another deserter! A coward or a sentimental communist! What the hell are you talking about? This is my country and I am going to defend it to the last drop of my blood. You are a jerk! Can't believe you were my best friend. You never had balls – never! It was obvious, it was even heard in your

music. You were and you are a weakling. You are leaving your country? Where to? To Russia? To Serbia? To Slovenia? Where do you wanna go? And... you've come to warn me, haven't you? Warn me about what? About my stand towards my country? It is our call! We need democracy, we need money, we need freedom, we can be, as our president said, a new Switzerland, even better... and yet, you are running away. Fuck off, go! Right now, clear off, get out of my sight! Go, you bum, you were always a bum!"

"This is not my war, this isn't your war. We are going to be used in others' interests; you know that, we all talked about it before you went to prison. We all agreed that we lived good lives. Do you wanna kill other people? To prove that you are a patriot? Do it! You are, in the end, the son of an ex-Nazi and a German mother. Go, and kill people! Blame others for your misfortune. Go around and rape women! You've become an animal. That's who you are."

"I'll smash your head before you get out of my house!"

"This house was given to you and your family!"

"Fuck off, you communist! Bugger off; go wherever you wanna go. Don't you ever knock at my door again!"

"Who came to visit you every Thursday and Saturday? Who brought comics and books? Who organised a concert in Via Roma?"

"I said go! We don't need cowards like you."

"Yeah! The bloody banquet has commenced. Enjoy it!"

Gregor screamed:

"Fuck off and don't you ever come back again. This is my house, this is my country and I am going to defend it, I am going to do what it takes!"

Ivo left and he felt only bitterness in his mouth:

'What happened to intellect: to the philanthropists, scientists and talented artists who would resist the war and hatred; whose peaceful and constructive efforts have been drowned by the clamour of their more warlike and destructive brothers?'

Hatred, fear and doubt widened the gap between brother and brother, man and man, and man and God. Godless times had dawned.

Ivo wasn't the only young man from his hometown who had left. An army of young, educated, urban men left: as war wasn't fit for the urban, cultivated mind. It belongs to the twilight of humankind. Ivo never wanted to be a number, to be manipulated by mainstream hysteria. He was a quiet thinker, a young man who understood the world that appeared to be and the world as it really was. He saw through advertisements, through mass media hypnosis, he saw through the pamphlets, phrases, emotions and passions. He was not a passionate fool; all he wanted was to live a life of respect and creativity. Creativity and respect were never born from blood, tears and utter human misery.

'Let them call me a traitor, a deserter, what difference does it make anyway? They'll need years to understand what they were getting themselves into.' Those were his thoughts on that cold morning when he left his hometown.

He thought of Veronika, *'Who would ever know where that strange, yet smart, girl has gone?'* He wanted to find her *'somewhere'*, but he knew that the Truba family didn't have a clue about her whereabouts; he heard as much from his mother's mutual friend. *'But, Pia... she left too, somewhere in London...'* he knew it would be difficult to find the *'lost generation'* again.

***

'No one is going to tell me who I am and what I stand for!' thought Gregor upon Ivo's leaving. *'Deserter, traitor and a sleazebag! He was always nothing but a sleazebag.'* He couldn't believe how much rage Ivo's words provoked in him; he couldn't believe that he was upset for several days after thinking those thoughts and he couldn't believe that those thoughts prompted his decision to go into the battlefield. He called his brothers, Baretta and Bedak, told them his decision, called them to join. What would thugs do anyway in such times?

When he came to the military headquarters to check into the army, to be sent as a volunteer to the battlefield, he was met with utter enthusiasm by officers who had known him well for a long period of time. When the chief of the headquarters came in they stood still when they looked each other eye to eye: Gregor Truba met Simon Odak. The two men who loved and loathed exactly the same women: Pia Odak and Luna Bonifacio. Thoughts were playing with their facial muscles, but the cool, rational brain took over that inner conversation: they were on the same side; they fought for their country, and the country was above love for daughters or lovers, the country was above everything, even above God himself!

In the darkness of the night, in the shadows of the streetlights military trucks were loading with arms, blankets, some medicine, young men and a casket of brandy per head. The tipsy soldiers sang patriotic songs and hung onto their crucifixes. One of them, with a freshly shaved head was the son of the proud father who came to escort him – Anton Truba. He held his stretched out arm long after the last truck disappeared around the corner. He wiped off a tear; he wished he could have joined again, but for the time being that pride of sending his son off was working miracles for him. And where was mother Elsa at that time? Yes, praying to the kind God who selected her son to be a hero and to keep him protected and alive! What honour had dawned upon the Truba family, what an honour! It was not only the Truba family who acted so proud and loud when asked about their son's bravery but Friar Marag also felt as if a slice of that cake belonged to him. And it did: he did all that was in the domain of his knowledge and power to help this *'strayed sheep to find its way back to where it belonged.'*

A new history was in the process of writing itself, the history of this region, but the new books would be written for the whole world, as this small region, with the Balkan countries, was a fertile soil for all sorts of experiments. People were burdened with a past, were dense with emotions and gifted with highly flammable personalities.

And it looked as if someone switched on the program and said:

"Let the Game begin!"

"Hurrah!" the hoards ran towards freedom and democracy that was waiting to be unleashed through the fabricated *'facts and truths'* of the mass media, the perfect propaganda and the absolute, insane bloodshed.

Democracy was coming, bringing a new world and new values, whilst Gregor Truba was riding the crest of that wave. No one knew, back then, that the mare on which Democracy was riding was lame and cunning.

***

On the following morning Friar Marag met his superior, Friar Dondi. Friar Dondi said:

"Our best ideas, ideals and passions don't come from God necessarily. What might look to you as God's will and plan, might be misinterpreted... just be aware, there are times when God doesn't speak to anyone because there is too much noise..."

Friar Marag thought, *'Your days are numbered, not mine.'* But he didn't say a word just bowed his head and went to the confessionary, meek and humble as he could be.

That morning he talked about civilian duty towards God and to the country, he reminded the young and old about their patriotic and Christian duty: to defend the country, to take up arms, to defend the honour of each and every citizen from past to present. Friar Dondi listened without any expression, only his eyes were fixed up towards the sky, which was hidden, but he always could imagine that cloudless sky regardless of the thickness of the church walls.

Friar Marag couldn't remember, his hand ever being kissed or squeezed so many times in his service, as on that morning.

He felt like a rock-star, the way Gregor Truba felt in his best days: a demi-god adored by the masses.

***

Alcohol, drugs and camaraderie sustained his will to stay more than his patriotic feelings. It was cold, creepy, scary and inhumane. Fear all around him. He lost weight, he didn't shave for days nor did he shower, he could only shoot when tipsy or drunk or when everyone would fire. He didn't have the guts or such hatred as Bedak had, to rape and to slit the throats of women and children. When asleep he would cry; he had dreams about Veronika, about Hugo coming and telling him not to kill, not to burden his soul, telling him to run away to save his sanity. In the morning the day would take its own course; his comrades, his brothers in arms, would lead his mind and his decisions: he was a soldier, he needed not his own mind, thoughts or feelings. He had to be obedient, and he was.

The commander of Gregor's unit was an unscrupulous man; actually not a trained military man, but a former truck driver, a raw and rough man from the mountains, everybody feared his fierce, uncivilized manner. It was late afternoon; they sat next to the bonfire, tired and hungry, when they heard sporadic fire from a distance. Several men jumped up and took up arms while Gregor still sat down fixing his shoe. The Commander grabbed Gregor by the lapels of his uniform, almost lifted him up and nearing his face to Gregor's, said:

"This is a war, you cunt, not a rock-concert!"

Gregor stood up quickly, trying to get the rifle in his hands, while the Commander beat him to it, took Gregor's rifle and knocked him on the head with its butt. Gregor faltered, fell on his knees and the Commander yelled:

"Up! Up! You city pussy! This is not a game. This is not an outing for a precious intellectual! This is not a university picnic. This isn't a bloody countryside shooting; this is a bloody war! We are defending our country. With whom? With weaklings, spoilt university students, mummy's boys! This is a War! With a capital W. I'll make men out of you even if no one was able to do it before me. You'll be the man, the man that fought and won this war under my command. Up and run, kill, kill, kill the bastards! Kill without selection and discrimination; kill everything that breathes on your way, without mercy, no mercy in war. Understand?"

Gregor was bleeding. He didn't know where the blood was coming from but it poured down into his right eye. He feared this man so much that he didn't feel any pain; his vision was blurry but he took his rifle and ran with the others, carried by common energy and ideas. He didn't have time to ask himself, *'Was it? Was it a common idea?'*

All they asked from him was to be obedient, not to ask questions.

He feared him even more when he was drunk, then his temper was uncontrollable, his speech rough and illiterate, his intentions criminal and he would lose control in a split second: rage and hatred would burn that little sanity that he showed every now and then. Any question that came to Gregor's mind he learned to cancel immediately or to dull with alcohol. He knew how important it was to fight this fight, to come back as a hero, to make his parents proud and ... to show Pia what he was capable of ... maybe, he thought, she might be following his whereabouts, most probably she had learned that he was a hero in the making. Under the rose he would jot down lyrics for his future songs that he would sing in front of a mesmerised crowd.

Many dreams later, it dawned on Gregor that Hugo's whispers, *'Long, long, long...'* actually meant, *'Wrong, wrong, wrong...'* but he didn't want to listen to Hugo's whispers as those whispers were only dreams, and dreams were made of nothing, anyway.

He didn't have any dreams of his own anymore; even the dream of the New Fantastic Country of their Own was blurred by blood, alcohol and fear.

***

The Friday evening news spoke about the advancement of the army in the region of Lika; Elsa was alert, eager to hear more as her son was fighting on that front. There were too many rebels there, *'primitive pigs'*, were her frequent comments. The doorbell rang and she put the sound up to hear the reporter's voice while opening the door, *'That could only be the Friar bringing some good news'*, she thought.

When she opened the door in the late, muggy evening, the sun shone through the door: there in front of her eyes the God of Bravery and Beauty stood, her son Gregor Truba in uniform. She jumped up and put her arms around his neck, roaring with laughter and shedding tears of happiness and relief.

A whole year had passed since he left home, yet it looked as if he had never left. All he wanted was a warm bath and a good meal. His father was eager to hear the stories straight from the horse's mouth, but Elsa said:

"Let him have a good rest, tomorrow we'll have the whole day to catch up."

That night Gregor slept a deep long dreamless sleep. Hugo didn't come to his dreams, but a few minutes before he came to a conscious state, he caught just a glimpse of someone's face: it was Veronika's face, she looked at him with disapproval in her dark almond-shaped eyes and said nothing. She just swung her head barely noticeably from left to right, from right to left. Then she disappeared, leaving him confused and full of doubts; he called loudly:

"Veronika! Veronika!"

Mother Elsa rushed into his room; his senses were overwhelmed with this fantastic aroma of freshly brewed coffee and cinnamon scrolls, and he felt home again; tears rushed and formed a little puddle held by his lower eyelashes; Elsa's voice sobered him up:

"Breakfast in bed?"

"Did she ever call or send a letter?" It was his first question.

She shook her head.

"Do you know where she could be hiding?"

"No. Not a word from her. Her choice; let it be!"

"Can we just shrug our shoulders and say – let it be?"

She replied with a short, *"Yes!"* and swiftly changed the topic.

That evening he heard some rumours; he heard that Ivo was in town; he came back from Amsterdam via London. Apparently, he was told, he met up with Pia; Pia called Veronika over; no one was absolutely sure but *'it was hearsay.'*

When he approached Ivo that evening ready to put behind their last brawl, he was met with a wall of silence and coldness. He said:

"You don't want to talk to me? Are you serious? We were best friends, we did everything together, yet you are the one who remained deaf to the country's call for honourable duty, and I went to the battlefield. Now, you think that I don't deserve your attention. You know what, you were and you've stayed a bloody nobody, a spineless worm. You ran away to Amsterdam, have you been welcomed with open arms – with milk and honey running through the streets of Amsterdam, for you and your friend Johnny? Or do you sit, with the same kind as you, in some café and smoke marijuana all day long? Or are you just a simple bricklayer working on a building there... what else would they offer you? You were building someone else's city and country while your own has been bleeding."

Ivo turned his back on him, Gregor grabbed him from behind, but a pair of strong hands grabbed Gregor by his arms. He turned around and his eyes met Simon Odak's eyes. Odak whispered:

"He is a worm, but you aren't any better. Hands off and don't dirty this holy uniform. Get out! Right now, before I knock all your teeth out!"

In that instant he was thrown out of the café on the road and many witnessed the scene. The amount of rage he experienced was never before experienced in his chest; it looked as if the chest was going to burst and his lungs and heart and other internal organs would blast out and spill blood and gall over the entire town. Nothing happened though, he rushed towards the other pub but on his way someone called his name and the man he met was his grandfather.

He told him how humiliated he was, yet again, by this sadistic idiot, blaming his ill fortune every time he met anyone from this family.

The next morning upon leaving Truba's house, Friar Marag asked Gregor to accompany him back to the church. They walked slowly and the Friar's calm voice and manner soothed his nerves.

They took the longer path to the church as the day was calm and warm and they were not in a hurry. Gregor was talking and the Friar was predominantly approvingly nodding his head. When they were approaching a house with a white façade and a clean lawn, the Friar said with a small enigmatic twinkle in his eyes:

"You've seen this house before?"

"Yes, I think so."

"In front of the house there used to be a small plaque, do you know what was written on the plaque?"

"No." Gregor scratched his clean-shaven head.

"Then... you don't know who lives in there, do you?"

"Not really."

"Never mind then." The Friar said and never hurried his step.

"Why, never mind? Should I know whose house that is?"

"You were friends with that young woman... the one who was the exact reason you were jailed absolutely innocent."

"You are talking about?"

"The one who apparently was very pretty, young people have such silly taste..."

"Are you talking about Pia?"

"Hmm, I think that was her name."

"She never lived here, I know where she lived."

"On, no, not herself. But her grandparents, that doctor, the plaque read 'Jure Odak, General Practitioner', his wife... she is of Serbian Orthodox religion, yes, he married a Serb. He is now as small as a little mouse. Yes, some time ago they were proud to spread such nonsense that she was related to the so-called genius, Nikola Tesla. Rubbish! They made it up to make themselves important as if they were of some 'better background'. I don't believe that story, after all, who was that Tesla anyway? Yes, yes, they still live here and I see her now and then going out to do some chores, shopping or who knows what, whilst the so-called doctor doesn't leave the house. Never mind, just wanted to tell you to whom the house belongs, and a little background of the owners."

The rest of their walk passed in discussions about the political situation in the country and about some organisations and countries that were pouring money and support for the army.

On his way back, Gregor took the longer way and passed by the house where Pia's grandparents lived. The house where the father and the Serbian mother of Simon Odak lived.

From the outside it looked like any other house in the neighbourhood. How it looked from the inside he didn't have a clue. He didn't walk the path made of square cut stones, but he walked through the grass, treading flowers and small plants carelessly; he looked through the window and saw a man sleeping in his armchair. There was nobody else in the house.

He pressed the buzzer and after a short time a tall woman opened the door. She smiled and asked:

"How can I help you, son?"

"Does Miro Anic live here?"

"I am afraid you knocked on the wrong door."

"I do apologise."

"Don't worry, son. To be honest I don't know any Anic family in our street. There are Anics two blocks further down towards the town, but here... as far as I know there are no families with that surname."

"Thank you."

"You are welcome, son. Is there anything else I might help you with?" she asked as Gregor looked quite confused and puzzled.

"No... not really, thank you and good-bye."

"God bless you."

'*So, you are Simon Odak's mother.*' Gregor thought while he hurried back home. The surname Odak didn't evoke any longer a fuzzy warm feeling, as it used to several years ago when it would evoke Pia's image in front of his eyes. That surname evoked an image of the courtroom, the two men who conspired against him and sent him innocent to jail; it evoked a fat, ugly image of the sleazebag who was his superior of sorts, who treated him like trash, yet he,

Gregor Truba, was a soldier, a volunteer who took a gun and went to defend his country while this clown just paraded in his uniform around the town and staged his plays as if he were still a provincial theatre director.

That afternoon he called Bedak, a ruthless psychopath who would do any sadistic act to take him out of boredom.

"Can you extract an important piece of information from a worm called Ivo Lucic, for me?"

"Sure I can."

"My sister is in London and I don't know where exactly she is, what she does and I don't have her contact number. Ask him to hand you her telephone number. No matter which method you use, I have to have it today. I'll pay you back, brother!"

***

When Ivo walked out of his building approaching his car he saw a uniformed man following him, he hurried, but the man hurried too; he slowed his walk, the man caught up with him and said:

"Get in the car. We are going to have a little ride."

Bedak sat next to frightened Ivo and switched the radio on. Ivo asked:

"What do you want from me?"

"I'll tell you, don't worry. Just drive nicely approximately ten kilometres out of town, towards mount Učka."

After half an hour Bedak said:

"Stop here. Look down, such a nice view, isn't it?"

"What do you want from me?"

"Look how deep and steep this slope is."

"Yes. I understand. What is it exactly that you want from me? I know you are Gregor's friend, we somehow fell apart, but he could have asked me anything he wanted... tell me what is this all about?"

"You live in Amsterdam?"

"Temporarily."

"Temporarily... till... what? The war ends? Then you'll come back?"

"No, I have some opportunities there, I thought I might take advantage of such opportunities."

"Oh, good for you. OK, let's make it short. Veronika's telephone number in London."

"I don't have it."

"I don't waste my time, and what I want to get I always get – in this or that way, but eventually I get what I want. Make it easy for both of us."

"Honestly, I don't have her number."

"Yet you visited her in London."

"I visited Pia, she called Veronika."

"Good. Call Pia and ask her Veronika's number, we'll drive back home, you call Pia, she gives you the number, you hand it to me and you are free. OK?"

"What if Pia refuses to give me Veronika's number?"

"Then it would be your fault. We drive back here, we don't have any further negotiations, I walk out of the car and shoot you, I push the car down the cliff and take a bus home. No one would care about you except your parents - believe me. No one!"

Late that afternoon, Gregor had the telephone number. He didn't call on that day; neither did he say anything to his mother about the number. He put the piece of paper with a number, scribbled by Ivo's shaking hand, into his wallet.

It took only several days for him to be, once again, the biggest star in the country. The papers and all the TV channels reported that *"Gregor Truba, the famous front man and the guitarist from the biggest and the best local band just came back home from defending his country with a Kalashnikov and patriot songs."*

Wherever Gregor walked God himself walked with him: he was met with reporters and handshakes, with cheers and tears, with screams and honours of various descriptions. He could sleep with any woman he wanted, and every morning when he woke up he felt emptiness in the pit of his stomach while trying to figure out, *'Who was that girl and where did he meet her?'*

The only girl he would think about with warmth in his heart was Veronika. Somehow he feared to call her for a so far unknown reason to him, yes, he feared to hear her voice the same way he feared that Hugo would come in his dreams and with his little tongue hanging out would stutter:

"Gogol, come back... long, long, long ... Yugo wants old Gogol."

The remedy to silence Hugo's cries (*wrong, wrong, wrong*), to reduce the fear of calling Veronika and the remedy for such intensity of fame, he found in the bottle. Every evening he would go out, sing in pubs and cafés with his pals and hit the bottle in order to suppress the intensity of some of his emotions.

Still, the holy duty to his country was the strongest emotion fed and supported by his family, by the family's dearest friend and by his own pals. Oh, yes, and the daily heavy dose of propaganda in all the all-available media outlets.

The month of Gregor's leave was nearing the end. He didn't want to think about anything else but the country's freedom, otherwise he might give in to some silly feelings.

Several days before his leaving the new mayor invited Gregor to attend a small party. The press was there and Gregor himself was the most important guest; he outshone the local politicians and even the famous theatre-director-turned-politician. As the evening progressed Gregor drank more than the others did. More than tipsy he was when Simon Odak told him:

"I've designated you to a new place."

"What?"

"You won't go where you were before, there's another battlefield where more boys are needed. You'll go there in a week's time, down the coast."

"Oh, really?"

"You better show some respect."

"To you, piece of shit?"

"You'll go from where only few come back alive, you singing-soldier. War isn't a game."

"What do you know about war, you, you little piece of shit? You sit here in your nicely pressed uniform, you parade around like a show-pony at a provincial Sunday fair, you eat and you drink at the expense of us as you always have, piss off, I couldn't care less about you. You play the biggest patriot, yet everyone knows that your mother is a Serbian crossbreed."

Simon grabbed him by his lapels and several men stood up. Gregor repeated:

"You play the biggest patriot, yet everyone knows that your mother is a Serbian crossbreed."

"Escort him out, he had too much to drink" said one of the men whose name Gregor had forgotten. He was escorted out, yet again he found himself on the street thanks to Simon Odak's odd power.

Drunk and deeply hurt, he made an absolutely demonic decision, but sober as one could be, he followed it up. He took out his father's old sniper rifle, which was hidden in the garage for decades, he cleaned it, put ammunition in, drove out of the town and tried it out.

For three days he sat in front of her house and when she came out on the third day, sometime in the late afternoon, he slowly followed her to a travel agency. She was a tall, lanky woman, still with a straight back and a steady walk. She walked in, there were a few people waiting in front of her; he crossed the road and climbed the opposite building. Up to the top he went, climbed the iron bars, opened the iron gate and found himself on the top of the building. He lay flat on his stomach and looked at the street through the gunpoint: the world looked different from that perspective. It looked as if it were on the palm of his hand.

His hand was steady and precise. She fell down like a long lanky tree cut in haste with a chainsaw. He climbed down, took a padlock and locked the iron gate that led to the terrace. He threw the key into a wastepipe; without any inhibition or fear, he came out of the building with the sniper rifle on his back.

There were other uniformed men carrying sniper rifles or firearms in the town, he wasn't the only one.

Now he felt free to go wherever his country wanted him to go, wherever Simon Odak assigned him to go.

His walk was brisk, he never turned his back, shortly he heard sirens, but the traffic on the street was slow at this hour; all he wanted to hear was a birdsong, but they were muted by sirens and loud music coming from a passing-by car.

With a slow but steady step he came to the church: Friar Marag was outside tending the garden. He saw him and waved his hand; Gregor asked:

"What are you going to do with this pile of leaves and twigs?"

"I shall burn them."

"Can you burn a rifle?"

"It won't burn completely, but yes, we can burn it and what would be left of it we can bury in the cemetery."

Gregor took a rake and collected more leaves, twigs and wood. He lit a fire and when the flame was big, steady, he took his sniper rifle and threw it into the fire. They sat at the low wall overgrown with ivy and looked at the fire. No one was there to see them, no one to witness what was burning in the fire. Gregor whispered into the Friar's ear, while the latter just nodded his head in approval; not a word came from his mouth. Smog was rising up high; it reached even higher than the tall cypresses which had grown around the church ground for several hundreds of years. They were silent witnesses; they choked on that smog, which was, at the same time, the secret and the truth about the burned rifle.

The very same day, Gregor Truba, had packed his rucksack and left: to the very same battlefield where he came from. He waited not for Mr Simon Odak to tell him where to go – he went where his guts took him, where his pals were – his Brothers in Arms.

That night Hugo came into his dreams and said nothing. He just looked at him and cried his baby-tears. They were unstoppable and bitter, they woke him up; he cursed and reached for the bottle.

"Give me a break, Hugo. Give me a break, brother." He said distressed.

***

When Gregor left, Friar Marag examined the ashes: the rifle butt had gone completely while other bits in the ashes were obviously parts of a rifle and that would be evident even to a small child. He waited a while; when the iron had cooled down, he collected all the pieces and wrapped them in an old blanket which he took from the dormitory, he tied it up with a long rope and took it to the church cemetery. When he covered the hole where he had laid the remnants of the weapon with dirt and dead leaves, he turned around to check once again that no one, except the cypresses, witnessed his deeds; he met the calm eyes of his superior, Friar Dondi.

Friar Dondi said not a word, but patiently stood there waiting for Friar Marag to tell him the story – *'What was it that he had just buried in the church cemetery?'*

"Friar Dondi, please, for God's sake, please, do not stand in our way."

"Whose way?"

"We are making history, this church of ours bled for too long, this nation bled and moaned throughout history, this is our opportunity to be who we are again."

"Are we going to be what you have envisioned us to be? How would you justify your efforts and deeds when God calls? What you have just done is a deed criminally entangled with the fallen ones, you are giving them your power."

"Friar Dondi, I am helping our people and flock to get back to their roots, to root out the Devil who presented himself as the Communist Party and the aggressor. They oppressed, they tyrannised this nation for decades, if not for centuries."

DETHRONED

"Those who came as false teachers and prophets have been the instruments of darkness, the accusers must criticise and put down in order to feel good about their own misdeeds. Think long and deep about my advice: from now on do everything that is in your power to make your future creations lead to the resurrection and life of your soul."

Friar Dondi said, and left Friar Marag in the cemetery cloaked in twilight: a deep grey sky, long dark shadows of cypresses and dark-grey tombstones.

Night fell on the church, the cypresses and the cemetery lightly, as it falls on any other day in these seemingly peaceful surroundings.

A few days later Friar Dondi went to the Serbian Orthodox part of the town's cemetery, where the late wife of the respectable Dr Odak, and the daughter of his old friend, Milovan Tesla, was buried. He read in the papers that an unknown sniper, while she was crossing the street, shot her. Upon reading it he knelt in front of the altar and prayed incessantly.

Evil has no nationality.

***

Prior to going back to the battlefield Gregor summoned up the courage and called a number. The phone rang and rang, and after a while a voice said:

"Hi, Nikki's not at home but you are encouraged to leave a message for her."

It was Veronika's voice. He didn't leave any message, but he called every following hour until someone picked up and said:

"Hi."

He said:

"Veronika?"

Silence!

He repeated:

"Veronika?"

"Who is this?" she asked.

"Gregor. Your brother."

Silence.

"Veronika, are you there?"

"What do you want from me?"

"To ask, how are you?"

"I am well and I read the other day that you are well, too. A shameless hero!"

"Let me explain."

"No need."

"I miss you, I am your brother."

"My brother has died and I don't have any now."

"Can we talk?"

"No. I don't have a family, and I don't need you. Please, don't call ever again. I don't wish to talk to you, I don't have the need to see you or any other person from that place, I am ashamed of you and the place I came from. Good-bye, you won't find me at this number as I shall change it first thing in the morning."

She hung up and he felt an incredible heat in his head, as if it were going to burst like a volcano.

That was the night when speechless Hugo came to his dreams and just wept and wept. That was the last night that Hugo ever visited his dreams; he came to say good-bye and he said it with his unstoppable river of tears; then he disappeared, for good, as a white mist in the glory of a rising sun.

After a short while, since Hugo's disappearance, Veronika started to frequent his dreams: stern and provocative without a word she would stare, not in his eyes or in his face, but in the distance, in some future where Gregor couldn't find his figure, like a ghost who would never see himself in a mirror. After such dreams the future looked to him as a future of broken mirrors.

Broken mirrors in seven thousand pieces. Those nights were nights of sweat and sudden awakenings; they resembled more the nights of a menopausal, worried woman than a war hero whose obedience was never questioned, whose decisions were ruthless. For his nightmares, his misfortunes and nights of sweats and broken mirrors he had an excuse and explanation: the enemy on the other side of gunpoint.

Not even the crucifix, which Friar Marag blessed for him, could bring any relief, only the bottle of good old schnapps, which was given in abundance by the locals to whom this army was a sign that God had finally opened His eyes. It looked like mercy from Heaven.

His peace was fragmented, his thoughts discontinuous and his speech harsh and slurred. Sometimes he would think of his comrades, his brothers in arms, more as a ruthless mob that ruled and roamed the villages where old people, innocent young women and children were left to wait for their uncertain future, as their men fought the same insane war Gregor did. They killed their animals, burned their houses and put bullets through their heads. He saw rivers of blood and heard horrid screams from innocent civilians: scenes that made him question his sanity. Every night was a nightmare, every other night he would see the eyes of pleading victims, of crying mothers and terrified children. Every other night he would see the eyes of his sister Veronika who didn't look at him directly but looked at his deeds speechlessly. He would scream waking up in a cold sweat, and she was often yelled at in the silence of the night:

"Shut up, you cunt!"

When his conscience tried to sneak in, he would silence it with more alcohol or a song, but his feeling that his comrades were uneducated, rural brutes grew day by day; he started to hate himself as he could occasionally witness that he had become one of them: Gregor Truba, who played the piano and guitar in his childhood and youth, who carried his brother Hugo on his back when Hugo wasn't willing to walk any longer, Gregor who played basketball and was considered to be the, *'Golden Boy'* in the neighbourhood because of his random acts of kindness towards everyone, he who tried to defend his sister whenever his mother would say anything against her, he who sincerely loved a girl whose words came out as beautiful poetry every time she spoke…

'No, I can't think of it… I have to defend my country.' With much difficulty he fell asleep and Veronika came and looked at him speechlessly and he was awakened by the horse's whinnying, by the thunder of machine guns, by curses and shouts. He was woken up and he couldn't distinguish what was the nightmare: his waking hours or his dreams.

***

As a premonition of something horrible that might happen, a dream came to a physically and emotionally exhausted Gregor.

A woman came to his dream.

She was tall and dark. He thought, in his dream, that somehow he knew this woman. In his dream, almost as if a little birdie whispered into his ear that the woman might be the girl he once loved. He couldn't remember her name but he kept on looking into the eyes of the tall dark-haired woman. She had eyes deep and moist with sadness and she had a little smile on her longish face. He said:

'Say something.'

But she kept on smiling giving him a chance to remember her image. As he was looking at the woman, she slowly, but surely started to age in front of his very eyes. When she first appeared she looked like a woman in her late twenties. Now he saw her in her late thirties: still statuesque, of elegant demeanour, with that enigmatic smile on her peaceful face. Then he saw her in her late forties, with the first white hairs on the edges, with deeper lines on her face and slightly sunken eyes only then he thought that he might have known this woman, she looked more familiar. Then she aged again by ten years and was in her late fifties, but she still smiled and his feelings of knowing her intensified, but when she appeared looking like someone in their late sixties, with her white hair, thin skin and tall, but with a more frail frame, he recognised the smiling woman. When the epiphany occurred, the smiling woman said:

'I forgive you.'

At that moment, just when the apparition disappeared from his dream, he felt a pair of strong hands around his neck: there was a strong man above him trying to suffocate him. Gregor in his death rattle managed to scream, but the man put his hand on Gregors' mouth and whispered:

'Regards from Simon Odak.'

Gregor wiggled his legs, pulled all his mighty strength into his tall athletic body and managed to grab the man by his neck. They tumbled around holding each other's throat, while their comrades watched that unexpected match which brought wild entertainment for a while. Then someone yelled at the top of his lungs:

"Stop! Cut it out!"

Gasping for air Gregor ran into the woods as if he were chased by millions of dead people, he ran for his life and after a long period of running, he stopped and vomited and cried till dawn. They found him as dawn broke, gave him some food and a drink of water and the commander of his unit said:

"Next time you run away you'll be considered a deserter. We shoot deserters on the spot."

The next destination they came to was a small village called Raduč. Next to the plaque where the name of the village was written, Gregor saw a woman standing. She was tall and slender; in her late seventies, she was smiling and nodding her head. Gregor took the rifle and fired into the vanishing apparition, then he threw himself on the ground and started to bark! Yes, bark as a dog and the rest of the unit broke into synchronised laughter, only Baretta came and knelt next to him. He said:

"Are you bloody crazy? Have some water."

"The Musician has lost marbles. The war is harsh on town folks; it isn't a rock concert.

He was taken to the local hospital while barking all the way. He barked there for some time, and after only a few hours was he taken back home where the hospital was bigger and doctors more knowledgeable than the provincial ones.

***

On the sixth day after his arrival at the local hospital, he recognised the woman who cried next to his bedside. It was his mother Elsa. He put his hand on her face and said:

"Don't cry Mum, I am alive."

On such words she cried even more. He heard that she never left his side those past few days. He told her that he was tired and a little bit sad and that all he needed was rest; he tried to reassure her that he would be back on the field as soon as he regained his strength.

When he saw his father, he nearly cried but he held his tears back. His father told him that he was very proud of him, while Gregor longed to have heard those words way back, when he was the front man, of a now all-forgotten-band. Gregor nodded his head and told him he was planning to go back to the battlefield as soon as he regained his strength.

When Friar Marag came in, the following day, Gregor Truba refused to see him. He only said:

"I am too tired to see anyone else but my family."

He asked his mother about Veronika, but Elsa just shrugged her shoulders.

"Don't even think of her."

"Yeah, I'll think of our country, Mum."

Elsa looked at him and said nothing.

When she walked out Gregor quietly cried. No one heard him. He wished Veronika could have heard him, his thoughts ran to the past, his jaw trembled, the vision of beautiful Pia came into his mind, but he called out asking for morphine – he had unbearable pain in his neck, he still felt those hands and fat peasant fingers squeezing it, which since that event didn't allow him to breathe freely. He could only stand the vision of the tall lanky woman as the morphine rendered him to the comfort of pleasant nothingness.

In the morning a nurse came in and said:

"You've recovered. I am so glad."

"Thanks."

"Do you remember me?"

"You look familiar."

"We live in the same street, I am three years your junior, but you know my brother Alan."

"Yes, I know him."

"I have all your records."

"Thank you."

"Would it be rude to ask if you could sign them for me?"

"Bring them over. What's your name?"

"Diana."

"That's a very nice name. Do you know, Diana, how long I am going to stay in this hole?"

"Not really. You seem fine, maybe just another day or two. There are not enough beds, anyway. We've had a woman here almost two years."

"Two years?"

"Yes, she was broken like a broken glass. Came all in pieces; when they sewed her up she never regained consciousness. Apparently she was raped over and over by a troop of drunken soldiers. She has someone big standing behind her, I mean, a big wig, otherwise life support would have been stopped long ago."

A strong and sudden fit of coughing, a rush of blood to his face, he held his stomach while Diana came closer and helped push him up against his pillow. She stood next to him offering water, asking questions, but after a short while Gregor stopped coughing, while the redness still lit his face.

"I've got to go now, Gregor. Who would ever say that I would strike up a friendship with the famous Gregor Truba. If you need anything, I mean, anything, please just the ring the bell and while I am on duty, I will be available for you whenever you need me. Call me even if you don't need anything but a bit of company or comfort."

She winked and as she was leaving his room, he called her back:

387

"Just one more question, Diana. The woman, the one you said is in a coma for almost two years... who comes to visit her."

"I think her family."

"I'll ask you something, but please, be discreet."

"Go on, ask whatever you want."

"Does a man come to visit her, a man in his, let's say early fifties, a man in uniform?"

"Are you asking about Simon Odak?"

"Oh, no. I don't know his name... but, I thought that my mate's wife was in hospital for a long time. The rumour had it that she was raped. Horrible, really horrible, but, never mind, never mention our conversation to anyone."

"Stay assured I won't."

When she left, he broke into a cold sweat, his heart was thumping and running as fast as the fastest animal could run in the wilderness, *'He must be aware that I have been here for the last week. He is going to try and kill me again and what would be a better place than in hospital? He knows the doctors; he has better connections than I have ever had. I got to get out of this place and get back to...'*

But where *'back to'*? To that question he didn't have the answer.

His friend Tomas came to visit.

"I've got to get out of here at any cost."

"I'll see what I can do for you, are you sure you are ready to leave?"

"It was just general exhaustion."

"Yes, you seem to be OK now. I'll talk with colleagues, I don't see any problem; you can be discharged this week."

"Tomorrow, if possible, today even better."

"Why such a hurry?"

"Hate it here. I need open space, my brothers are fighting and what am I doing here?"

Diana came in:

"There are some journalists talking with your doctor. They want to take a few photos and write an article about our hero."

"You see, Tomas, that is precisely what I am trying to avoid."

"But that was your life – there in the spotlight, plus you've never been too modest or shy. Tell people how our brave boys are defending our country. Don't be modest; it is a bigger pride to be a soldier in such circumstances than a rock star. They see you as the full package: a soldier, a hero, a rock star and the guy next-door, go for it! Give us hope and courage, especially those guys who proudly hurried to the frontline ready to give their lives for the fatherland."

Regardless of his unwillingness, they took a few shots and asked him only a few questions. The next day the article was on the front page, his picture in the hospital bed, his mate next to him, under the picture it read – *A Soldier and a Musician Gregor Truba with his best pal Dr Tomas Berlic, and a nurse by his side.*

His discharge papers were signed that afternoon.

The telephone rang unceasingly, friends visited in groups, once again he felt like the biggest star in town – Gregor Truba, the front man of the most popular rock band in the region. When the night fell he felt like the biggest loser ever – fear crept under his duvet, uncertainty and doubts, a cold, cold heart that froze all his future plans. He went to Veronika's room, looked up at the ceiling, there were still the words written by her hand inspired by Hugo's wish:

"Lonnie in the sky with diamonds."

He felt like crying but he didn't, he was a man, a soldier in that important period of history of his young country.

On that night, once again Gregor was woken up by a disturbing dream; but this time is wasn't Hugo or Veronika, nor the tall lanky woman; the man who came unannounced was her youngest son – Simon Odak.

The dream had no topic, logic or storyline. He fell asleep and the man came and looked at him with his cold and unemotional eyes, and that look woke him up instantly; yes, that simple look pricked up his skin and soaked him in a cold sweat. He woke up shouting and repeating the same sentence:

"He is up to something! He is up to something! He is up to something, I know it!"

Mother Elsa rushed to his side and he threw himself into her arms. He wanted her to hold his heart in her hands. But he didn't know there was no safety, no peace for his strayed heart as his private Armageddon raged in his interior: the battle of the light of the original Gregor Truba and the darkness of his synthetic self, brought by the trumpets of the New World which was emerging on the ruins of many lives that never welcomed the fast approaching lies and terror.

With lies and terror, money poured in from all over the world to this little country to support those lies and terror, that lie itself could be presented as the truth and terror as freedom fighting.

Blindness fell upon the country as a thick layer of dirty snow; blindness fell upon them as sleep fell upon that kingdom from a fairy tale and almost all the inhabitants of the kingdom fell under the spell. Sleep, amnesia, madness, yet they all believed their awakening had just taken place on a collective level. How wrong, how wrong that perception was, as many would need a number of years to unveil the veil of the collective amnesia.

IV

Heroes

Motherhood

Nikki felt exhausted after the whole afternoon of rehearsal. She didn't have the nerve to listen to Caesar's lamentations; with years, his state of mind and soul deteriorated, so she couldn't cope with his problems as often or as well as before, or with the same dedication as she used to a few years ago. He became delusional, full of self-pity and bitterness, he fought with his aged lover often, and more often than not, came out bruised from their clashes, humiliated and downright exhausted. Not even money, the prime reason why he hooked up with the moody pianist in the first place, could soothe his wounds. His cocaine use escaped his control – what a pathetic figure he cut even on an ordinary day! He no longer needed an excuse to get off his face – a party or a crazy outing, simply he would entertain and treat himself to a drug whenever he wished. His speech became incoherent, confused and irrational and Nikki couldn't put up with him on a regular basis. Except on the occasions when she was in a good, steady mood, which in all honesty, was quite rare.

Seven years had passed since she arrived in London and her situation hadn't improved greatly. She was aware of the fact that in her-so-called country a war was raging, she heard it almost every day on the radio or TV, but she disassociated with it all long ago. Whenever she would hear people speaking her language she would turn and change direction. Since Pia left she suffered a form of depression, mood swings, a divine nostalgia for times that would never repeat themselves, yes, she was young but already felt as if she had lived long enough to understand the nature of human life on this planet – plain misery spiced up by promises and lies. Democracy - such a worn-out word, used up, depleted, a medium to fool the fools. She ran down the stairs, into the Tube, caught her train and threw herself onto the vacant seat panting. On the opposite seat a young woman was seated. She knew by her physiognomy that she came from the same country; if she could find another seat or if she weren't that tired, she would most probably take off and land her bottom elsewhere, but she just sat there looking for some strange reason at the young woman. Not directly, but glancing as if she would read something particular on her face. She wasn't pretty, neither was she an ugly girl, but what drew Nikki's attention was the way the girl looked randomly at people. She looked at them as if she wanted to befriend or rob them. After a short while the girl opened her bag and took out a newspaper. She unfolded it and covered her face by spreading it out wide. From the first page a uniformed man stared at Nikki: he was blond, tall and had a faint smile on his face, while across his figure big bold letters said– *The Saga of a Local Hero: Gregor Truba, Soldier and Musician.*

She swallowed an invisible dumpling that almost choked her.

His eyes! They were not the eyes of Gregor Truba, the man Nikki used to call *'brother'* many years ago. His eyes were the eyes of an old man, a man who had lost something quite precious… something indefinite, perhaps his soul. She discarded this thought, she talked fast to herself convincing herself that she couldn't care less about *'any of them'*, she just didn't belong there any longer: not to *that* place, neither to *that* family. But, from the main page of the newspaper Gregor Truba looked at her with his sad, tired eyes with much intensity and it seemed to Nikki that she was mesmerised and glued to the chair by that gaze.

"Where did you get this paper?"

The girl looked at Nikki for a while then she said:

"My mother sent it to me."

"May I buy this paper from you? I'll pay handsomely."

"Why should you pay handsomely? Are you a Croat?"

"No. But my husband is."

"You don't even speak the language."

"No. But my husband would be glad to read the paper. I'll pay whatever you ask."

"There is an interview in this paper with a man that I used to adore, so my mother sent it to me."

"I'll pay whatever you ask… Please."

"Sorry, but I'd like to keep it, Gregor Truba was the idol of my generation."

The train was approaching the station, the girl folded the paper and was about to put it back into her bag when Nikki snatched it from her hand and ran towards the exit pushing a few men aside and jumped out as soon as the doors opened wide.

"Stupid cow! Stupid slut!" the girl yelled.

Nikki ran up the stairs pushing protesting people, the girl tried to run after her as if she were running after someone who had stolen all her belongings. There was a parked cab; Nikki ran in, closed the door and looked at the girl full of rage standing there pointing her middle finger.

Nikki felt ashamed and sorry. She waved at the girl and blew her a kiss and the girl poked her tongue out, believing that she was being mocked and laughed at.

When she locked the door of her small apartment she put the kettle on. While preparing coffee she couldn't tell why her hands were shaking – whether because she stole from an innocent victim or because of the content of the paper.

She took a cup, lit a cigarette, sat on the sofa and spread the paper out in the middle then slowly started reading the interview.

After reading it all, she sat quietly smoking cigarette after cigarette for three quarters of an hour. Then she said to herself, *'From bad to worse. That's why I don't miss you, none of you – heroes!'*

What Nikki Barlow never learned was that the interview Gregor Truba gave to the newspaper was mere propaganda, his words were twisted and his pride oversized and emphasized.

At that time Gregor Truba was already aware that in the long term the winners and the losers would be one and the same.

She put the paper back in her bag hoping that on her way to work or back she might meet the girl again, apologise and give it back to her. But she never ever met the girl again and after several months she threw the paper away.

The only thing that bothered her on some, unconscious, level were Gregor's eyes, but she would dismiss the thought if it surfaced. Once she had a dream about him, she dreamed that he was a young boy, way back when Hugo was alive, and they played board games and laughed together. That actually never happened in her childhood, they never laughed together.

"The only person I miss is you, Hugo" She smiled at his photo as she prepared breakfast that morning, *"... you and 'your beautiful Pia', my sweetheart."*

She always remembered his words, *'Lonnie, Lonnie is Yugo's 'yllo.'*

"Lonnie was Hugo's hero; Nikki's nobody's hero." She quietly said to herself, and that very thought brought an epiphany, release and liberation. Nikki decided to get pregnant and have a child on her own.

A smile lit her face. She wanted to love and to care for someone the way she loved and cared for Hugo. She wanted to be someone's hero again; she just found out how to end her loneliness and longing. Before she went out she winked at Hugo's photo and said:

"Who knows, you might come to me again."

*** *

After such a decision, Nikki eyed men differently. She looked at them as a *'potentially good piece of meat that could be useful or used.'* She wanted a good-looking man, healthy and intelligent. Went through the list of her acquaintances or colleagues, at least those that she was sure were not gay, as in her profession gay men dominated. And for Nikki, since the last quarrel with Caesar, she couldn't put up with gays for longer than she had to. She had had enough of unstable and moody men, unstable and moody people in general.

She thought of several so-called boyfriends that she had – useless material! Then the thought came – Dean Bloxham. What could she get out of Bloxham? Good looking – check! Healthy – check! Intelligent – check! Bonus: fairly responsible (judged by his relation to his brother and his mother) and on top of all – reasonably wealthy.

She found his number and the reason to call.

"Dean, I know it has been a while, Nikki's here."

"Nikki! Lovely to hear from you! How come you're calling me?"

"Aw. Have you ever heard from Pia since she left?"

"No, unfortunately I haven't. She left, not even Andy has any clue. Any news?"

"I heard some rumours... thought you might know more... never mind. Sorry."

"Oh, don't be silly, sorry for what? What kind of rumours?"

"Can't talk about it over the phone."

"How are you doing, Nikki?"

"Same old stuff."

"Do you wanna meet up?"

They organised their meeting on the coming Friday. She was off on Friday; went to the hairdresser and after a long time she had a nice haircut and re-freshed her colour. She bought a new pair of jeans that fitted her perfectly and a blouse, kind of see-through and a nice, quite provocative, bra.

She looked lovely on that Friday evening; looking at her reflection in the mirror she thought, *'Why don't I look after myself more often?'* then she waved her hand – she wasn't a show-off, a Barbie-doll-material.

He gave her a kiss on the cheek and said:

"You look so lovely Nikki, as time passes by you look sexier and so woman-ly."

"A woman I am, am I not?"

"A hell of a woman. A boyfriend?"

"No, I attract cheats... or, perhaps men can't be faithful? What do you reckon?"

"With age we all become wiser, I'd say."

When he asked about Pia, Nikki said that she heard rumours that Pia was quite ill, living overseas at a place where she had wanted to live. She was making up the story based on assumptions, but knowing Pia well, her assumptions were not far from the actual truth. In the end, she said, she didn't know if that story was just weaved out of assumptions and rumours, but her strong feeling was that he might know something, given that Dean and Pia were really close before she left.

"I am glad you called, Nikki. I am really glad. Often I thought of you, and can't tell you the exact reason I never called. Maybe I never treated you right, but I would love to stay in touch."

They met up several more times and after the latest outing when they drank a fair bit of vodka and wine, she said:

"I keep a bottle in the fridge, let's go to my place."

From that union that lasted only another couple of months a baby was conceived, just the way Nikki planned it. When she was two months pregnant, she said:

"Dean, I am not good at relationships, neither are you, let's call it quits."

"I am happy at the moment, why should we?"

"I am not the one that can commit for the long run, neither are you yourself marriage material."

"Who speaks kids and marriage? We can hang together for some time…"

"I last, approximately, two months. Then I freak out, commitments freak me out; you know that."

"We can stay friends, can't we?

"Sort of. But let me sort out several other issues. I'll call you in several months' time."

"Are you seeing someone else?"

"Not really, but I might."

"Science fiction. Is someone coming from the future?"

"I'd say so!"

He packed up a few things that he kept at Nikki's and headed to the door:

"Call me now and then."

"I'll miss you, Dean."

"I bet you will."

Seven months later Nikki Barlow, also known as Veronika Truba, had given birth to a healthy, plump little boy. She gave him a beautiful name, the best name she could ever think of – Hugo. In the birth certificate it said– Hugo Truba Barlow.

Sober, combed and nicely dressed, Caesar came with a bunch of flowers and a basket of fruit, some Lindt chocolate and a teddy bear.

"I was positive that you'd call him Caesar. How unfair!" he said laughing and mocking her.

But Hugo was his name and that was the happiest day of her entire life. When she brought him home, she took off the picture from her fridge and brought it to the baby:

"Look Hugo, your little nephew."

Her son smiled and kicked his little legs as if the boy in the picture were real – free and happy, liberated from the picture-frame on the fridge.

***

When Hugo was three, by mere chance Nikki met Dean in the local bookstore. She was looking through the titles, Hugo was in a pram, and someone tapped her on her shoulder. It was Dean Bloxham, the father of her son.

"It has been awhile, Nikki, you look radiant."

"Oh, Dean, who would expect you here?"

"You never called. Never mind, I thought we might stay friends."

"Err… I've had a baby… haven't had time to contact anyone."

Dean looked at the handsome blonde boy. There was so much tenderness in Dean's eyes that Nikki almost choked when she witnessed it. He said:

"What a handsome fella. He looks nothing like you, lucky father, hey?"

"He looks like my late brother Hugo, believe it or not."

"What is his name?"

"Guess?"

"Hugo, I guess."

"Hugo it is."

"How are you doing, Hugo?"

"OK. Your name?" asked Hugo.

"I am Dean. Your mother's friend."

"A friend."

Dean looked at Nikki and asked:

"Married now?"

"No."

"Is he seeing his father?"

"Yes." She quickly lied, smoothed Hugo's hair and said:

"We've got to go now. Hugo, say 'bye-bye' to Dean."

"Bye-bye to Dean." Hugo waved his little hand.

Nikki pushed the pram through the door but couldn't manage with the bags hanging off it; Dean helped.

"Do you wanna a lift?"

She hesitated; he took her bags and said:

"Around the corner."

He helped her to get the pram, the child and the bags into the apartment. He put the milk and some fruit into the refrigerator. Hugo took a toy, a car and handed it to Dean:

"A car."

"Yes, a great car. Do you want me to play with you?"

Hugo brought a picture book and handed it to Dean.

"You want me to read to you, don't you?"

Hugo nodded his round head full of blond feather-like hair. Dean sat on the floor; Hugo sat on his lap, put his thumb in his mouth and looked Dean in his eyes. Dean commenced to read.

Nikki stood speechless next to the dining table looking at father and son. She wondered, *'Is there a doubt in Dean's mind?'*

After half an hour Dean stood up and said:

"I'd better be going now. Hugo, it was lovely to meet you… and, of course, to play with you."

"Thanks for the lift."

"Don't mention it. You have such a lovely son. Adorable."

Hugo crawled on his knees, hugged Dean's calves and said:

"Stay with Hugo."

"Hugo, sweetie, let go. Dean has to go, darling."

"No!" said Hugo and pursed his lips.

Dean squatted next to him, took his head into his hands and said:

"If you let me go now, Hugo, I might come back again. How about I come tomorrow to see you again?"

"No! Stay!" said Hugo.

Nikki tried to reason:

"You have to eat now, Hugo, then you'll go to bed… and tomorrow afternoon, perhaps, Dean might visit again. But you have to let go of him now."

"No!" said Hugo again.

He'd never done that before. Not even to Caesar, the one he really liked. He would just wave and repeat to Caesar's *'See you again'*, *'Again Caes."*

"How out of character his behaviour is! Sorry, usually he is quite obedient."

"I can stay a little longer if you think it's OK… or shall I come tomorrow, I'd really like to see him again… only if you agree, what about your boyfriend?"

"You can come tomorrow late afternoon."

"Dinner time?"

"Dinner time."

He kept on coming as the bond between him and the boy grew stronger still, and Dean found himself on both sides of a very strange kind of nourishment, the feeling he'd never had for anyone. Figuring out when Nikki gave birth to her son really wasn't a matter of high and complicated mathematics. He knew that they were still in some sort of a relationship, but as one always judges everything from one's own prism of understanding and behaviour, he was very doubtful about Nikki's faithfulness to him. He wasn't faithful to her and she knew it since the time they dated way back when they first met. It always stayed that way; he couldn't resist the call from other women. He never really loved Nikki, he liked her; she had a fantastic body, but quite a cold heart, well, like all other British girls he knew. There was something in her that he liked so much, apart from that fantastic body, but on the other hand there was something about Nikki that emitted a strong message – I am self-sufficient and strong, back off!

A few days before Hugo's fourth birthday, Dean picked him up from the kindergarten on Nikki's request. He did that more and more often. When they came to sign him on as a person who can come and collect the child, they put on the official papers that he was the child's uncle. A few days before Hugo's birthday Dean bought some clothes for him: a white shirt and black shorts with suspenders, a small bow tie and he changed the clothes Hugo was wearing. He combed and sleeked back his untamed blond hair, then he took him to a professional photographer. The photographer had his studio in the neighbourhood for at least the past thirty years, or as long as Dean could remember. Dean gave the photographer one photo and told him:

"I'd like you to take it from the same angle with the same lighting. Take ten pictures and I'll chose from those ten."

When they finished the photo session, Dean changed him back into his jeans and T-shirt and treated him to an ice cream. He said to Hugo:

"How about if you keep a secret from your mother? You don't tell her where we went today, and in a few days it'll be your birthday, Hugo, then I'll buy you something special. How's that?"

"You'll buy me a bike?"

"Maybe."
"I won't say a word if you promise a bike."
"You little rascal!"

Hugo's Birthday

Nikki asked Dean to take Hugo out on that Saturday so as to give her time to prepare food for the party.

Some ten kids were invited, some of the mothers that Nikki was on friendly terms with, two girls from her dancing group, indispensable Caesar and Dean were invited, too.

Dean took Hugo to the bike shop and Hugo nearly choked with excitement. He was given the opportunity to choose and he couldn't make a decision. Dean had a word with the sales person to decide which one would be the most appropriate for Hugo. They came back later than Nikki told them to come; all the guests had already arrived. Nikki was a bit apprehensive and nervous; when Dean rang the bell she was ready to yell and be snappy, but when she saw Hugo's radiant face and Dean holding a brand new bike, her eyes filled with tears.

'Mummy, mummy, Hugo's got a bike! Dean got me a bike!"

She pressed her eyes and tears started to roll down her cheeks, for her little son sounded just like her dearest late brother when he used to call:

"Lonnie, Lonnie, Yugo loves Lonnie."

It was a short party, they cut the cake in the end, sang *'Happy Birthday to Hugo'* and the guests slowly disappeared one by one. Caesar stayed longer, Dean took Hugo out to ride the bike. Caesar had become so difficult and emotionally draining. His relationship with Mr Lukas was on the brink of disaster but none of them had the balls to end it. Caesar said that he gave him *'Less and less satisfaction and money'* but at this point in her life Nikki had no understanding or compassion for his problems. He left an hour later, empty and disappointed just as he had come earlier that morning.

When Caesar left and Nikki tidied up the lounge-room and the kitchenette, she called Dean to bring Hugo upstairs.

She put him to bed and it took some time for Hugo to calm down and get over all the excitement brought on by the presents he had been showered with. The bike especially made him mad with excitement.

She expected Dean to stay a little longer, to share a glass of wine, but when she came out of Hugo's bedroom, Dean was already standing at the door:

"I hope he had a great birthday."

"Thank you Dean, you really made him happy today. Thank you, you are such a good friend."

He went down a few steps; she was still standing at the door when he said:

"Actually, I have something for you."

He walked back up those few steps reached for the pocket of his leather jacket and pulled out an envelope, shoved it into Nikki's hand and quickly and swiftly stormed down the staircase.

"What on Earth!" she said and closed the door.

Nikki poured a glass of wine and sat on the settee. She opened the envelope and found two pictures and a bank cheque. There was a small note pinned to the cheque which covered the details of the recipient and the sum of money.

She looked at the pictures; one of them was frayed at the corners. It was bitten by the tooth of time: yellowish and colours faded to one or two shades. There was a young boy in the photo sitting on some sort of high chair at the photographer's. The boy had a white shirt, and a black bow-tie around the collar. He had a pair of black shorts with suspenders, his smile was wide, hair blond and sleek, a twinkle in his eyes, yes he looked exactly like her son. The other picture she looked at was a picture of Hugo, in the same outfit with the very same smile, with the same eyes, combed and resembling a little angel.

"I guess the message couldn't be conveyed any louder."

It was just a matter of time before Nikki got asked about her pregnancy.

"What now?" she asked herself loudly and drained the glass.

On the refrigerator, next to Hugo's old picture, Nikki put two new photos: one of her son and the other of his father when he was of the same age.

Then she looked at the note, it said:
"It might help, a little."
There was a bank cheque that brought tears and tenderness to her eyes, simultaneously.

***

When Dean came over several days later to see Hugo, Nikki said:
"Let's not talk about it."
"How much longer do you intend to keep it from him?"
"Let's not talk about it right now."

The following year, when Nikki enrolled Hugo at school, she had to nominate a person who could pick her son up from school: Dean Bloxham, the child's father.
She asked Dean:
"Shall I name you as the father?"
"Sure!"
"Will you talk to him about it?"
"Sure I will."

When he was driving Hugo back from school he asked:
"Where do you wanna go?"
"Home, I guess."
"Do you want me to take you somewhere fancy?"
"Yes... but where?"
"I don't know; do you have any idea?"
"I'd like to go fishing."
"It's too late. But we can go on Saturday, yeah?"
"If Mummy agrees."

"She will. Hugo, she definitely will."

It had been not so long since Hugo had a conversation with Nikki about their status as a family:

"Mum, are we a family?"

"Sure we are a family."

"Most kids have a mummy, a daddy and a granny and a pop. It's just you and me, isn't it?"

"We have our friends. You have Caesar who is very kind to you, you have Dean, Anna and other friends."

"How come I don't have a father? Seems everyone has one but me."

"Yes, everyone has a father. You have a father too, Hugo, he just doesn't live with us."

"Where, then does he live?"

"He went back to his country."

"That's silly."

"But you have uncle Dean."

"I guess, I have him... but he is not my father."

"We can talk about it when you grow a little older, how about that?"

"OK, Mummy."

It was a rainy Saturday and Dean decided to take Hugo on a shopping spree instead of fishing. He wanted to buy some warm clothes for him, a winter jacket, a pair of gloves and proper winter shoes.

When they bought the clothes Dean took him to a café. They ordered some sandwiches and a warm drink.

"You are so good to me, Dean."

"Hugo, every child has a father to take care of them, and you have me, I do take care of you."

"You do, but you are not my father. My father went back to his country."

Dean scratched his head.

"Does that make you sad?"

"I guess... In a way... you know, everybody has a father."

"How about this, Hugo. From now on you call me father."

"I can't do that!"

"Why can't you?"

"Because you are my uncle Dean."

"What if I am not? What if I were your real father and the one who went back to his own country turned out to be just a fictional character, one like Peter Pan or... Aladdin? You know, people that never really existed, only in a story."

"I wish you were my father."

"What if your wish could be granted?"

"But how if he's gone?"

"I told you before. The story that your father went back to his Neverland was a made up story."

"Why would my Mummy make it up?"

"Because she didn't know what to say."

"But she never lied to me."

"She didn't really lie. She... she... I don't know Hugo, maybe we can talk, like, all three of us, we can talk and each explain things to the other."

When they came back Nikki had a catnap. They showed her the clothes and Dean took three photographs from the fridge and laid them on the table.

Now all three were sitting at the table.

Dean pointed to the photograph and asked Hugo:

"Do you know who this is?"

"This is Mummy's brother Hugo. I got my name after him. Mum said that she loved him almost as much as she loves me. It means – a lot."

"Correct!" Dean pointed to the other picture and asked the same question:

"And, who'd that be?"

"Hugo. I mean this Hugo, is I."

"Correct!" Dean pointed to the third photo, the yellow one, frayed at the ends.

"And who's that fella?"

"Hugo."

"Hugo, who?"

Hugo looked at Nikki. She was sitting and listening attentively. She shrugged her shoulders and looked at Dean.

"Hugo, I." Said Hugo full of doubt looking alternately at them not knowing why all this confusion and mystery.

"No, Hugo. This little fella looks like 'Hugo, I', but it isn't. This little fella is Dean Bloxham when he was your age. You remember the day when I took you to the photographer? I gave him this photo of me asking him to take one of you, dressed exactly in the same clothes."

"I remember; why did you do that?"

"To show them to your mother and to you."

"Mum, do you like them? We look alike, so, so much alike."

"You know why we look so much alike, Hugo?"

"I don't know."

"Because I am your father, Hugo."

"Are you?"

"Yes, I am."

"That's nice."

"Are you happy?"

"As long as you stay. I guess you will not go back to your country."

"This is my country, Hugo, I can't go anywhere else."

"Oh, that's good then."

"That makes you happy?"

"Very much so."

"If you wish you can sometimes come with me to see my house and spend a few days with me. You can meet my brother, he'd be a real uncle to you, and my mother... your grandmother."

He looked at Nikki. She sat there quietly, playing with breadcrumbs on the table. Hugo said:

"Is it true that I have a real uncle and a grandma?"

"It is."

"When can I see them?"

"Whenever you wish."

"Why did they never come over?"

"They might come."

"So, I have a family."

"You've always had a family, and you've always had your mother and me... it is just that you called me 'Uncle'. You can call me father or dad from now on, if you wish."

"I do wish."

"Well then, I am not 'Uncle Dean' anymore."

"Hmm, Dad."

Nikki stood up and walked out.

Hugo hugged Dean and said:

"Anyway, would you like to play, I got a new game for the play station."

"Let's check it out!"

***

"What would you say if I told you I were a father?"

"Nothing that comes from you would surprise me. Elaborate, please!"

"Do you remember Nikki?"

"One of your girlfriends, wasn't she? How could I remember her? You had simultaneous relationships... all the time."

"I wouldn't call it that, nor would I agree that it was – all the time. But anyway, Nikki was that tall, good-looking girl who hated admitting that she was Croatian."

"Nope!"

"You met her on several occasions. You must remember Nikki?"

"Sorry, but I don't. You were saying... you were a father. I guess Nikki's the one. Or one of them."

"You are still bitter."

"Bitter as..."

"What happened on that day?"

"Forget it!"

"Tell me. You need to tell me. I am your brother. You'll feel better."

"How can I feel better by plainly telling you?"

"You would and you will. What happened on that day? Everything has changed since that day."

Andrew took his guitar and started picking the strings. After a while he said:

"On that day I got a letter from Pia. You do remember Pia, don't you?"

"That's the real connection! Pia! Let me interrupt: Pia was Nikki's best friend. Do you remember Nikki now?"

"Yes. I remember."

"You received a letter from Pia on that day?"

"She went to Australia."

"What for?"

"Who will ever know? She left without any explanation."

"What did she say in the letter?"

"She killed herself."

"No!!"

"Yes, she did."

"Who said so? So, it wasn't a letter from her but from someone else telling you that she had killed herself."

"No. She just wrote a poem and told me that she used to love me. She finished the letter with Sylvia's verses:

'The woman is perfected.

Her dead body wears the

Smile of accomplishment.'

"Yet, Andy, that doesn't mean anything."

"It does. Pia killed herself. That cognition filled me with dread. I feel as if I could have prevented it, I still feel as if I were, somehow, for some reason, responsible for her moodiness. I really, really loved her and I never really told her. Never told anyone."

"I don't know what to say."

"You asked, now you know."

"I don't believe that, otherwise Nikki would have told me."

On the very same evening he visited Nikki.

"What happened to your friend Pia? Are you still in touch with her?"

"My heart bleeds when I think of Pia. She just left with that loser and I have never heard from her since."

"What loser?"

"Nicholas O'B... whatever, the Irish devil, the unscrupulous cynic, liar, cheater, a really good-for-nothing bum."

"When did they leave, several years ago?"

"More than that; several years before Hugo was born."

"You remember my brother was in love with her?"

"Many men were in love with Pia. She was an extraordinary person and friend, but few really knew her. She never loved anyone, I can tell you that. She didn't even love my brother who was, just as she was, admired by many. He was a musician, a good-looking bloke, a heartthrob, very much in love with Pia. She was his girlfriend, but never in love with him."

"Wow! An Ice-Queen."

"Too intelligent, too sensitive and sensible. Not for this world, that's how I perceived Pia. Why do you ask?"

"Andrew said something silly..."

"Silly like?"

"Oh, never mind."

"No, you can't 'never-mind-me' now. Tell me what he said!"

"He said that she had committed suicide."

"That can't be true." Said Nikki and her fingers started to dance.

"That is an awful lie!" Screamed Nikki and threw the glass she was holding on the floor. Milk spilt and the puddle grew large in a few seconds.

"Why would he make up such a horrible lie?" She choked and almost started to cry but Dean came closer pressed her arms next to her body, hugged her and said:

411

"It is a rumour, only a rumour. I can ask... it could have been made up by Andy just to cope easier or... something."

Nikki was in a foul, horrible mood for the rest of the day.

For years she had been haunted by the thought – *'Why didn't she ever write? Not a single word. Nothing. As f there were never anything! Why? Why? And why?'*

She feared that the rumour wasn't just a rumour, the last sentence from Pia's letter read:

"Nikki, I'll miss you very, very much. I fear I won't see you ever again."

Way back then, Nikki feared that this sentence might bring heartbreak to her sooner or later.

"He said that he would write a story about it. A story that would bring him relief."

After more than five years, that evening Dean Bloxham spent the night at Nikki Barlow's. He spent the night with a woman who was the mother of his son.

There was a feeling of lightness as the small family sat at the table and ate their dinner.

***

The next morning telephone buzzing woke Dean up.

Nikki rushed to answer it.

In those eleven years living in London it was his third attempt to contact her.

"Veronika, I am in London. I'd love to see you."

"How did you get my number?"

"Does it really matter? I'd love to see you."

"I am not the person you knew any more. I am nothing to you; you are nothing to me. Don't make me change my number again, don't call."

They had coffee while Hugo was still asleep. On Sundays he slept in, and if Nikki hadn't woken him up, he could have stayed asleep till lunchtime.

Dean asked:

"Who was it?"

"The person who used to be my brother."

"I know nothing about you, Nikki."

"Nothing much to know. My brother was a killer, went to the war support-ed and promoted by my father and grandfather. My mum was a Nazi-lover and church-floor-licker. They were all obsessed with big ideas, with their own grandeur and importance, they hated passionately the way a sane and sophisti-cated person would love. My mother was in love with a local priest and I bet it was more than just spiritual love that she felt for him. Interesting, hey?"

"How do you know that?"

"Know what?"

"That your brother was a killer."

"I read it in the papers. Someone called me one day and told me he killed a woman on the street with a sniper rifle. The woman was Pia's grandmother."

"Did you believe it?"

"I don't know what to believe. I have cut all ties with my country, with my family. I don't even wanna talk about my mother."

"What about Hugo?"

"He was the only one who had good intentions and a pure heart. He had Down syndrome and my mum was ashamed of him. She hid him in the house and took him out only on rare occasions."

"How did he die?"

"A car ran over him."

"Just like Bobby."

"What exactly happened to him?

"He was a troublemaker, poor soul, always unsettled, but good-hearted. To cut a long story short, he went to Amsterdam and after a short while we received a message that he was run over by a car. Just like that. After that I went to Amsterdam as if I wanted to find the cause of his death. A few years before that, our father passed away and Mother took it badly. Bobby ran,

Andrew was lost and sad because of our father and some other issues that he had at that time, and I just simply disappeared to Amsterdam. And... what now? What are you going to do with your brother?"

"I have no brother. Hugo had passed away long ago."

"You are a harsh soul, Nikki, aren't you? But still, you are my hero."

Third Day in London

On the first day upon his arrival in London Gregor Truba called Veronika. She told him off.

On the second day of his stay in London Gregor Truba visited his friend Davor, and on the third day in London he went to a bookstore.

He bought a book and had lunch at the bookstore café.

The book he bought was a collection of poems written by a woman he used to love. He heard that she *'made it'*, that she had a *'great life in London.'*

He ordered a meal and a cup of coffee.

In the mirror, on the opposite wall, he looked at himself: that wasn't the Gregor Truba that he used to know. He looked ten years older and was, at least, ten kilograms heavier than he should have been. He had dark circles under his eyes, and the eyes themselves looked like the eyes of an old tired man. Disillusioned and disappointed.

"Nevertheless…" he said loudly and took the book which was lying next to his plate. He took it in his hands, then he put it back on the table – he'll read it later.

There was a magazine there, he took the magazine and leafed through it.

He smiled at the very peculiar coincidence: there was a story in the magazine entitled *'Pia's Poem'*.

"How strange." again he said it aloud.

He was in the habit of speaking to himself aloud whether he'd be alone or in the middle of a crowd.

He looked at the cover of the small book; it read *'Pia's Book of Poetry'*. Once again, he looked at the magazine story – yes, it was entitled *'Pia's Poem'*.

"How strange." he said even louder this time.

He ordered a glass of wine.

The young woman didn't even look at him; she just placed a glass on the table. The wine spilt a bit and a few droplets stained the book. He protested noisily asking her:

"Why, are you a stupid cow?"

The girl just indifferently moved forward.

"Bloody foreigners! Stupid Brits!"

No one took notice of him.

He went back to the book, wiped off the droplets of red wine.

Then he looked at the magazine again. It was a literary magazine with literary reviews, with several poems and several short stories among other content. The longest story was *'Pia's Poem'*, written by Andrew Bloxham.

Loudly, with an angry tone, he commented:

"A short story by Andrew Bloxham. What a jerk!"

Then he took a big sip of wine and sank deeper into the chair.

He started reading the story that was titled *'Pia's Poem'*, the story written by Andrew Bloxham.

Pia's Poem

My memory's fading. You tell me what's real.

My story began long before my remembrance. My remembrance was as long and winding as a dirty country road.

I told you my story, but was it really objective?

I remember the day when someone brought quinces and put them on the table. Against a dark mahogany table they looked as if they were made of brass. They looked rather unreal, as if painted in the 3D technique.

As I told you, I was happy on that occasion, their smell made me feel loved for some reason.

Yes, I told you – I was happy, but I wasn't. The quinces' smell brought a great deal of sadness to my day. It was the day when they tried to conceal Lila's death from me. They tried to mask it with a smell. Yes, we mask things with smells.

Even as the brass quinces went on perfuming the house, it proved to be a rotten day, concealed by all that sweetness and by mother's forced laughter.

My father said *'no real man cries'*, and the relief he obtained by saying so was expected to be my relief.

They brought in the quinces and I said I was happy; again, there was expectation that I might show gladness, for they thought that I loved quinces. I said the same to you, on that day when I started to recount my story.

My story was made up.

Stories are made of feelings, not of events.

I told you about the event, but through the prism of false feelings.

I can recount it to you now, but overshadowed by different shades of feeling and you'll see what a difference that makes.

On the day when my father was taken to hospital I was happy. They told me that I was going to get a bike, instead. Instead of the truth, that's what I mean by *'instead'*. Yes, I was happy, I was going to ride a bike.

It was grey. I didn't like the colour, but I said I did.

I came to the hospital a month later riding my bike. The hospital wasn't far from our home. Mother was walking and I had already learned how to ride. On our way to the hospital she cried, but she blamed the wind, blamed the little fly, blamed the onion-sticky fingers. She plainly cried. I was riding my grey bike.

Dad never came back.

They told us that we couldn't see him – yet. Maybe tomorrow.

I rode back whistling. Mum cried. She blamed the wind and the little fly. And I wasn't really aware of the sheer magnitude of either reality or feelings.

A few years later Dean left for Amsterdam. What the hell!!!! Amsterdam! Why, out of all the destinations this world had to offer did he have to choose Amsterdam? Bobby was killed in Amsterdam: some car ran over him. As if he were a rabbit.

I blamed the car, the lousy driver, the wrong weather and the laws in Amsterdam. But, I never blamed Bobby. He smoked. I never knew that. Mother said not to blame anyone as he had freely chosen such a script. Bobby never liked *'happy endings'*. I did, and believed if we said so, we'd believe so… if we believed so, then it was real.

When they said that Dean had gone to Amsterdam, I wasn't ready as yet to show my real feelings. I kept on pretending to read the label on some jar. The jar was red; even thought it was made of clear glass - it was red. The contents were red. I was reading the label keen to figure out what was inside. Strawberries. Sweet strawberries. They sweetened his departure. I buried my head into the dish and ate two jars of strawberries with extra sugar on top.

Mother cried. She blamed the menopause.

I couldn't blame anyone. I just ate and ate as if this were going to be my last meal. After that, after his departure, I hadn't eaten for more than two weeks. My mother cried. Begged me, telling me that I was *'all that she had left"* as if I were some, rather expensive piece of furniture. She loved her antiques. It was solid confirmation that we belonged to the *'right family'*. It looked as if I were the last piece of antiquity in that household.

I said – I wasn't keen to see the Rembrandts, that I was *'more than happy'* to stay with her among the antique furniture.

But I wasn't.

I concealed my feelings with the red strawberries.

Bobby used to conceal his feelings with grass.

Dean – with his travels.

I said, I had been predominantly happy throughout my youth. Mother took good care of me. Besides, she had money and antique furniture. She had everything. She even had me. We were both conscious that – having everything makes one feel absolutely happy.

I started recounting my story telling you how happy I was. Blissfully happy: we always had *'everything'*.

Dean never came back. He went in search of Bobby. Bobby was already *'elsewhere'*, but at that time Dean still believed that he would find him. I was happy for him, even jealous (only a bit), for I thought *'How on earth could he sustain such faith?'* But Jesus resurrected!

Bobby didn't. No one did. Father didn't. Even though they said they were *'expecting a miracle'* because father was a strong, healthy man and had a brilliant, focused mind. They said he had a *'perfect family'* worth fighting for. He wasn't as lucky as Jesus was. Or the family wasn't as perfect as it needed to be to summon a mighty wish to fight.

We were blessed. In a way.

He lived a month longer than the doctors really expected. I learned to ride my bike just to tell him that I did, perhaps to make him proud of me, or … maybe, somewhere in my childish mind I believed that this fact would somehow enhance his recovery.

It didn't.

That year I was utterly sad. Beneath it was all dark, perplexingly deep, but I concealed my utter sadness with reading books. I assume that I had learned a lot, who wouldn't learn a lot, who wouldn't learn from Dostoyevsky? He wrote about death and sadness. He worked it all out for me, so I was just a passive reader. Death and sadness thus happened to someone else, in some other stories, Dostoyevsky's.

I lied to my mother about my choice of literature. I told her that I was reading something else. I found a writer whose name I had forgotten long ago and told her that I was reading his simple, uncomplicated and entertaining stories. The ones that all other kids read at that time. Back then everyone watched *Pippi Langstrumpf,* later some kids went on reading it. I didn't. I kept Dostoyevsky's book under my bed, wrapped in a scarf, as if he were a dead seer, hidden, undiscovered as yet. It was Lila's scarf I wrapped him in. I suppose that, too, was the way I mourned her death. I never knew where she was buried. Mother said that it wouldn't be appropriate to bury Lila in our garden. The garden was always perfect, and death wasn't. It was scary; I denied death as if it were unreal. How brave, arrogant and naïve that attempt was: to deny our sole certainty!?

I told you that I had six girlfriends but I never loved any of them (that's why I left each of them... except the last one).

But this wasn't true, either.

Mother liked none of them.

I met a girl named Apollonia.

Those were the times of *"The Godfather."* I met her on the street: unusual place to meet Apollonia – the daughter of an Italian immigrant. They didn't walk the streets just like that. There was no scene around from a romantic movie on that day, on that street when I met Apollonia.

A figure of infinite beauty.

I saw her eyes and my heart raced. My feet raced and I foolishly followed her. She turned her head twice and hurried. I hurried and she started to run. I ran, caught up with her and breathless said:

"Don't be afraid, I am breathless not because of running but because of your beauty."

I squatted down, picked up a daffodil from someone's garden and extended it to her. Her eyes were pretty, big with wonder. They shone. She didn't say anything she just took the daffodil. It was yellow, like the quinces on our antique table. I walked next to her speechless. When I summoned enough courage to talk, I said:

"I am not speechless because I am dumb... but, because of your beauty."

She smiled.

I smiled.

I took her bag and carried it to the park. When we reached the park, she said:

"May I have my bag now, please?"

"When am I going to see you again, beautiful, nameless girl?"

"I walk this road every day... Apollonia."

"Apollonia Road?"

She laughed.

I laughed.

But really believed at that moment that it was the name of the road. I walked that road many times before, but when I met her, I forgot all other names. Including mine. She asked what my name was and I said:

"Call me Michele, Apollonia."

She just smiled gently with tight lips, shaking her head barely visibly as if she knew that I had fallen madly in love and that had she triumphed again.

Bobby told me not to *'mess with Italian girls."*

Bobby was jealous. He always was. He was redheaded and short. He had a bad temper. He was quick as quicksilver. Once he got in trouble with Stefano. Yes, the one who was Apollonia's brother.

Mum said not to *'mess around with Italians'*. When I told my mother that I *'loved Apollonia'*, she just waved her hand, unwilling to even consider the possibility of loving an Italian-immigrant-daughter. Waving her hand meant *'we don't mess or mingle with Italians'*.

I said that to Apollonia and she said that her brother didn't like us, either. Apollonia's father owned *The Gelateria*. I used to buy an ice cream there occasionally. One day, as I went in there, he rushed over and said:

"Leave her alone!"

He didn't have a gun, or anything that a seventeen-year-old scared boy might have imagined after watching *'The Godfather'* over and over. Only, *'That particular look'* in his eyes was enough to convince me that there might be unpleasant consequences if I didn't obey.

I loved Apollonia and that gave me courage. So, *'that particular look'* was not enough to convince me or ward me off, even though I was scared. I didn't say a word to Apollonia but each day I went on carrying her bag to the park where the bag exchanged hands and we exchanged our kisses.

Shaken by the certainty that God was never present when he was needed, I lost my occasional and weak trust in him: on my way home I got beaten – badly. I couldn't walk for days. Mother said that she had told me *'not to mess with Italians'*.

Apollonia changed schools. A year later she left for Rome to study. I had never been to Rome, never wanted to go – why should I care about the Sistine Chapel or Caravaggio's work?

From that day on, the day I was badly beaten, I never met Stefano again. Bobby said if he ever met him, he would *'kill that Italian bastard'*. I was happy that Bobby never met him again. What a terrible, terrible temper Bobby had. Paradoxically, he had a mellow heart, and as sweet as dark-yellow quinces.

I never mentioned Apollonia again.

Then came the four girls that I really didn't love, but did care for in my own way. I remember their names because I had written them down in a sort of dairy. I had a thick book where I would write some sketches of my daily life. Not on a regular basis, not in structured sentences. More like – jotting down: "Failed exam... Bobby's a bastard – he stole from Dean... Al Paccino said: *'Cavalleria Rusticana?! I think I got tickets to the wrong opera. I've been in New York too long...'* got to memorise this line... Beatrix got on my nerves, can't stand her high-pitched voice... Four library books due on Monday... Cathy called... shall I or shall I not? Not pretty enough? ... Tuesday cinema with Dean."

That's how I could still remember their names.

I ended up going out with Cathy only because she wanted me so badly. I liked pretty girls. One can't date an angel like Apollonia and not care about a girl's appearance after that. But Cathy! Was she an artist in the art of opulent persuasion? Oh, yes. All I learned from her was plainly sexual. Fine!

Then I met Emma and after her Simona.

I hopped Simona would awaken in me the same sweetness Apollonia did, but Simona was *'just another pretty girl'*, there was plenty of intellectual vacuum around her.

I don't want to talk about it any longer because I wouldn't like to leave the impression that my speech is absolutely derogatory when it comes to ex-lovers.

Emma and I, we lasted the longest. This time mother didn't mind the girl's background but she had found other faults as time went by. Mothers are skilful at finding faults with girls, as their potential rivals and threats.

Bobby liked Emma. For hours, for days they could laugh together. They had the same sense of humour. They behaved as if they were brother and sister.

But then he left without any warning or need for an explanation. He just said he wanted to *'live elsewhere'*. Yet another battle he won without glory. I said that I didn't miss him at all because he was always a troublemaker. But I missed him terribly. I feared for his future knowing him too well; knowing his temper, I mean.

In 1990, I met a woman I fell in love with deeply. From my side it wasn't an ordinary love – it was pure madness. I never told anyone how much I loved her, no one – including herself. I wasn't even prepared to admit it to myself.

I read her poem.

It blew me away.

I read her poem before I met her and thought that it was written by an older, experienced woman and even though the poem was fresh and mellow, it had that depth which can only come through a great variety of life experiences.

I learned it off by heart.

I walked in its rhythm, whistled it often as if it could just as well have been a song. While whistling and reciting it in my head, I would imagine the woman who had written the poem. I gave her the face of Meryl Streep: she was beautiful, mellow and mature enough to come up with such a perfect order of words and emotions. I even called it *'Meryl's Poem'* although it had a different title.

Dean used to write little poems. When I lend deeper thought to his poems, I might correct myself and rephrase: Dean used to write soulful, meaningful verses which could easily bring memories of my father, which could at the same time easily sadden and mellow my heart. I used to love some of his poems but I never admitted it, for I believed that it might show some of my hidden weaknesses.

It was quite a cold evening. Dean had been coughing all day. He asked me to accompany him to the poetry evening. It was held in a small dark café downtown. I was hesitant because he was getting ill and this place was full of smoke that one could cut with scissors. Dean has those big brown eyes and he knew how to look in a person's eyes if he wanted to make them do as he wished. He looked in my eyes with the right dose of sadness, precisely enough to make me change my clothes without a word and get the car key.

I was driving; he was coughing.

I said:

"Do you really…"

"I really do!" he cut my sentence and I started to hum *'Meryl's Poem'*.

As soon as we walked in, Dean lit his cigarette and ordered a beer. I just swung my head helplessly; my eyes were already hurting.

Dean read his poem and I was close to tears. He had his way with words, awakening feelings of sadness, awakening pictures of father's departure, of mum's absent-mindedness written on her face like on a blackboard with a blunt dirty-white chalk. It looked to me that evening as if he had known for a long time that he was predestined to write this poem, to awaken those exact feelings in my heart.

I pleaded, he was coughing, smoking and drinking cold beer, but I pleaded to no avail. When Dean starts to drink his beer, you'd better not plead.

I sat sulkily in the dark corner while he talked to one of his friends. He introduced me to a young woman. Yes, she was pretty and I was sulky and unfriendly, I couldn't care less; all I cared for was Dean's cough and his reluctance to go home. Father used to cough a lot the year before his departure. Dean had father's nature: independent, stubborn but subtle in a way. The pretty woman was a quiet one. She didn't talk a lot. Without saying a word, she stood up after a while. She took the mic and started to read. I didn't care; all I wanted was to take Dean home.

But I recognised the poem.

It was *'Meryl's Poem'*.

She just renamed it. She had stolen it! I stood up quickly and came closer, to hear it better, or to see her better.

Shamelessly she read *'Meryl's Poem'*.

I almost protested, but as I came closer and looked into her eyes I stopped as if I were trapped by her melodic voice and her purple eyes. In the dark her eyes looked purple.

I approached her when she finished reading and said:

"You read it so expressively."

"Thanks!"

Her name was Pia.

Pia.

She said in the poem that *'she was dethroned from love'*.

Half-drunk on our way back home Dean told me that Pia didn't just read the poem, but that she wrote it. She was a Poetess.

Pia was a Poetess.

It wasn't Meryl Streep's.

It was a young woman's poem.

A beautiful young woman of few words. Probably she spared her speech, she spared her words for her poems.

I changed the title. I didn't call it *'Meryl's Poem'* because it was now, rightfully –

'Pia's Poem.'

On that day when I met Apollonia on Forest Hill Road, I changed the road's name. From that day on, for me it was – Apollonia Road.

I met Pia on Apollonia Road on 22 September 1990. She never noticed me, and I simply said:

"Pia."

She lifted her glasses up looking puzzled.

She looked absent-minded; she didn't remember Dean. She didn't know who he was. I said *'sorry'* and walked away. Pia yelled:

"Wait up!" She just remembered, but she never called him Dean. I never knew that his nickname in those circles was Jacques. So, my Dean was Jacques. Like Jacques Prevert, perhaps.

There, on Apollonia Road I fell in love with Pia, but still wasn't aware of it. It took me a few years to admit that. I considered it to be a stroke of good luck that among a number of fruitless encounters the only woman who would ever embody beauty and brains would be Pia the Poetess.

I said that I was happy the day I fell in love with Pia. That day was overshadowed by yet another death.

We got news – that Bobby was run over. I cried in the shed as one would cry for a real brother.

The first time I kissed Pia, she said:

"Don't expect me to love you. I don't fall in love, and I don't see myself sharing my future with anyone. I am free and independent; I have never stayed long with anyone because of the fear that someone might get to know me. The art of loving is not my art, I can write poetry and that's the only field where I feel knowledgeable, confident and surrendered. Otherwise, I don't surrender."

"I never wanted you to surrender. All I wanted is to be friends... may I say, I want a lasting friendship... even when you go..."

She looked at me long before she repeated my last words:

"A lasting friendship... even when I go?"

She shrugged her shoulders and headed towards the park down Apollonia Road. Although I used to carry Apollonia's bag to the edge of the park, I had forgotten carrying it, her brother had beaten out of my brain most of the memories containing slides or pictures of Apollonia... except for the Road I named after her.

I said I was happy with such a relationship.

But I wasn't.

Everyone believed that we both wanted the kind of relationship we had. I never wanted it to be that way. I wanted to tell her how much I loved her... I wanted to recite to her all those sweet verses lovers speak to each other. But I never did. Pia reserved all those words for her poems, I always felt like a stranger on her pages. They were not my home. The verses were written for someone she was yet to meet, that someone she yearned for. It wasn't me.

But I loved her and had learned to develop the art of not showing my love, almost denying it. What a tiresome art it was, what a weird artist I had become. Did that harden my soul and silence my honest speech?

She would disappear and I didn't know for many, many days anything about Pia. She would come back with a poem and a kiss. Something was burning within me, I could hear little explosions inside, but the major part of my art consisted in keeping the surface motionless. After some time that surface became – a stranger. I would look at the surface in a mirror and the mirror was absolutely indifferent, almost hostile... Still, sometimes in that mirror I could grasp some fragments of me or of my late dad, there were some hints of Dean's words or gestures, some of Bobby's anger and lots of Pia's unspoken emotions hidden underneath, which aroused an unknown melody in my soul.

Love!

Did Pia love me without wording it? Is love a person? Is it an attitude? Could it be an orientation of character to the world as a whole, not just toward one person?

Whom did Pia love?

Does 'love' mean the absolute absence of a conflict?

I said that I never feared anything.

But I did.

I feared confrontations with Pia. Feared all that leaving.

I said it was the way we both liked it.

But it wasn't.

Underneath my outsized pride I knew Pia was never 'mine'. I found myself to be completely under her spell, but kept silent, 'disinterested and distant', believing that only 'disinterested and distant' could I keep her by my side.

She kept on writing and winning and I resigned myself to the idea that we would always divide ourselves between poetry and silence, and among the little cracks that parted those two – a little bit of love.

Pia was hardly ever happy. Happiness is a state of mind, nothing else. But she was predominantly in a state of mind which demanded an absolute surrender to it.

The day dawned full of clouds. Pia called almost in a hurry wanting to see me. While we were walking down Apollonia Road, Pia said:

"Today at 11 o'clock I am departing."

"Where to?"

"To Australia."

"Mm."

I said nothing.

Nothing to her.

To Dean I said that I didn't mind.

But I did.

I cried inside.

Mother finally smiled. She heard that the Poetess was going away. Far away, indeed. She heard it from Bobby's friend, who still used to come and visit as if he hoped that Bobby might have magically appeared from thin air. That friend of Bobby's, whose name I don't remember any more, never liked women of few words, the moody ones. I remember him, not particularly but only because he said that he never liked Pia's poetry, in his words she was *'worse than Sylvia Plath.'* He said that she was *'suicidal material'* and that he hated such whims. I hated him; so I forgot his name. I assume when you deliberately forget someone's name you show utter disrespect or hidden hatred.

Mum said it was about time that I got a new car.

There, on Apollonia Road, Pia said that she wanted to go to the airport alone. She never liked a *'public display of affection'*. I replied that I was not an affectionate guy, anyway. She kissed me and went away. I felt so alone on that day looking at Pia's back getting smaller down Apollonia Road.

I got a new car. I told you I was happy because of it, but I wasn't. It was just a car, after all.

When she left, for days I read Plath's poetry.

I never read Pia's poetry again.

There was only one poem of Pia's which I truly liked and loved. It was *'Meryl's Poem'*.

The rest were just self-torturing expressions of the wounded soul.

I never asked her if she planned to come back or if she was going for good. No difference.

Dean left. Why did he leave?

Amsterdam.

I said to myself that I would never go to Amsterdam, or Australia.

There I was: all alone with mother and our antique furniture. I had a new car. How happy was I supposed to be? I had everything.

My new car was a fancy one: its bonnet was adorned by a little black horse propped up on its hind legs.

It is needless to say that she never called and never wrote a letter.

She didn't and I said I had forgotten her.

Anyway, she had a neurotic nature and her thoughts were like some dark river threatening to flood my sanity. I was drowning in love and despair, losing ground, losing self-respect and identity. I breathed Pia, recited Pia, imitated Pia, waited for her, bled for her, I almost exhausted my desire to go on living while she was absent writing her poetry.

It was August 30th, the day was warmish and I was driving along a riverbank. Suddenly, someone waved their hand and hoarsely called my name. I slowed down.

It was Marcus.

He said that he was home for the holidays.

"Where do you live now?"

He said, *'Sydney'*, but I never knew he lived there.

He said he saw Pia several times.

He said she lost lots of weight.

I put my dark sunglasses back on.

Pia!

I said:

"It was a long time ago. I barely remember her."

It was a lie.

I did remember her each day.

He said:

"Lucky you", pointing his hand towards a little black horse propped up on its hind legs, *"...you always had everything. Even as a child you had everything..."*

"Yeah, I was pretty lucky."

"Even with the girls. You always snatched the best-looking ones. I remember that Italian girl. Good Lord, she had a piece of arse!!!"

Her brother beat the crap out of me!

Physical pain! You can touch it, locate it and eventually heal it.

I got back home and, as always, mother kissed me.

There was a pleasant smell of quinces on the table. I closed my eyes to invite memories with the smell of yellow quinces.

I opened my eyes and looked at the quinces again. A letter was there – resting against a vase full of flowers. It was addressed to me.

It was Pia's letter.

It said:

"I want you to know that I used to love you. But you couldn't save me from myself. That unbearable emptiness of Australia inspires only a death wish. I hate it here, that's why I've come to this nothingness – only to torture myself. It is done:

-   The woman is perfected.

Her dead

Body wears the smile of accomplishment. -"

What was the name of that friend of my dear Bobby who said that she was like Sylvia Plath? Suicidal. I hate that man, I always did!

I couldn't even cry, I remember her asking me:

DETHRONED

"A lasting friendship… even when I go?"

London 2004, ©Andrew Bloxham

*** *

Gregor Truba sat there as if he had seen a ghost. He had no wish to talk, not even to himself loudly or quietly, no wish to talk at all.

He stared at the letters as if they were alive accusing himself of, if not all of his deeds, at least – some of them.

As he stared at the letters he had an infallible nudge that there was a figure standing on the other side of the café intensely staring at him. He turned his head quickly and there she was: a tall lanky woman with a faint smile on her face, with kind yet sharp eyes. He took a glass and threw it in her direction, took the book and ran with a slight limp through the open door. The young waitress didn't even yell after him, as he ran without paying for his meal; she was glad he had left. The magazine stayed on the table, opened on page 53, where in bold grey letters it said, *'Pia's Poem' by Andrew Bloxham.* She took the plate and the empty glass, then she put the magazine away.

"Huh, what a character!" she said, *"Bloody Russians!"*

He visited two more pubs, had a few more beers but couldn't rid himself of the story. He knew that the story was about *his* Pia. He took out of his pocket a piece of paper with Veronika's address and her telephone number. The world was a small place, she might be hiding in London, but he had his connections, he wasn't a *'War Hero'* for nothing, he had his connections and privileges.

The taxi took him to South Kensington. It was late afternoon; the shadows were dark and he felt as if it were really late evening, as if it were really cold, the kind of coldness which he could only be found in his heart when facing this world. In an attempt to fight for his heart, for the last sparkle that was still there alive, he had to see his sister Veronika.

After waiting an hour, he saw a man with a young boy walking towards the building. The child reminded him of someone, he had blond hair and a strong build. The child ran and the man said:

"Wait up, Hugo!"

It sent shivers down his spine. Without thinking, with a slight limp, he crossed the road. He said to the child:

"Lovely name."

"Thank you, dear stranger."

His father smiled, Gregor said:

"What a lovely boy."

"Yes, Hugo is a very friendly boy."

"Hugo. That is a beautiful name."

"I got it after my uncle Hugo. He died long ago."

Gregor's eyes filled with tears, no, he was a *'War Hero'*; he was not allowed to express such feelings. He barely managed to squat, the leg he'd been shot in prevented him from being and feeling like the old Gregor. But for the sake of this little Hugo he made an effort, he blocked the pain.

"I used to have a brother whose name was Hugo, too."

"That's nice. Where is your brother now?"

"He passed away."

Dean said:

"Hugo, it's time to go home. Say good-bye."

"Good-bye, sir."

Gregor said:

"I am Veronika's brother."

"Who is Veronika?" asked Hugo.

Dean said:

"I am not sure she wants to see you."

Gregor extended his hand and Dean squeezed it:

"Gregor."

"Dean. I dislike interfering, but she appeared to be disturbed by your call."

"I haven't heard from her in more than eleven years. How is she?"

"I guess she is fine. Hugo's our son."

Like a hurt child Gregor started to cry covering his face with his chunky, strong hands.

His shoulders shook while he was sobbing. Hugo wriggled from one foot to the other, pulled his father's arm and asked:

"Why is he crying? Is he homeless?"

"No, Hugo, he isn't homeless."

"Is he sad?"

"Obviously, he is."

"What are we going to do? Are we going to invite him up and give him some warm soup for dinner?"

Gregor said:

"Don't tell her I came. It might scare or disturb her even further."

Then he turned his back and quickly, with a slight limp, crossed the road.

Hugo asked:

"Does he know my Mummy?"

"Yeah, he does, but look, maybe it'd be better if we just don't mention this meeting. Agree?"

"If you say so."

Half an hour after they entered the apartment Nikki walked in. She was wet through as heavy rain poured outside, she said:

"Oh, bloody rain, I am soaking wet."

Then she went to the bathroom. When she came out Dean said:

"My mother expressed the desire to meet you and Hugo."

"When?"

"Whenever we decide. Might as well be the coming weekend."

"Oh, God, I ran away from a family, am I building a new one now?"

"Nikki, my paranoid girl. Maybe families, after all, are not as bad as you'd like to believe. Not even your own."

"What do you know about my family? Nothing!"

Branka Čubrilo

***

On his fourth day in London Gregor Truba found himself at Gatwick: back to his hometown.

The flight wasn't a long one but it was filled with memories: the ten-year-gap in his mind-hidden compartment, the years that he worked hard to wipe out.

While the plane was taking off and the houses become smaller and smaller, a look at his own life came from a different perspective.

He remembered countless sleepless nights, chills and fires, thunders, shouts, cries of people, domestic animals, howling of winds, deep snow and drunken parties. He was a soldier, not a musician any more, he had to be ruthless, no one needed a poetic soul, or any of *'that crap reserved for university students'*; he was a soldier defending his country and the interests of … and the interests of whom?

Nightmare after nightmare; fear after fear; paranoia and lies. Endless and countless lies, a forest of thick lies so that he couldn't tell the truth from a lie any longer, and it became irrelevant and all the same. He didn't know who he was anymore, he wore the uniform and sang songs, he drank alcohol and witnessed those who drank blood from both sides; he drank his tears and saliva dreaming of times when he was free to roam beaches, chase seagulls and write songs.

After several months on the front line: a leave of absence, back home from being a scared-when-sober and hero-when-drunk-soldier to the full-time hero to everyone. His mother was the proudest woman in town; then he had an over-proud father, then the man who claimed to be the family best friend, a friar who was so ambitious that his ambition bordered with the unscrupulous, then the numerous friends who cheered him and there was no end to it.

Then one day when he was on leave, he read the morning paper. There was a short notice:

"After several years of constant struggle to regain her health, yesterday at 11 am, in the hospital of Sacred Hearts, the prominent, well known gallery owner, poetess and philanthropist Luna Averna Bonifacio passed away. The tragic events that preceded her health deterioration have not been fully disclosed for the sake of the investigation that is still in progress. Utter respect to her family and friends. In her lifetime Luna Averna Bonifacio had reached out to help many of the less fortunate in our region. She helped young artists, writers and musicians by organising charity events, donations and promotions through her Gallery."

The story continued with details about her burial and some other information that Gregor found uninteresting. When he opened the last page, there were countless obituaries in remembrance of Luna Averna Bonifacio from family, friends, organisations, city council and government institutions.

He said nothing. He felt nothing. He commented nothing when people discussed it in the local cafes for days. Nothing to do with him, he barely knew her!

In none of those obituaries did he see Pia's name.

Several days after *'the biggest funeral in the history of our town'* he met a group of several young men. Someone called his name:

"Truba, Truba, you motherfucker!"

He squatted down as the other man fired at him and then he ran for shelter as fast as he could. The other men fired as well, they were drunk but one said loudly:

"Simon sends his regards!"

Gregor took out his gun and yelled:

"Come over here!" and fired in the air.

The siren was heard, the boys ran away, only one ran towards him, fired again and Gregor felt excruciating pain in his left leg. He wasn't sure where exactly he was shot, but he couldn't stand on his leg; while lying down he shouted for help but no one approached. Two uniformed men came up, they were from the special police force; upon examining his leg and asking some questions, they called the ambulance.

The plane was caught in turbulence and it dropped a few meters; some people screamed, some sighed loudly; Gregor thought that it wasn't turbulence at all, hence he said loudly:

"You people don't even know what real turbulence is! You don't have a clue, you clueless idiots!"

No one paid attention, he sank into his *'ten buried years'* comfortably as one would into childhood days filled with fun and wonder.

If he ever wanted to discuss it or admit it, then yes, his childhood days were filled with fun and wonder: he lived in a house close to the sea, he spent three months every summer from early morning till late afternoon on the beach exploring sea-life, exploring boats and floating clouds, filling his mind with beautiful images and impressions, feeding his soul with a myriad of changing pictures, smells, sounds and stories, the stories and sounds that would lead him to become a creator himself, to create fine music on his piano and on his guitar. He thought often about real existence of the soul, as he would often find himself in a state of pure bliss liking and loving the sun and the stars, seashells and breeze, trembling air and seagulls' cries.

He never thought of himself, as part of some exclusive nation while his mother would scold him:

"Don't you say that; you are better than all of them!"

"But, why?"

"You are from my side German and a pure Croat from your father's side. We are better than any of them."

He knew, always, that it was faulty teaching. He never gave it a thought; he even ridiculed his mother on many occasions. So out-dated, so old-fashioned, so narrow-minded!

He was mild-mannered when compared to Veronika. She would protest loudly, she would resist, oppose and argue... or, moreover, she would do something outrageous: like bite, pee into someone's lap, cut braids or spill paint. She would get her message across in a very specific way, the message that couldn't be forgotten easily, or perhaps – ever!

She left – he stayed.

She couldn't stand the idea of war and killing, or couldn't find any excuse for murdering. Prior to her leaving, Gregor found her at the kitchen door eavesdropping on a conversation that was taking place between her mother and Firar Marag to what Veronika with a straight face said:

"Grand ideas from a fine preacher – whenever killings in cold blood occur en masse, it is obvious that behind them are manipulation and bloodthirsty designs of creatures who are somehow not quite like the rest of humanity, I mean, the rest of us."

She walked out without any expression of emotion on her face.

Mother screeched, the Friar wisely lifted his hand up and whispered something to what Mother crossed herself quickly.

"Who was Veronika?" he said loudly but there was no one to answer that question.

He witnessed murders, raping of woman, bitter beating of old people and children, looting and devastation all in the name of democracy. Terror and dread, fear and hysteria, breakdown of families, households and spirits. He was there all the way to be a witness, Veronika left without a word.

Veronika changed her name and was not his sister any more.

'Was she wiser? Was she quicker? Who was she?' He repeated loudly: *"Who was she?"*

After he was shot in the foot, he never walked straight again. He, kind of, limped and that left him devastated: a good look can easily be damaged and lost. Those ruthless years, deeds and thoughts had toughened his, once mellow, eyes and cut strong vertical and horizontal lines across his forehead. The wind had beaten him and his previously soft skin, became harsh like the skin of a rogue.

He never loved or liked a woman again; he consumed women as one would consume food or drink, as someone would consume a fine casual scent or a blatant transparent lie.

On that short flight he asked, mostly loudly, *'Who was Veronika?'* but he never asked himself – who he was, as to impose such a question Gregor Truba needed yet another flight into the future and back into his past.

His eyes always looked sad and tired, as he couldn't sleep well. Since he came back from the war he couldn't sleep any longer: two to three hours at best. Then he would get up and read for a short period, or just simply look through the window at the rare passers-by or changing pictures. He was never sure if that was his town anymore, too many people had left; too many friends had been lost forever.

During the night, lonesome visitors and suppressed events in walking hours haunted him. To him the dead and the living were equally present, equally alive and eloquent.

That tall and lanky woman came so often and presented herself as if she were some sort of a benevolent spirit, but he knew she came to torture him even though she smiled, occasionally she sang some folk-songs whose rhythm and rhyme he couldn't stand longer than a few seconds. He was often awakened by Luna's cries, pleas and curses that sounded as if they were coming from some other dimension, a faraway lonesome land where even wolves feared to roam. He would see her nakedness; her wrinkled body and felt terror as she was approaching with her vacant eyes, rotten smell and cold breath.

Then he was haunted by long columns of people and animals, not soldiers but such innocent people as did not participate or want that bloody war:

438

women, children and the sick. He mourned horses: a number of beautiful, strong and well-fed horses. Sad long columns: cries, laments, curses and promises. If they were to be seen from the air, up from the moon, they would probably look like an endless centipede made of humans and animals.

He would be awakened by the stench of urine, or just any other stench, a smell of blood and alcohol. The stench of smoke and arson, of the scorched land and wood... and awakened by the numbing and sickening smells and sounds in the middle of the night: owls flying overhead, bats and grenades.

Panic in the pit of his stomach. Hatred multiplied by thousandfold.

But still, in his ear this voice was ringing, a thousandfold louder than all grenades, fires, cries and screeches: Friar Marag's words asking for obedience towards the country, nation and, God himself.

And the Friar said that God gave them the right to fight for their freedom, God granted them the right to kill, to set fires and to disperse. The Friar knew it, as he was God's emissary, God talked to him, therefore God knew which nation was the chosen one! If Friar said so, it should have been so. His father fought all his life for this idea, his grandfather left their land for Germany and fought for the idea all his life, his Mother's words and heart were clear and, what else would ever be needed to convince him that he was right. The media was telling the truth, Germany and the USA were telling the truth, the world was ringing with truth and Goebbels said – *'If you tell a lie big enough and keep repeating it, people will eventually come to believe it.'*

A better world was promised, more light for everyone, the country was going to be a *'new Switzerland, just more prosperous'*, that was exactly what Mr President said, even though he had been a Communist General under Tito, who cared, he was supported with so much money and enthusiasm from all corners of the world, why wouldn't he, Gregor Truba, be on the right side? He might score a medal, a prestigious rank or some material gain, as winners always make new rules.

"We have the Yanks behind our backs, and Yanks bring democracy, freedom, free-trade, money and a good life."

That was the belief and the slogan of that time.

Gregor Truba was on the right side.

Only one thing he couldn't stand: when night would fall, his nightmares became violent and never-ending.

***

When the war ended in victory and glory, as a logical consequence, democracy and freedom came to the shores of Gregor's existence. Not only Gregor's but many people's. The celebrations were loud and happy, killing brought freedom and happiness. Who were those ethnic Serbs, and when did they come? Only yesterday?

In the books of current history, it is said that the first Serbian Orthodox Monastery in Croatia was Krupa Monastery, built in the year 1317 by Stephen Uros II Milutin of Serbia. Members of the Orlovic Serb Clan settled in Lika in 1432.

In 1690, in the small village of Raduč, in the region of Lika, the Tesla family had settled. Nikola Tesla's grandfather Nikola was born in Raduč in 1788. He was a soldier, a border sergeant in Napoleon's army, as Lika and Croatia belonged to Napoleon's Illyrian Provinces, and during his military service he was awarded a Medal of Bravery. Nikola had married Ana Kalinic from Raduč and they had four children: two sons and two daughters. He had sent both his sons to study at the Military Academy in Austria where his younger son Josif, obtained a degree in mathematics.

His other son, Milutin, didn't have a natural inclination or interest in the rigid discipline that the Military Academy called for; hence he left the Academy and followed his soul's call. He was a born poet and philosopher, a deeply spiritual soul, a natural educator and negotiator. Those qualities led him to the seminary, to study to become a Serbian Orthodox Priest. He was the best known and best respected Serbian Orthodox Priest in that region, an ecumenist, a poet and a philosopher, deeply involved and devoted to spiritual and secular life of a wider community. For his exceptional efforts and merits in develop-

440

ment of good relations between different religions, he was awarded the Imperial Medal from Emperor Franz Joseph I, *'Order of the Cross of Merit of the First Degree.'*

In the year 1822 he married Djuka Mandic, a daughter of Gracac's Serbian Orthodox Priest, an exceptionally talented woman who was able to recite sonnets and tomes of poetry, a woman who was an inventor of many devices and household supplies.

As a priest, he was transferred to the new parish in Smiljan, a small village not too far from his native Raduč.

There in Smiljan, Lika, on the 10th of July 1856 the most distinguished scientist of all time was born – Nikola Tesla, the fourth child out of five children that were born to Milutin and Djuka Tesla, the Serbs from Lika.

Therefore, when Gregor Truba said, *"Who the fuck is Nikola Tesla... some lunatic-Serb"* it wasn't really him talking; it was the ignorance of mind and poverty of spirit, distraction for the sake of distraction as warmongers promised to *'build better houses and breed smarter minds'*.

But when he lit the house where Sava Tesla was born, a small white-stone house, he didn't know who Sava Tesla was. She wasn't only a descendant of that worthy family, but she was Pia Odak's grandmother. How could he have known that Pia had such an impure bloodline? Had he known that, who can tell if his lighting of that modest house would have been a more joyful deed or a more sorrowful and shameful one?

But when the war ended celebrations started with joy, followed by sorrow and culminated in shame for many disillusioned souls and for many years to come.

In the beginning there was that sweet scent and taste of euphoria that characterises small nations and justifies the unjustifiable. It was almost like a drug, fine heroin for the undeniable heroes.

Songs and celebration, fireworks, rifle-fires, and arrogance-and-fame-loaded crowds, such were the everyday scenes throughout the country. And hatred prevailed still. The heroes were proud, loud and all-deserving: houses of expelled citizens were granted to numerous innocent war victims; state pensions and awards where handed out in abundance; high ranks were given to many who were not trained or schooled in military schools. Many were just lay people, but truck-drivers became generals, welders – high-ranking officers.

Peace was celebrated and the future seemed to dawn as the brightest that history in this part of the world had ever known.

Sometime, in the year 2007, there was a third attempt on Gregor's life. The first two appeared to be *'accidental'*, though; he knew only too well who stood behind those orders.

He came home late. The shadow on the wall pulled back quickly as he turned his back around. Gregor walked into the house and hid in the corridor. The shadow followed, walked into the semi-darkness and pulled a pistol out. Gregor took an iron bar that was taken down from the window that very morning and approached slowly, quietly behind his back. With a swift movement he put the bar around the man's neck and tightened it. The man started to choke, to cough and kick his legs and arms. Gregor never loosened his grip until the man fell down onto his knees. They were both on the floor – the man lying in the foetal position, and Gregor kneeling next to him. He pulled out a small flashlight and shoved it into the man's face.

He recognised him: the man wasn't a local, he came somewhere from the inland, the place where people had never seen the sea, a *'corso'* or a café, library or any institution. A pure hick. But an evil one: one of those, who on the suspicious merit of being a war-volunteer got himself a nice house along the seaside. The one that had never been on any vacation as he had never earned any, a crook, to whom the *'Holy Nation'* became the key for opening any door. A small cheat, cheap thief and intellectually inferior in any circumstances. He came to Gregor's hometown when the mud of war brought a lot of scum to the surface.

"What do you want from me?"

"Just some money!" He cried.

"You, bastard. Liar! Who sent you?"

"No one did."

"I can kill you here, in this darkness, without blinking an eye, don't you know that? No one knows you anyway in this place, you poor beggar, you peasant!"

Gregor hit him with his fist straight between the eyes.

The man burst out sobbing. Gregor hit him again without warning. The man tried to get up, but Gregor hit him across the face with his foot. The man tried to reach for his pistol, Gregor started to kick him with his feet until the man uttered:

"Don't kill me! Please, do not kill me!"

"Who sent you?"

"I can't tell you."

"I'll kill you right here but not with a pistol. You'll experience a horrible death. I'll bring down a claw wrench and will slowly take out each and every tooth from your mouth."

"Odak."

"Simon?"

"Yes."

Gregor opened the zip on his jeans, took his penis out and pissed on him. He said:

"Urine heals wounds."

The man said nothing. When Gregor finished urinating, he put his penis back in his pants, zipped up his jeans, spat on the man and said:

"Be wary. Very, very wary. When you see me, cross the road. But don't walk – run! And never, ever, think of revenge. You have lost already, be sure, you have lost all you have, already, including your shitty life."

He turned around and saw his father standing at the end of the corridor in his dressing robe. He came closer and said:

"Get lost otherwise the night will swallow you."

The man, on his knees, walked out of the house sobbing.

Gregor found the man's pistol, took it and said to his father.

Branka Čubrilo

"Get dressed. I am not going to kill him, just give him back his pistol. You have to witness it."

***

It was two o'clock in the morning and Simon Odak slept in his innocent dream. He couldn't have known when Jozo would execute his mission, but he knew he would, this Saturday, or a few days after, it wouldn't make much of a difference.

Jozo obeyed Simon's commands; he was good to him on several occasions. He learned to listen and to obey; he knew that Mr Odak knew how to generously reward his obedience. After all, he gave him a permanent job in the new government: a job where he wasn't asked to come early in the morning or leave late in the afternoon; a job that he had already been doing for a number of years, but without a wage, a holiday and unexpected and generous bonuses. Who wouldn't be loyal and obedient?

Gregor didn't ring nor did he knock at the door. He broke in; with his broad, strong shoulders knocked the door down and walked in with the pistol in his hand. His father stood at the broken door. Gregor went straight into Odak's bedroom. Many years ago he walked through this corridor and he still remembered some paintings he passed by as he was heading to Odak's bedroom. Odak was already awakened by the noise, he stood up, opened the drawer on his bedside table, but Gregor said in a low voice:

"Close it! Yep, close it! You are not going to get your gun out as I am pointing mine at your head. Be good and calm, understand?"

"There must be some misunderstanding, young Truba."

"Oh, you remember my name?"

"You were a worthy soldier, a great patriot."

"Hmm. Why is it then that you want to put a bullet in my head? This is the third time that you ordered my murder, isn't it? Or were there more, but I wasn't aware of them?"

"Why would you think it was me?"

444

"Because it was you, we both know it. We both know why you want to see me dead. You opened the investigation and it didn't lead you anywhere. Who stood behind the rape of your beloved mistress? I don't know."

"Who killed my mother?"

"I am not responsible."

"I was told you lit my grandfather's house."

"Bullshit!"

"What do you want from me now?"

"To warn you. There is a man at your door. I am not alone. Come over, have a look. This man is my father. He fought for this country in times when you and your worthy Odak family were on the right side of the law. You were Yugoslavs, communists, the righteous ones. My father was a fascist. He fought for this country in WW2 and ever since until this liberation. Yet, you and your Odak clan prosecuted him. Not only once but, many times. You followed each and every move he had made in the past forty years. I went to the battlefield, yet the Odak family still occupies the most influential positions in this country. How is that possible? You order a crook to kill me? That was a mistake. I am not afraid of you, but you don't know me well, you can't even imagine how mad I am. I do not shy away from anything. Understand? Anything! We can negotiate now, talk like men, I can go home and forget all about you and your hit man. As for you, stop being obsessed with the science fiction story – that I raped Luna and killed your mother. Stop that nonsense. I have been to hell and back while you were sitting in your fine leather chair, in your ironed uniform and acting in yet another role. You have to understand well that I do not shy away from any bizarre or horrendous act."

Without expecting an answer, without the fear that Odak might shoot him in the back, Gregor turned around and walked away.

Simon Odak's fingers trembled for several hours after Gregor Truba left. He was no longer a young man; he didn't have such steady nerves as he used to. Luna's horrendous death and his mother's cowardly death changed him somehow. Yes, he wanted revenge but he feared it too. Gregor Truba wasn't a young boy anymore, but Simon Odak was almost an old man. Only the thought that the preparations for his post as Defence Minister of the country were in progress could bring him some feeling of power and control. After all these years of absolute silence from her side, he stopped thinking of Pia. But for her quiet disappearance he blamed, once again, the man who claimed that he had nothing to do with Luna's misfortune and his mother's death.

***

Two men were summoned into his office on the same day, but at a difference hour. Friar Marag was slightly restless, but nothing gave that away. He still stood straight, firm on the same spot, without changing his position. His eyes calm, resting on the same object.

Jozo Prka was the name of the first man he called in.

The Friar welcomed him to this town when Jozo showed much dedication to *'their cause'* in the early days of fighting for freedom. He knew his father, even grandfather, none of whom were very bright but were big patriots. To be a patriot brightness wasn't necessarily needed, obedience and readiness were in demand. There are those who are called to think and those who are called to obey and to act. For those who are called to act brightness could be an obstacle. The Friar's philosophy was, *'The more of us, the stronger we are.'* No need for selectivity, there was a need for the strongest, most extreme feelings.

When Jozo walked in beaten like a mangy dog, the Friar listened to his story attentively, without any trace of feeling on his almost sculpted face. Upon hearing his story, the Friar called a doctor and organised urgent hospitalisation. Then he calmly called two men to come over: Gregor Truba and Simon Odak, who appeared to be sworn enemies but who, unquestioningly obeyed, the same master.

Five years had passed since Friar Dondi abruptly opted for early retirement. It looked as if he had decided upon it overnight. Not a single sign, he just wrote a letter of resignation in haste and without further questioning church authorities accepted his resignation and Friar Marag was appointed as the new Head of the Church.

Friar Dondi took up residence in his old house by the shore, surrounded by cypresses and pines and prayed there incessantly, eating only once a day a slice of bread dried by the wind and the sun, a sip of water to make his prayers flow easier. His eyes were pointed up to the heavens and maybe for the first time in his life he felt helpless.

But Friar Marag thought that finally he had reached his much deserved post. He hid his pride behind his sculpted face while Elsa Truba could hardly contain her excitement when news of it reached her. She almost felt as if there were a part of her own merit in such an achievement by her best and dearest friend and ally.

***

When Simon Odak walked into the Friar's office it appeared to him that the Friar was fast asleep: his eyes closed, face smooth but motionless. He stood on the threshold for several minutes, which dragged and seemed as if they would keep on dragging for eternity. The Friar had heard him entering, breathing, but he kept his eyes closed for a while. When he opened his eyes, he smiled at him and made a gesture with his hand:

"Please, do sit down."

Odak kissed his ring; Friar Marag smiled and withdrew his hand and continued:

"You know this hatchet has to be buried?"

"Can you be more specific Father?"

"Young Truba is a good man. He was a good soldier; his father is a good man, a good Croat. Your moves aren't wise; we can't turn our back on our brothers or show anger. Our enemy is common and our country is young; we are united by our holy nation. The Ministerial chair has been offered to you, and you have to be wise, to know who your friends are. You have to avoid making enemies out of good people at all costs. I'll see that everything runs

smoothly for you, I'll pray to God for you as well, what we expect of you is only to be wise and cooperative."

Simon Odak sat there almost obediently as a schoolboy would, listening attentively. Friar Marag's face and eyes were calm, benevolent, full of understanding and compassion. At least, that's how it appeared to those who would look at him for the first time or through a blurred window.

"Luna Bonifacio was…"

"I know what happened to that woman! Forget it! After all, she was, God forgive me, a loose woman, the one who easily could ruin a good man's reputation. Forget it now and forever."

"Who killed my mother?"

"That was an accident. Some people knew who she was."

"Friar…"

"Odak, your mother was of Serbian heritage, yet this country trusts you, it trusts you enough to put you in the highest position thanks to your loyalty and dedication throughout the war. All I am asking of you is to forget the past, it was a war, it has ended, but we have to be wise now… I shall repeat and ask you once again – please bury the hatchet and forget the past. Thank you for coming."

Odak stood up and accepted the offered hand. The Friar blessed him as he kissed the holy cross, then he left in haste. The Friar stood next to the window hidden behind heavy curtains; he looked at Odak's back until he disappeared behind a grove of olive trees.

Gregor was hesitant to go: he was never sure what kind of feelings he harboured in his soul when it came to Friar Marag. There were moments when he even feared him. Yes, he feared him as his eyes were at times so deep and dark and he looked at Gregor as one who was possessed by a demon. Could it be that, after all, Veronika was right about him? She never liked him and had the guts to show it from the very first time she was able to show her emotions or feelings towards anyone. On the other hand, Friar Marag had helped him on numerous occasions. He was always there to help and to guide. To guide! That was the word that Gregor had trouble with. He felt guided by that man, by his mind and his wishes. At times Gregor felt used, manipulated, spat out. Oh, he wished he had a firm belief and opinion about this man, it would be so much easier, because Gregor was never at ease when he was around, especially since the Friar became Head of the Monastery.

Short courtesies were exchanged, *'How is your mother doing?'* and *'I hope that all's well now.'*

Then abruptly the Friar said:

"You have to bury this hatchet! I know he is a pain. He is not the most honest of men, but he has his merits and above all he has connections. Forget the past and move on. We can't afford to have disagreements and hatred among us. We still have enemy eyes on us."

"He ordered my murder several times..."

"I said, forget the past... he will not bother you any more, he knows where he stands, he knows that my opinion counts. And you too, you have to think more about your future. The war has ended; we are victorious, and now is the right time for you to take your rightful place in our society. I see you wallow in apathy. Don't destroy your soul with such useless emotions. You served your country; you were ready to give your life for it just as your father was in 1941. We have gotten rid of intruders once and forever, you ought to teach your children and the children of your children what they have done to us over the centuries, they have to remember it for many generations to come. Come over here and have a glass of wine." Said the Friar while pouring wine into two glasses.

When those with a not so pure intent go through the motion of seemingly doing good, being outwardly personable while appearing to be good human beings, they who do have that connection with their inner voice and intuition can see through subtle levels that these creatures have evil motives.

"I'll do as you ask of me, Friar."

Gregor turned his back and left without taking the offered glass of wine. While walking away the Friar's voice followed him:

"Send my blessings and love to the family."

'*... or just to my mother...*' Gregor thought, briskly walking through the corridor; again an uninvited thought popped into his conscious mind, *'Was she right?'*

Yes, was Veronika right, did she feel or know, on some different level, something he didn't know? He would never come to answer that self-imposed dilemma, as he knew he would never ever have a chance to talk to Veronika. She disowned them all long ago.

***

He adjusted his seat and looked at the sky: the sky is not there for some people and it isn't absent for others, nor does the sun shine only on the select few who have been arbitrarily chosen.

He dozed off.

Up there in the sky he had a dream about Hugo after many years.

He appeared as a four or five-year-old boy and smiled at him. He looked in Gregor's eyes and said:

"Thank you for visiting, you see Hugo's back, I am a healthy boy now. Gregor, Gregor, Gregor save your soul..."

He jumped up and the plane was slowly dropping down ready for touch-down.

He thought:

"What now?"

***

DETHRONED

Gregor Truba had never married and never had kids of his own. He had several women but his attitude towards women was the attitude of a womaniser. Long ago he resolved that women served only for entertainment and pleasure. Since he came back from the war he never looked at a woman with the same eyes. He was demanding, domineering and showed a sadistic streak if disobeyed. He lived like a hero from cheap romance stories: a hero, a war-veteran and an ex-musician that still rocked the scene. He tattooed his body heavily, he covered his eyes with dark sunglasses, the ones that the army provided with other generous gifts: bourbon, whiskey, top guns and rifles and other macho gadgets.

After the war ended there were so many celebrations, daily celebrations, but also daily blow-ups of local cafés, institutions and *'enemy'* houses. People were clearing and straightening up old debts and ancient claims. After the war total chaos prevailed everywhere: in the economy, education, politics, human relations and the most disturbing thing of all was – the lack of money for the masses. There was plenty of money for a few: politicians and those in power; a new elite was born on the backbone of the working and the middle class until it altogether disappeared. Poverty everywhere, just arrogant soldiers and a torrent of individuals armed with the lawless law and heavy arms ruled the regions. Every town had their rulers and every village their potentate.

But the flag fluttered on every corner, it fluttered proudly, and intoxicated masses sang patriotic songs: loudly, loudly, proudly!

With his guitar, with his rumpled hair, unshaven and heavily tattooed, Gregor Truba sang loudly and proudly but without heart. His heart that once beat strongly for the country, for the idea, for freedom seemed to have withered away. Not even beautiful young girls could squeeze any emotion out of such a heart. He felt as if he were a dead man. He couldn't live like that any longer, with the maxim *'lie and intimidate'*, it got stuck into his throat and he was happiest when alone with silence.

Such introspectiveness never skipped the attention of the zealous Friar. He called him once again and asked him what would be his preferred job or involvement, for he would be able to help him out, yet again, to find himself. To guide him towards the light.

Yes, those godless creatures were everywhere around him, spiritually wicked and in high places of the Church and the new State, in education and art, in economics and the media; now he had the opportunity to join that merry lot in their feast in the dawn of human indecency. When money and power talk, human decency is silenced. Gregor Truba silenced, once again, the voice of a decent human and was promoted to the post previously held by his archenemy, Simon Odak; he was appointed as the theatre governor.

On the most intimate level, on the deepest level, he dreamed that Pia Odak or Veronika Truba could see him, watch his plays and applaud in the audience. He never wanted to think about those two women deliberately, willingly, but there was something deep inside that was nagging and knocking on the doors of his conscience. But his beloved mother Elsa was his audience, his admirer and his zealous supporter and promoter.

Her remarks were:

"From the very beginning my son Gregor was different. I knew from the moment he was born that he would merit something extraordinary. Not only was he gifted musically and theatrically, he was gorgeous, he was kind and above all, he was one of the first to join the liberation army as a volunteer."

She aged well, never showed any sign of aging, she aged the way emotionless cold women age, as if those cold emotions had frozen her face and defended it from wrinkles and truth. She was the proudest woman that walked the streets of this town, as if it were her own town: she proved that it was, she was the mother of the celebrated and gifted artist and the bravest soldier, Gregor Truba.

She was a German woman and pride grew stronger every time the radio emitted the latest song *'Danke Deutschland'*, she knew she was on the right side and their time had just begun, just as her father promised many years ago, just as Friar Marag promised on that blessed day she met him.

Crime, pillage, terror and impoverishment continued and had worsened year by year. Those who *'had made it'* kept the situation the same, a continuous *status quo*: chaos served the masters. For the majority who had lost everything, they still held that the most important thing was the holy flag waving in the wind – *'Oh, the wind, the wind is blowing through the graves the wind is blowing, freedom soon will come; then we'll emerge from the shadows.'*

Freedom came from the graves and the shadows.

With the sacrificed soldiers, horses, towns, life and the sacrificed future for many generations to come. *'Oh the wind, the wind is blowing...'* and the beautiful flag was triumphantly dancing, freedom had arrived!

V

Pia's Diary

The Night Has Grown Colder

Sydney, December 1993

Dear Sapphire,

What do I know about the man called Nicholas O'B? Nothing. It has been a month since we arrived in this big unknown. Yes, I let myself into this adventure just for the sake of adventure. I grew tired of lies, deceptions, family frauds, fake love and lovers and met this misfortunate fellow that I almost fell in love with, and in the process of almost falling in love I had almost broken the innocent heart of Andrew Bloxham who made monumental, but failed, efforts to hide his real emotions. I wish you could see me, what I wanted to say is – I wish it were more obvious to me that you can indeed see me, that you are around as I can feel, but not see, your presence. Nevertheless, as you have probably witnessed I felt something for Nicholas, something that was the closest feeling I ever had to what I used to feel when I was around Gregor Truba. No, I didn't love him either, because I never wanted to entrust my love and faith into the hands of an unreliable man. Or, into the hands of any man as you know, I don't trust men, being the daughter of Simon Odak

I found nothing here worthy of such a mighty trip and my intellectual starvation just eats my bones. On the other hand, Nicholas is such a stimulating companion, yet, at times, he can be demanding and he clearly demonstrates signs of possessiveness and even jealousy. Oh, God, only you know that it is the main thing that would turn me away from men. Possessiveness.

He won't look for work and it is a constant pain trying to explain that he can't live at my expense. He has a talent, he is quite a storyteller, but that doesn't impress me in a way that would make me enjoy paying for his keep. Finding a job, isn't the easiest thing if you are learned and clever. Here, beauty doesn't help either, as when a woman is clever, educated and beautiful, they say, 'We don't approve of tall poppies'. Outrageous and almost primitive:

that cult of mediocrity. I'll let you know more about it as I expand my experiences and collect all the local wisdom and pearls.

Let's talk about Nicholas. His mind is not far from brilliant, his talent unpolished, he may appear to be a rough diamond, but his habits are the habits of a demon: he drinks like a fish, he is a chain-smoker, he swears like a drunken soldier and is often under the impression that he is God's gift to mankind. To women as well, for that matter and in the current situation, to be precise, he thinks that he is some sort of a gift awarded to Pia Odak. You know, Sapphire, that no man was ever an award for me. I don't need such awards; if a literary award comes along, that is something I might celebrate, but only with you. No need for others' eyes.

Currently, I am trying to make some sense out of this experience, or shall I say, adventure; I can't predict how long we will last; so far I feel a bit overwhelmed being around someone so intensively. I need to find my own place and see if there is any sense in this city, anything that might interest me or keep me here a little longer, I can't really say that I miss anything or anyone but you.

Nicholas walked in and said:

"I am off to the beach, are you joining me?"

"I miss great libraries, not beaches, go ahead. I'll stay in and look for some job that interests me and makes sense."

"Come with me and we'll dream, we'll make up stories and conversations whilst making fun of people and seagulls."

"I need my privacy."

"Oh, who dares to intrude into Pia's solitude?"

What was he: a man or a boy? An actor or a whole theatre? Nicholas O'B had so many characters under his hat, which was only natural for a writer of fiction. She had her demons and characters that never left her alone, but the nagging question was – *'Did she really need a moody man around her? A man who came home tipsy, a man who swore instead of saying, 'Thank you very much!'*

She left this question unanswered for some time.

"Why don't you ever make dinner?"

"You mean... cook for you?"

"Well, yes!!"

"I am not your cook. I am a free woman, someone who does what she feels appropriate in certain moments or situations. Do you really believe that I would cook for you? That I would wash your clothes?"

"I didn't mention the clothes, I take my clothes to the laundry."

"Oh, good on you! Then take your arse to the restaurant if you want dinner. Make some money; at least, buy food in the grocery store, yeah? I am paying for the rent and buying food for both of us, and may I ask – how do you contribute to this, let's call it, household?"

"I'm your man!"

"Don't make me laugh, indeed, do not make me cry! You know you can't talk such filth to me. I don't depend on any man, you, on the other hand, depend on me."

"But I am writing my novel."

"Yes, you've been writing your novel for the last five years. You talk about Andalusia, about people you met there, about food and wine, what have you done since? Nothing. Nothing, Nicholas O'B! Understand me now: I am not impressed by your worthy efforts."

"What if the novel wins..."

"Just stop it! I am capable of doing exactly the same. Indeed, I have started my own novel, and yet, I haven't even mentioned it. I am working to pay my rent and feed us both and in my spare time I write. I won't miss an opportunity while I am in this odd country to record my daily experiences."

"I brought you here."

"Wow, that's something!"

"Do you want to argue?"

"No. All I want from you is to make some money and share the expenses. OK?"

"Then I wouldn't be able to write."

"Bad luck!"

"Pia, you have changed."

"I haven't changed, Nicholas. I have always been like this: it is just that you never really got to know me. We don't know each other. What you've been seeing lately is the best version of Pia. If you don't start to contribute, you'll see her much uglier version."

"Pia, I love you."

"Don't play that card. Find yourself a job for a start."

She would not give in. He was a charmer, swift with words, and often prone to extravagant deeds, but nothing really impressed Pia.

She commenced her novel and all she needed was at least an equal share of responsibilities. It fell on deaf ears.

On the 20th of December, Pia Odak wrote a letter. It was addressed to Andrew Bloxham, London, UK.

On the same day she packed just one bag, leaving several useful things for Nicholas: two chairs, a rented double bed, some cutlery, a plate and one saucepan. She had not left a letter for Nicholas, for he was such a clever man that she assumed – it would dawn on him as soon as he opened the door, what exactly had befallen him.

She went to the Office of Births, Deaths and Marriages.

She filled the papers and changed her name to Sapphire Bonifacio. She thought of Nikki and the reasons why she never wanted to carry birth names. Yes, the times were crazy and people even crazier; she never wanted to identify with any group, the only person she would love to identify with was her late mother, hence she lovingly took up her nickname as her first name to carry proudly.

Once she had done that she felt like herself: the real Pia that was hiding inside, the real Sapphire.

Then she took a map and searched for the location where she would start her life as Sapphire Bonifacio, free from her past, her holy nation and from pestering men. In the last two months she laughed heartily for the first time. She couldn't care less about the so-called uncertainty.

***

On the same day, December 20th, but much later when the day showed rusty colours, Nicholas O'B came to the place he called home. It was a small unit in the *'affordable'* part of the city where nothing exciting ever happened, yet it was not too far from the Southern beaches where he would go fishing while pondering about his characters and winding paths of his story that were set far away, all the way down on the lacy shores of Andalusia.

That afternoon he thought about Pia. He wasn't sure what he genuinely felt for her, but there was that feeling which he wanted to deny, or simply to nullify. He really didn't want a woman that was self-sufficient and who had a much stronger creative mind than he had. But on the other hand, she was a rare diamond which he thought he had to polish in order to see his own face in a myriad of its facets. He was drawn to strong women, creative and in a way wild, those that wouldn't cry on his shoulder nor ask him for any kind of help or empathy. And empathy was what he lacked; therefore, he needed a strong companion that never complained. With Pia it was a bit different, as she was way too confident and self-reliant. She wouldn't blink her eye if he left, hence he wanted to convince her how much he loved her, more than he was prepared to love anyone. He needed lovers for his stories, not for the sake of love itself, but with Pia it looked as if she was in search of that same – love for the sake of a good story, love as an experiment, love as an idea.

When he was heading home he prepared a speech, he inserted some words of apology, or a tone that rang like apology, a casual apology, but still he had to voice somehow that she would keep that role of *'temporary moneymaker'* or *'someone who was in charge'*. After all, wasn't he Nicholas O'B? The novelist, the man women liked, adored? Pia even left her boyfriend because of him and ran away without turning her head back. But he never assumed what Pia's real reason for leaving her boyfriend and rainy London was.

The door was opened.

He walked in and there was no one; the living room was empty, the little kitchenette too, he looked into the bedroom… the bathroom.

He called her. No answer. He sat and lit a cigarette. No beer. Not even money in his pockets. He went down to the pub and had only one beer, as that was all he could afford. There was a young woman sitting alone at the bar. He struck a conversation.

Her shift had just ended. She commented:

"Irish?"

"Yeah."

"What are you doing here?"

"Came to have a couple of beers and just discovered I have no more money."

"I'll get you a beer."

"That's fantastic. What's your name?"

"Fiona."

"Bloody Fiona, that's my mother's name. Are you Irish yourself?"

"My parents were born here, but, yes, my ancestors were Irish."

Fiona paid for three more rounds as he promised to come by the next day and to pay her back. She said:

"No, don't pay me back, tomorrow you shout."

He went home tipsy. The door was opened. The lights were off. He walked in and called Pia. Silence. Just bloody silence!

He cursed:

"Where's that bloody bitch!?"

But silence prevailed.

Fully dressed with his shoes on he threw himself on the bed and covered his face with the duvet. For half an hour he was listening attentively for when she would walk in, but drink got the better of him and he fell asleep.

DETHRONED

The sun was high when he woke up. There was no smell of Pia's morning coffee, there was no sign that she went to work or that she had been in since yesterday.

"Has she gone?" he asked in disbelief.
"She hasn't! Can't be!" he continued talking to himself.

Midday passed, then three o'clock, then five, then she never came. He was hungry, there was some food in the fridge, some in the pantry; he didn't even know what to do with it! He opened a can of baked beans and ate it with a fork straight from the can. He went down to the pub and said to Fiona:
"Pia's gone."
"Is she your girlfriend?" she asked this question judging by his expression. He nodded his head.
"I don't have any money."
"Have a beer, it's on the house." Said Fiona and smiled.
'*A lovely Irish girl*' he thought, but loudly said:
"Bloody moody Croatian bitch!"
"Is she?"
"Pain in the arse."
"Were you married?"
"God, no!"
"You'll get over her, mate! Have a beer and stay here if you don't have any place to go to right now. I'll finish at eleven."

Yes, that was Nicholas O'B at his best. He could charm any woman with his puppy eyes, green with hints of emeralds in the middle, with dimples in his cheeks; tall and statuesque, hellishly good looking, and smooth talking when needed.

But he promised himself that he would '*find the bitch wherever she was hiding*', he would never admit that he was in love with Pia. Not him, not Nicholas O'B.

A Chance Meeting

Sydney, 29th December 1993

Dear Gemma,

I have changed my name; I am you now, are we for yet another step closer to each other? I called myself Sapphire and I love to carry your maiden name, as I know that you didn't belong to Dad's family with the exception of my beloved Granny Sava. I myself was at odds with the Odaks as if I didn't belong to that family, strangely enough. My dad was an immature man who loved only himself; he couldn't feel or show any feelings for others unless expecting some big favour. He didn't love anyone, not even you, not even Luna; he never came to his mother's funeral; don't you think that these facts and his deeds never haunted me?

When it comes to the Bonifacios I feel almost the same: strangers as they were obsessed with things of the past, things that could never be changed or repeated, they never cared about people but things, possessions and ideas. Luna was no one's daughter, no one's darling and no one's friend. She was your sister, that's why I tried to put up with her. Who knows, how she is doing now? When I think of her I think of a cat, a creature who has nine lives. In all those horrendous happenings and changes I bet she found her way of staying on top of the game.

Look where I have found myself. On some days I'd like to laugh, on some days to cry, but you know, I'd like to give myself a chance to stay away from the madness that is happening over there. The puppets are playing their games, pulled by the strings in the hands of the grand masters. How repulsive! I can't even create here. But, as paradox has it; here I can't even write the way I'd like to write. I feel some unexplainable emptiness here: emptiness of the human soul. What is a piece of writing if the soul hasn't been immersed in it? What's a poem if the poet looks for words that rhyme? I am looking for a job, hoping to find it in academia, as I have just worked for one month in a local drugstore. You should feel the difference between the Old Continent and the mentality of 'equality'. Average is good enough. Beauty is 'OK', there is no gradation, and soul-deep, examination of circumstances or people. Everything is the same and equal. Just naïve and superficial, it hinders my writings.

I left Nicholas, as I knew he was a leech. He had a way with women, he was aware of it, but alas, did he really believe that his charm would win over Pia's intelligence and insight?

I feel lonely Gemma, and I miss you more than ever. I miss Veronika, my dear Nikki, and am often painfully tempted to write her a letter or to call her, but for the time being I still believe that it is better to leave people to their own struggles, to let them find their own way out. She left her family with a resolution never to come back. I have to see what I can come up with and create what I can call 'a new start', just out of curiosity so as to figure out who the real Pia Odak, aka Sapphire Bonifacio is. So often people tell me that they don't know me, to many I appear to be quite mysterious, but to be absolutely honest – I am often puzzled over the entity within me that governs my decisions, deeds, or my entire life. Who's the thinker in my head?

You were the only person I could be at ease with when we were together, and only with you could I be myself – the quiet creator of my daily life. More often than not I wonder what my life would be if you had stayed with me?

After a year of numerous little jobs Sapphire Bonifacio, known as Pia Odak, applied for a position at the University of Sydney once again. The letter came and she was ready to quickly go through it and throw it into the rubbish bin, but it wasn't material for the rubbish bin. She had been accepted and the smile of contentment brought two little dimples into her cheeks. Soon after she moved closer to the university campus and rented a small house, bought a dog and a small car. In her spare time she talked to her dog, she fed birds in her backyard and slowly but steadily progressed with her novel. Her life seemed pleasant, but deprived of meaningful conversations, relationships or outings. It was just a boring life, not fit for a young, intelligent woman.

But she had resolved not to complain, nor dwell on her weaker side, but to be consistent in her writings and mission to bring out the real Sapphire in her.

Sydney, March 23rd 1994

Dear Gemma,

My novel is nearing its end. Yes, it took me quite a long time to finish, but I wanted to take time and write it very precisely and to remain honest to each and every thought and feeling of mine. I wanted to ponder deeply about the many facets of my life and life in general. I don't know what to call it, not as I am thinking of the title, but to give it a certain genre. I live in a society obsessed by material things and plastic beauty; people are just consumers, tools in peace, and collateral damage in war. There are new genres in literature; new trends are established and the world is obsessed with vampires and creatures of darkness who dominate this pop culture, as their masters and manipulators heavily approve of that kind of 'literature' to mould young thoughts in a perverse, nihilistic and aggressive way. People are unable to deal with reality and suppressed memories alike and they have a desperate need to read books of horror, watch films of murders, the macabre and the apocalypse in order to neutralise what lies underneath. I often think – what would you say if you had your turn? I remember that sophistication of thought and word that you cared about so much. Often, when I think of you I wonder where you could have gone with such a fine soul? So many things are happening right now that are denying the human soul or the spirit right in the face of it. Ugliness has taken over as a new means of culture, manipulation of our commodities and money; there is deterioration of society and culture, and I witness every day the sad deterioration of the educational system and the dulling of young minds. Sadly only few see and recognise such crime, even fewer find ways to verbalise it.

I have found myself in this strange land because I couldn't live with lies, exalted but primitive emotions brought by false promises by foreign economic cannibals. People are like little mad flies caught in a web of illusion that they counted when big decisions were made far away from their dwellings and lives.

I have resolved to stay alone for the rest of my life. Don't be saddened by this decision of mine, as you already know that I dislike the way men rule this world and everything that belongs to this world including women. I grew up with a father who was a disgusting pig without realising it, believing as any man in this part of the world believed, or for that matter, probably in any part of the world where man is in power, that they have to dominate woman. They have done so from the beginning of this world and I am not positive that they would let go of such a sadistic practice in any near future. I meet men and they adore me just because I am pretty, and pretty degrading that fact is. Western media portrays woman as a lower species, our children are not receiving proper education while they are surrounded by violence brought by main-stream news and media. There are children who are being imprisoned in sex-slave trades, forced into prostitution and pornography. Women are having abortions while rape and sexual harassment are everyday occurrences; it has become 'normal', while Governments and economies are falling apart like sand castles, for our leaders, our Men, are corrupted liars and spineless worms.

This world doesn't belong to me. I do believe that this physical world is just a projection, an illusion of a young mind or soul and in their ignorance and greed they are destroying anything that is in their way. I am a free soul, I belong where you belong and have no wish to be a toy in the hands of today's men. They seek to break down any society, as they did in our country, to destroy the lawful means in any society. I fear it is just the beginning. I am not a part of it – a part of a man's world; I am a sovereign leader of my own land – Pia's Land.

I miss you terribly even though I know you are there, sitting beside me smiling and approvingly nodding your head... sometimes I think my thoughts are yours, my hand is only recording them.

Five years had passed and nothing monumental had happened in Sapphire's life. She tried to publish her novel but without success. There were clear reasons why she couldn't succeed in a place where the whole nation proudly lived by the childish maxim *'We cut down tall poppies.'* She really couldn't figure out what exactly *'tall poppy syndrome'* was but with time and rejection letters she understood that she was in the wrong place. A place that didn't need profound thinkers, a place where women didn't need to be beautiful and intelligent: one or the other, but not the whole package. Such women could bring only trouble and no one needed trouble in such a *'peaceful and friendly environment'* – Just don't create any trouble with your intelligence, we have plenty of our own, and it shouldn't come from a woman.

The closest she got to striking a publishing deal was with quite a respectable publishing house, but when she met the editor in person, he, upon reading her novel asked:

"Why don't you simplify it? Do you want your readers to think or do you want them to enjoy?"

Pia's thought was that it was high time she went overseas, but still she didn't know where, as this world was full of editors similar to this one.

Often she would ponder about her family connection to Nikola Tesla and those stories weaved and spread about his mysterious character. She found herself to be the happiest in her isolation, the most fulfilled when immersed in a kind of written thought that would reflect her own.

There was one unusual and unique description of Nikola's oddity: he wore gloves all the time and declined to shake hands; he felt extreme discomfort when in the company of overweight, obese people – he fired his employees if they gained wait.

"How civilised it is to know one's measure in everything, particularly food intake. People eat, animals indulge."

Similar comments came from the Tesla family. To be cultured doesn't mean only to say *'thank you'* or *'you are welcome'*, there is a culture of food, clothing, of thinking, of deeds and manners and it needs many generations over many centuries to bring it to the highest level while it needs only one generation to destroy it as if the culture had never existed. She declined to listen about the war on the territory of former Yugoslavia because it was a made-up war, a war of the media, lies and ignorance. They sold their souls quickly, denying light and adopting a new religion: kill, kill and kill.

***

She took a chair and dragged it to the *'Foreign Books'* section. She picked several books written in Italian for the sake of reading in Italian. She sat on a little stool and read a book of poetry. As she was reading, a voice above her head, as if Lucifer's voice were coming directly from *'Inferno'*, in a deep husky tone read the verses with her:

Through me the way into the grieving city,
Through me the way into eternal sorrow,
Through me the way among the lost people,
Justice moved my high maker;
Divine power made me,
Highest wisdom, and primal love.
Before me were no things created
Except eternal ones, and I endure eternal.
Abandon every hope, you who enter.
All hope abandon ye who enter here."

"Canto Terzo." He said.
"Straight from Inferno – here we are again."
"I promised myself that I would find you no matter what."
"You have found me, Nicholas. What now?"
"How could you leave me without a word, you thoughtless, heartless beast?" he asked as he was squatting down to bring his eyes to Sapphire's level.
"As you know – I am a heartless beast, am I not?"
"I thought that you were only pretending to be one, only showing a false self, but indeed, you are who you are. You were not acting but plainly being yourself, a hellish creature."

"Thank you, Nicholas. Wise words, delivered impeccably in the friendliest of manners."

"You expect me to be friendlier? It took me six bloody years to find you, to track you down and I almost gave up. You see, we were meant to cross paths again, otherwise how would I meet you here reading 'Inferno' waiting for me. I thought that you had emigrated back to the old world."

"I had many thoughts about it, but no, I am still here, still resisting the devilish temptation to go back where the concentration of hatred and chaos is the densest, hence floating from project to project from idea to idea..."

"From man to man?"

"Oh, get lost!"

"No man in your life, or you had left me because someone cleverer or more solvent came along?"

"Do you really think that the world revolves around man as such?"

"For the majority of women – yes!"

"Let it be."

"Still superior?"

"Always superior."

"Coffee?"

"I'd be happy to say no, but I am not sure how it would pass."

"Won't strangle you or anything like that. I'd just love to talk to you. I can't believe that six years have already passed."

When they sat at the table she looked at him peacefully. She couldn't say that he had aged but it was obvious that his lifestyle left a mark underneath his eyes and around his lips. It was obvious while he was trying to light a cigarette, his fingers were clumsy and shaky, and there were other numerous but little giveaway signs as to what kind of life Nicholas led.

"And... your novel?"

"Started and stopped, started again, stopped again. Doing shit jobs, sleeping during the day."

"What do you do?"

"Working in the Irish pub from five pm till midnight, after that I stay and drown my sorrows till morning."

"Poetically said, but I don't trust you have any sorrows... unless you don't have anyone to support you. Where do you live? I mean, with whom do you live now?"

"That's a good question. When you left I met a girl who worked in a pub and she offered me to stay at her place until I found a job, as I told her I had no money. She helped me to get a job in the pub and to stay with her for some time. Pia, we are the same, my dear, as soon as someone shows love, we run away. Poor soul, she fell in love and wanted me to stay 'indefinitely' and that scared the shit out of me, so I did what you do best – ran without a trace. My story just kept repeating itself in those six years: I would find a girl, or a woman, and she would take me in and support my creative endeavour until two things happened – she would fall in love and I would run away, or she would demand of me that I find a job. I couldn't do that. I can only work in extreme cases, like the one I am currently in – that there's no one who can pay my bills. I loved only one woman and that was you, Pia."

"Yeah, yeah, I have heard this but you know that I do not believe in such declarations. I don't even believe in love in that form, Nicholas. I think you were with me because you love gorgeous women, I was an intellectual challenge and I could afford to keep you at that time."

"For Christ's sake, do you have a soul?"

"A very fine one, indeed."

"But you never show it, isn't it so?"

"More or less you are right."

"Ah, Pia, Pia. What about your novel?"

"I have no right audience here."

"Try it somewhere else, I know you can't compete here with model-turned-author kind of writers, but why don't you try it back in London?"

"It isn't urgent, my novel is waiting for the right time to be published. It might still be too early for it."

"We should keep in touch."

"I have no wish, Nicholas."

"Tell me then, how is it that you think you are not heartless?"

"I am happiest when I am alone."

"I am happiest when I am alone with the wind! I heard this phrase before. What if I go down on my knees, you know me, I am a shameless bastard and right now I would do anything to persuade you to give me your phone number. I won't bother you, I won't fall in love with you, I won't promise anything; all I want is to be friends again. Show me your human side."

"I have a full-time job, a dog and the most beautiful view. I have an extensive library, a great collection of classical music and two reasonably loyal friends. I can't fit you into my life, not right now."

"Where can I find you?"

"Don't try. Sincerely, I don't need trouble and we know that you bring only trouble."

"I can change."

"God, no! I don't intend to change anyone, I always liked your eccentricity and this brutal honesty, but right now I am better off without it. Can't you take 'No' for an answer?"

"I can't."

"Your ego has been gravely wounded, hey? But look, you too are better off without me; you know how difficult I can be."

"I can handle you, I have always managed to handle you and your moods."

"Nicholas, good-bye, I have to go and don't you dare follow me or try to figure out where I have gone. I am gone, gone for good!"

Sapphire paid for her books, walked out and stopped the first approaching taxi. Nicholas stood at the door with his hands in his pockets looking at the car blending into the colourful traffic. Whatever thoughts Nicholas might have had in his head one was certain –he never felt any remorse for his misconduct, no pity for any of his victims and zero ability to empathise; he stood there with his hands deep in his pockets and a smile on his face. He went back to the library and said to the librarian:

"I went out and came back because I couldn't leave without telling you that your lovely smile and your smart eyes made my day."

She quickly put a hand on her mouth to cover surprise and embarrassment, but somehow she couldn't stop smiling at him. He put his elbows onto her desk and said:

"Please, tell me that you are not married, engaged or have a boyfriend, that would crush my intention to take you out and make you the queen of the finest restaurant."

It didn't take him too long to persuade her to give him her number. He shoved it into his pocket, winked at her and headed towards the door. When he was almost out of the library, he, seemingly confused, came back and said:

"Err, my sister took several books, she just texted me that she has forgotten 'The Divine Comedy', can I take it and you put it on her name."

"Go ahead" the young woman said with a mischievous smile.

"Sapphire Bonifacio, isn't she?" he looked bewildered when the librarian said:

"Sapphire Bonifacio, the woman you talked with, isn't she your sister?"

"Sure, sure… It is just that you make my brain freeze when I look at your eyes."

The librarian shook her head, Nicholas said:

"I've just come back from Ireland, can you help me find the way to her place if I take public transport, cabs are too costly for me."

The librarian showed him a map and how to get to Australia Street, Glebe by public transport. He kissed her hand, she pulled it quickly but when her eyes met Nicholas' she quickly blushed as he said:

"I'll call you in a few days."

Then he walked out of the Library and threw the piece of paper with the librarian's telephone number in the first rubbish bin. Pia's address, he hammered into his mind, and the way the librarian showed him to get there.

"So, Sapphire! That is why all my attempts to find Pia Odak failed over the last six years."

***

As any other person Sapphire had her same unmistakable morning routine. She was an early bird: getting up before dawn, writing for several morning hours with a pot of warm coffee on her desk. The first step in her routine would be to open the windows in her study. The study faced the house next-door, shielded by several tall pine trees. Every morning while opening the windows she saw a man of an uncertain age in his garden, performing an unusual dance. Initially she thought him to be a swirling dervish, then some martial-art master, but then she researched a little bit more and was quite positive that the man with a little pony-tail on the back of his head was a master of aikido art. Sometimes she would watch him behind pulled curtains; on a few occasions he would see her and put his hands on his chest in a prayer position and bow down. She would quickly pull away, somehow embarrassed, as she felt she was intruding into his privacy.

She gave him the name, Aikido Master, and saw him only in the early mornings when he was practising his amazingly beautiful and silent art. In those last five or six years she never really saw him at any other time but early in the morning. She would leave in the morning herself, and come back at dinnertime, then she wrote a little more or she would simply read and research or converse with her mother via her letters. She loved that kind of solitary life; she built stories and bridges out of the finest material and felt as a Master herself – the Master of her invisible, yet for her, real world.

Then the Master's routine somehow changed in the last two weeks. She would see him on her return home standing behind the hedge, slightly smiling with his hands on his chest in a prayer position, and when Sapphire's eyes met his, he simply bowed down with a faint smile as if it were painted permanently onto his placid face. He made her feel honoured in a way by that simple, yet kind, gesture. Initially she would just nod her head and smile, but lately she started to put her hands together on her chest in a prayer position and a pleasant smile would come without intention or any effort.

She saw him every day for a fortnight and on the 7th of June he wasn't there. She almost missed him as his smile would permanently reassure that the world was a kind place where each and every day one was exposed to kindness of a fine human being, rather than watching the horror of the evening news.

Sphinx, her six-year-old Sicilian mastiff ran towards her excitedly. She poured more water and food into his bowls and went into the house.

She came out three times that evening as Sphinx was howling and barking, but there was no one, it was a quiet street, civilised and discrete neighbours; she blamed the possums or some stray cat.

When the evening was quiet again, Sphinx wasn't heard any longer; she had already been working for several quiet hours. She heard some noise coming from her bedroom, like a dull jolt that she couldn't identify. Slowly, she went into her bedroom, she knew that she had already closed the window, but when she came closer to it someone's hands grabbed her: one arm around her waist and the other hand pressed her mouth. He was a strong, a tall man skilled in such a performance; she couldn't bite his hand. Quickly, he took her hands and tied them together with a silken scarf behind her back. He walked her into the kitchen and sat her on the chair, then he took a rope and tied her to the chair: legs and arms. Then he faced her and said:

"Sapphire, you lied to me."

"You are drunk, Nicholas. This, what you are doing, is a criminal act, don't you know it?"

"A lie is a criminal act, too. You had left and changed your name. You are not Sapphire Bonifacio, but Pia Odak. You left me like a piece of shit, isn't that a crime?"

He kissed her lips, the horrible smell of alcohol irritated her senses, she screamed:

"Untie me, you brute!"

"Why brute, beautiful Pia? You left London with me, you loved me, didn't you?"

"I thought you were a decent man."

"I was, Pia, I was a decent man. Look what you have done to that decent man he drinks and he is utterly unhappy."

"Untie me, right now!"

"You are not in a position to demand. You have to listen now."

She screamed again:

"Coward! Leave me alone, coward!"

He sat next to her and ate biscuits and oranges that were on the table. He fed her with oranges and she bitterly spat them out of her mouth. He laughed as any sadist would in such a perfect, sadistic scene.

The wind opened the kitchen window ajar, Nicholas stood up and closed the window and when he turned back there was a man standing in a funny robe behind Sapphire. He had a little bun on the top of his head, an oriental man with yellowish skin and without any expression on his flat face.

"What is this? Is this a circus day?"

The man said nothing but commenced his fine dance. He danced in Sapphire's kitchen so finely as if he were performing in some world famous theatre in front of the finest audience. Sapphire's face lit up with wonderment and ardour. As he danced, drunken Nicholas lost his balance several times while trying to grab him by his arms or neck. Any attempt to defend himself was ridiculed by the new elegant and effortless movement of the smiling man. He danced him to the entrance door and kicked him out as if he were a rag doll.

The Master untied Sapphire and she ran into the garden to check out on Sphinx. She was lying on her side without signs of life. They knelt down and the Master said:

"She was poisoned, let's take her to the vet, quickly."

They sat at the veterinary hospital in complete silence for three hours. A nurse came out and said:

"She will be fine. We'll keep her in for another two to three days."

Sapphire's eyes filled with tears, the Master put his light but manly hand on hers, he looked at her eyes and simply smiled.

When they came back home she said:

"I can't thank you enough. I don't know if I should notify the police about this incident."

"Don't! He won't be back. Cowards don't return if they know there's someone wiser than them."

Then with a light step, as if he were dancing again, he left her car and entered his house, the light went off as soon as he entered.

***

For several months they kept on bowing and smiling at each other every morning or on the occasional chance meeting in early evenings.

Sapphire kept her dog inside, but since that incident she never heard from Nicholas any more, though, she was always wary – the thought that he might return and cause more trouble never left her.

She never talked to her Master again, but was happy to see him through the window in the early mornings.

Then one day she decided to buy some literature about aikido and as she read a form of peace fell upon her, she felt as if her mother were next to her breathing into her hair, whispering kind words of encouragement until this idea was firmly formed in her head.

She summoned the courage and prepared a little speech and knocked on his door one pleasant, almost warm evening towards the end of that year.

He opened the door, bowed and let her in without saying a word; he just kept on smiling as if he knew which words bothered her exactly.

Branka Čubrilo

They sat on a low futon, after a short silence she said:
"Would you be willing to teach me your art?"

He nodded his head, then quietly said with a smile on his face:
"When a disciple is ready he finds his master."

After only several lessons Sapphire understood what had been missing in her life all those years, she wrote in her diary:

Sydney, December 29th 2000

Dear Gemma,

Not only do I think, but I am positive that the force behind mine and the Master's meeting was – you. When I put the dots together everything leads to you and with that early training and understanding in the bud, I can freely say that you made a great effort to connect us again. The Master doesn't say much, he knows what he knows and he shows what he wants to, but he leads with wisdom and kindness. He said I was ready to receive his knowledge and through his knowledge that is slowly streaming from his into my consciousness, the light to understanding shines bright. I can see your hand leading me to this moment; even the so-called misfortunate reencounter with Nicholas was nothing more than a pebble on the paved road to my enlightenment. No, no, no, I am not enlightened, but the mere fact that I was, somehow chosen, to meet this man brings enormous joy. Joy is the word, my dearest Gemma, as I haven't known such joy since I was in your care, since we were creators of our days, creating art, love and joy from our energy and mutual understanding of what love should look and feel like. Oh, love; people search for it for an eternity, but isn't it just in one's breath? No one has to travel in order to find it or to buy precious items and jewels; no one has to beautify themselves or to pretend to be wealthy or wise. The simple formula for love itself is that utter simplicity of living through breath and movement in absolute synchronicity and that willingness to listen to life's gentle murmur that liberates from the illusions of this world. I found a man who teaches me about love without ever mentioning it, without the profanity of words, he teaches me the art that is beyond words and the love that is beyond love itself.

I was in such a state only when with you, that was this sacred feeling I was after all my life; there was that melancholy of mine which knew that this material world made of illusions and lies is just appearance and that beyond it beauty lies.

I need not write any more of my poetry or any novel, neither am I in need of travelling to the end of the world in the childish belief that I might meet you again. When I practise what he teaches me, when I listen to his timeless words and when I drink from his inexhaustible source of wisdom and kindness I am united with you. I am immersed in love; I am one with you and the love by which this world was created.

Now, I assume that my journey has ended, and at the same time it has just begun. I have found what I was looking for, and I have just embarked on the most beautiful adventure I could ever have imagined. No lust could ever replace this novel feeling of unity and completeness; only few know this truth, as only few are willing to search, to listen and obey the order of the divine. My beauty didn't bring love and my literary talent never brought peace. I touched love and peace when I allowed the higher law and order to govern my mind and heart; still and always, I will be convinced that your divine energy led me right where I am at this moment.

This profane world, where an average human dwells, is utterly manipulated by many different sources: some are totally ignorant the others purely evil. We are like leaves carried by the wind of events and human emotions from one misfortune to another. And we never stop believing, in this comedy and illusion that we are tied to the material world in which hidden masters pull the strings of all worldly events, 'crises' and affairs in general. My Master never talks about evil and wrongdoers but about the vast spiritual potential we have inside of us. He said it once in a simple sentence, 'Accusers must criticise and carp, and their wicked need has put us down in order to feel good about themselves. Let's practise.'

Branka Čubrilo

We have been conditioned from birth to respond to externals, hence we are kept distracted by responding to outer stimuli. I learned one cannot follow two masters: if one sees life as evil, it will become so, therefore it will become good if one sees life as good, for whatever we think in our hearts we become those very same thoughts.

There is still so much to learn from the Master and I deeply, sincerely hope that this is just the beginning of our sacred relationship, which will only grow stronger day by day. He gives me the kind of inner strength and peace that I have never experienced before, and when he talks I am aware that he talks from the source, which I often touched in my silence. I am often overwhelmed by the fact that I have had the privilege to walk through that door closed to many.

Sapphire's life revolved around two things: her spiritual practice and teaching at the university. Life became light and meaningful only practising those light movements and letting the mind go off mundane affairs that had the sole aim of polluting people's minds or keeping those minds imprisoned. She felt liberated to the extent that on some days she even thought there was no thinker in her head, the thinker had disappeared, that critical voice in her head, the one that measures and weighs, evaluates and judges. When it ceased to exist there was splendour was all around, the feeling of oneness with the world, which was overwhelming to the extent that it often brought tears to her eyes.

The Master invariably wore a smile on his face and at every moment he knew where to lead. To Sapphire's never-ending gratitude he said:

"Thank that divine spark within you, not me. There are few that would be ready to follow our path. It is not that the path is hidden, it is that people's hearts are not ready to recognise truth."

The lightness of thought brought the lightness of being and the world became Home, regardless of how many wars were fought in this world in the fake name of *'democracy and freedom'*; she had experienced that holy peace and there was no going back to lies and illusions.

478

Ten years had passed and the Master said:

"Are you ready to travel to meet the Grand Master?"

She put her hands on her chest in a prayer position and bowed her head down.

Sapphire Bonifacio looked ageless and timeless: her movements were governed by the most sophisticated energy. She looked rather as if she were floating, and when she spoke, her words were melodic and sweet; she had a magnetic personality and people and animals alike were drawn to her as they used to, in the ancient times, be drawn to the wisest sages and seers. Under the governance of her Master, Sapphire started to experience a paranormal phenomenon: his movements were as swift as lightening and he would appear behind her in the blink of an eye; in the same manner, he would disappear from her sight only to be seen in the other part of the room. Not only did he possess great power, but also such subtle speed that one could never perceive its origin or destination.

He asked her to pack lightly as they were going into the mountains.

"Aikikai?"

"No, not Tokyo. Far up in the mountains were my father lives."

***

Sydney, June 2nd 2011

Dear Gemma,

You are as real to me as the Master is. Thank you for being around and arranging the events in my life. I feel so grateful for your gentle guidance and whispers. For me, poetry doesn't have to be written any more as I live my poetry through my thoughts and my movements, my art. I have found my perfect expression, my divine art that has liberated me from this web of illusions and suffering. Wrong is the premise 'Ignorance is bliss', but it is certainly the root of all obstacles on the spiritual path and spiritual progress. Ignorance is total blindness to the nature of one's real self, yet the world of appearance is a world of ignorance, thus suffering and misery.

No person could ever have given me such a feeling of oneness and unity as these holy teachings my Master showed me. We are travelling to Japan, meeting his father who was the Master's teacher of this fine art and who still lives high in the mountains where many climbed in search of his wisdom and help. The Master said I am ready to meet someone who has more knowledge than he has, as he claims that he has passed down to me all his knowledge.

I am honoured, grateful and full of anticipation to meet this man. As always, be behind my back and comb my silky hair, as I can feel your hands when you are touching it.

***

When they arrived they were met by a frail old man; he could hardly weigh over forty-five kilograms, his skin was transparent covering his protruding bones, but what Sapphire had witnessed was beyond comprehension for an average person. But the average never even knew that the Old Master existed and lived over a hundred years in the mountains. He was stronger and quicker in his body and mind than any man five-fold younger could ever be.

He greeted them by bowing down his white head and smiled at Sapphire in a very amusing way.

When he talked he looked straight into her eyes and the Master translated:

"You come from the linage of a great man. He was beyond wise; he came from a different dimension to this one in an attempt to advance humanity. You don't know human lust for flesh and for material things just as he never knew them. Welcome to our humble home."

Then he bowed his white head low and Sapphire did the same.

The next question the old Master asked was:

"What do you want me to call you?"

"Call me Pia, please."
"Good, short and simple. Pia, hmm... that suits you."

Unplanned Voyage

Mount Hotaka, Gunma, April 5th 2017

Dear Gemma,

Almost six years have passed since I arrived here with the Master: breath-takingly beautiful country, absolutely wise and enlightened company of my teachers and an incredibly loyal and good-natured family; all this brings a deep, utter experience of silence and contentment. I feel as if I had always been here, one part of me totally belongs to these people: their language of wisdom and love is the same language that you used to speak when talking to me and other people as well. Their language of wisdom and love is the same language my Granny Sava addressed to everyone. The Old Master talks about my great-great-granduncle Nikola Tesla, as if they were contemporaries and more than friends, as if they came from the same family that resides who knows where in this vast and unknown universe.

The language that I have been learning from them is something that I can't even describe; the discipline that they teach me and the moral codes and conducts are all I have ever needed to learn. Since your departure, this would be the first time in my life that I have experienced the feeling of belonging. I was just like you, I never belonged to anyone until I met my Master and he taught me all those principles that I had known already, they were almost as if they were buried somewhere underneath that fake Pia, the person of blood and flesh that represented me in the world. But I had never been comfortable with this image that was so generously given to me by mother nature or just by the luck of the draw from our healthy and beautiful genetic pool: the Bonifacios, the Odaks and the Tesla family. Granny used to say that I was the only one in the family who was 'somehow the real Tesla child'. I have never known what she really meant by that. I think now that I have learned genuine kindness, love, silence and generosity; I am closer to understanding that notion of hers. She was the epitome of wisdom and understanding.

I am writing to you today because you came to me in my dream last night and you know that, I just want to acknowledge it and let you know through written words that I have heard you, I have experienced your light breath and your whispers. But there was someone else who came with you; it was a young man who had lost his life a long time ago. As I loved him very much, somehow I took the blame for that misfortunate event in which he lost his life.

He came in the same clothes he had on the day of his passing. He asked me, with his little tongue hanging down and dripping saliva:

"Pia, do I look smart enough?"

"Oh, yes, Hugo, you look adorable." I told him in my dream last night. He laughed and said over and over that I was his 'favourite Pia' and he told me that you are now his 'favourite Gemma'. Thank you for sending him over as I can see that he is fine and we had a beautiful conversation where he informed me that there was another boy called Hugo now and he belongs to Veronika, too, just the way he did long ago. He told me to go and find him and that is how I would save Veronika. I wanted to ask many more questions but he put his index finger to his lips, saliva was still dripping down from the corners of his lips, there was an incredible light around him and then, you came, you took his hand and both of you waved and disappeared into the light.

I recounted this dream to my Master and he asked:

"What did he want to tell you?"

"To go and find Hugo."

"Are you ready for it?"

"Yes, I am" I said to my Master this morning.

He told me to pack my small bag and promised to organise my trip to To-kyo and the flight to London.

I don't know where to start looking for the 'other Hugo', but the Master just smiled, and the Old Master said, 'There are some things you just can't fight'. I know, deep down, that I shall be led by you and Hugo on my journey, the way I was led many times before.

There are only a few things to take with me but there are people, trees, some rocks and a brook that I have to visit and exchange thoughts and feelings with before I leave.

I don't know what feelings I have, or will have, upon leaving this place and my Masters.

There is no confusion but one clarity: We all are One.

Many years have passed since I left my hometown, since I left London but within me there is that eternal feeling of being at One with everything: air, breath, trees, brooks and mountains, with Masters and you, and all I feel is everlasting love. The Old Master said:

"Only one song left for Pia."

I still don't know what the exact meaning of it would be, but I have all the time on my side to figure it out.

Dearest Gemma, you know that today is my birthday. I am, apparently, fifty-six years old today, I have never felt lighter and more carefree; I feel like Hugo when he was walking this planet – free, simple and utterly content.

All those words were just because of you, even though, I know clearly that you are too well aware of each and every thought of mine. When I put it on paper it seems to me as if it is, somehow, more real. The thoughts come from me, I suppose, but then, I am aware that they might as well originate from you. The only difference is that I took the time to write them down. I don't miss you anymore, I just absolutely enjoy whenever you are around, and thank you ever so much that it is so often.

***

On the following morning Pia woke up before the horizon's line lightened. She went into the forest and walked to see her friends: animals, birds, trees and rocks that she met while she stayed at the Old Master's house. She performed her morning dance and swam in the cold mountain stream. When she came back she met her Master standing next to the house. Her bag was packed and his too.

Tears welled up in her eyes, but she heard his voice in her head:

"I am always with you."

The very same words his father, the Old Master, spoke to her the day before.

When they came to Tokyo she remembered his warning:

"Don't lose your focus in the big city."

He didn't say anything, he didn't ask her to come back; he just bowed down with his hands in the prayer position on his chest. She did the same and then took up her light bag and lost herself in the faceless multitude. She wanted to turn her head back to see him, maybe for the last time, but she resisted such temptation as she knew him too well – he had already disappeared, and his mind and heart were open to welcome a new disciple, ready and ripe to embrace timeless wisdom.

She followed the voice:

"Passengers for flight number seven-zero-two Tokyo to London gate seventeen."

When she was high up in the air, when Tokyo looked like a *Legoland* from the bird's eye view, she pulled the blind down, put the eye mask onto her eyes and sank into inner silence.

She never worried about money, as she never spent much of her wage when she was a lecturer at the university, and in the mountains her savings remained untouched. She just thought of which hotel in London would have a free room for someone who just turns up, but once again, she remembered her Master's words:

"Follow and It will take you exactly where you must be."

She learned that lesson long ago, but it didn't carry the same connotation or conviction by the Master's side in the mountains as it did here in a tremendously hectic London.

Did the spirit of her late mother, or the spirit of sweet innocent Hugo lead her, or was she just in tune with her intuition, she took a taxi and said:

"To the Ritz Carlton, please"

Was that the only hotel she remembered existed in the centre of the city, or was that the voice of her inner wisdom? It didn't really make any difference, as she walked in, she said to the young receptionist:
"A single room, please"
He looked at her with a smile on his pleasant face and said:
"I am sorry madam, we don't have any vacancies."

She stared at him unwilling to accept that answer for acceptance would imply suspicion as to the existence of her benevolent companions. The Master told her that everything was ready and that she had to *'follow her inner knowledge and voice.'*

She wanted to ask herself, *'What now?'* when the young man repeated:
"I am sorry madam, we don't have any vacancies."
She looked at the young man's wristwatch and it read – half past eleven, *'Where does one go at half-past eleven?'*
It wasn't the right time to figure out if Theodor Lukas was still alive and living at the same address,
When she turned back to the receptionist, the young man wasn't there any longer; he was replaced by another smiling face, a colleague that came to do the night shift. He asked:
"Ma'am is everything OK?"
There was a nametag on his impeccable uniform. It read: Hugo Bloxham. She smiled. He looked at her; without thinking, she said:
"Dean and Andrew Bloxham were my friends when I lived in London."
"Ma'am maybe my father Dean and my uncle Andrew are the very people you knew."
"Hugo was the name of my dearest friend Nikki's late brother."
"Ma'am my mother's name is Nikki and she had a brother who passed away long ago. I was named after him. It can't be a coincidence."
"I have such a strong need to hug you."

He repeated that there was no room available for her that night, he wrote his mother's address down and said:

"Nikki lives alone, she is a night owl. Take a taxi, you'll get there before midnight."

***

Nikki had two different kinds of feelings: she was surprised that someone buzzed at this hour and she was afraid of who that midnight visitor could be. She decided not to respond. Quickly, she switched off the side lamp and closed her eyes. Since Hugo left she never felt secure or sociable.

It buzzed again, but she kept her eyes closed.

Then the telephone rang. She was absolutely suspicious, but she answered the phone. It was Hugo. He asked her if her visitor arrived safely.

"What visitor? I have none. Someone though, rang, I don't open the door at this hour."

"A woman, with a slight accent, she knows you, she knows dad and uncle Andrew; I gave her your address."

"Are you mad? You are a kook, just like your father, you trust people just like that. What's wrong with you? How could you..."

"Whoa! Hang on; I didn't meet her on the street. She came here at the Ritz, wanted a room here, then she saw my name she told me she knew my mother, father and uncle Andy."

"Hugo, always, you are always so silly. What am I going to do now with that woman? I don't even know who she is."

"Let her into the building but don't open the door. Ask her from behind the closed door where she knows you from? Easy as that, don't panic. I'll call again as soon as I can, OK?"

She opened the window and peeped out into the darkness. There was someone standing downstairs with a small bag next to her. Something very particular struck Nikki's attention: the way this woman stood, her figure, the way she held her body… She summoned some courage and in a quiet voice she called:

"Did you ring my bell?"

"I did Veronika, I did. Pia is here."

Nikki screeched, screamed and cried, all at once. Then, in her pyjamas and her slippers, she jumped over two or three stairs the way she would twenty-five years ago. When she came out, when the streetlight lit Pia's face, Nikki's jaw dropped and in disbelief she said:

"This is not you. This is an apparition, a spirit of you, the same way I see my Hugo, that can't be you."

"Veronika, my dear Nikki, it is me, Pia. Pia Odak, your best friend and your lost sister."

"But you should be over fifty now, and you look exactly like you did twenty-five years ago, it can't be true… or could it be that you have had all possible plastic surgery done to keep you looking that way? Even in the dark I see that you've never had anything like that done. Let me touch you Pia, let me touch you; let me hug you. Oh, Pia, it is you! You even smell like my Pia."

They sat on a settee and teary Nikki said:

"Why, Pia, why on earth, did you desert me? All those years without a word from you! Do you know how many times, how many long nights I spent thinking about you, there wasn't a single logical conclusion that I could come up with to soothe my hurting ego and my sad soul. Not a word! Not a word from Pia."

"I made the same choice as you had made years ago. I just left because I had to, just as you did, Nikki, just as you did. It couldn't happen in any other order. You see, just like you, I had changed my name officially. Changed it into Sapphire Bonifacio and then back to Pia Odak as the Old Master liked it better. I was prone to please him as he and his son were the only two men that I respected and trusted."

"Let me make the biggest pot of coffee, as I know there will be no sleeping tonight, there's so much to catch up with."

"I won't be going tomorrow morning, if you can put up with me, I would like to spend several days in London."

When Nikki went to the kitchen Pia observed her – her figure, her movements, noticing all the barely visible signs that one shows of habits and character. Pia wanted to read how much life had changed her best friend from long ago. Her movements were slower and her temperament seemed to be, somehow tamed, somehow mellowed. She was slightly overweight, especially in the area of her hips; she looked like a solidly built ship. When Nikki laid cups and biscuits on the table she sat next to Pia and looked at her observantly:

"It is almost unbelievable that you haven't changed a bit. You don't look a day older, how is this possible, Pia? I know that you were different from all the other people that I had ever met, but you look as if you carry all the peace there is in the world in your heart and the beauty of your face is intact. Your willowy body hasn't aged, what is it Pia? Is it that famous Tesla gene, is it that, somehow, on some telepathic level you receive from him a form of energy that comes from a fountain of youth?"

"It may be the genes, it might be some connection that I am not fully aware of with the genius Tesla, it might be my daily exercise or the wisdom that I drank from a most sacred source."

"Whoa! That sounds crazy! Tell me more about your scared source."

"I met a man, an Aikido master, who taught me precious lessons and practices over the last sixteen years. These last two years we spent in the mountains with his father, who happened to be the wisest Master in Japan, most probably – in the world."

"What a privilege! But, what kind of life did you lead?"

"I'll tell you now, day by day since we parted."

Then Pia started to retell Nikki her meaningless and lonely life in Australia until the day it took a turn she never thought it could take and brought her such insight and so many rewards. The day when drunken Nicholas came to her house and tied her to the kitchen chair. The day when a silent shadow walked through the window of her bedroom and danced bewildered Nicholas out of her house and her life forever.

"*Amazing, amazing... typical of you. So, you gave up your work at university and city living in order to learn, to dive deep into that silence and to become one with it? Haven't you missed anything that worldly pleasures have to offer?*"

"*Our time on this planet is short, we don't own our lives. The Master said that we come into existence when yin and yang energies interact; hence we disappear when those energies separate. Therefore, should we find ourselves alive in this world, we must let this life run its course, never be attached to it, but also not throw it away. We must make the best use of our time now. If this body of flesh and blood is impermanent, how much more so are non-tangible things like a name, a title or reputation? I changed my name because Sapphire was within me; I left my title Doctor of Philosophy, for it was time I were free for new knowledge. When I let it all go I made room for a new awareness, my journey hasn't come to an end, every day is a new opportunity to learn more.*"

"*Tell me about your writings? Now that you have new insights you can soar high like an eagle. With such knowledge you can reach many people, change their lives, perhaps, be famous or rich.*"

"*People exhaust themselves for three things: fame, social status and wealth, as soon as you achieve fame, it breeds anxiety since you become fearful that people who are jealous of you might damage your reputation. It is much the same with social status; you fear that a shift in politics might take it away. When you acquire wealth, you'll be afraid that you might be robbed. Anxiety never ceases and only those who see through the illusions of fame, social status and wealth are not burdened by fear and constant anxiety. No, I think I had no calling to write any more or to preach anything. I love my quiet existence; my Master said, 'If you can dispense with reputation, then you are free from care. Reputation is only a visitor, but reality is here to stay.' And now, you tell me about Hugo Bloxham.*"

DETHRONED

"When you left I was, sort of, devastated. In this cold city I never really had many people I could call friends, apart from stuffed-up-with-all-kind-of-substances Caesar and a few girls that had a very different view of friendship. Anyway, I missed you; I missed some sort of normalcy and simply decided to have a child. I thought of Dean – I used to like him; he was of good stock. Several years after Dean understood that the child was his, we kept a sort of loose relationship. He fell in love with the boy and in the end asked openly if he was his son, which I admitted, and that's how Hugo earned a father. Later on, Dean insisted that Hugo carry his name. I agreed as, in all fairness, what do I really have to do with this made-up name – Barlow? At least the child would have a father and his name. His mother invited us only once, and on that occasion she never spoke more than three sentences. She treated me as if I were some sort of a rare plant, sitting at her elegant table not knowing which fork to use. She thought that all Croats were barbarians, but when Dean told her that my mother was of German origins, she wrinkled her nose and said under her breath, 'Oh, Germans...' with a facial expression that read 'I've just seen the most gruesome scene.' But, you know what? Hugo had his father and his uncle Andy and that was fantastic for him. Dean as Dean, never really committed as a man, or as a husband, which he never really wanted to be, but he was a good father to his son and that was all that mattered to me in the end. You know me, when it comes to men: mistrust and hurt! He married sometime in 2003 or 2004 and he is still with his wife. He has two boys and Hugo visits them regularly. I was very grateful to him for including Hugo in his family and for supporting him. When Hugo was a teenager, sometime between the ages of twelve and sixteen, he was a real nightmare. I feared he could really have taken an irreversibly wrong path, and I earned hundreds of white hairs over those few years and dozens of new wrinkles with each new day that passed. But I loved and understood him, as he was a carbon copy of Veronika Truba in her youth: disobedient, unruly and free-spirited. I just prayed that some common sense from the same Veronika Truba would have been inherited as well. Contrary to what my indifferent mother did, I just tried to love him uncondi-tionally and never ceased to talk about love. I still don't know how he finished

high school, but at that age Dean stepped in. I told him about the trouble his son was causing every day with so much zest and dedication; then Dean offered an unusual deal: a college paid for and lovely holidays he'd pay for, a stable family and a brand new car in exchange for his wild ways. It might have been that Hugo had already used up all his wild cards and extravagant deeds, but after a while he enrolled into college, cut off his hair, passed his driver's licence and, with Dean's help, again, he got a two-day-job at the Ritz. He moved out that year and became a proud elder brother to his siblings. When he moved out I cried my eyes out, as I felt that I really had no one on this earth, but soon his visits became more frequent and reminded me of my old boy, little Hugo, who had a kind heart and fine manners. I still can't believe that chance took you to the hotel and that your sharp mind gathered who he was by putting two and two together."

"It wasn't a mere chance, Nikki. There is no such thing as chance. This universe calculates everything, every little detail has already been arranged and put in its place; when the butterfly bats its wings somewhere in isolated Japanese mountains it causes an effect in smoky London."

"Everything is predestined, you say?"

"No, I didn't say that, I just said a simple truth, but to know the universe and how it has been arranged and organised needs much more knowledge than humble Pia has. My great-great-granduncle Nikola Tesla famously said, 'Our senses enable us to perceive only a minute portion of the outside world. To know each other we must search beyond the sphere of our sense perception.' When I met Hugo at the Ritz, I heard a voice in my head which said, 'Lonnie's here. Hugo loves Lonnie.' So, the boy came and he was labelled as Hugo Bloxham, he smiled at me and I knew it was you smiling at me."

"But that coincidence of you choosing the Ritz and Hugo just commencing his night-shift... it is mindboggling, isn't it?"

"Maybe."

The telephone rang and while Nikki spoke to her son, Pia fluttered off in her velvety dream on the wings of that butterfly that bats its wings somewhere in the Japanese mountains. Nikki lifted Pia's legs onto the settee and covered her with a blanket. Then she sat next to her and observed her, as she fell asleep, for a short while.

'Why did she come after all this time?' she didn't ask that question.

When Pia woke up she found her friend having breakfast on her feet, scoffing the remnants of her sandwich; while she tried to gorge her coffee over the sandwich, she looked at the wall clock and said with her mouth full:

"As always, I am late. Please, feel at home, I'll be back in the evening. Here is my number, right here on the table, call me if you need anything or wish to meet up for lunch."

"I'll be fine."

It was a rainy day. She felt no need to call anyone she knew in London. She preferred to stay in, probably read and make dinner for her and Nikki later on. She looked at some memorabilia displayed on Nikki's fridge, walls and shelves: photos of both Hugos, then the only one photo of the Adriatic Sea, most probably taken from her terrace, Pia's book on her shelf, Nikki's diploma and some sort of Award for a performance that dated way back, Caesar's photo on a red Vespa, sadness in his eyes... Nowhere was Gregor's picture.

She stood next to the window watching the rain. She never missed the rain. Before she could have missed some locations or habits, but she never missed the London weather. Then her eye caught three tall men in the street holding another young man. She opened the window but still she couldn't hear anything for rain was drumming down. One man punched the man that the other two were holding, in his stomach. She frowned, *'Ah, big cities'* she uttered. Then, as if her eyes cleared and sharpened, she looked again and recognised the boy they were holding and beating. It was Hugo.

She ran down the stairs and said in calm voice.

"Let go of him!"

"Who the fuck, are you?"

Pia started her dance, the same dance by which her Master elegantly walked out of her house bewildered Nicholas almost twenty years ago. It was the finest art, astonishing scene to witness: a tall, slim woman, with long loose hair, lifting lean legs high, swirling around and moving her arms slowly! It looked like a scene from some movie, only the protagonists, all except one, were confused and in disbelief. The dance became more intense; three tall men couldn't catch her in her swift movements then believing her to be an apparition, one by one they ran away, leaving Hugo's seemingly lifeless body on the pavement.

She took him in her arms and carried him up as if he were a child. She put him on the couch and brought a cloth and a basin of cold water. When he regained his conciseness, she said:

"Let's call your doctor." Then she took him to the surgery.

***

Nikki came earlier but Pia wasn't home.

Nikki thought, *'Her presence brought such peace, the whole apartment breathes deep tranquillity."*

She brought some prawns, as she knew Pia enjoyed them greatly. She started to prepare dinner, knowing that Pia would return for dinner. She was singing after such a long time. Mumbling rather than singing, she stopped when she understood that it was one of Gregor's biggest hits. Pia brought back memories; she dug them from some depth in Nikki's innermost basement where her suppressed memories lay so deeply buried that she didn't think anyone would ever go there or venture to bring them back.

When Pia came back it was late. Nikki was worried though she knew that she shouldn't worry about a grown-up woman. Pia said:

"Hugo is fine. I took him to the doctor's and they rushed him to hospital. But he is OK now. His life is out of danger, a few broken ribs, broken nose and head injuries, but the doctor said he would be all right."

She told her what happened and Nikki just stood holding onto a chair. Hugo said he didn't owe them any money; he had never met them before. He was just a random victim. They took his wallet; they were on drugs.

"You saved my boy's life." Said teary Nikki.

"Your mother blamed me for Hugo's death years ago."

"My mother! A mean, dishonest creature. Pia, you saved my son's life. I wanna go to the hospital now and see him."

"Let him sleep now, it is late. But first thing tomorrow morning."

Nikki's anger was visible around her lips: vertical sharp lines indicated that old bitterness sat there permanently, her eyebrows almost touching were stopped by those two vertical deep lines. She said:

"This world has gone bonkers. I wish I could have some other choice but to be stuck in this rot, but there's no alternative."

"What bothers you the most?"

"It is a big lie, I knew that from the very beginning, but somehow, childishly, naively, I believed that my leaving for the UK might change something. It isn't any better here: people are blind and obedient, poverty has reached epic proportions and politicians are the very same liars as those we left behind in our chaotic country. These here, appear to be, slightly more 'sophisticated' liars, sophisticated my arse! Look at the state of their world: they have no remorse for their misconduct or their wrongdoings, no pity for their victims, zero bloody ability to empathise. They'd rather legitimatise their murderous intent by coating over with terms such as 'wars of liberation', you see how liberated we are, how liberated all the countries are where they set foot and set up their 'democracy'. I don't have a country any more – fine! But I left in the naïve belief that in any, so-called 'Western country' I might find more freedom and democracy. What a lie! These morons milk us daily of our light, their banks steal our money, they suck our talents, awareness and our soul, and this is, my dear friend how they have sustained their endless materialism on which they thrive. These bloodsuckers have infiltrated every nation, religion and race, they're in every walk of life, and there is no government or nation that can claim immunity from their presence.

I hated with all my heart that sinister priest, my mother's 'best friend and confidant' as he was one of them: a creature that seeks chaos and division while preaching 'Christian values'; I had recognised him when I was a young child and knew that my own mother wasn't any better than he was. He was among the powerful that pulled the strings in our country. Poverty everywhere: but the problem of our economy is rather a spiritual problem. When one has no food in their pantry, roof over one's head, when one has to fight for one's mere survival on a daily basis, then that is all that one has. No time, space or belief in any spiritual advancement or involvement with one's soul. Let's kill the notion that humans have a soul! That is their slogan. We have become mere instruments, a robot-like brainwashed mob, that the president of the country where we were born by 'mistake' called his people 'Small-tooth livestock'. Am I angry? Yes. I live in a world that I despise."

"What about: Hugo, your fantastic ability to express your inner light through painting little vignettes, your keen interest in philosophy and poetry? Finer things?"

"That's exactly what I was telling you: they try to kill everything by forcing us to watch so-called 'reality shows', they choose 'stars' from those shows and write and report on them every second of the day, we are bombarded by so much fake information and brainwashed to follow the wickedness and sickness of their minds."

"When Hugo gets better, just focus on him more. You won't change anything, but you can colour your life in brighter hues."

"Oh, Pia. I envy you. I always have. I am so happy that you saw through my brother, you saw through everyone, I wish I could have had more time to spend with you and learn more from your inner inborn wisdom. I don't have wisdom, all that has remained is pure anger."

"Anger is not good for your soul."

"Oh, I don't even believe in the soul any more. Or if there were a soul within me, it was sucked out of me by this mad, fake, greedy society. No one is interested anymore in hearing about human virtue, goodness and harmony. In this society people place importance on materialistic pursuits rather than building human relationships. Relationships have become shallow and superficial, as everyone is bending to social and peer pressure to get approval or outwit others. And you know, my dearest Pia, when you lose all your vision and

ideals, when you become absolutely disillusioned, you understand that simply accepting life as it is does not make you happy. So, here I am – disillusioned and unhappy."

"Oh, Nikki! Wisdom is the ability to recognise our own strengths and weaknesses, and the strengths and weaknesses of others."

On the next day Nikki called Dean and told him about Hugo's incident. Pia told her not to mention her at all.

"But, aren't you coming with us to the hospital?"

"I'll be off in the afternoon. Just call me and let me know how he is doing and I'll go with peace in my soul."

"Where are you off to?"

"Our hometown."

"I have never visited since I left."

"Neither have I."

"How come, now?"

"Something remains to be completed. What happened to your family? I assume they have benefited from the change. My family may well have benefited too, but only my father's side of the family, though."

"Very likely they did benefit. My brother was a soldier in the patriotic war. I assume he has benefited. I don't know anything; I mean anything, about anyone. I have never asked. Mainly, here, I was ashamed to speak of my origins as people looked down on us, as if we came from some really barbaric planet. Serves us well, from what I saw on the streets of London, in department stores and in the government institutions I would rather never speak that language again. In front of churches women with scarves, loud and demanding, asking for money, donations, 'justice' et cetera. I pretended to be from Prague, as my Slavic accent gave me away. I would say 'I am from Prague' and would never get that many dirty looks as when I told the truth. Even Hugo thinks that we came from Prague."

"I never took sides anywhere. I have never been bothered with such stupidity. Sydney wasn't any different: full of prejudice and people fed by manipula-

tive media. They don't think critically; they swallow the news and repeat it as parrots would. So, you don't know what happened to Gregor Truba?"

"Not really. He called three times and each time after he called I changed the number."

"Do you want to come with me?"

Nikki just smiled and shook her head.

As Pia was leaving, Nikki said:

"Are we going to stay in touch?"

"I don't own a mobile phone as I don't want anyone to track my insignificant movements. I don't have Internet connection for I don't need it, I dislike it, and believe that it is yet another way to control people. I don't even have a permanent address for there is no permanency in this illusionary world of ours. But, we'll stay in touch – think of me every day at six o'clock in the morning and I will do the same. That is how we'll stay connected. Talk to me every day if you wish."

"Go, Pia! Go quickly as I feel like crying so heavily that I might get a nervous breakdown."

"Nikki, it isn't complicated. It is so simple once you cut through illusions."

"Yeah, I know it all theoretically, but like the majority in this world, I am trapped too, and I have convinced myself in this mass hypnosis that there is no way out. I have lost this battle because I believed that I would be cleverer than any shitty government and would be able to do things my own way. Yet, I am now, sitting in some insignificant third-rate clothing shop and selling cheap clothes, trying to convince people that the 'stuff is of a high quality at an affordable price'. Shit!"

"Change it Nikki, you don't have to do what you dislike so much."

"It's too late for me, Pia. I am happy to see that you have stayed the way you were, that you did it for both of us. Free and awakened."

***

The plane took off; she heard that Hugo was getting better and she stopped thinking of Nikki, she thought of her Master.

'Why did he want me to travel back? What is it that I have to find or to face that I haven't dealt with? Is it a person? An event? Or just a memory that has to be unearthed right there on the same ground where it had been buried many, many years ago?'

She put the headphones on and the soothing music added to the feeling of lightness. It was a feeling of dizziness due to the mild turbulence of the small plane. In all honesty, she was not sure about the origins of her dizziness: was it caused by the mild turbulence or was it that strange feeling one gets when going back, after more than twenty years of absence, to face one's own past?

When the plane landed, there was no one waiting for Pia, as no one knew she was coming. Probably no one knew or remembered that Pia Odak or Sapphire Bonifacio had existed.

But in this assumption she was wrong.

A taxi took her to the centre of the city where she took a room in a hotel. She opened the window that was facing the school she attended thirty years ago. It had not changed - just the tooth of decay left its marks.

She took a deep sigh and sat on the floor to meditate.

When she opened her eyes, she checked the time: it was early evening, the sky was streaked by red and gold lines, the air was light and heavy at the same time as there were light and heavy feelings on Pia's chest.

She closed the door and said to herself:

"Tomorrow is April 15th, I can't believe that twenty-five years have passed as if they were twenty-five days. What a dream! What a nightmare!"

Was It Metamorphosis?

"When Gregor Samsa woke up one morning from unsettling dreams, he found himself changed..."

When Gregor Truba woke up on that mild April morning in 2017, from a long unsettling dream, he found himself changed. Indeed, he found himself manipulated – altered greatly.

Gregor Truba was an ordinary man. He always portrayed himself as an honest, hardworking man with a sharp sense of justice and belonging. Belonging to his country, to the dream. The Big Dream.

But, on that particular morning, April 15th, while his head was still resting on the pillow, he heard himself talking as if he were talking to some other person who had their head on the same pillow:

"Today is the 15th of April. I can't believe that twenty-five years have passed as if they were twenty-five days. What a dream! What a nightmare! What had happened to my dream, to my country and my countrymen? Poverty, lies; poverty, lies! Poverty, crime; poverty, crime! A vicious cycle for the past twenty-five years: all is broken, this is a paradise for criminals and fools and I am one of them. Was that my Big Dream? Was it that I was dreaming my father's never-fulfilled dream? Was that my mother's dream or was that the dream of the priest who manipulated many? Whose dream has collapsed as if it were a sandcastle? My dream has, and the dream of my friends that fought the fight for foreign bankers, foreign companies, big investors and domestic criminals? Bravo, Gregor Truba, you have lost! Bravo, Gregor Truba, you were used as any other brainwashed fool! There is no past, no present and no future. Bravo, Gregor Truba, you have contributed with all your limited resources, but you have contributed greatly with your heart. With the heart that was powered by mother Elsa's heart and father Anton's heart and by millions

of unwise hearts that are empty, now that the blood has been drained out of them."

He screamed, a loud scream as a wounded animal would and slowly, with a walking stick in her hand, mother Elsa walked in. Her German accent by now was so strong that even her own son sometimes struggled to understand her as she sounded as if she chewed pieces of steel while talking.

She came closer, sat on his bed, took out a pill and handed him the pill and a glass of water.

"Swallow it. Schnell, Schnell!"

He obeyed her command but then he looked at the eyes of that, by now, old woman and mighty anger lifted his arm, with all his strength he threw the glass against the opposite wall. The glass still half-full hit the wall and broke into numerous pieces that slid down the wall washed by clear water.

Mother Elsa sighed heavily, and Gregor said:

"Your crazy hero. But, nevertheless, a hero he is and you earned the prize."

"Stay in bed today, son. Stay in bed."

"Don't patronise me! Don't talk to me as if I were a retarded child. I am not Hugo, I am Gregor Truba; I do whatever pleases me."

"OK, son, do whatever pleases you, but just stay in bed for today, as you see it's come on again. You'd better stay in the house."

"Locked in this house with you."

"Stay... please."

"You have ruined everything. Look around you! Where is your husband? Oh, he left! Why did he leave? Oh, he can't provide! Why couldn't he provide any more? He wanted to give up his life for the country and the country has no job to offer. Not for him, and not for his son. Where did he go? Well, no one knows."

"I'll bring you breakfast. God, what have I done wrong?"

"What have you done wrong? Ask your friend, he might know. He taught you how to listen to that particular God. He had instructed you in everything. Where is he now? He never comes along? Why doesn't he? Is he scared of your

*son? Does he have dreams of dead people visiting? No! All he had ever done
was to give instructions in accordance with his God."*

She left his room quietly while he was shouting and swearing.

He had a shower, then they had breakfast in silence. His mood had changed
and he seemed to be more docile.

When he dressed and combed his hair he looked handsome: he always had
a good sense of dress, his tall body was still strong, though overweight, but he
knew how to choose and match the right clothes. When calm and under the
influence of his pills, he acted as if he were perfectly collected and civil. It
looked as if he had never been a soldier, a man of arms; a man who killed the
people who were floating through his dreams, easily and frequently.

As in life, so in death, as in death, so in dreams: Luna was his most feared
and at the same time, most loved and loathed regular visitor. Theirs was, by its
nature, a sacred timeless alliance, which knew no borders of life and death; an
alliance that they carried from day to day, from night to night, one she encouraged and maintained wherever he believed she resided.

He never had much money, but that morning as on many others, mother
Elsa took out the exact amount of money he needed for his coffee and the
morning papers. She handed it to him; he wanted to kiss her hand, but he
changed his mind and planted a kiss on top of her head:

"Thank you, Mother. Dankeschon."

"Bitteschon mein Sohn."

As a little child that would obey effortlessly, he put the money in his pocket and patted her back again. She straightened his shirt and patted his chest,
uttering the last warning:

"Take care son. Be back for lunch. Take care, don't talk politics."

"Jawohl Elsa, Jawohl!" he said teasingly and off he went. In the middle of
the street he looked back as she called after him:

*"You forgot your pills, take two of them at half-past one if you don't man-
age to come home on time."*

Who visited his dreams last night he wasn't sure, but somehow he knew that everything had changed and he looked at the world with different eyes: as he walked downtown, he noticed the façades of old buildings falling apart, as if the town survived the apocalypse; the shops were empty and deserted, the streets dirty and rubbish bins overflowing with stinky rubbish that hadn't been collected and carried away for weeks. He noticed passers-by with long faces, people that looked through the rubbish bins in order to find scraps of food. Poverty and desperation on each and every corner poked at him. Europe was elsewhere, but his country and the lives of his friends, brothers and comrades were given as a gift to those that would walk the streets of the country into the future.

"Who will walk the streets of my youth? My innocent youth?"

Then he remembered the best remedy – *'Change the train of your thoughts – Change the mind's pattern immediately!'*

He bought the daily paper and climbed the stairs that led to the terrace of his favourite café. From there he had a stunning view regardless of the season or time of day: he would see the ever-changing colours of the sky, the ever-changing colours of the sea and the constant movement on the two main roads and in the port. He could sit there all day long and look at young girls that came out of the high school. The same high school that he attended thirty years ago. He loved and loathed his hometown, though he knew that he would not ever be able to leave it for good in the way Veronika Truba, his former sister, did.

He pulled his chair out of the small table where the sign *'Reserved'* was written. As soon as he sat down, a young woman brought him his *'macchiato'*. She said:

"Anything new?"

"New York, New Jersey, New Caledonia."

"OK! Anything old?"

"I am old."

"OK. Enjoy your 'macchiato' and paper, dad is still not around."

Branka Čubrilo

"I have all the time one could possibly have, at least that is what they left us. Useless time."

"Sorry, I've got to go, there are customers waiting for me."

The young woman rolled her eyes and swiftly left.

After some time had passed Gregor folded his paper and took off his glasses. But as soon as he put them down on the table, he put them back on in a hurry. He spotted a tall woman, lean and leggy, sporting a pair of black jeans and a tight black T-shirt. She had dark long hair and walked elegantly. He looked at the apparition and said:

"Luna, Luna, every time you appear you look more and more real. I wouldn't be surprised if you sat here, next to me, in the full light of day."

The woman sat a little bit further and started to scrutinise the four-page menu. When she moved her hair with her left hand, with two fingers precisely, his heart skipped – *'Could she ever materialise again?'*

The woman talked to the young waitress and he knew that she was very much alive and present on this terrace. His eyes stopped, he stared at her so intensely that the woman didn't dare lift her head as she felt that intense gaze on her face.

He called her quite loudly:

"Luna! Luna, is it you?"

The woman kept her eyes glued to the menu. He stood up and walked slowly but the *'apparition'* was still there – sitting and examining the menu. He knew he had taken only two morning pills, no more no less, he hadn't drunk any alcohol, but Luna was sitting there ignoring him as if he were not real. When he came close, he lightly touched the chair and asked:

"May I sit down?"

She lifted her head and looked at his eyes. She smiled but didn't say anything. He sat down and said:

"It can't be possible. You are not Luna. She died; I know that for sure. You are not her daughter, either, as she passed away alone. You could be only one person, but only if you were frozen in time."

She looked at him without saying a word. He covered his eyes, then he looked at her and again he said:

"Where have you been all these years, Pia?"

"It is a long story Gregor, but it can be narrated in two sentences: I left home when the epidemic of madness was cast upon this country: when hatred speaks, reason cries, doesn't it? Since then I've lived in London, Sydney and somewhere in Japan, in some place you've never heard of."

"Pia. Pia Odak."

"Yes. It is I."

"I used to love you, Pia."

"It was a long time ago, wasn't it?"

"A very long time ago, but, you know the heart is a rather tricky instrument. It doesn't measure time but only emotions. I still remember the intensity of that love."

"We were very young."

"Yes. We were young. What happened to you? You look like you have come from some other time. You look like you had at least fifteen plastic surgery operations to keep you looking almost the same as twenty-something years ago. You have lots of money?"

"Not a lot, but some money."

"How many operations have you had?"

"A few."

"Oh, I see. How do you see me? Still handsome?"

"If you get a buzz out of it, then let me tell you – yes, still handsome."

"I lost contact with you, I lost contact with Veronika and I lost contact with my mind. I think I went cuckoo in this war, in all this madness that engulfed this country. I lost so many friends, we all lost our loved ones, jobs, savings, human decency, kindness and basic human goodness."

"They who are involved are confused but they who watch are clear minded."

"Yes, how strange, Pia, that only today I came up with the same line of thought. I thought – it was all an illusion and a lie, my downward spiral of a selfish, purposeless existence that sought to justify itself by killing others. I killed people Pia, in the name of freedom and life. I killed people, Pia... not soldiers, not enemies that I was supposed to kill, but I killed people that were not soldiers, that were innocent."

"Don't talk about that. Look at the sky."

"Oh, don't please! Don't say that. That is exactly what my Mother tells me – Change the subject. Pia, I was thinking about that today, that the Big Lie happened and we all rushed towards it with open arms and ready hearts. How can one justify war when it is always fought in someone else's interests? It has never been worse in the past fifty years. It has never been worse and it is going to get even more miserable, we have new owners, big guns: our saviours! They saved us from ourselves. Did you know that everything has been looted: big companies and factories, the shipyard, the state roads, water, forests, every-thing has been privatised, bought with no money, abducted from the people and the state that owned it. Whoever could steal, abduct, falsify and illegally appropriate did so. Thoroughly and with the help of those criminals from abroad. Nothing's left for the people: no work, just skyrocketing unemploy-ment, no social security, no worker's rights or medical care. Nothing! Not a thing! Anyone who held any position stole and looted, your father too, don't you know it?"

"I don't. And I don't feel intimidated because of his deeds. I don't take re-sponsibility for anyone's actions, why would I take responsibility for his?"

"Is he still alive?"

"Who?

"Your father?"

"I don't know. I arrived only yesterday; I haven't seen anyone yet. You are the first person I've met this morning, if we are to exclude the receptionist and the young waitress."

"He ordered my murder several times, don't you know that?"

"I don't feel responsible for his actions and decisions. I know nothing about you, people. I came from London last night after twenty-five years of *absence. Just as your sister never contacted you or your family, I haven't spoken to my family either. Does that satisfy you?"*

"It doesn't. Nothing satisfies me, Pia. Nothing! I am nobody in this country no one is anybody. There is a fistful of jackals that had stolen everything that could be possibly stolen and the rest including us, the people, are as people from the government call us – livestock! That is precisely what we are – livestock!"

"I can't help you, Gregor."

"No one can help me or anyone else in this country. It is robbed, sold out and split up into many bits and pieces. We are a big nobody in many pieces and now the Lords are coming and tailoring new laws. We have new Lords. They don't even speak our language, they don't know our local culture but they will rule our land – and here we are, a gang drowned in lies."

After a short pause Pia said:

"I think I'll go now."

"Don't' go, Pia. Stay here with me a little bit longer and I'll tell you who was who in this last bloody war. I'll tell you who your father was and I'll tell you who the Holy Father was, who the enemy was and who made money. I know them all..."

"I opt not to listen. I have to go now."

"I know who killed Luna and I know who killed your grandmother."

Shivers went down Pia's spine. She took a big sip of water and collected her belongings in her bag. He continued:

"It wasn't me who killed your grandmother. You know the priest. He told me to shoot her in her back. I didn't even know who she was, I was just ordered to kill her."

Pia hurried towards the bar, he followed her:

"I didn't kill Luna, either. She was raped. I wasn't involved. I just showed the guys where she lived. They did it! She begged me. But you know, you know that evening, that last evening that I ever saw you, the evening I played the *guitar at your graduation party. That night I had promised myself to seek revenge. But I would never kill Luna. She was raped and taken to hospital. I didn't kill Luna. She reminded me too much of you, I would never do that..."*

She gave a banknote to the young girl and without waiting for the change she rushed down the stairs and quickly unlocked her room. Her heart was beating as a wild animal's. No amount of wisdom that she acquired from her Masters came to her rescue at this moment. She rushed into the bathroom and threw up in the sink. She looked at her reflection in the mirror and said:

"Run away, Pia. Run away now!"

***

On the same day, in the late afternoon hours, Pia put her hair in a bun, on the top of her head; she put a small hat on and covered her face with big dark glasses. Carefully, she examined the street and when she was sure that there was no imminent danger lurking, in a brisk walk she headed towards Southern Shore Road. She turned her head several times but no one was following her; she stopped at number twenty-one and pressed the doorbell. It took a while before she heard the echo of someone's shoes on the wooden floor. A man opened the door and she recognised him at once: her uncle Boris.

She took her glasses off; she took off her hat and said:

"Uncle Boris, good afternoon."

In disbelief he looked at her, then he opened the door wider and showed her in, saying:

"It looks to me as if you have been resurrected."

The first truth she learned was that almost no one benefited from the war that was fought, now, almost twenty-five years ago, apart from several unscrupulous people, including her father. The second truth she learned was that her father was lying on his deathbed ridden with cancer, no hospital wanted to keep him. He was at home, with a carer, waiting for his time to come. Nothing could save him: his ministerial chair, his connections, money and wealth that he had accumulated in those years of war, chaos and despoilment. Uncle Boris said that he had played hard, with tough players and remained on top of the game for a long time. He said that her father, his brother, had all the qualities of such a player: he was cunning, unscrupulous, heartless and soulless, interested only in personal gain and fame... *"...as was always the case, regardless of the position: an actor, a theatre director, a high ranking officer or a minister, mercilessly and ruthlessly he climbed up."*

"He was different."

"He even denied Mother's origins."

"He always did. He always had manipulated facts and people too. When did he get ill?"

"Two years ago. Now it is over six months that he's been bed-ridden. He can't even get up anymore."

"Do you visit?"

"Sure I do. He talks about what he will do when he 'gets better' or 'when he gets back on his feet' unaware that he won't be as good as he was."

"Did he ever mention me?"

"Only lately. Just a few days ago he was half awake and half in a dream state, he said, 'I hope Pia will call in today', on which the carer commented: 'He's been calling for her lately in his sleep.' Obviously, he would be glad to see you."

"Not sure about 'glad', but that is his conscience speaking. It is heavily loaded. So, what happened, uncle? What happened to uncle Ivan, to you, to the Bonifacio family? I've had no contact with anyone over the last twenty years."

"If I look back, I can now say– maybe that was your smartest choice. That war brought chaos, hatred and poverty and this country will not recover for many years to come. It has never been worse, but we haven't seen the most horrible of it yet."

"Can it get any worse than this?"

"Don't be naïve. I bet you haven't lived under a rock all these years. When you ask what happened to us I can sum it up in several sentences. Nothing much happened; we were all wiped out from good jobs, good living standards

and we were reduced to poverty… or bare survival. Your father had profited, but at what cost? I believe that you'll have the right to inherit his wealth."

"I need none of his wealth. Shall we go and see him?"

"Go by yourself."

"That would be better."

Pia's Last Poem

A middle-aged woman opened the door. Pia said:

"I am visiting Simon, please let me in."

"He is fast asleep... may I know who you are?"

"I am related to him, don't worry, if you don't trust me, call his brother Boris."

The woman let her in.

Everything was exactly the same as it was before. She put the kettle on the stove, and the woman said, *"I can make you a cup of coffee"*, but Pia just ignored what she said and continued to take out coffee, sugar, a cup and a saucer slowly, deep in thought.

When she made herself a cup of coffee she took it up and walked into Simon's room. He was fast asleep, but the aroma of coffee made him open his eyes. He said:

"Thanks Sandra, that was a good decision, a warm cup of coffee. What a delicious aroma."

Pia sat on the armchair next to his bed and said:

"Do you still take three spoons of sugar?"

Hearing that voice in a semi-darkened room he propped himself up quickly, looked at Pia, cried loudly from pain and said in disbelief:

"Luna!"

"You always think of her. It's me, Pia, your long lost daughter. I heard Luna passed away."

His breathing was heavy, blood rushed into his cheeks and they were red for the first time in many years. He adjusted himself on his pillows and grabbed her hand:

"Pia, am I dreaming or am I dead already?"

"None of it, Simo. You are alive, still alive, and yes, I am your long lost daughter Pia Odak, also known as Sapphire Bonifacio."

"I can't believe it right now. Pia, where have you been all those years? Where and why have you been hiding?"

"It is a long story, Simo, as one could easily build a long story over such a long period of time. But let me be concise: I left the country, as I never wanted to be a part of such collective madness. I went to London and didn't find what I was after. I went to Sydney where I had found even more emptiness. I went to Japan and grasped the meaning of peace through glimpses, and the meaning of my own existence. You see, I never believed in group mentality but rather relied on my own intelligence and free choice. You know that I have always rebelled against authority in my own way. You know that I never liked it when someone else decided on my behalf. When some other person, institution or any authority such as a government made decisions on my behalf. Whenever possible I rebelled against them. Do you think that I could have been an urban, cultured mind and allow a bunch of lunatics to lead me into their mentality? You tell me, how are you doing now?"

"Oh, I am doing reasonably well. I don't know whether or not you have any knowledge of my extraordinarily successful career. I was the alpha and omega of decisions on top government's issues and politics. I have distinguished myself and became the pride of the Odak family, the only one to have made the right choices when the chips were down. Your worthy uncles, they were always 'worthy lawyers' and my family never took me seriously, calling me an 'actor' or an 'entertainer', but there was more to it. I showed them what I was made off! War is the time when one shows what one is made of. I was fearless and sharp in making decisions and proved to be an extraordinary leader, I have retired as a Minister."

He started to cough and then cry from the pain in his chest. Pia sat there motionless, holding a strand of her long hair with two fingers.

"Have you heard about my political career and my achievements?"

"No, I haven't but for me you are still the same Simo, my father who never really cared about anyone else but himself."

"Don't say that, Pia. Don't say that, please. You know that it isn't true."

"On the contrary. You cared only about yourself as you do right now as well. Whatever you have 'achieved' you have not impressed me nor the Odak Family."

In one gulp, he swallowed his coffee. Pia remained silent. He looked at her and said:

"You haven't changed a bit. Look at your flawless skin, the clarity and sharpness of your eyes just as when you were a teenager, there are no wrinkles on your smooth face..."

"The eyes when they are about to lose their sight tend to be extremely sharp in noticing details."

"Why have you come now? Why after all those years of silence, did you miss me?"

"I did not miss anyone, Simo. I was taught not to miss and not to love. Yes. My mother took her own life and she was the only person I have ever sincerely and completely loved. You married my mother who knows why, not out of love as you, yourself, never knew what love was. You married her, most probably, so you could be closer to Luna, who had been your lover for many years. That was the reason my mother took her own life, I understood that years later. I came back from school and found her bleeding; she cut her veins, that scene had never left my memory but had frozen within me and isolated me from love for the rest of my life. You were there, hidden, with Luna, trying to cover up the truth that you two were there when she took her own life. It could be possible, I am almost positive about it, that you two pushed her to it. This case was never investigated as everybody took it for what it seemed at first glance: a melancholic, weak young artist took her own life. People said that she was unstable, given that she was always compared to her twin sister who, as we know, had psychopathic tendencies: cold, unscrupulous, calculated and manipulative. A perfect match for Simo Odak. Yes, that is the abbreviated version of the story. I was only a child and couldn't grasp what had really happened, but after that

event I had never trusted men again. Then in my youth I served you as some sort of pimp without knowing it. Yes, pimp! You would ask me to bring my girlfriends over and you were the king of the party. You liked those young girls, innocent but ambitious luring them in with false promises of an acting career. Your 'friendliness' with my girlfriends, even my male friends, was notorious. It took me years to understand what it was. Do you remember, when you were drunk that you tried to get under my sheets? Do you remember it? Do you remember that I once threatened to expose your drunken visits to my grandpa and your brother Ivan? Do you know what would have happened if your brother Ivan, the general attorney, had learned how you treated me while I was a teenager? Or your brother Boris? Don't doubt they ever suspected it. Even your mother, my granny Sava, occasionally asked me about your drinking or your behaviour when drunk. I faced life with a straight face. I never told anyone that you would come into my bedroom naked, or into the bathroom when I was having a shower. You told me that it was 'natural'. It wasn't natural. I feared men and I was ashamed when with a man I liked. I couldn't open up; I couldn't trust and let go. I was always on the alert, disgusted with your domestic habits and daily advancement in my girlfriends' pants. You convinced me that it was 'normal'. I thought for a short period in my life that it was OK. You would now probably justify your orgy with my girlfriends as always, saying that 'it was their choice'. But they were young, naïve and believed that you would help. They believed that your name opened doors to fame and success. They believed that I was happy and blessed to be your daughter. I was ashamed. You were the brute of this family; that is the reason why you place so much pride on your political career. No decent man would climb over dead bodies to get to where you have positioned yourself. So, Simon Odak, your family wasn't proud of you. I was never proud of you either, I am not proud of you now. I pity you now, that's all."

"You are blaspheming against God."
"Which God? Mars? The Odaks' God?"
"Is that the reason you have come here while I am ill and fragile?"

"*I don't know the reason why I came exactly, but as we are here right now, I'd like to let you know who you were to me. You deserve to know it.*"

"*I smell roses! Oh, what an overwhelming smell. Can you smell it? I feel as if I am going to suffocate from that smell.*"

"*The nose is the most sensitive to fragrances when it is about to lose its ability to smell.*"

He propped himself once again on his elbows against his pillows and cleared his throat:

"*Whatever you are saying isn't true. I was left to be a single father and I took good care of you. I had money, I had fame; you had all the doors opened. You could do whatever you wanted to do. You enrolled in the best schools and graduated from the best university. I gave you an opportunity to be who you are. I turned you into who you were; you inherited all my talents. You can't come to my house now and talk nonsense, rubbish! I don't owe you anything, Pia. I gave you life, education, connections, a good name, I gave you every-thing and as a 'thank you, Simon' you came here on my deathbed to trash me as if I were some sort of a monster. I fought for this country and made the right decisions as a military man and as the Minister. People respected me, they asked for my counsel, for my guidance, and the state appointed me to the best duties, as I was wise and trustworthy. Don't you dare talk to me in such a manner! I haven't seen you in over twenty years, don't you dare come to my home and tell me what I have or haven't done right. I know who I am; I know what I have done and what I have deserved, in this family and this country alike. If you have come here to give me a hard time, I can tell you right now – Go! Go, wherever you came from and leave me alone to die in peace.*"

"*When one begins to weaken their will one pushes their body to the limit, just as those who are about to lose their minds become aggressive and argu-mentative. You are not willing to admit that everything comes to an end hence you make your speech of strength to cover your weaknesses. I shall go now free as a bird. I pity you. I pity you, Simon Odak.*"

Then she walked out without turning her head back.

She was sitting on the balcony of her hotel room overlooking the harbour. It was late evening; there was a lit candle on the table, a small bowl of various nuts, a bunch of tiger lilies in a vase and a book. She read a verse, closed the book and closed her eyes. This town looked like the town she used to know. Now she didn't know anyone anymore because she didn't want to.

The only memory she kept for good was the memory of her late mother. She took a pen and wrote in her diary:

Fiume, April 15th 2017

Dear Sapphire,

Here I am, back to where it all started. It all looks the same, yet everything is so different. I think we've lost: human decency has lost. Just lost, greedy souls looking at me as I pass by. God has his favourite planets and their fine inhabitants; this is where he dumps the unworthy, to learn lessons in Hell. But the masters of this ungodly place have hidden the simplest knowledge: underneath this web of illusions which they skilfully manipulate, endless love exists, it has always been and it always will be, but unless we unveil the lies and untangle the web we shall not see it. Love is not physical contact between two people, as it is usually portrayed in romantic stories. Neither is love what has been shown in television shows, films and what media want us to believe. It can't be grasped by intellect, mind or a poem. Only a few mystics have reached the depth and reality of such love and only they are the ones who do not speak of it. I leave you now with my last letter and my last poem, as I don't need words any longer:

Raindrops and dewdrops on the petals
Of flowers

516

DETHRONED

On the petals of sapphires and in the spheres of
Speechlessness
Light and darkness reflected and caught in
A thought of yet unawakened ones:
Some mourn darkness
Some mourn light
But there was neither darkness or light
Just raindrops
Back then when the sky was kind and the world was young

Good-bye Sapphire, my next destination shall be Japan: back to the raindrops, dewdrops and to my Masters for a while. Follow me as you do, inspire me as you always have, make me follow the 'coincidences', and please, do come to my dreams and to my different distant planet where issues of the great dualistic struggle between life and death have never fully formed from this circle of my consciousness, although, even now, I refuse to believe that one cannot find the answers, as all the treasures lie concealed simply inside oneself, therefore making one dig deep, refusing the destruction that was created deliberately to imprison the advancement of the human soul, and to deny the existence of the human soul would be the same as to deny life itself.

On Sale Now!

For more information
visit: www.speakingvolumes.us

On Sale Now!

For more information
visit: www.speakingvolumes.us

On Sale Now!

For more information
visit: www.speakingvolumes.us

Sign up for free and bargain books

Join the Speaking Volumes mailing list

Text

ILOVEBOOKS

to 22828 **to get started.**

www.ingramcontent.com/pod-product-compliance
Lightning Source LLC
Chambersburg PA
CBHW030744030726
47497CB00001B/120